UNSEEN SCARS

Unseen Scars is a work of fiction. Names, characters, places, and incidents are the product of the author's imagination or are used fictitiously. Any resemblance to actual events, locales, or persons, living or dead, is coincidental.

Willow River Press is an imprint of Between the Lines Publishing. The Willow River Press name and logo are trademarks of Between the Lines Publishing.

Copyright © 2025 by S.B. Labate

Cover design by Morgan Bliadd

Between the Lines Publishing and its imprints supports the right to free expression and the value of copyright. The scanning, uploading, and distribution of this book without permission is a theft of the author's intellectual property. If you would like permission to use material from the book (other than for review purposes), please contact info@btwnthelines.com.

Between the Lines Publishing
1769 Lexington Ave N, Ste 286
Roseville MN 55113
btwnthelines.com

First Published: February 2025

ISBN: (Paperback) 978-1-965059-28-9

ISBN: (eBook) 978-1-965059-29-6

The publisher is not responsible for websites (or their content) that are not owned by the publisher.

UNSEEN SCARS

S B Labate

For those who have carried invisible scars-this is for you.

The Lord is nigh unto them that are of a broken heart; and saveth such as be of a contrite spirit.

Psalm 34:18

Prologue

Life has always been a strange concept to grasp. Some days life is a literal miracle and other days it's an utter mystery. There are so many ups and downs that impact our lives, and the decisions made along the way. There are so many lessons learned and some that we must unlearn to carry on. Some people live to be a hundred and others are born only to die a few seconds later. Life is full of so many unpredictable events that it is impossible to understand everyone's life story from a mere glimpse. No one can know what life will bring tomorrow or the next, which is why appreciating everyone in your life today and in the moment is so vital. Who knows if tomorrow they will simply vanish? Vanish physically or vanish mentally from the person they once were.

Many of my friends and family know of the past that continues to haunt my dreams. Others cannot know from their simple glimpses or from small talk and nor I to them. The demons that would wake me from the safety of my dreams have become something that I have learned to live with daily. You see, many people today do not realize that I am a twin. They don't realize that I once shared everything from my looks to my dreams with a little boy who is now a mere memory of the past. A memory of good and bad times. Now when people look at me, they see an eighty-something year-old-man with little to no grey hair and wrinkles outlining every high and low from my life. I was once a little boy, a scared and confused little boy. Scared about what life would have in store for me. Now, no one will know that the gravestone we will all be staring at today was not just a stone, but a man. That man, Henry Gene Clark II, was my big brother and the bravest man I have ever known. No one will know his story except those who were closest to him. My brother kept things to himself and was never one to let people in to see the real him behind the deep stares and stern voice. He never wanted anyone to judge him based on his past. He wanted people to simply respect him for himself and not based on the sympathy one would without a doubt have after hearing the story of his past. He was a good and humble man.

Today is November 30, 2019; and the sky is slowly revealing that the winter season is coming soon while the trees are beginning to lose their identity. I made my way through the quiet and eerie cemetery, leading the way for family and friends. Near the back of the cemetery, overlooking a beautiful and serene lake, I saw a tent and chairs set up for my expected family. Positioned perfectly centered under the tent was a chestnut-colored casket draped with an American flag across it. I tightened my hand, which was wrapped in the support of my wife for balance and stability. I remembered that I was surrounded by endless support of those who knew and loved my brother, and I could not help but smile. Oh, how he would have loved to see all this attention. He would have loved and been embarrassed, all at once, by the amount of love being shown for him.

Unseen Scars

I knew this day would be coming. For years now I have watched life leave my brother's memory. Before his final days on this earth, he could only remember his loving wife, Jane. Occasionally, he would remember me, his little brother. I watched as they folded that beautiful American flag into the tricornered shape and hand it over to his now tearful wife. My sincere wife weeping to the side of me was now gripping onto my hand tighter and tighter. I could not help but reminisce on the life my brother and I shared together. Oh, how life has changed and moved on faster than I could have ever imagined. Who knew that one day we would be surrounded by our wives, children, and grandkids? We were just two boys trying to figure out our place in this world what felt like only a few years ago.

I stood there listening to the minister preach about life and the importance of love when I saw someone through the crowd who caught my attention. I did not recognize the stranger's face, but it felt familiar to me. He stared back at me with a sense of confidence I had only ever seen once in a man, but that was decades ago now. The way his eyes conveyed feelings and his tall and thin stature was familiar. I had seen someone like him before, but I could not place the time. He had a pretty woman next to him who kept her eyes down. She had on a hat that hid her face from onlookers like me. I must have zoned out from the service because the next thing I knew my wife, Leanna, squeezed my hand as she normally does when trying to get my attention. I turned my head to find the minister along with the rest of the service attendees looking in my direction waiting. Maybe that was why that strange man was staring at me. He, along with everyone else, was waiting. Waiting for me to speak. It was my turn to talk about the life of my big brother, Junior.

In the pocket of my suit jacket, I pulled out a paper with my wife's writing scribbled on it. The writing of words used to describe my brother. It was too short. How can there be a limit to how much I could say about him. He was my big brother, my protector, my hero, my friend, and my safety for so long. I released Leanna's hand and looked at her for an encouraging nod of her head signaling that I could do this. I made my way up to his beautiful casket, smoothed out the paper about my brother and turned to face the crowd of attentive family and friends. That is when it hit me. Why should I be given a limit? Why should there be a limit on describing the life of someone who made an impact in not only your life but on many of those around him? I folded the now smooth paper back up and placed it back in my pocket. I took a deep breath and began my speech, my story... our story:

"Today, we come together to talk about a man we all loved. We celebrate a man who spent his life protecting his family and friends. An honorable man. A man of his word. A man who was always there to help at any given time. A man who would have given the shirt off his back to anyone who needed it. A man who was more than 'Mr. Clark, Alzheimer's patient for 10 years.' Henry Gene Clark II— Junior as he was known by those who knew him best— was, and will always be, more than just a gravestone. He was my protector on this earth for eighty-seven years and will continue to be my forever protector in heaven until the day I leave to join him again," I felt the tears coming in. I quickly closed my eyes pushing them back for another time as I took a deep breath and continued with my speech. "For Junior and me, our story goes back seventy-nine years ago to Charleston, South Carolina. Life was a whole lot simpler back then. We were... young. I was only five years old... can you believe that?" I winked at my beloved five-year-old great granddaughter Violet, who smiled back at me. "And Junior was only eight years old at the time. We came from a family of five—our dad, Henry Gene Clark, our Momma, Katherine Francis

Clark, and finally our little brother, my twin, David William Clark. We were a close and tight-knit family. We were the picture-perfect family of the 1930s.

"We lived in a small little white house outside of town, giving us the privacy Daddy always wanted. It was a charming home away from all the commotion and fast-paced life of living in the city. The structure was a two-story and two-bedroom home with a burgundy roof and chimney which helped create a 'homey' look. We had a chicken coop in the back where we got our eggs every morning. The chickens would roam free during the day, and we locked them up at night. Between us three boys, we took turns each night locking them up. As well as chickens, we had a little garden out in the back that we tended to after school. We had a handsome front porch enclosed with a white-railing and with four steps leading up to the doorway. Walking through the front door, the staircase was immediately ahead giving a perfect view of the bedrooms and bathroom above. Adjacent to the stairs was our living room, which gave way to the dining room, kitchen, and back door. Junior, David— or Davie as we called him— and I learned how to walk on that porch. When Momma was a young girl, she had always dreamed of one day having her very own porch. She always said, 'memories on a porch make a family.' We used that porch almost every night making memories enough for a lifetime. That is why Junior, and I always had a porch our entire adult life. You see, those nights on our porch were spent telling ghost stories, singing, learning to dance, and enjoying the company of one another. Daddy would pull out his guitar and he and Momma would sing together. Their favorite song to sing was 'Keep on the Sunny Side' by the Carter Family. Junior, Davie, and I would strum along in our heads and dance around the porch without a single worry in the world. That porch... that house was our world during those days.

"We were close once, you know, our whole family. We three boys, we shared a room together. Davie and I had a bunk bed which we thought were swell to have back then. Davie slept on the top bunk, of course; that was Davie, the man in charge! Our bunk bed was on the wall closest to the door which was closest to Momma and Daddy's room. Junior had a single bed across from us next to the window looking out at the woods. Junior was our role model growing up. Many times, we would just lay in bed staring at him reading a cartoon or book just admiring him, which believe me, annoyed him. We were, as many younger siblings are, the annoying little brothers who would not leave him alone. But deep down, I knew he loved being admired by us. He loved being the role model and the older brother.

"You see Junior—or as some of you call him, 'PopPop'— was very reserved and introverted growing up. He wouldn't show his emotions all that well or reveal the sensitive man that hid behind the mask he wore. I never saw him cry out of sorrow or show any worry for Davie and me. He was the popular boy at school. He was athletic and top of his class. In our eyes, Junior had it all. He looked identical to Daddy; dark hair and blue eyes, which received a compliment from all the ladies. He was the baseball star at age eight and the boy who aced every test he took. He made life look so easy and uncomplicated that there was no reason we should not have looked up to him. If Junior could have only known how to deal with his emotions, I would tell you he was a perfect person. But emotions were something he had to learn through experience, and boy, did we both get that.

"Why am I telling you all of this, you may wonder? Because I want you all to know the man behind the mask of grandpa, father, and husband. I want you all to know the experiences that led him to become the man he became. The veteran, the loyal husband, the tentative father, and the giving grandfather. I want you all to hear his story before he is lowered into the earth and remembered only by the stone that will forever judge him by the number of years he lived and not by the life he lived. Home was everything to Junior, and that is where I will begin. Seventy-nine years ago, in a small town called Charleston, South Carolina..."

Chapter 1

It was October of 1940; I was five years old when the United States initiated the Selective Training and Service Act. The Act required healthy and able men between the ages of twenty-one and forty-five to register for military services. At that time, Daddy was a healthy and fit twenty-seven-year-old man working as a foreman at the Cigar Factory, who fit their profile becoming a prime candidate for the draft.

Without any hesitation, Daddy volunteered to serve the United States due to the tensions rising in Europe. He volunteered with his best friend and a man we had considered our surrogate uncle, Thomas John Adler— or as we called him, Uncle Tommy. They volunteered together to enlist into the United States Army. Pride took over them as they received their papers confirming approval to serve. They were known as, 'volunteer draftees.'

Our Father was a stout and sturdy, handsome man. He had dark features, thick dark hair, and light blue eyes which, to Momma's dismay, made him popular among the ladies in town. Daddy owned a deep and husky voice which made him a powerful and immediately respected man throughout the community. He was a hard and dedicated worker at home and at the factory, ensuring that he provided for his family.

Daddy grew up in Raleigh, North Carolina which is where he met our beautiful mother. He was the only child of Donald Henry and Dorothy Jean Clark, Granddad and MawMaw. Daddy, like Junior, was athletic and the baseball star of his community back then. Daddy was Granddad and MawMaw's pride and joy. He was their perfect son, and they could not have been more boastful of him as he grew up.

Momma and Daddy grew up together in Raleigh and began courting at the age of fifteen. They were high school sweethearts and friends since grade school. The two of them were unmistakably best friends and spouses all at one time. He treated our Mother like she was the only woman in the world and oh, did she love that.

With us kids, he was a hands-on father, the type of father any child would have dreamed of having and the man I admit having aspired to be like. Most nights were spent with Daddy gathering us three in the living room to help us with our homework or just to teach us something important about life. He would never play favorites with any of us, which is difficult to do at times when having multiple children. His goal, as he would always say, was to make us 'productive men in society.' So, naturally we three looked up to him. Many in town would call us his three little shadows.

Momma— Katherine Francis Clark— was the absolute essence of classic southern charm. She would never leave the house without having 'her face on' or without her best dress perfectly pressed and ready to wear. She had long blonde hair and mesmerizing hazel eyes, which both Davie and I inherited. Momma's voice was pure and sweet as if it came directly from Heaven's streets. When she would sing, she had this angelic voice that could make anyone radiate with pure happiness. Her voice was comforting when woken up by a nightmare in the dead of night. She was the safe arms we three would run to when we were frightened or sad. Just being locked in her arms made every bad thing life would throw our way disappear entirely.

Just like Daddy, Momma was the only child of Johnnie Lee and Vera Mae Williams, Pa and MeeMaw. Momma was born and raised in Raleigh, with dreams of moving to the oceanside in Charleston, which MeeMaw and Pa could never understand. She was the diamond of their eyes. She was their entire world.

The beauty and elegance Momma held will stay in my mind and heart forever, but the safety and love she provided us is something I will forever long for.

Just before Junior was born, Daddy lost his parents unexpectedly after a robbery turned deadly. Since then, MeeMaw and Pa became the only family Daddy really had. They took Daddy in soon after and were beyond thrilled when Momma and Daddy were wed just months after their High School Graduation. It was only after the birth of Junior, a few months later, that Momma and Daddy decided to make the move to Charleston, South Carolina. Like any parents, MeeMaw and Pa were far from pleased with the idea. It took them some time to accept this decision, but they did. They knew how much Momma loved the beach and small-town feel Charleston had, especially the small-town gossip. And gossip was like Momma's second language.

Just ten months following their wedding, Henry Gene Clark II — Junior — arrived on August 12, 1932. This made Junior a Leo, a natural born leader, fitting him very well. From the time he was born, he was independent and loved taking charge. He knew what he wanted in life at such a young age; it was inspiring for Davie and myself. At the age of eight, Junior's goal was to earn the Eagle Scout award and to someday work in the steel industry. He had the heart of an old soul and always aspired to greatness in everything he did. Daddy would often call him 'his little forty-year-old man.' And again, this personality trait resonating in Junior was the reason Davie and I looked up to him. He was Daddy's look-a-like and was undoubtedly destined for greatness.

Three years after Junior, Davie and I entered the world on May 21, 1935. I was born James Lee Clark — or Jamie. Momma instantly fell in love with James Cagney's performance when she viewed Footlight Parade, and she named me after him. My middle name, Lee, came from her father, Johnnie Lee Williams. Daddy took over when naming Davie and chose David William Clark. William after Momma's parents to pay respect to them for all they did for him. David...well...Daddy just loved that name.

Davie and I were identical twins, as identical as our bunk beds. We looked the same on the outside but were completely different on the inside. Davie was our own personal comedian and would pull the most immature yet creative pranks we had ever seen. He loved a good laugh and being the center of attention. His favorite prank by far was stealing Daddy's shaving cream and putting it on his sleeping victims' hand before gently touching the brim of their noses with a feather and then waiting for them to whack their face with a hand full of shaving cream. Not many found this as hilarious as Davie did, especially the one who was sleeping — which was typically Junior. Davie's humor and light outlook on life, along with his infectious smile, are things I would eventually see in my youngest son years later.

Davie and I had light blonde hair and hazel eyes hidden behind by round glasses we were forced to wear due to our horrible vision. But

Davie somehow was able to make those round frames look in style, while I just looked like the typical school nerd.

I was born a full five minutes before Davie, which meant, of course, that I was wiser and more mature than he, being I was older and all. I was known as 'mister serious,' as Momma would sometimes call me. I truly did not know how to have any fun back then. Rules and exceptional grades were all that I knew or cared about. I could not throw a baseball from the pitcher's mound to first base, but I could tell you everything there was to know about long division. In school, I was the kid who would read all the instructions before beginning an exam or before playing with any toy. I was the true definition of what you would now call a "nerd", in the 1930s and 1940s.

Regardless of the differences between Davie and me, we were each other's best friends. We shared all our dreams together and spent many days in the backyard going on little adventures. We would climb through the woods and pretend to be explorers, while Davie narrated everything we did. Together Davie and I built a fort in the backyard made of tree branches, wood planks, and wire, filled with blankets, pillows, and writings of our goals and aspirations for life. It was our fort, The Clark Fortress. This was Davie's and my own place to retreat to, which no one except us could enter. We did practically everything together. Even when Davie would play baseball, I would sit in the dugout and just watch him and support him along the way.

I could not have imagined going through my life without him by my side. We began life together. And to be honest, I always thought we would end life together. Even to this day, as an eighty-four-year-old man, I still wonder what he and I could have accomplished growing up together. Our last family photo still sits at my bedside today. It was one of the last valuable items I was able to take from our childhood home before being forced to escape abruptly leaving all our memories behind.

Our story took a turn when the Selective Training and Service Act began. Daddy was going to be leaving home to serve our country in one of the greatest wars the country had ever been a part of. He was set to leave March 3, 1941, for training at Camp Croft in Spartanburg, South Carolina. This meant we only had one more Christmas and just five more months left being a complete family. Daddy and Uncle Tommy were leaving and the normality we all knew would soon come to a shattering end.

At the time, Uncle Tommy was a twenty-three-year-old single man who worked with Daddy down at the Cigar Factory. Daddy took Uncle Tommy in as the little brother he never had. Uncle Tommy lost his parents to disease when he was only 16 years old and since then he had been working hard to stay on his own feet. Uncle Tommy was a tall and slim-built man with dark hair like Daddy but with deep brown eyes that showed every single emotion he felt. Uncle Tommy walked with a sense of confidence; a confidence that could not be taught but was gained through life experiences.

Uncle Tommy was a man full of life and love. He adored having us as his surrogate family and spoiled us three as though we were blood nephews. He would show up at our house with gifts for random occasions. For instance, one day he came over with three toy guns exclaiming "Happy 10th Friday of the Year!" He was a man you would have never guessed was orphaned and left to fend for himself without any nearby or willing relatives to take him in. Daddy met Uncle Tommy when he and Momma were new to Charleston. They became instant friends and soon Uncle Tommy became a daily guest for dinner at the

Clark residence. We loved Uncle Tommy, and he loved us. He was our family not by blood but through unconditional love and friendship.

It was Junior who would eventually reveal the main reason for Daddy's seemingly quick decision to volunteer. During a conversation between Junior and Daddy, Daddy confessed that he decided to serve to protect Uncle Tommy. As I said before, he took Uncle Tommy in as his little brother. He protected him, supported him, and loved him as a brother. Uncle Tommy made the decision to volunteer, and Daddy felt obligated to volunteer with him. He wanted to ensure his friend would be safe. And after many discussions with Momma, he submitted his paper to join the United States Army.

Uncle Tommy and Daddy seemed to be apprehensive about the possibility of a long and not altogether unexpected war with Germany. And once alone, Daddy would retreat to the darkness of their room, engulfing himself in angst. Through the following months, we began to understand the toll this would all take on Momma. With each passing day, her singing lessened and the silence grew.

The confident mask once worn by our father faded as the months passed. When around one another, the humor between Daddy and Uncle Tommy remained strong. But as the months flew by, their effortless laughter faltered.

As adults, Junior would always say we lost Daddy the day he came home from the war, but I still believe we were losing Daddy before he even left...

Sunday, March 2nd, 1941

It was the day before Daddy left for Camp Croft and we spent the entire day at home together as a family. Daddy woke up early that morning and began anxiously packing for the uncertain adventure that lay ahead.

I, along with my siblings, woke up late that morning. I woke to the pain of my stomach as it growled to the smell of eggs and sound of bacon being prepared. I clenched my eyes tight again at the noise of our bedroom door creaking open slowly. Quiet footsteps made their way across our bedroom floor, careful not to step on the squeaky floorboard.

"Junior?" I recognized Daddy's voice whispering to my still sleeping brother. "Son? Are you awake?"

Junior, who wasn't making any coherent responses, moaned, rolled over, and covered his head in bed sheets, desperate for more time in his dream.

"Wake up son ... come with me. Wake up Junior, come with me for a walk before breakfast. Let's try not to wake your brothers," Daddy whispered, pulling the bed sheets down and lifting him up to a sitting position. "Come on son..." Daddy laughed quietly at Junior's still sleeping state. "Get your jacket and slippers on and come with me."

Junior mumbled something and sleepily searched the floor with his feet for his slippers. I played sleep, carefully watching Daddy pull Junior up, put his jacket on, and lead the half sleeping Junior out of the room with one eye slightly opened. The door was pulled gently to a close as he was careful not to make a loud sound that would potentially startle two "sleeping" boys.

"Davie...Davie...," I whispered, looking up to the top bunk as I waited for any sign of movement from my sleep loving brother. But nothing stirred above me.

Through the haze, I found my glasses and pulled myself up to climb to the side of our bunk bed. Davie was still in a dead sleep, undisturbed by Daddy's whispering or the delicious aroma of bacon and eggs that slowly filled our bedroom. I left Davie to sleep and tip-toed across our room to the window positioned over our desk that was on the wall between Junior's and our beds. I searched the backyard frantically for any signs of Daddy and Junior walking but saw nothing.

'Where are they?' I thought desperately to myself.

I grabbed my jacket out of the closet, slid on my slippers, and crept softly out of our bedroom. I searched upstairs first, listening closely for any sounds of people talking in Momma and Daddy's bedroom; nothing. All I found was daddy's duffle bag packed with our summer family photo laid out on top of it. I crept to their bedroom window to scan the other side of our backyard and saw them. They were walking along the edge of the woods together, side by side talking. Daddy looked serious, occasionally using his hands to explain something while Junior kept his eyes down to kick any rock nearby. I cracked the window slightly in hopes I might hear some part of this oh-so important morning conversation. That was until I heard a stern yet somehow polite 'ahem' behind me. I spun around, almost throwing myself off balance, and found myself staring at Momma.

"And what conversation are we eavesdropping on here?" Momma said with a slight smirk.

She walked over towards me, slowly and full of grace. The guilt inside of me heightened the closer she drew near. I hated breaking the rules, and I hated even more being in trouble. Momma would always tell us that private conversations are meant to be private, and it was not right to listen in unwelcomed. I knew I was wrong, but I just had to know what was so important and so urgent.

'Why couldn't Daddy talk to Davie and me too?' I demanded in my head.

I was so angry with confusion as I wondered why Davie, nor I was included in this morning conversation. And before I could find the words to speak, Momma had me in her arms, lifting me into a warm and understanding hug — oh, how I miss her hugs. One thing I loved about being little was being held by her.

"You know Daddy's leavin' tomorrow and he has important things he needs to discuss with your brother—" Momma began to say before I rudely interrupted her.

"But why," I said before I could even think of the impoliteness of my actions. "Why... Why not us? He hasn't spoken to Davie or me about nothin'. What makes Junior so special that he gets a special conversation with Daddy? What about us, Momma?" I tried sounding confident and more mature, instead of like the sensitive and hurt child I was.

"Sweetheart, your brother is the oldest son and will be the oldest man here. There are certain ... responsibilities he is laying out for Junior to uphold. Such as taking care of you and Davie while he is gone. I know—" She cut me off before I could interrupt again. "You don't need to be taken care of ... I know. But your Daddy wants to make sure you two will be okay. He wants to make sure Junior will help around the house more and not cause me any more trouble. I am sure your daddy will make time today for you and Davie as well and talk with each of you. But right now, it's Junior's time. It is also close to being time for breakfast. So, go wash up, wake your brother, and get downstairs before the eggs I just made get cold."

I didn't move nor speak. I just continued to stare straight in her eyes, desperate for her to take me seriously—to understand me.

"I know you are upset and yes, you have every right to be. You are only five years old, and your Daddy won't be home for a while, but please try to understand." Momma's voice was becoming increasingly stern with me. "You know your Daddy loves you and your brothers equally. Now, go—wake up your brother—wash up—and come down for breakfast."

She kissed my forehead, sweetly placed her fingers under my chin, and gave me a smile. I don't know how she always managed to instantly calm me down. All I know is that the anger that had been brewing inside of me was gone at once. I gave her a quiet smile and nod before sliding off her lap to run back to our room to wake Davie up for breakfast.

Like always, breakfast was amazing but somehow never enough. Between us three boys, our stomachs were like bottomless pits with the ability to eat pounds of food without gaining any weight. That's not so true anymore at the age of eighty-four—now I can't seem to keep the weight off.

By the time we plowed through our first plate of food, we heard the all too familiar rhythmic knock at our door.

"—Knock, Knock, Knock, Knock, Knock—" pause "—Knock, Knock—"

"UNCLE TOMMY!" Davie exclaimed as he jumped up to his feet before the final two knocks were sounded.

Davie sprinted across the living room to the front door where the silhouette of a man stood. Momma let out a noticeable sigh by Davie's loud and abrupt exit from the breakfast table. Daddy could not help but smile at Momma's lack of enthusiasm. Without hesitation, Davie flung the door wide open to reveal Uncle Tommy standing there in a blue collared button-up shirt and khaki pants with his typical khaki-colored suspenders. He always wore those khaki pants and occasionally alternated between a blue or green shirt. He always combed his hair back with a few hairs hanging down freely on his forehead. This was his signature look.

Uncle Tommy opened his arms wide and painted a silly smile across his face before screaming, "DAVIE! How is the man of the hour on this fine morning!?" He picked Davie up and swung him around in circles before holding him upright in his arms. "Not causing any trouble, are you?"

"Yep!" Davie said proudly, in between his infectious giggles.

"Excellent! What's life without causing a little ruckus?!" Uncle Tommy hollered. "You remember what I have always told you and your brothers, don't ya?"

Davie placed his right hand over his heart and calmed his face expressions into a serious stare before reciting, "If you can't be good—then be careful." This caused them to roar in a hysteric laughter together.

Behind the two of them, soft giggles from a woman whose voice I did not recognize took my attention. Uncle Tommy didn't come here alone this time.

While setting Davie back onto his feet, Uncle Tommy shouted to the woman who had been hidden from view behind him, "Joan, dear. Come in and meet my family!"

Through the doorway walked a charming and elegant woman. She was gorgeous; she was one of the most gorgeous women I had ever laid eyes on. She had on a knee-length pink dress with puffed shoulders and a black bucket hat. Her sable brown hair curled into her hat so tightly that not a single strand was touching her perfectly fixed face.

"Tommy! How are you holding up?" Daddy responded as he stood from the table to greet his friend and new guest. "And who is this lovely lady? You can't be the unfortunate dish that has been hangin' around

Thomas, are you?" Daddy offered his hand to the beautiful woman while Uncle Tommy rolled his eyes.

"Joan... I'd like you to meet Henry. Henry and family, this is my girl, Joan. Joan Margaret Pye." Uncle Tommy put his arm behind Joan's back and smiled proudly. "The future Mrs. Thomas Adler...has a nice ring to it, don't you agree Hen?"

"Oh Thomas...please." Joan blushed at Uncle Tommy's playful comment. "It is a pleasure to finally meet you all. I have heard so much about you all from Thomas," She smiled slightly, you could tell she was nervous. Her voice trembled but still held its elegance. Elegance I had ever only seen in Momma.

"Hi Joan... My name is David," Davie held out his hand to greet Joan while standing next to Daddy with his chest puffed out to act like a manly man.

"Well hello Mr. David," Joan returned his smile and took his hand without hesitancy. I had never seen Davie blush so red before.

"It's a pleasure to finally meet you Joan," Daddy picked up the still blushing and now giggling Davie. "Tommy's been keeping us from you. Come in and meet the rest of the family. Enjoy some breakfast before our three bottomless pits of so-called children eat all the food."

Uncle Tommy closed the door behind Joan and remained at her side as they walked over to the breakfast table. "Katherine, Junior, Jamie, I'd like you to meet the love of my life—Joan."

"Joan, it is so nice to meet you." Momma stood up to hug her neck as though they'd already met. "Please take a seat, I'll get you a plate from the kitchen."

"Oh, why thank you—" Joan sweetly responded while taking a seat in the chair drawn up by Uncle Tommy. "Mrs. Clark, your home is gorgeous—"

"—Oh dear, please, call me Katherine," Momma smiled over at Joan while fixing her and Uncle Tommy a plate. "And thank you so much…we do love this home."

"Katherine," Joan smiled as she relaxed some more. "It is so nice to meet you. Thomas tells me you make a delicious apple pie. I was hoping you could give me some baking tips," Joan spoke to Momma while giving Uncle Tommy, who was now in the living room talking with Daddy and Davie, a smiling side glance.

"Oh, of course I can give you some tips, but I couldn't give you the recipe no matter how much Tommy asks for it," Momma said loud enough to get Uncle Tommy's attention.

Uncle Tommy chuckled re-joining Joan at the table with a contagious grin on his face. "Oh, Katherine, I'll never get that recipe from you, will I?"

"Never," Momma smiled handing him over the plate of food.

"Worth a shot!"

"So, James and Junior? Am I remembering your names correctly?" Joan's eye met mine.

"Jamie…" I whispered, embarrassed by my own voice.

"Jamie," she corrected with an undoubtedly beautiful smile. "And you are Junior, am I correct?"

"Yes ma'am," Junior, unbothered by her beauty, answered.

"Well, Thomas you really weren't lyin' were you. These two are completely identical!" Joan exclaimed as Davie took his seat next to me. "And Junior, you really are a miniature version of your Father."

Uncle Tommy gave the plate to Joan as he grabbed another chair and joined her at the table. "I told you! The only way to tell Davie and Jamie apart is that mole under Davie's chin. Other than that, you are on your own."

"Mrs. Clark—"

"—Katherine," Momma corrected.

"Katherine," Joan smiled. "You and Henry really have beautiful children. So well-mannered and polite. You two must be so proud."

"Well, don't let them fool you, especially this one," Daddy tickled Davie under his arm, causing Davie to laugh hysterically. "Beyond that innocent smile and laugh, he is a complete menace."

Davie's infectious laugh caused the whole table, including Junior, to join in his hysterics. During the remainder of breakfast, we enjoyed each other's company and our conversations for what felt like hours. Momma stood up to do dishes, reminding me that we were still at the breakfast table. Daddy joined her in the kitchen to help her wash and dry all our empty dishes. Meanwhile, Davie had Joan locked in a conversation all about his and my personality differences and how being five minutes older does not truly make an actual difference in maturity. This, of course, I disagreed with.

I looked over at Momma and Daddy in the kitchen and saw Momma whisper something into his ear. Daddy turned his head in my direction to which I turned away from, hoping to avoid any eye contact. I rejoined the conversation with Davie and Joan, learning that he was now discussing how much fatter my face was compared to his own.

"Jamie," Daddy called out to me, which I pretended as though I did not hear. "James? I know you can hear me."

I could not pretend anymore; the whole room was now quiet with their eyes on me.

"Yes?" I finally answered with an innocent look on my face.

"Come help me with the car please," Daddy told me as he headed to the back door between the stove and the laundry room.

"Me? Wh—Okay – Umm—Yes sir," I know I sounded confused; I was.

I walked into the kitchen past Momma and towards the back door being held open by Daddy. I glanced over at Momma, whose face I could have sworn revealed a smile. Ignoring her, I stepped out the door and onto the grass. Daddy closed the door behind me, picked me up to throw me over his shoulders and walked towards his 1930, classic red-colored, Ford Model A sedan.

"So, Jamie. Your Momma told me you were trying to listen in on Junior's and my discussion this morning." Daddy was calm as he opened the passenger side door for me to sit me inside. I kept quiet. I knew I was in trouble for sure. Daddy smirked slightly, closed the door, and walked around the hood of the car to climb into the driver's seat. He shoved the keys into the ignition and revved up the engine.

"Whe—Where are we going?" I stuttered out my question.

"The river. I wanna talk with you for a little while if that is okay with you?" Daddy responded while turning the car off the grass and onto our driveway.

"Yeah—yes sir. Talk about what?" My mind began racing with thoughts of being in trouble and being lectured. The anxiety of awaiting a lecture was killing me. "I—Daddy I'm sorry for eavesdropping. I know you and Momma always say if we aren't invited into a conversation, then we should stay out of it. I—I was just curious. I didn't hear nothin' anyways. I'm sorry Daddy, plea—please don't be mad at me." I was pleading with him at this point while my stomach turned with just the thought of being yelled at. I thought I was about to throw up the breakfast I just scarfed down.

"Whoa—whoa—whoa...Hold on, son. I'm not mad..." He laughed to himself without any further explanation besides, "no one is mad at you."

We pulled out of our driveway to turn right out onto the road towards the direction of the river. We would usually go to the river all together as a family. Momma would bring a picnic basket full of sandwiches and fruit while Daddy would bring the fishing poles and bait. It was one of my favorite things we did together as a family.

We sat quietly as we drove down the familiar road out to the river. Only minutes passed by before we turned down the same dirt road we always took. Eventually the dirt turned into grass, and I saw the glimmer from the water shine as the sun hit. Daddy brought the car to a quiet and slow stop before getting out. A lump developed in my throat making it difficult to swallow the saliva that filled my mouth from the anxiety building inside of me.

'I know I'm in trouble—I just gotta be—' I thought desperately.

Daddy opened my door quickly and pulled me out without waiting for me to make a move. He placed me at his side, and we walked side by side, father and son, hand in hand along the riverbank. It was a beautiful and quiet day. It was March; winter was already fading, hinting at a hot summer that would soon arrive.

"I don't know when I will be home. I don't want to get your hopes up that I will be home in a few months or a year. The conflict taking place in Europe is serious and even though America has remained neutral, it is only a matter of time." Thus, Daddy began his lecture. "You, you are a smart boy, Jamie. Yes, you are young, but you are a smart and very intelligent boy. I have never really been too worried about you, Jamie. You are smart and have a decent perspective on this world, more than any five-year-old boy I have ever met... even Davie."

He smiled with me at the relief of Davie not hearing that comment. "I talked with Junior this morning because I need him to understand the responsibilities that I am leaving him, the responsibilities I need him to take care of, such as taking care of your Mother, Davie, and yourself. He is the oldest boy. He will be the man of the house. But I have a special job for you...I need you to be his sidekick, can you do that?"

"Like Robin?" Daddy's blue eyes met mine with the power and confidence I had always admired.

Daddy giggled at my remark. "Yes—yes, exactly like Robin. Anyway, I am telling you this because I need you to know that I might be gone, but I won't forget any of you. I won't stop being your father when I'm gone. I will be able to write to you, and I will be able to receive letters from you. I just need you to try and remain strong for me; be brave just like Robin. Be happy for me, and smile when you think about me. You can be sad and cry when you need to, it is okay to cry. But also try to remember the happiness we all share together. The distance cannot take away the memories we all have together and the love we share. Keep doing well in school. Be the very best Jamie you can be. You may share your brother's looks, but there is only one Jamie Lee Clark in this world, and he is you. I'll be home as soon as I can be... and when I am back, I want to hear about everything I have missed. Can you promise me that?"

I could not help the tears that began to fall from my eyes. Every tear that fell burned down my cheeks.

'Why my father?' I questioned quietly in my head. 'Why take my father away? He makes our family complete. Who will play guitar at night after we have a long day at school? Who will help me with my arithmetic? Stay strong...Jamie...Stay strong.' The rush of thoughts at one time began making me dizzy.

I must have taken too long to respond or looked heartbroken because the next thing I knew Daddy stopped me from walking. He turned to face me kneeling to meet at my eye level. His eyes were like mine, glistening with tears.

"Listen—I might—I might be far from home —" his voice broke, "but I promise I will never be far from your heart, or your mother's and brothers'. Keep me there and you will never be alone, okay?"

I wrapped my arms around him and held on tight. He was my father. My father, who knew how to be both strict and loving all at once. A man who taught me that love was a 'manly' thing to feel as well as having pride. I say this even to this day, regardless of what eventually happens, my father is one of the reasons I am the man I am today. For all the good reasons and even all the bad.

We stood there together, father and son, for close to an hour before heading back to the car for home. As we turned back down our driveway, I saw Momma, Uncle Tommy, Joan, and both of my brothers outside enjoying the beautiful weather. Momma and Joan were locked in conversation on the porch while Uncle Tommy taught Davie how to swing a bat like Babe Ruth. Junior stood out in the yard tossing the baseball high in the air before running to catch it. It seemed like just a normal day; yet, in just twelve hours our lives would be forever changed.

Momma stood up at the sight of the car returning home and ran across the yard to meet us at Daddy's typical parking spot with her usual beautiful smile across her face. He brought the car to a stop before leaning out the window to give her a kiss.

"Well, hello there beautiful," Daddy said smoothly. "Jamie and I went out to the Ashley River and discussed a few things, didn't we son?" I nodded in return. "Now, how about a big cold glass of sweet tea?" He patted my leg and gave me a wink before hopping out of the driver's seat. He wrapped Momma in his arms as he kissed her again, this time more passionately. They were so happy and so in love with each other during those years. I never thought anything could change that.

I continued to sit there lost in my thoughts, my mind pulling me back to the river with Daddy. My door pulled open, ripping me away from my thoughts, landing my mind back in the car. Momma stood there at the door with a proud smile to greet me.

"So, Jamie! What did you and your Daddy talk about?" Momma leaned in to ask me in a whisper.

"Sorry Momma, you can't hear a conversation you weren't invited to." I smiled foolishly at her.

"Oh, is that so!" Momma tried to keep a stern face but was overcome with laughter. She grabbed me under the arms and pulled me into a hug. I could not help but laugh along with her. She put me down on my feet and I took off running across the yard. She closed the passenger's door firmly before chasing me with laughter.

The rest of the day we spent like this, laughing, eating, and playing. It was a day full of beautiful memories that I will never forget. Memories that have lasted me an entire lifetime. Memories I held onto when life became almost too difficult to bear. These were simpler times, happier times. Some of the happiest of times for the Clark family. This was the way our life should have continued, but life doesn't always work like that. Life is full of unexpected curve balls that you can never truly be prepared for. You just have to keep on moving to make it through those hard times to find the blessings on the other side. Unfortunately, life at that little white house would never be the same after March 2, 1941. And we had to keep moving forward to survive.

Chapter 2

March 3, 1941

 I can't begin to tell you how much I didn't want to go to bed that night. My brothers and I all tried to fight the urge to fall asleep as we piled in Momma and Daddy's bed. We stayed up talking and telling stories until one by one my brothers and I drifted off into our dreams. I woke up the next morning in my own bed still exhilarated with memories from the day before.

 That was when the devastating reality hit me...

 'It's the third!' I screamed in my brain.

 I searched feverishly for my glasses that had been hanging off my bed post. I grabbed them and slammed them onto my face immediately clearing my vision. Hurling my body off the bed, I made it to the closet in just a step or two. I flung the closet door open reaching for any type of clothing I could wrap my hands around. I ripped off my bedtime shirt and awkwardly threw on whichever button-up shirt was easiest to grab. I hastily glanced over to both of my brothers' beds assuming each would be empty, but Junior was still sleeping. I focused my eyes up on Davie's top bunk, searching for his tightly curled-up body under the sheets, and found him lying motionless, lost within his dreams. The only sound in the room was the soft snoring of my two sleeping brothers, who remained unbothered by my spastic and frantic movements.

Still dazed and confused, I peered out our bedroom window, investigating the still and dark woods.

'What time is it?' I wondered.

I scanned the room for our clock a time or two before my squinting eyes found it on the desk.

'Two in the morning,' I read the time in my mind repeatedly. 'How? It feels like it should be later.'

Sighing deeply with perplexity by the time shown, I threw back on my bedtime shirt and somberly climbed into bed. As the pillow swallowed me, my mind filled with anxiety as I thought of the day that lay ahead of us. Anxiety of the unknown hindered my ability to drift peacefully back to sleep.

Instead, hours seemed to pass by endless thoughts and images of things that may or may not happen. Eventually I was able to slip back into a restless sleep. A sleep filled with dreams of war, death, and the burials of faceless soldiers.

My dreams that had once been filled with nothing but happiness and joy turned into total darkness. Before this night, the most frightening dream I had ever dreamt was when I was only three years old. I dreamt that I had been chased by a swarm of bees endlessly around our home. I woke up in full screams while flailing my arms to fight off the murderous yet imaginative bees. When I finally woke, I found myself drenched in sweat with Momma and Daddy breathlessly by my side. My brothers, of course, teased me incessantly without sympathy. Junior — Junior taunted me about it until I was at least four years old.

Lost in the fog of my current nightmare, I heard a distant sound of an all too familiar voice.

"—Where is my jacket?" a hushed Junior spoke.

"—March along, sing our song, with the Army of the free—" Davie sang noisily above me while tapping our bedrails.

"Davie—shut up—" Junior snapped at him.

"—count the brave, count the true, who have fought to victory. We're the Army and proud of our name. We're the Army and proudly proclaim—"

"Davie, shut up!" Junior barked at him.

"What?" Davie remarked. "I'm a true patriot, Junior, what can I say?"

I opened my eyes slightly to peer out at my relentless brother.

"You can't even sing…" Junior recanted, while searching through our closet for his jacket as he stroked the skin above his lip. It was as though he was mimicking the behavior of a man with a mustache. "I need to get ready to go to the train station — you and Jamie also need to —"

"—I can't believe you actually think you have a mustache coming in… you are eight years old…" Davie rolled with laughter on the top bunk.

Junior sighed with frustration as he turned his attention back to the closet.

I sighed at the ridiculous brotherly arguments my twin tried to initiate when literally our entire world was about to change. I guess that was what made Davie so special. He could always find the light in everything regardless of the weight of the situation.

I slid out of bed and made my way to our bathroom to wash up for the morning that lay ahead. As the water rejuvenated my face, my mind was left with an unfaltering uneasiness.

'When would I see him again?' I was starting to panic.

The lump in my throat returned from the day prior, making it increasingly difficult to breathe.

'Hold it together... hold it together...' I repeated to myself while staring into the mirror.

"Jamie?" Junior called out from the other side of the door. "Jamie? Can I come in? I need to brush my teeth too, you know."

"Yeah—yeah, come on in." I unlocked the door, allowing him inside the now steam-filled bathroom.

Junior had already gotten dressed and was ready to leave. He had on knee-high grey socks, black shorts, a white, button-up shirt with a dark blue vest, and a grey jacket to finish his look. He was very spiffy as we used to say. Looking at Junior dressed up and ready to leave lead me to wonder about my own self. I had no idea how to match clothes...and how could I send my daddy off into the unknown wearing clothes that didn't match.

"Junior..." I was hesitant, afraid to get the typical judgmental look from him. "I wondered—would—would you mind helping me get dressed—you know –for today?"

"Gee, Jamie..." he rolled his eyes while spitting out his mouthful of toothpaste. He looked down at me with his head cocked sideways with attitude. "You don't even know how to get dressed by yourself? You're such a baby..."

As I looked down to the ground with embarrassment, his attitude changed instantly.

"Oh—fine—" Junior sighed greatly. "I'll be there in a minute. Let me just finish brushing my teeth and I'll be in to help you. Go ahead and pull some stuff out you like. Might as well get Davie too."

"Gee Junior, thanks!" I shouted as I hugged Junior tightly before I ran straight out the bathroom for our bedroom. As I rounded our doorway, I nearly ran into Daddy.

"Whoa! Whoa there speedy—Now if you'd only learn how to hit a ball, you'd be a phenomenal baseball player, little man," he smirked down at me.

"Sorry Daddy, I was trying to –"

"Figure out what to wear I reckon? Yeah—I just helped your brother with that. Come on let's find you something sharp to wear today," he clapped his hand on my back and lead me to our closet.

We passed by Davie who was still admiring the clothes Daddy had laid out for him to wear. Davie picked up the red vest and held it across his chest with a toothy grin across his face. I knew from that look he thought he looked good.

"Davie," Daddy shook his head at his noticeably cocky son. "Instead of standing there admiring yourself, go wash up and get dressed, please."

Davie smiled without a complaint and threw his khaki shorts, red vest, and the rest of his attire over his shoulder as he strolled out of the bedroom.

"What about this green vest?" Daddy turned, holding out a bright green vest, the very one Momma got me last year for my birthday. "Green—now that'll look good on you I think."

"I don't want to wear that vest. I want to wear... something... different," I said disappointedly.

"Something more mature you mean... okay—okay—what about...this?" Daddy pulled out a short sleeve, white button-up shirt, and laid it out on my bunk. He then walked over to my dresser and pulled out my dark grey shorts with matching suspenders. "Oh, I can't forget. It's not complete without this —handsome—mature—blue bowtie! And—of course—a black cap! Now that will do it! You are not only mature but stylish as well. Just enough to send me off properly. How about that?"

All I could answer him with was a simple smile. That black newsboy hat was my favorite growing up. I wore it almost every day to school. So much so, that Momma grew tired of seeing me in it and would purposefully hide it and place my other hats out around the house. It was her way of trying to force me to wear those instead. She was sneaky like that.

I dressed quickly finishing my outfit with my favorite pair of black shoes. Satisfied and confident with my look, I tore down the staircase to get a plate full of breakfast. Junior was already sitting happily at the kitchen table, indulging himself in a plate full of scrambled eggs and grits. house

"Wow ..." Momma announced as I hopped into the kitchen licking my lips at the smell of her mouthwatering cooking. "So handsome! You are very fine-looking this morning, Jamie...such a man—Now...before I get all emotional, come on, grab a plate, and eat up quick. Your daddy is out putting his bag in the car. Where's your brother? Davie —" She hollered. "David William Clark! Get your behind down here or we are leaving without you!" Momma shouted, stomping through the living room to the bottom of the stairs, with every bit of her attention set on our bathroom.

"Okay! Okay! I'm coming!" Davie yelled while running down the stairs holding his red vest firmly in his left hand and his hair still untidy. One of his black socks was pulled up and the other down around his ankle. "Sorry, Momma—the bathroom was being hogged up by them…"

"Oh no it wasn't! Momma, he overslept like he always does! Don't you lie your way through this one. You —"

"Henry Gene Clark! That's enough from you! That's enough from both of you! Now sit down and eat your food. We are leaving in ten minutes, and if I hear any more fighting from any of you, I will gladly leave you behind." Momma spoke to all of us with an undeniably stern face. "Your father will be gone for some time. He needs to see you three getting along and working together before he boards that train. So, behave. Junior, you're done eating. Go outside and help your father — now."

Junior left the table with an obvious sigh which was caught by Momma's eyes. I sat quietly at the table, minding my own business, gulping down every inch of food off my plate. I did everything I could to avoid even looking at my troublemaker of a twin. Davie had a tendency of making people around him either extremely joyful or incredibly angry, sometimes all at once.

I took my plate over to the sink to clean it off appropriately while Momma frantically tried to smooth out Davie's untidy hair. Eventually Momma gave up and shoved his grey hat on his head to cover the mess.

Soon, Daddy and Junior came in announcing that it was unfortunately time for us to head to the train station. That lump in my throat revealed itself again.

'Stay strong… Stay strong,' I reminded myself.

With some reluctance Momma removed her apron, smoothed out her dress, and grabbed her handbag. Together, as a family, we walked out the front door one by one, piling into the car. I, unfortunately, was forced to sit between my still bickering brothers. Momma sat calmly in the passenger seat. Her eyes glancing over to Daddy who had become noticeably quiet, his face appearing to be carved from stone. I could sense the grief and distress he was fighting back. Momma softly put her hand on the back of Daddy's neck in an attempt to relax him.

"So," her voice was soft as she interrupted the loud silence in the car. "...are we meeting Tommy at the train station?"

"Yes. He told me he wanted to take Joan. I'm assuming they are walking since Tommy doesn't own a car ... Joan will probably need a ride home though," hinting for her to offer her a ride, which Momma caught. "They seem good together. What do you think?"

"Most definitely. I have never seen him like that over a girl. He's never seemed so... attached." She responded as she pulled out her makeup powder to continue powdering her face. She wanted to be sure she was the best-looking wife of the station. "Did you notice she calls him Thomas? He looks more like a Tommy than a Thomas, but it is sweet seeing her doting all over him. Tommy needs someone like her to help keep him a little less wild."

"Daddy?" I whispered, timid about interrupting their conversation. "You will write to us, right?"

"Of course, Jamie. Whenever I can, I will be writing to y'all. I'll be at Camp Croft for about a month before leaving for New York. I'll try to keep you as informed as I can. Remember what I told you ... I will always be with you. Just please, you three, take it easy on your mother for me. Help around the house, mind your manners, and be respectful to her — and to each other." Daddy glanced in the rearview mirror, trying to make brief eye contact with Davie and Junior, who almost immediately looked down.

We drove, deep within the silence of that dark red sedan, riding through the country to the train station. To this day when I close my eyes tight, I can still smell the aroma of leather that wafted from those seats in that sedan.

As we entered the city, we remained quiet. Each of us appeared to be looking at something outside or inside the sedan to distract us from the difficult reality that was about to take place. Momma placed her hand on the back of Daddy's neck again without saying a word, just giving him a gentle smile, to which he answered with only a faint smirk. The sound of a sniffle came from Daddy just before he turned his head back quickly to the road. Looking in the rearview mirror, I saw a tear fall from Daddy's eye. As he drew in a deep breath, the glimmer of the tear was gone. He put on a strong front for us all, but — in retrospect — I now know how much he was hurting.

When our car pulled into the train station, my heart sank deep within me as the reality came crashing down. Thousands of people— men, women, and children—were running frantically throughout the station. Women were desperately hugging their men goodbye as tears streamed uncontrollably down their faces. Children, as young as newborns, were saying their goodbyes to their daddies without fully understanding the events that would soon occur.

Off to the side of the crowd I spotted my dear friend, Margaret, from school. Margaret was a freckle-faced girl with curly brown hair, whom I met the first day of kindergarten. We were assigned to sit next to each other and had been friends ever since. She and her older brother, Ernie, were crying, hugging tightly onto their daddy. Margaret's cheeks were red as she wailed hysterically with her arms tightly locked around his neck, refusing to let go. Her momma stood behind them, as she didn't have any words that could comfort her sobbing childrens' emotions.

I was lost in a daydream; my eyes transfixed on all the families around me who were saying their goodbyes to the ones they loved. The sound of the trunk slamming shut brought my mind back to my own family, and our story. Daddy confidently marched around our car with a secure grip on his bag and a fake smile upon his face.

"Alright... let's figure out where I need to go now," Daddy said with noticeable sorrow.

"Hey there Clarks!" A familiar voice pushed its way through the crowd.

It was Uncle Tommy. He was waving boisterously as he forced himself through the crowd with Joan close behind. Joan looked stunning; her hair was pulled up into a tight bun with one of those sideways hats women wore back then. She had on a very patriotic red a-line dress with a white belt across her waist. She wore a practiced smile as she followed Uncle Tommy through the crowd in our direction. She and Momma greeted each other with a hug and immediately started complimenting each other on their 'dashing' styles. Uncle Tommy strode straight up to the three of us with his arms opened wide and his trademark smile plastered across his face.

"Well now gentlemen! Seems like you three are going to be the men of the house for a little while." Uncle Tommy looked proud as he spoke, placing his hands on his hips. "Especially while your Daddy and I, along with the rest of these fine gentlemen, get those Nazi's in order, huh!"

"Well Tommy, the U.S. has not declared any war just yet, so..." Daddy attempted to remain optimistic for the sake of our emotions.

"Oh right...right. You are absolutely right there Hen—! Don't worry boys, we will be back before you know it!" Uncle Tommy declared after catching Daddy's warning eyes.

"Uncle Tommy!" Junior, unbothered by the silent conversation they were having in front of us, beamed with curiosity. "Will you write to us too?"

"Yeah, Uncle Tommy, will ya?" Davie chimed in. "We want to hear stories!"

"Well, of course, I will! And Joan will keep you up to date too. Now, is it alright if I talk with your daddy for a moment or two?" Uncle Tommy patted Junior's shoulder and nudged his head at Daddy.

"Yes sir..." Junior mumbled, clearly disappointed.

Uncle Tommy and Daddy walked off behind our sedan to discuss something that seemed to be serious as indicated by the strained look on Daddy's face. I tried to read Uncle Tommy's lips, but to be honest, I had never been good at that. The only thing I could decipher from their conversation was Daddy pointing at the train and Uncle Tommy only nodding as a response. I figured they were discussing where they would need to report.

"Junior, Davie, Jamie, come with Joan and me please. Daddy and Uncle Tommy will catch up in a minute," Momma put her hand out for us as a signal for us to follow.

We were headed toward one of the train compartments when Joan suddenly stopped us to say, "Thomas said they were assigned to this compartment together."

I looked up at the rusty, maroon-colored train, towering over my brothers and me, that was placed near the back end of the train. The familiar voices of Daddy and Uncle Tommy resonated over the subtle hissing given off by the train. I turned my head and started scanning for them while the whistles continued to blow, and what seemed like thousands of people continued to chatter at an increased volume. I finally found them sauntering towards us, joined by a man in a uniform as the three of them seemed to be conversing over a piece of paper. The man in uniform gestured at the bags held in Daddy's arms before pointing to the back of the train.

Daddy and Uncle Tommy nodded with the man, then he turned away from them, walking off. Uncle Tommy grabbed Daddy's bag and left Daddy with us as he headed off towards the back of the train. Momma greeted him with a tight embrace before she finally broke her own private rule, which was not to cry. A sincere smile crept onto Daddy's face as he held her tighter.

In her ear, Daddy softly spoke, "I will be okay... I love you Katherine... and when I'm able to, I will let you know where I am. Everything will be okay," Daddy rubbed her back gently as Momma's tears slowed down with each word. "When I come home, we will go on vacation together as a family and continue our life together, okay? How does that sound?"

"You better come home, you hear..." Momma leaned back in his arms, met his eyes, and distracted herself by straightening his tie.

He gave her a confident side smirk before kissing her like it would be their last. It was one of those embarrassing 'parent' kisses, you know? The ones that make your lip curl up in complete and utter disgust out of embarrassment.

"I will be back home before you know it my darling. Stay strong for me," Daddy said resting his forehead onto hers to look in her eyes more closely.

"I love you Henry," she said as her voice cracked.

"I love you too," he smiled back.

Soon after, Uncle Tommy returned with his arms wide open to swiftly pick Joan up off the ground to wrap her in a deep embrace. Joan was now blubbering in tears like Momma, so Uncle Tommy desperately tried to bring a smile to her face.

It seemed like a long time passed before Daddy pried himself from Momma's grasp and turned his attention onto us. He strutted over to the three of us, kneeling to meet Junior's eye first.

"Remember what we talked about?" Daddy asked him specifically.

"Yes sir," Junior straighten his back up with confidence as he answered.

"Good man. I love you Junior," Daddy told him softly before pulling him in for a hug.

"Oh—" Junior, who had been holding his hand out for Daddy to grasp, was caught off guard by his hug. "I love you too, Daddy." he replied, deepening his voice for maturity.

Next, Daddy turned his attention to Davie.

"Now...David," Daddy tossed Davie into his arms to hug him tight. "You, my little menace, had better behave yourself, you hear me? Do not drive your mother mad, okay?"

Davie giggled as he responded, "Okay Daddy."

"Good man...I love you," Daddy rested his head onto Davie's.

"I love you too Daddy and I'll be on my best behavior! Scout's honor!" He held his right hand over his heart as he spoke. As Daddy lowered him to the ground Davie blurted out, "Bring me back somethin' foreign!"

Daddy was in hysterics as he turned away from his comedic son and was now facing me. His eyes found mine and I beamed thinking, 'finally my turn.'

Daddy knelt to me as he had done with Junior and spoke to me as a man. "Stay strong for me, Jamie…" Reaching under my arms, he pulled me up and into a strong hug. In my ear he whispered, "remember what we talked about… I may not be here, but I am always in your heart. I love you so much… Be brave for me."

The tears I tried so desperately to hold back began to pour out unabated. I tightened my grip around Daddy's neck and refused to let go just as Margaret had. I knew I must have looked like a baby to onlookers and I knew that without a doubt Junior would tease me for it later, but I didn't care. At the tender age of five, I thought of Daddy as my world…he was the security I had known. He was a hero…he was my hero. He was my role model and my best friend. He was everything to me, and I knew that soon he would be boarding that train, and I would have no idea when I would see him again.

Daddy rubbed my back and kissed my cheek before putting me back onto the ground. Before he stood back up straight, Daddy wiped away the tears from my eyes, clearing my vision behind the glasses. After the fog was gone, I found Daddy smiling sadly at me with tears of his own swimming deep within his eyes.

"I love you Daddy…" I cried out before taking a deep breath as I wiped away the new tears from my eyes. Gathering myself, I offered my hand for him to shake—man to man.

Daddy, seeming pleased, gripped my hand and firmly shook it before responding, "I love you too Jamie." And his tears could no longer be controlled. "Alright, alright…" Wiping away his own tears, he stood up taking a deep breath and put his hands on his hips as he looked over at Momma. She could only manage a weak smile before leaning into him for yet another hug and kiss. She put her arm out and motioned us to join them as their arms welcomed us into one final family hug.

In the midst of this, I could hear Uncle Tommy speaking with Joan quietly off to the side telling her, "When I get back, we're getting married! You're my girl. And if you'll have me, I am your man."

"Oh, yes, Thomas! Yes!" Joan shrieked, throwing her arms around his neck. "I love you, Thomas John Adler. Always and forever!"

At that time, a high-pitched noise from a whistle ripped through the station, pulling all our attention away from one another and onto the train. Daddy and Uncle Tommy looked at each other and nodded with a silent agreement. They each turned to Momma and Joan respectively and kissed them one final time.

Uncle Tommy moved over to us for the last time. His voice was steady with complete over-confidence, but apprehension lurked within his eyes, "Stay strong you three! We will be home soon." Standing up tall and straight, he saluted us with a familiar and goofy smirk. The three of us gathered ourselves, standing tall to return his salute which would signal our final goodbye.

Daddy moved his attention back to us with uneasiness.

"Now...remember...y'all behave yourself, okay? I don't want to see a letter from your Momma complaining about any of y'all's behavior. Be good to each other and to her. Alright, now give me one more hug." Kneeling for us all to reach, the three of us gave him one more hug. Our arms all locked around his neck. I wanted so much to stay in that moment forever, to stay there, innocent at the age of five wrapped in my Daddy's arms. However, he had to leave. Regretfully, I knew that you couldn't avoid the inevitable.

Daddy unlatched our arms and gave us a wink before jumping up to catch up with Uncle Tommy. And together, side by side, Daddy and Uncle Tommy walked to the men forming a long line to board the train.

It was a slow and time-consuming process; but we, and the rest of the crowd, watched every single man board the train.

The train began to build up steam and puff out heavy smoke from its stack. Whistles blew and the wheels squealed and stutter-skipped to a start. Before the thick smoke devoured the clean air, I was able to see Daddy sticking his head out the window with Uncle Tommy by his side. Both wore identical fake smiles with hints of worry. As the train began to pick up speed, they waved goodbye.

The smoke began to dissipate, leaving us with the fading sight of the train moving further away. Everyone at the station continued to stare into the distance, as we also stared into the unknown that was leaving us empty with loss.

After a while, families began to slowly walk out into the parking lot to begin their new lives. Once Momma and Joan gathered themselves emotionally, they began shuffling us towards the parking lot. Joan was preparing to say her goodbyes to us when Momma interjected.

"Come home with us," Momma told her, grabbing onto Joan's hand. "Come have a late lunch with us, won't you."

"Oh, Katherine thank you. But you don't have to," Joan answered with a few tears rolling down her cheeks. "I shouldn't—I don't want to intrude."

"Don't talk such nonsense! The boys and I would love for you to come home with us. Don't go home and be alone right now. Tommy is family to us which means you are family," A gentle smile crossed Momma face. "—deal with it Joan."

Joan grinned honestly, wrapping her arms around Momma for a hug. "Oh, thank you. Thank you, Katherine. It really, truly means a lot to me."

"We will have each other to get through this." Momma reassured her. "Alright boys! Hop on in. Let's go home."

During the entire drive home, both Momma and Joan discussed what they would cook and prepare for our late afternoon lunch. Eventually they agreed upon biscuits and gravy. This was by far Uncle Tommy's and Daddy's favorite meal to eat for breakfast. We pulled up to our house a little after noon and somehow, from simply pulling into the driveway, the solidarity was already noticeable.

Everyone gathered inside and Momma and Joan left to immediately begin work in the kitchen. They didn't skip a beat. I figured they worked hard to keep themselves busy for the sake of their own emotional well-being.

Davie assumed a position on the couch and Junior grabbed a book to read to waste some time. I, on the other hand, went outside to the Clark Fortress to process things and have some needed alone time. I laid down on the old blankets left intentionally by us and stared up at all the scribbles and drawings from Davie and me over the past few years. All those doodles and dreams from those days had seemed so important at the time. But as I looked back on them now, they just seemed unrealistic and almost foolish.

My mind swiftly took me away into a seemingly never-ending supply of thoughts. 'Where could he be right now? What could he be doing? What was he thinking? Was he scared or exhilarated with this adventure? Were they all pumping each other up for the training that laid ahead?'

Slowly, my thoughts gently pulled me into a deep sleep of dreams about the train and men marching in uniforms. My dreams had brought me to Daddy, and I didn't want to leave it. I wanted to stay within that dream until the day he returned to us. I wanted to stay with him inside my imagination. I wanted to—

"—Jamie! James Lee Clark! Lunch is ready!" Momma hollered through the kitchen window. "Come inside now, please!"

I rolled over with my back facing the entrance of the fort, ignoring my seemingly 'happy' mother. I did not care if I was acting up or being emotional at that moment. I did not care if I seemed rude or unpleasant to our guest. I could not understand how anyone could act as though everything was normal. How could anyone pretend like life could continue as normal. I was angry. Angry at Momma. Angry at the world for taking away someone so vital in our life. I even found myself angry with Daddy. I was angry with Daddy for volunteering to leave us.

Squeaking of the back door opening behind me drew my attention, but I remained in place. I knew it was either my Momma coming out to get me, or one of my brothers sent to find me. But I didn't care. I wanted to remain subdued in my thoughts.

A soft sigh was exhaled from behind me, and I knew it was Momma.

"Dear, you need to come inside for lunch." She rolled me over, forcing me to look at her. "I know this is not easy for you… it's hard on all of us. Daddy isn't gone forever…he will be home again. And until then, we all need to remain strong and continue moving forward…just like your father said. He would want us to all enjoy being together. Together…We need to be together during this time."

I continued to stare blankly at her, not satisfying her with a response. I knew I would not be able to make any coherent sounds due to the intense emotions I was experiencing.

From the house, I could hear plates and forks clattering and the distant giggles of my brothers and Joan. I had no interest in joining their laughter.

"Okay then. You just lay here the rest of the day. No lunch or dinner for you unless you come inside that house and act like you are part of this family. Lay here and think things over. Just think about what your Daddy would want." Her eyes filled with tears, but she was able to hold them back for the stern lecture. "James, you need to stop thinking about yourself and think about your family right now. When you're ready, your seat at the table may or may not be waiting for you." Momma stood up, brushed off her dress, and aggressively turned away to join everyone inside.

'I shouldn't enjoy myself... not while Daddy is gone,' I thought, 'but Daddy wouldn't want me to lay in here the rest of the day either. Ugh...maybe she was right. Daddy would want me inside with everyone. What do I do?' I laid there alone, listening to everyone inside laughing and talking. I heard Davie saying something, undoubtedly with his mouth full of food, to which Momma responded with a 'quit talking with your mouth full!' My stomach began to grumble as I thought of the delectable food prepared by my Mother and Joan.

"Ugh...Fine. Fine. Fine!" I mumbled to myself as I crawled back out into the sunlight.

With attitude, I sauntered over to the back door following the smell of biscuits. I took a deep breath before opening the door to find Momma waiting for me to make the right decision.

Without any hesitation, she grinned at me. "Wash those hands and grab a plate."

I gave her an apologetic smile in return before walking hastily over to the sink to climb up onto the step stool to wash my hands. I grabbed the remaining plate and filled it with the best-looking biscuits and the 'graviest' looking gravy I had ever seen. My stomach rumbled with joy as I took my seat.

"I am glad you joined us. It just wouldn't have been the same without you, Mr. Jamie," Joan winked at me placing her hand on my cheek. I couldn't help but smile foolishly.

We sat at the table for what felt like hours eating and talking with each other about everything and anything that came to our minds. No one, thankfully, ever mentioned my momentary absence from the table. Momma pulled out an extra apple pie she had made the night before, saying she'd thought we would need something a little sweet to cheer us up. Joan's eyes glazed over with excitement at the sight of the pie, especially after hearing Uncle Tommy talk so much about it.

"So, Joan, where are you living in town? You had just moved out here recently, right?" Momma asked.

Joan lowered her head a little with slight embarrassment. "So, I haven't really told you about me yet. I moved here a year ago from my hometown in Columbia, South Carolina. I am actually a schoolteacher over at the boys' school... I teach first year. So maybe next year, I'll teach you two," Joan smiled over at Davie and me.

"Oh, really? Then you just missed teaching Junior then!" Momma responded. "When I was younger, I had always thought about becoming a teacher, but we had Junior so young and these two followed soon after. Anyway, I just think it is such an honorable position to hold."

"Thank you, Katherine," Joan blushed from the praise. "I appreciate it. I have really enjoyed teaching. Anyway, I rented a small room in that tan house just outside of town. I walked to the school most days which is how I met Thomas actually. He began to plan his trips home so he would 'accidentally' run into me. He said Henry used to drive him home, but he decided if he walked home, he had a chance to get to know me a little more. Well, a few days ago he asked me to live at his house while he was gone so I wouldn't have to pay any rent. So, that's what I did. I moved in all my stuff, which wasn't much, just a few suitcases. So, I live in Thomas's house not that far from here," Joan remained timid. "I know that it isn't very accepted for a woman to just live with a man without being married… But I just felt like it was the right thing to do… please don't think bad of me, Katherine."

"I don't," Momma beamed. "You and Tommy work well together. I have never seen Tommy so smitten with anyone. He never introduces us to any of the girls he has ever courted; you are the only one. So, from that we can see just how much you mean to Tommy. You aren't just some random girl he picked out. You've been good for him."

"Yeah, we've never seen Uncle Tommy with a girl before," Junior mumbled, his mouth full of apple pie.

"Junior, please don't talk with your mouth full," Momma sighed slightly while shaking her head.

"We can't help it, Momma," Davie chimed in, mouth full too. He did a little dance in his seat before saying, "This apple pie sure tastes good!"

I giggled watching Davie intentionally make Momma more frustrated by his lack of manners. I couldn't help but laugh. Davie was the king of pushing people's buttons just enough to make them slightly aggravated. Momma didn't say a word to him. She just put her hands on her face in disappointment and gave Davie the look.

Joan giggled at Davie's little seat dance before she stood up from her seat. "Well, Katherine, boys, it's getting late. I really should probably head home. Thank you so much for this delicious lunch and making me feel so welcome here." Joan took her plates off to the sink followed by Momma with hers. "Katherine, if you or the boys ever need anything, please do not hesitate to ask," Joan said gently touching Momma's hand.

"Oh Joan, and you know you are always welcome here." Momma gave Joan a tight hug. "Let me get the keys and I'll drive you home."

"Oh no. It is okay. I think a quiet walk is exactly what I need right about now. It'll give me some time to think, breath in some fresh air, and walk some of that food off," Joan held her flat stomach as though indicating she had gained weight. "But, please, let me help you clean some of these dishes before I leave," Joan insisted.

"Oh, don't be silly. I've got three capable men right here who wouldn't mind helping their old mother," her eyes glared down at all three of us, as if daring us to complain, but we were still sitting at the table, indulging in pie.

Joan responded with a simple smile before making her way to the front door. "Thank you again, Katherine. I will see y'all again soon. Let me know if you get a letter from the men, and I'll let y'all know as well."

"Of course, we will! You should come by for dinner at least once a week. The boys and I would enjoy that!" Momma told her as she followed her to the front door.

"That would be lovely. I might take you up on that offer, especially if there will be more of that apple pie," Joan smiled over at Davie. "Thank you again for dinner. Have a wonderful night."

"I'm so glad you enjoyed it, but you're still not getting the recipe." Momma smiled. "Walk safely, you hear. Goodbye Joan!"

The three of us stood up to rush behind Momma to watch her from behind the screen door. We watched her walk away, out onto the sunshine while we yelled and waved our goodbyes to her as she turned out onto the main road heading back for the city.

"Alright boys..." Momma sighed with her hands on her hips. "...let us get this cleaned up, shall we."

We agreed without argument and completed our home chores before concluding our day with our own, individual activities. Momma made her way to the porch to enjoy the early evening breeze. Meanwhile, the morning arguing between Davie and Junior ceased to exist. We were all trying to behave ourselves as instructed by Daddy.

Junior picked back up where he left off in his book while I laid out on the floor staring blankly at the ceiling. Davie found his little toy Army men and began acting out military training exercises.

The three of us didn't speak again till we turned in for the night. We climbed into our beds, each of us pondering endlessly in our own minds.

The silence was soon broken by Davie, who could no longer control his inner thoughts.

"Junior?" Davie whispered from above me. "Daddy... he will be okay, won't he?"

"Of course. This won't go on very long, Daddy and Uncle Tommy said so themselves. Now...go to sleep." Junior turned over in his bed so his back would be facing us.

I hung my glasses on my bed frame and did everything I could to get comfortable but horrible thoughts took over my imagination. I couldn't rest until I felt assured.

"Junior... everything will be okay, right?"

"Oh gee, yes Jamie! Like I said already...this will be over soon! Now, leave me alone and go to sleep!" Junior hissed at me, lacking any sympathy.

Unseen Scars

I laid there for what felt like hours. I laid there thinking of everyone this would be affecting. My mind even raced to Margaret and Ernie. I wondered how they were handling this new and unwelcome change.

Then the thought crossed my mind again, 'What would life be like from here on out? When will Daddy come home? And how do you keep moving forward in a situation like this?'

I had always struggled with that thought. No matter how old I become, I will always come back to that same question—how do you move forward when life pushes back against you?

And the answer, I concluded, was simple…family.

Chapter 3

November 20, 1941

Every day was one day closer to a year since we all watched Daddy and Uncle Tommy climb aboard that maroon-colored train headed off for Camp Croft. Since then, we would receive a letter from Daddy once or twice a month followed by an occasional phone call. We had been hoping—if not expecting—Daddy to be home in the next few months. However, despite all the hoping and expecting, we actually had no idea when he would be coming back. Things over in Europe had changed so much that there was, unfortunately, no return date anymore.

So, with Daddy gone, Momma decided to get a job with Southern Bell as a telephone operator. It was her way to help during this uncertain time. She, along with many other women across the country decided to pick up jobs over the next few years to help the American economy.

Even with the growing tensions overseas, America had remained neutral. And we remained that way until the tragic date of December 7, 1941.

Unseen Scars

I think we had all been expecting to enter the war, I just don't think we were as ready for it as we thought. From the occasional phone calls and letters from Daddy, we learned that he and Uncle Tommy had been stationed at Fort Lewis located in Tacoma, Washington. With his location being so far from Charleston, it made it impossible for any chance of visiting. This, of course, increased tensions within our own family.

Momma had been amazingly strong through it all, including all the firsts — first birthdays, first holidays, and first anniversaries, all without our father being there. She always made sure we felt safe and hopeful throughout the past year. She put us first, trying hard to be both mom and dad when we needed it. She worked full time at Southern Bell and at home. Food was always on the table on time and the house never lost the cleanliness it had always maintained before all of this began. Momma also did her best to hide the pain she felt from us. She made sure to maintain the innocence that remained in us by not allowing us to take on the responsibilities of adults.

Junior became increasingly distant as the days went by. He had always had a more difficult time expressing his feelings — but since Daddy had left, it became worse. He began to bottle up all his emotions, resulting in a strain on our relationship as brothers. Momma noticed his change in attitude and did what she could to come up with activities to help bring us back together, but nothing worked. We'd still sit on the porch at night together, and Momma would sing from time to time, but Junior wouldn't stay outside with us for long. He would excuse himself so he could lay in his bed to just 'think.' Momma wouldn't fight him on the subject, too afraid of what might happen if she did. We did as much as we could to be there for Junior, but we eventually just learned to let him work through his issues alone.

Davie, for the most part, stayed the same. He matured a little bit since Daddy left but he kept the same spark he had always had. Just to be clear, Davie being more mature only meant he started to pick up after himself and do his chores without being asked. He kept his humor and continued to play jokes on us when he found it most suitable. Davie tended to handle stress and change with humor and wit. Not to say that he didn't express his disappointments as well, but he did so in a healthier manner. He'd sit down with Momma or me just to vent about the frustrations he felt. But not long after, he'd just be laughing again. Davie would try to find the humor in any situation. That was what made him so special.

Then there was Joan. Joan moved back to Columbia with her parents a month after Daddy and Uncle Tommy left. She had been coming over for dinner most days until she officially moved on April 20th, 1941. The day before she left, she came over as she always did, but wearing a smile that was more forced than her natural easy one, and she was more tearful than usual. During dinner she broke the news to us that she and Uncle Tommy were expecting a child and that she would be moving back in with her parents. Momma was honestly thrilled for her — even though, back in those days it was very much frowned upon to be pregnant without being wed. But that was Momma. Momma could see beauty and happiness in everything and everyone she laid her eyes on. Even when that person could not see the beauty in themselves. This gave Joan the comfort and confidence she needed to reveal her pregnancy to us. When Joan did tell us that she would have to move, Momma instantly began to cry. Joan explained that her parents wanted her to move home so they could help her throughout her pregnancy. We were happy for her but devastated to see her go. She and Momma had become close friends within those few short weeks, making saying goodbye that much harder.

Once Joan left, things became just a little darker in Charleston.

November 30, 1941

We received word from Joan that she gave birth to a beautiful baby boy named Thomas Clark Adler. Momma teared up when hearing that Joan gave her son the middle name, Clark, after our family. We were all so thrilled for her and Uncle Tommy. And we were even more thrilled when we received a letter from Uncle Tommy the following week.

The letter read:

Katherine and boys!

Can you believe it? I have a son! Thomas Clark Adler was born November 10th, 1941 at 5:45 in the afternoon. He weighed 7lbs 12oz and was 21 inches long. He is beautiful. Joan enclosed a picture for me in her letter. He has got a nice head of hair. Dark hair like me! And fortunately, he has his mother's nose, ha ha. Joan did say he has long toes like me though... poor boy ha ha. I hope you will all have a chance to meet him soon. I know Joan misses y'all. I hope you are all well! Will keep in touch.

Sincerely, Tommy (Uncle Tommy)

"How about that? Oh, they must be so thrilled! Junior, you weighed 7lbs 12oz too, when you were born. What a coincidence!" Momma exclaimed to Junior, who remained unamused. "Although, you were shorter when you were born... only 19 inches long."

"How about us Momma?" Davie beamed across the table.

"You two, my darling boys, only weighed five pounds each. Both of you were 18 inches long." Momma remembered. "I believe Jamie — you were 5lbs 5oz and Davie — you were 5lbs even."

"Ha!" I laughed to my brother. "I was bigger!"

Davie only responded with simple mockery of facial expressions.

Ignoring us, Momma turned her attention to Junior beside her. "Once your Daddy and Uncle Tommy come home, maybe Joan and Little Tommy will come home as well. Then we can throw Little Tommy a first birthday party next year right here? How does that sound?" She ran her fingers through Junior's hair while smiling down at him.

"Yeah..." Junior scoffed before returning to his book he left on the couch. "Like that will ever happen."

This was the last bit of exciting news we received that year. The next time we received any type of word regarding the war or any possibility of Daddy and Uncle Tommy coming home was on December 7, 1941.

And that...that was not good news.

December 7, 1941

John Daly interrupted our radio time:

We interrupt this program to bring you a special news bulletin. President Roosevelt has just announced that the Japanese naval and air forces have attacked Pearl Harbor, Hawaii, as well as the principal Hawaiian island of Oahu.

All of us sat immobilized around the radio in silence.

My thoughts began running rampant. 'What would this mean for the United States? Would we declare war — or would we not?' I could feel the panic welling up within me. In Daddy's last call, he stated they were continuing to train at Fort Lewis in Washington, but harrowing thoughts, and "what if's" still came to my mind. 'What if they travelled to Hawaii since our last contact with him? What if he had been injured there? Was he safe? What would all of this mean for us? What does our future look like now?'

Later that day, it was announced that 2,403 people were killed during the attack on Pearl Harbor. Junior, as always, returned to the solace of our bedroom where he expected not to be disturbed. Momma, as she always did, let him be. Davie and I remained in place in the living room. My bones and joints felt as though they had been frozen into place. I was afraid. Afraid of what this would mean for our country and our family moving forward. Afraid of the possibilities that could turn into reality. Afraid of the world I once saw as safe. More than 2,000 people lost their lives, and countless others had their lives destroyed by having to now live with that loss. My small mind, innocent and new, struggled with the devastation that was taking place.

'How was it that a world, a world that seemed so good to me, become so evil?' I wondered. 'Has it always been evil? Have I just been naive or simply a child?'

For the first time since I have known my mother, she was unable to remain strong. She retreated to the silence of the porch. The porch, where we would all come together as a family, now was a place of needed serenity. Davie and I watched as she paced up and down the porch lost in thought.

I glanced over at Davie as he too noticed Momma's uneasiness. We stood together and made our way to our weary mother. She was sitting quietly in the rocking chair Daddy made years ago, slowly rocking back and forth in the cold weather that had taken over Charleston and staring off at the world as though she were waiting for an answer as to why this was happening. Part of me thinks she may have been waiting for servicemen to come up our driveway to inform us that Daddy was one of the 2,403 people who were killed in the bombing. But no one came. Daddy had said, he was in Washington State. So, for now, he was safe.

I was unable to watch her sit, lost in her own despair any longer. I placed my hand on her shoulder as I tried to find some way, any way, to ease her pain. For a while, she did not speak. She simply placed her hand on top of mine to let me know that she knew I was there beside her.

Several minutes passed before she finally turned to speak with me.

"Oh, Jamie. My dear, come here." Momma wrapped me in her arms and pulled me onto her lap. "Davie, my darlin', come here too."

Davie walked over to us, and accepted Momma's extended hand. Davie wrapped his arms around her neck, as he pulled himself onto her lap next to me. We sat there, just the three of us, in the calm of the night.

"Momma..." Davie whispered barely audible. "Daddy won't be coming home for a while...will he?"

"I don't think so, my loves," Momma sighed. "I don't believe he will be home anytime soon. But...at least he was not in Hawaii, right? We need to remain strong and hopeful..."

Davie and I both remained silent in Momma's arms.

"I know this isn't easy for any of you. I can't imagine the pain and confusion you three are experiencing, but we must stay strong. Don't you dare let this world take away all the things that make you two so special. You understand me?" Momma's voice changed, becoming more serious as she spoke.

"What makes us special, Momma?" I asked.

"Well, for one, Jamie, you never let this world take away your heart. You care for people regardless of things they do or don't do. And you see things, others can't. Things that make a difference. Don't let this world ... this unfortunate world take that away from you," Momma smiled as she squeezed my arm tight.

"What about me, Momma?" Davie sat up straight to look at her, slightly annoyed that she had not yet mentioned him.

"You, my darling boy," Momma couldn't help but laugh at him. "You have a way of finding the humor in life when everything seems dark. Your smile and contagious laughter are like a candle in the dark. Don't let this, or any hard time take that from you either." Momma kissed his cheek and Davie smiled slyly, content with her response. "No one can be a better you than you... So, both of you two stay true to who you are. Daddy... will be okay... I know he will be. As will Uncle Tommy."

"Momma, what about Joan and Little Tommy?" I asked.

"Joan will most likely stay with her family to give Little Tommy the best life she can offer him until they return home. For now, we will keep up with them through letters and maybe a phone call if we get lucky," Momma looked back at the house and noticed it was getting late. She stopped the chair and redirected our conversation. "Now, let's head back inside. I think we have given your brother enough space for one night. So, let's find him and get dinner cooking. Would you two want to bake a cake tonight too?"

A simple smile was enough for both of us to slide off of her lap and run inside with eagerness. Momma had the ability to bring joy when joy seemed to disappear.

We tried our best to push all that was out of our control, out of our minds. Therefore, we spent the remainder of our evening baking and listening to the record player to take our minds off the rest of the world.

December 8, 1941

We all struggled to get up and go to school the next day, as we were eager to stay near the radio for any more news regarding Pearl Harbor and the war. Thankfully, we were released early so all kids and teachers would be home to hear the president's speech. That speech— which is now more commonly known as the "Pearl Harbor" speech or the "Day of Infamy" speech — was delivered by President Franklin D. Roosevelt. All four of us gathered around the radio to hear the news that would soon change the United States of America forever.

It began:

"Yesterday, December 7th, 1941, a date which will live in infamy the United States of America was suddenly and deliberately attacked by naval and air forces of the Empire of Japan. The United States was at peace with that Nation and, at the solicitation of Japan, was still in conversation with its Government and is Emperor looking towards the maintenance of peace in the Pacific. Indeed, one hour after Japanese air squadrons had commenced bombing in the American Island of Oahu, the Japanese Ambassador to the United States and his colleague delivered to our Secretary of State a formal reply to a recent American message. And while this reply stated that it seemed useless to continue the existing diplomatic negotiations, it contained no threat or hint of war or of armed attack. As Commander and Chief of the Army and Navy, I have directed that all measures be taken for our defense. But always will our whole Nation remember the character of the onslaught against us. No matter how long it may take us to overcome this premeditated invasion, the American people in their righteous might will win through absolute victory...

The president continued to tell us all about the people killed, the ships damaged and lost, as well as the other locations the Japanese attacked. He finally ended the speech with,

"I ask that the Congress declare that since the unprovoked and dastardly attack by Japan on Sunday, December 7th, 1941, a state of war has existed between the United States and the Japanese Empire."

It only took thirty-three minutes after President Roosevelt's speech for Congress to officially declare war on Japan. After the announcement was made, Momma picked up the phone for a long-distance call to MeeMaw and Pa all the way to Raleigh, North Carolina. Momma took the phone into the dining area and began whispering so we could not hear. Trying desperately to take our minds off the new announcement, Davie pulled out our peashooters and beckoned me to follow. Davie and I took them out front as to not disturb Momma or Junior. Junior, seemingly undisturbed by the news, lay, unbothered, on the couch reading his favorite book, The Moffats by Eleanor Estes.

Davie and I ran out to the front yard desperate to reclaim any of the innocence the war attempted to take away. We jumped from the porch, ducked, and rolled while shooting each other repeatedly. We ran off into the trees one by one pretending we were off in war together. When Davie would get shot, he would dramatically fall over and give a detailed play-by-play of all the injuries he sustained.

After close to an hour of being shot with a pea from every possible direction by that rambunctious brother of mine, Momma beckoned us back inside.

"Boys!" Momma hollered from the porch. "David—James—inside please!"

I had just fallen into a pile of leaves after being shot in the head by one of Davie's sniper shots from his position high in the trees. I picked myself up off the ground to gather myself together, as Davie dropped from the tree with an unapologetic smile on his face. We crossed the yard, making our way to the porch, and climbing the steps. We walked through the front door to find Momma standing in the middle of the living room. She was grinning from ear to ear, about ready to bust with excitement.

'What could she be so happy about?' I wondered.

"Boys...I just talked with your MeeMaw and Pa and they have decided to come out here to visit us for a little while! They should be here on Saturday! How—ugh" Momma grabbed the book out from Junior's hands to get his attention. "How exciting is that? Something that will help us all take our minds off everything."

"Ow!" I clapped my hand to the back of my head. "Davie, quit shooting me!"

"Davie come on ... just a few minutes of your attention please." Momma sighed putting her hand out for the peashooters we were still holding. Reluctantly, Davie and I handed them over. "Isn't it exciting? We haven't seen them in years. We will be picking them up at the train station Saturday morning. So, we need to think of sleeping arrangements. They can have my bed and I'll sleep in Junior's bed. We can put you three down here. Junior can sleep on the couch and Davie and Jamie on the floor. Yes, I think that will work..."

Momma was pacing around the living room pointing and trying to imagine where each of us would sleep. You could see the excitement in her eyes as she thought about seeing her parents again. In her search for light when all seemed dim — she found it with family.

Without speaking, Junior got to his feet and stormed off to the stairs.

"Junior, where are you going? Not your room again," Momma placed her hands on her hips while watching her eldest son climb the stairs. "Junior!?"

Junior pivoted his feet with force, locking eye contact with Momma. "Yes, ma'am. I thought I would enjoy my room for however long I have it — you know, before all my privacy is completely taken away from me." With his voice unfailingly stern, he continued to speak. "I don't want to hear any of this. In case you didn't notice, Mom, we just declared war. What does that mean for us? Oh, well why don't we invite family into town, celebrate, or play with peashooters? Who cares if Daddy is going to war? You don't, obviously. So, since you don't care about your husband or our father, I will be in my room." Junior turned to storm up the stairs before Momma's voice stopped him cold, in his tracks.

"Excuse me!" Her voice slicing through the air like icicle daggers. "Henry Gene Clark, you come back down here right now! Don't you dare talk to me like that, as though you are the only one in this household struggling! I am missing my husband. You and your two brothers are missing your father. Not just you! People across the entire nation are missing their fathers, sons, brothers, husbands, and even women are leaving. You are not the only one in this house, or this nation going through something, so don't you dare act like it. It is not fair for anyone involved. But it is what it is. You can go lay in your bed some more to mope around and separate yourself from us further, or you can be the man your father thought you would be and we can work together as a fam—"

"A what? A family!? I am tired of seeing you smiling all the time as though everything is fine. Because it's not fine! Don't you ever cry?! Do you? You put on this fake attitude with us as though everything is normal. Nothing is normal!"

"Junior—"

"No! In case you hadn't noticed, Dad is gone! Uncle Tommy...he's gone! And you? You sing! You smile! Like everything is okay and it's not! Just! Let! Me! Be!" Tears poured down his beet red cheeks. The veins in his neck pulsated with each word spoken.

I had never seen Junior this angry before, nor had I ever seen anyone yell at Momma. How could they? She was perfect.

Momma and Junior stared at one another while Davie and I tried desperately to blend in with the wall. Momma remained calm, unmoved by the words spoken by her eldest son. She took a slow, deep breath, turned, and walked out the front door without hesitation. Junior stood his ground, breathing deeply staring at the wall directly across from him. Momma was outside somewhere, desperately trying to control her emotions before saying anything she knew she'd regret.

'Daddy told me to be the sidekick...I was Junior's sidekick when things were difficult,' I reminded myself. It was my job to help take care of things around the house too. I knew things needed to be fixed but they were just too far broken to mend at this point. 'You have to try, you need to try,' I reminded myself again.

"Junior..." I whispered to my older brother who was still breathing deeply. "Listen, Jun' we—"

"No, Jamie, you listen. This—" he threw his hands up as though trying to show me something I couldn't see, "—isn't right! Kids shouldn't be expected to go along with life as though everything is perfect when it clearly isn't. And that is what we are. We are kids. I'm done living life like it's perfect—"

"But—" I tried to interject.

"No! Dad...Dad...he promised. He promised he wouldn't be gone long! He promised! And Mom... she... she isn't helping!" Junior's body began trembling with rage.

"Junior... you can't blame Momma—" Davie tried.

"Yes! Yes, I can! Dammit! Davie, you think you're so cute and that you understand it all, don't you! You think you're so perfect... you just make jokes to hide your disappointment... you don't fool me—"

"Junio—" I began.

And you..." Junior pointed angrily at me. "You are so damn sensitive..."

"I—"

"Would you grow up already!" Junior shrieked. "You act like a baby all the time! You act like a little girl! You think Dad would be proud of you?! Oh, please! You're supposed to be growing into a man and you're not! You're the exact opposite! Yo—"

"Okay!!" The anger spilled out of my mouth.

Junior stepped back quickly at the unexpected anger that ripped out of me.

"I'm tired of this! You can't continue to act like this, okay? None of us deserve this from you! I miss Daddy just like you miss Daddy! Momma is doing her best bein...being alone and dealing with everything! And you...you act like you don't care about anyone! You know, I'm sure Little Tommy would love to meet his actual daddy instead of looking at a photo. But that's what this world has come to. Maybe instead of feeling sorry for yourself, you should start—"

"Enough—enough—enough," Momma, remaining calm, stepped back inside.

Momma interrupted me when I was at my most heated. My fists were clenched and trembling with an anger I had never felt before.

"David and James," Momma's voice was steady with patience and understanding. "Go outside and play. I need to have a word upstairs with our 'man of the house.'"

Davie and I sat in our fort in complete silence until Momma called us back inside. Junior was sitting at the dining room table, his eyes red and puffy, refusing to look up from his seat. Momma didn't look at him or speak to him to give him any further instructions on what to say or do next.

"I...I want to say that...I'm sor...sorry..." Junior stuttered. "Please... forgive me."

"Okay." Davie and I said together, confused, but appreciative with the sudden change in attitude.

Junior stood up and took his place back on the couch with his book and continued to read as though nothing had ever happened.

"She must of hit im," Davie whispered while looking up at Momma, who refused to take her eyes off the sandwiches she was preparing.

"Why don't... we get the table ready..." I whispered to Davie who nodded in agreement.

The rest of the day was spent in silence as the tension between Junior and Momma loosened with casual conversation carried on by Davie and me. For once I couldn't wait to go to sleep. I had never seen Momma so angry with any of her children. Nor had I ever seen Junior so irate. If this was a new normal for our home, I didn't like it

December 12, 1941

Finally, school was over for the week. I met Davie in front of our elementary school as we did every afternoon before biking home together. Following the incident at home the other day, we quit walking home with Junior. Typically, he would wait for us, but now he'd leave without us. It was as though we didn't exist to him anymore. Which, I guess, was fine for us. As I said in the beginning, Davie and I had each other. And that was enough for us at that time.

The day prior, December 11, 1941, Germany declared war on the United States. The mere thought of Daddy being involved in an actual war began to hit us harder. I remember waking up that morning to Davie crying to himself in his bed. And the kids at school were quieter since most of their daddy's were now in a similar situation as ours.

The dynamic around town had begun to change completely. The preacher and his wife, Kenneth and Mary Taylor, lost their only son in Pearl Harbor. He was only nineteen years old. Grieving and mourning had begun to feel like the new reality of the world. Happiness became less noticeable in this once cheerful place.

We still had not heard from Daddy. It had been November since the last letter, and we began to worry. Momma said it was probably due to the change in the way of the world since the last letter.

"A lot has happened since then," she'd tell us when we'd question her.

Joan called us after hearing the news of war being officially declared. Momma told us she could hear Little Tommy in the background babbling away. He was already 1 month old. Momma would not tell us much of her and Joan's conversation, but only that Joan was worried. She was worried for Uncle Tommy but also of the possibility of little Tommy never having the opportunity to meet his father. Fears similar to this were on everyone's mind during those days. Everyone was worried about what this would mean for Americans overseas and on the home front.

We biked together through the city and out to our quiet home in the country. Neither one of us spoke while we pedaled home. We turned down that familiar driveway when we saw the unfamiliar sight of a thrilled and excited Junior, who stood by the mailbox on our front door, with what seemed to be a smile across his face.

"Oh, look whose already home..." Davie rolled his eyes.

"Is he—is he happy?" I asked Davie, as we pulled our bikes to a halt.

"JAMIE! DAVIE! IT'S DADDY! A LETTER FROM DADDY!" Junior yelled waving an envelope back and forth. "HURRY! HURRY!" He tore inside the house without looking back.

Davie shifted his eyes at me before we pushed off the ground almost simultaneously. We peddled as fast as we could, stopping just in front of the front porch, where we jumped off, rushed up the stairs, and through the screen door. Momma was in the kitchen hugging tightly onto Junior, crying. Momma was in the kitchen hugging tightly onto Junior, crying.

"Come on y'all!" Junior shouted still waving the envelope. His smile was undeniable. "Let's open the letter together!"

"We're coming, we're coming!" Davie shouted as he and I darted through the living room.

"Hurry up Jun'," I nudged him as he fumbled with the envelope.

"I'm trying! I'm trying!" Junior barked back with annoyance. "Ah-ha! I got it!" He yanked out the letter and flattened it before reading:

> Katherine! Boys!
>
> I'm sure by now you have heard the news of Pearl Harbor. I am sorry that I haven't written y'all in a while. It's been hectic to say the least. I don't know exactly how to tell you this, but as you can imagine, enlistments have been extended. This means we will

Unseen Scars

be sent to ████████████████████████
████████████████████████████████
██████

    I know this wasn't what you were hoping. I too am disappointed. We're hoping this will be over by next year. This wasn't part of the plan, I know... I want to be home with you four. I want to be there for all the moments I know I'll miss. Junior, I'm sorry son. Please continue to stay strong for me and take care of your brothers and momma for me. I know that is a lot to ask of a 9-year-old... but unfortunately, these are the times we're living in. Davie and Jamie... same with you two. Stay strong and hopeful. Help your Momma around the house and keep working hard in school.

    Darling, I can't imagine how hard this is for you. This wasn't part of our life plans... but thank you for continuing to stay strong for me. I promise I will make it up to you when I come home. A vacation... anything you want. I promise as soon as I can, I will be home. Right now, America and my brothers need me to be here.

    Can you believe Joan and Tommy had a son? Tommy — our Tommy — a father. It's hard to believe. Joan sends pictures and it's amazing how much he looks like Tommy. Tommy is so proud to have a son and plans on marrying Joan as soon as he is home. It has really given Tommy something to hold onto while we're over here. I'm happy to hear his middle name is Clark. Personally, I think Clark is a good name. Ha Ha.

    Things have been okay here. But I have a feeling that things will change very soon especially over the next few days. I will try to keep you updated as best as I can. Keep listening to the radio for any developments.

Stay strong my beautiful family. I'll be home before you know it. And I will make it up to all of you. We will be a family again soon.

Love to you all,

Henry/Daddy

Our tears were unleashed. We had all been crying together as Junior bravely read through the letter. Momma gripped tightly onto Junior as he spoke. This wasn't the news he had thought he would read. We all knew that war had obviously been declared... but I think deep down we were hoping that Daddy, for some miraculous reason, was coming home. But now, everything was uncertain yet again. It was no longer an issue of 'When will Daddy come home?'. It was now the much bigger issue of 'Will Daddy come home?' The word 'war' had never felt more real than now. Life would never be the same again, and that innocence a child holds would be gone forever.

Chapter 4

December 13, 1941

"David... James... wake up. Y'all need to get up and get ready to pick up MeeMaw and Pa from the train station. You better get with it," Junior said while throwing on his blue vest. "I'm going down to eat breakfast... now you two hurry up."

Since Daddy's letter had come in, I guess you could say Junior had been trying to be a better brother. It was as though he had been reminded to be nicer to us. He wasn't perfect, but he was trying.

"Okay...Okay..." Davie mumbled as he forced himself to stay awake.

"Get up, the both of you... don't make me come back up here," Junior said as he turned away to go downstairs.

"Since when did he become the boss of us..." Davie murmured as he dangled his feet over the bunk bed ladder.

"Who knows? Remember he is the 'man of the house,'" I replied mockingly as I got up to pick my clothes out for the day.

"Oh yes, I remember...Don't fall asleep again, Jamie, or the nine-year-old 'man of the house' will deal with you himself," Davie slammed his fist on his chest, mocking Junior's sudden rise to power.

I laughed at my silly brother's perfect imitation as I reached in the closet to grab my red vest and khaki-colored pants to put on. Before heading off to the bathroom, I grabbed Davie's matching red vest off his bed post.

"Come on you Menace! Get dressed!" and I threw the matching red vest at him.

It took us around an hour before we were all ready to head off. We got there around ten that morning; Davie and I were still yawning. Momma could barely hide her excitement, constantly fixing our hats to ensure we all looked appropriate for MeeMaw and Pa. I was so nervous; I could not even remember what I learned in school a month ago let alone what my grandparents looked like. Last time we saw them, Davie and I were only three. Thankfully, Momma brought a photo of them with us, but even that picture was taken three years prior. I was worried I wouldn't be able to recognize them in the crowd.

The train station was not nearly as busy as the day we dropped off Daddy. Being at that station brought back so many memories of that day — the beginning of the unknown. Now we are back at the station, but this time voluntarily. I saw my friend from school, Ralph Evans. He was at the station with his family welcoming his aunt and uncle into town. Ralph's father was stationed in Hawaii during the bombing of Pearl Harbor. He survived, but according to Ralph, the stress was impacting his mother horribly. His aunt and uncle were coming into town to help take some of the stress off her and to help her take care of Ralph and his three younger siblings.

Ralph met my lingering eyes and smiled. We nodded at each other before he turned away to join his family. I continued to look around the station searching the crowd desperately for a familiar face.

'MeeMaw and Pa should be here somewhere...' I thought.

"Do you see them?" Junior asked me impatiently.

"No..." I responded.

"Yeah... we are a little too short for you to be asking us Jun'," Davie answered standing on his tippy toes, trying desperately to see around us.

"Ahh!!" Momma screamed.

I jumped at the sound of her unexpected burst of excitement. She would not say anything coherent besides jumping and pointing. She stared at us as though we were supposed to see something that would make us just as happy, but we saw nothing. Momma bent down to Junior and pointed through the crowd of people. Junior's eyes glistened with happiness as he started smiling and waving as he saw them too. I tried so hard to look at where they pointed, but all I could see was dozens of older men with brief cases walking around with determination and women standing in crowds gossiping about whatever there was to gossip about.

'Why and what do women gossip about?' I remember wondering at that moment.

Then — I saw them. At first, I saw a small and plump older woman with short ebony brown hair waving with a noticeable smile across her face. She had a genuine look about her and wrinkles that outlined all the memories in her life. The kindness and honesty in her tawny colored eyes reminded me of someone, my Momma. This older woman had on a maroon dress that fell to her shins, a beautiful black coat and a black handbag which was gripped tightly in her left hand. I looked over at Momma's picture and recognized her immediately as MeeMaw.

Behind her and attempting desperately to catch up, was a tall and lean man with thinning blonde/grey colored hair. He had a thick grey mustache and wrinkles around his kind, bespectacled eyes that twinkled bright blue in the sun.

'That's where we got the glasses from!' I thought enthusiastically to myself as I checked again with the photo to confirm the identity of the man.

I was correct — it was Pa. He had a handsome suit on with a grey coat to keep him warm. Pa worked hard to keep up with MeeMaw while carrying two travel bags. Their eyes lit up with joy at the site of Momma, their only child.

"Katherine! My darling baby girl!" MeeMaw exclaimed as she was finally able to wrap her arms around her daughter. "Oh, how I've missed you so much. Oh, you look exhausted! It must be those long hours at work causing those dark eyes...Oh, my dear! Oh—oh—oh, my grandsons!"

Momma rolled her eyes slightly at MeeMaw's comment but continued to smile. "Oh, Momma and Daddy, I have missed you too!" Momma hugged the tall and lean man whom I had assumed to be Pa.

"Vera, Vera, you are going to strangle the poor boy," Pa laughed as MeeMaw hugged Junior so tight he began turning red.

"Oh, I am sorry, Junior," MeeMaw was tearful. "I have just missed yo — oh my twins! Come here and give your MeeMaw a hug!"

I looked over at Davie, who already had eyes on me, and I knew then; I would be first to greet her. "Hello," I stuck out my hand for her to shake, "My name is Jamie—" MeeMaw ignored my hand and gripped onto me so tight I began to get dizzy.

"Last time, Katherine—last time I saw these two precious boys they were just barely out of diapers! Now..." MeeMaw let go of her tight grasp to stare at me, "...I'm assuming you don't use diapers anymore right..."

"Uh..." I began.

"No ma'am, we still use them," Davie smiled sarcastically.

Davie's remark caused Pa to cackle so hard he began to cough. MeeMaw gave Pa a sly smile while she walked up to Davie. "You are exactly as your Mother describes!" She grabbed onto Davie for a tight hug and Davie's arms flailed for help.

I turned to greet Pa but saw Junior already engaged in a conversation with him. I held back and gave Junior his time with our grandfather.

"Well, Katherine," Pa began, "he still is the spitting image of Henry, isn't he? Junior fits him quite perfectly." He smiled at Junior before turning his attention to me. "Well, Jamie is it?" He put his hand out for me to shake and I took it firmly. He and Momma looked a lot alike once you got close enough to see the resemblance.

"It is nice to meet you, sir," I said strongly, standing up straight and tall.

"Sir? Now you may call me Pa," he winked at me before turning his attention over to the gasping Davie. "You must be the little comedian."

"I'm not that little. I've grown 4 inches since last year," with his hands on his hips, Davie responded with sass and confidence.

"Oh, he's still little," Junior's eyes rolled.

"Well, good afternoon, young man," Pa put his hand out for Davie to shake.

"Good afternoon, Pa." Davie gripped Pa's hand and shook it firmly.

"Alright... Well, why don't we get your belongings into the car, head home, and get some lunch started," Momma offered with her arm wrapped loosely around MeeMaw. "How does that sound?"

"How about I cook dear? You look much too tired," MeeMaw smiled honestly while Momma sighed.

I glanced over at Pa who was smiling knowingly at his wife's remarks to their daughter. This was their relationship, and family was family. Pa's eyes found mine again and he winked. I could not help but smile back at him.

We got back to the house a little later than Momma planned. MeeMaw wanted us to drive by our elementary school, the old cigar factory where Daddy had worked, and Southern Bell to see where Momma now worked. MeeMaw gave her unwelcomed opinions on why she thought Momma shouldn't be working and how women should be at home. Momma attempted to explain why she decided to work, but I am not sure if they ever saw eye-to-eye regarding that issue. Pa just sat in the passenger seat quietly looking out the window smiling as though he was just enjoying what appeared to be the familiar banter between Momma and MeeMaw. I assumed by his lack of reaction, they did that a lot while Momma was growing up.

Davie gave MeeMaw and Pa the tour of our elementary school from a street-side view. He gave them his directions on how to get to both of our classrooms and an hour-by-hour schedule of our days. Davie loved telling them about school, and they loved listening to him. They looked impressed with Davie's undeniable enthusiasm about school; but little did they know, school was just a huge social time for him. Junior and I took school seriously whereas Davie thought of it as a social club.

After finishing the tour of our city, we finally arrived back home. Momma and MeeMaw immediately began work in the kitchen while my brothers and I carried their bags inside. After searching through the pantry, MeeMaw and Momma decided to cook-country fried steak with mashed potatoes. Listening to MeeMaw and Momma in the kitchen made me understand how much Momma needed her. Momma needed someone to talk to, someone who would understand what she was going through. And MeeMaw needed her just as much. It made me feel happy, knowing Momma was happy.

We men sat in the living room listening to Pa tell stories about his younger days and stories of Momma growing up. We found out that MeeMaw and Pa live out on a farm in Raleigh, North Carolina. He told us about the crops they grew and the cattle they tended to. I wanted so desperately to visit them and learn how to take care of cattle myself. We had chickens at our home, and we had a garden, but it sounded nothing like what Pa had. We learned things about Momma and Daddy's childhood too. For instance, we never knew Momma practiced ballet as a little girl. We also didn't knew that she and Daddy had once skipped school to steal Pa's boat to go fishing. After that incident, Momma and Daddy were not allowed to see each other outside of school, but that clearly did not stop them.

Pa laughed and said quietly to us, "I'm glad our punishment didn't work."

It only took MeeMaw and Momma an hour or so to cook lunch and get the table set. You could see how proud MeeMaw was as she set the table getting ready for lunch. It had been a long time since our house felt full and complete.

"Alright boys! Get up and wash up for lunch," Momma yelled from the kitchen. Junior was first up, running for the stairs, followed by Davie, then me. "And don't you three make a mess!"

"I got here first!" Davie yelled.

"No, you didn't, you child! Back off and wait your turn like a good brother!" Junior snapped back pushing Davie out of the bathroom.

"Don't call me a child, you emotional nine-year-old!" Davie yelled back while grabbing the bar of soap out of Junior's hands.

As they argued back and forth, I left them to sit patiently on the staircase waiting for my turn. I realized Pa was not on the couch anymore. This got my attention so I listened intently for any whispering downstairs. Tuning out my arguing siblings, I caught onto whispering coming from the kitchen. I crept further downstairs hoping to hear their conversation.

"—well, they've been saying the war could last longer than five years—" I recognized Pa's voice.

"— I hope not. The boys would be devastated if Henry was gone that long." that was Momma.

"Honey... your father and I were talking and decided it would be best for you and the boys if you came home...to live in Raleigh with us... at least until the war is over," MeeMaw pleaded.

"No." Momma responded quickly.

"Katherine... we could help with the boys. You wouldn't have to work. It would take the pressure off you." MeeMaw continued to plead. "We live on a farm, the boys would work, learn, and take their mind off Henry's being gone. The boys need a father figure and currently they don't have that...an —"

"Momma... this is my home. This home is our life. That porch... each of my babies took his first steps on that porch. Junior fell off that couch when he was five years old and knocked out his first tooth. That fort out there... Henry helped Jamie and Davie build that. And this town is where Henry and I have lived since we got married. I can't — we — cannot leave this house." Momma softly explained to them.

"Junior just started talking to me again. Moving him away from the only connection he has left of his Father...I just...I can't do that to him. Henry still has a chance at coming home alive and I won't move my family without Henry being home. So, deal with my working and looking tired because this is my family, my home, and my decisions. Please."

"Okay... okay..." Pa's voice was calming. "Just remember if you need us... you and the boys are always welcomed with us. For any reason. We will protect you and will always be there to help you. Okay?"

"Okay, Daddy." Momma said calmly.

"What are you listening to—" Junior whispered into my ear.

I jumped at his voice losing my footing on the staircase. Steadying myself, I pushed Junior up the stairs and into our bathroom. I shoved Davie past the sink, pulled the confused Junior in, and shut the door hurriedly.

"What th—" Davie began, his face full of soap and water.

"Shhh—" I hissed while throwing him the hand towel.

"Jamie... what's going on?" Junior asked.

"Boys? Are y'all ready for lunch!" Momma yelled up.

"Almost Momma!" I answered quickly.

"Hurry up before lunch gets cold!" Momma hollered.

"Yes ma'am!" I screamed back before focusing back on my brothers. I lowered my voice for them, "I overheard MeeMaw and Pa talking about us moving up to Raleigh—"

"What... no! I'm not goin—" Junior began.

"Momma said no..." I clarified before his anger got the best of him. "—but Pa—" My voice became solemn, "—Pa said... he heard the war could last up to five years..."

"Five years..." Davie mouthed.

"How does he know that...?" Junior could not believe what I was saying.

"I don't know Jun... He didn't say—" my eyes locked onto Junior. "—Junior... what if it does last five years...?"

"Look...Jamie, we don't know how accurate that is. Like Daddy said we need to just stay hopeful... okay. We have each other right..." Junior was talking as though he was trying to remind himself of that too.

"Yeah..." I sighed.

"We all need to stick together...okay...Just like Daddy told us..." Junior said with his voice steady. "We're brothers..."

"We're brothers..." I agreed.

"...the best of brothers..." Davie for once, remained serious.

"—I guess we need to go downstairs or Momma's gonna come up here," I said softly.

"Alright, I'll head down. Get washed up Jamie. And look...I know how you get, okay. Don't worry or stress out too much about it. Pretend like you heard nothing, okay? Get your head on straight before you come downstairs. Okay?" For once Junior was acting like the older brother. "Davie, are you done?"

"Almost Jun'." Davie answered while drying his face off.

Junior left, making his way downstairs to join our family. I went into our bedroom to clean off my eyeglasses that got fogged up from the steam in the bathroom.

'Everything is okay... everything will be okay,' I told myself.

Junior was right. I had to calm myself down before I went downstairs. I didn't want Momma to know I eavesdropped on their conversation, or that I told my brothers what they discussed. So, I had to act normal. This for me, was more difficult than for my brothers. I was—as Junior always said—more emotional than them.

Once calm, I walked back into the bathroom to wash my hands and face. But—Davie was gone. I could have sworn I did not hear him leave to go downstairs. I blew it off and continued to wash my hands and face. I reached to grab for the hand towel in its normal spot, but it was gone.

"Ugh...Davie..." With my glasses off, I was left with nothing but blurred vision. I almost grabbed a new towel out of the cabinet when I saw the blurred blob of a towel hanging off the side of the hamper. I stretched my arm out to grab the barley dirty hand towel when—

"BOO!" Davie jumped out of the hamper with dirty clothes flying out with him.

"AH!" I hollered as I leaped back, hitting the wall behind me. "DAVIE! Come on ..."

"What—I was trying to calm you down..." Davie laughed. "You were all worried about possibly moving to Raleigh... I was only trying to help..." he smirked.

"Oh yeah Davie... I'm relaxed now, thanks—" I threw the dirty clothes back at him.

"You are welcome," Davie said smugly.

Eventually, Davie and I made it downstairs to join the rest of our family. We had a good late lunch, talking and telling each other stories. We found out that MeeMaw and Pa were the ones who gave both Davie and me our matching teddy bears when we were babies. Davie and I kept those bears with us on our beds every day until the day we were separated. I named my bear Winston and Davie named his Rufus. And to this very day, I still have Winston and Rufus. After all these years, I have managed to keep those two bears together, and they will be together until the day I die.

Junior, later, showed off a photo of Daddy in his uniform to Pa and MeeMaw. It was a photo Daddy sent to us earlier that year to show us his 'new look' as he wrote in his letter. Pa looked so proud to see his son-in-law dressed up in uniform. MeeMaw carried on and on about how handsome he looked, and Momma could only smile as she listened to all the compliments about her husband. I couldn't help but smile too. I was proud of my father, then and now.

After supper, Junior, Davie and I were sent upstairs to get ready for bed and to clean up our bathroom and bedroom for Momma. We said our goodnights to Pa and MeeMaw as they unpacked their belongings in Momma and Daddy's room. Momma made her way upstairs to tell us she had the downstairs all ready for us for bed.

"Why do we have to sleep down there? Our beds won't be taken," Davie asked curiously.

"Because dumb dumb—Momma needs her space and privacy. She doesn't need to share a room with you and Jamie." Junior said to him smugly. "And trust me I know what that is like."

"Like you're so wonderful to live with…" Davie responded.

"Because… I need my privacy. Anyway, the floor is made for you two and the couch is ready for you, Junior. Goodnight, my boys." Momma kissed each of us on the cheek before going into what was now her bedroom and closing the door for the night.

We set off downstairs to turn in for the night. Junior jumped on the couch smiling while Davie and I tried to get as comfortable as we could on the floor. Davie sighed staring off at the ceiling and I joined him, lost in our thoughts.

"Junior…" I started.

"Goodnight, Jamie," Junior responded before I could even talk. "Goodnight Davie. Don't let the bed bugs bite…oh yeah, that's right!

Don't let the floor bugs bite." He snickered in the dark thinking he was so clever.

Davie mocked him with incomprehensible words and soon I drifted off to sleep. I dreamed of living on that farm with cattle, goats, and chickens up in Raleigh, North Carolina. I did not have to go to school anymore, I was just a farm boy. But things quickly became dark...

'No, no, no... I don't want to live here! Where is Davie...? Where is Junior? Why can't I find anyone? Momma? Daddy?' I was alone...alone in the dark, stranded on a farm I had never been to before. 'Daddy!?' I screamed desperately in my dream. My voice echoed throughout the endlessness of the night, signifying further just how alone I was. Off in the distance, surrounded by dark and eerie woods, I saw a shadowy figure standing alone. From the distance between us, I was unable to tell who the shadowy figure was. The figure stood as still as the night around us. The hair on my neck stood up at the sight and my pulse increased with fear. Somewhere in the dead of night around me, an echoing pop rippled through my eardrum followed by a horrifying scream. A scream that you would only hear in the movies. But from where? I searched around me for the source but found nothing to pinpoint the scream or the pop. Misty fog surrounded me, pulling me deep into the darkness. I fought desperately to break free, but nothing was working. I couldn't be silenced. I couldn't be taken. I tried to get away. But it took me.

"Jamie...? JAMIE...?" Davie's voice came through my thoughts.

"No...No...." I muttered.

"Jamie...wake up!" Davie fiercely shook my body out of the dream and back to reality.

My eyes snapped open, ripping me from the darkness and into the morning light that shone on me through the window curtains. The safety of familiarity of my home steadied. My breaths slowly began to relax with each passing second as I lay there. My glasses were being forced onto my face to help bring clarity to my immediate surroundings.

"Are you okay?" Davie's face was mere inches away from me.

"Yes... I—I –I think so..." I breathed. "I'm sorry...I'm sorry—"

"You okay Jamie?" Junior was sitting up on the couch, still waking himself up.

"Yeah..." I sat up, my mind still spinning. "I'm sorry I woke y'all up..."

"Don't worry about it..." Davie told me. "What... what were you dreaming about anyways?"

"Probably something dumb...like always..." Junior scoffed, standing up to head to the kitchen. "Probably had a dream his clothes didn't match for school...or he was naked in front of school. Yeah! That sounds right! Naked in front of the school! Am I close, Jamie?"

Ignoring my seemingly back-to-normal, harassing older brother, I focused on Davie. I didn't know how to tell him about my dream. I didn't know how to tell anyone. What did it mean? What did it signify? If I knew then, what I know now, I would have told my family to run and hide away. But...there was no running. There was no way of knowing what was to happen. No way for anyone to know.

We spent the remainder of that day, and many of the days ahead, enjoying our time making memories with our grandparents. Pa took us fishing down on the Ashley River, something we hadn't done since Daddy left. MeeMaw and Momma brought us a picnic, just like we did when Daddy was home. Life had not felt so normal in an awfully long time.

Later that day, Pa tried to teach us how to shoot a pistol in the backyard. Junior was the first to learn and he did well. He shot each and every target Pa laid out for him. I flinched at the sound of the pistol and was too afraid to shoot it, which of course brought much ridicule from Junior. Pa forced me to at least hold the gun, which resorted in me shaking and crying uncontrollably. While Davie encouraged me, Junior mocked and harassed me. It just made me nervous, holding a gun. I did not like guns. Daddy never forced me to hold a gun, said I'd learn when I wanted to. I ran inside embarrassed and humiliated, and I found Momma. She allowed me stay inside away from my much tougher brothers and spend time with her and MeeMaw instead.

This was far less than enjoyable. MeeMaw and Momma were gossiping. Gossiping about girls Momma had grown up with who turned out to be nothing more than 'hustlers' as MeeMaw referred to them. I eventually left them in the kitchen and snuck off into the fort where a picture of Daddy was now hanging proudly. I lay there thinking of Daddy and how much he was missing. I enjoyed getting to know MeeMaw and Pa while they were visiting us, but the void of Daddy's absence was still present.

Pa tried to give us that fatherly figure back that we three had desperately missed in the time Daddy had been gone. And it was refreshing. Pa could never take Daddy's place of course, but his presence was needed and accepted by each of us.

So, to say we were devastated when they had to leave was an understatement. Saturday, December 20, 1941 was a quiet day for the Clarks. It was another sad moment at the train station watching loved ones board a train leading off to another place leaving us alone.

It was only five more days before Christmas—our first Christmas without Daddy. So, we said our goodbyes and early "Merry Christmas" while we hugged each other tight and cried. It was sad seeing them go. I would miss seeing them every morning and every night. I would miss their hugs and the laughter. But—I wouldn't miss sleeping on the floor.

"Now Katherine, you just remember what your father and I told you," MeeMaw said.

I had been so lost in the many adventures of their visit that I almost forgot about their plea to Momma the first night they arrived. So, when MeeMaw said this, my mind rushed straight back to the nightmare from the first night. I still had no idea what that dream could have meant for us, but Momma's response reassured every insecurity I had.

"We will be okay," Momma hugged her tight. "I love you, Momma."

We watched them board the train leaving us on that platform alone with nothing but hope and strength as we looked toward many more days without Daddy. It is never easy being the one who leaves, but it is never easy being the one left behind, either. Family is something we all should hold onto and appreciate. Even when you are miles away, family will always be there to guide and help you. You never know when that family, whether they be near or far away, will end up being the only thing you will have left in this world.

I know I didn't...

Chapter 5

May 21, 1945

"Happy Birthday to you, Happy Birthday to you! Happy Birthday, dear Jamie and Davie! Happy Birthday to you!" Momma sang to us while holding onto a decadent chocolate cake especially baked by her with a few candles on top for us to blow out. Meanwhile, Junior sat with his head resting in his hands as he stared off at the wall.

We turned ten years old today. It had been four years since we'd seen Daddy... four long years. We would still get letters from him, once or twice a month, but each letter was shorter and shorter. We could feel Daddy losing hope with each letter received. Even though he would tell us to remain strong, I could feel that was getting harder for him. It was a relief knowing that Daddy was still alive. After everything that had happened during that war, we were fortunate. By that time thousands and thousands of Americans had died fighting in Europe and in Japan, so each letter we received was a blessing.

At this point, it had been twenty-one days since our last letter from Daddy, which wasn't normal. It made us worried regarding his safety and well-being. However, since no one had come to our door in uniform, we just assumed he was busy. After all, he was in Europe during one of the greatest wars in history.

Junior, on the other hand, had lost all hope in ever seeing Daddy alive again. And with each passing year, he became more and more distant from us. He was almost thirteen years old, which to Junior meant he was a true man. So, he decided it was time for him to have a job. He managed to get hired on as a paperboy, and he took his job seriously. He really wanted to help Momma out by contributing to the grocery budget and paying some of the bills. Every morning, he would wake up early and head into town on his bike to deliver newspapers before school. Momma was proud of him for helping us, but sad to see his childhood leaving.

"Alright Davie and Jamie...make a wish and blow out your candles together!" Momma directed.

Davie and I smiled at one another and thought of a wish that would be good enough for our tenth birthday. I got it; my tenth birthday wish was for this war, that had taken so many lives, to be over. We assumed Daddy and Uncle Tommy remained in good health, because they were still deployed. I guess, in a way, that was a good thing, as it meant — well — it meant that they were alive. That was something to be thankful for.

We had not seen Joan in four years either. Once she had little Tommy, who was already over three years old, we heard less and less from her. Her life and ours had changed substantially once war was officially declared. We continued to write her, but we had not heard from her for over a year. And we understood. She had a job to do. She was a single mom to a little boy who had never once met his father. She had to change her perspective and focus on what was most important, her son.

"Got yours?" Davie whispered.

"Yep!" I responded proudly. "Are you ready?"

"I'm ready!" Davie nodded.

We grasped hands and closed our eyes tight before blowing out the candles for our tenth birthday. The candles burned out quickly leaving us in the dark. It always felt magical blowing out the candles on your birthday, especially being a twin.

According to Momma, we'd held hands since we were born. She told our birth story every year, always ending with, "As soon as they laid y'all together...you reached for each other and held hands."

And when we first started walking, we would walk — side by side — holding hands. So, we made it a tradition to hold hands and blow out our candles together on our birthday. In this huge and magnificent world, he was my person. We were meant to share this world with each other, and we were meant to be together forever.

But just because things are meant to be, doesn't mean they always happen.

As the smoke settled, I saw Junior sitting unamused in his chair, ignoring our joy and excitement. But it didn't bother me. After MeeMaw and Pa's visit, Junior, if possible, became more distant. As each day passed, I could feel my brother slipping further and further into isolation. Further into an abyss of anger and depression. I knew that as he got himself deeper into the dark, it would only become that much harder to get him out. So, I longed for — and hoped — that my birthday wish would come true, ending the war, and bringing everything back to normal.

"Oh, my goodness! Happy Birthday, my baby boys!" Momma exclaimed while clapping with much enthusiasm. "Alright! Alright! Present time! Junior... Junior! Oh, goodness, Junior come help me please! Go upstairs, where I showed you, and get their gifts. I will start cutting the cake!"

Junior groaned loud enough for everyone to hear. He wanted Momma to know how much he detested her request.

Nonetheless, he left to go upstairs and returned with two gifts in his hands. I looked over at Davie who was practically drooling as Momma cut each of us a slice of chocolate cake. Junior placed the two gifts on the table across from us. The first gift was a smaller and flimsier gift, wrapped in green paper and green bow on top. Taped across was a white envelope with familiar writing on top reading, 'Davie.' The other gift was stockier than Davie's. It was wrapped in blue paper with a blue bow on top and a similar white envelop taped down with the familiar writing, 'Jamie.'

Momma loved cards. She use to always say, 'giving and sending cards was a reminder of the love and respect you have for one another.' Cards were a must in our family.

"Alright boys!" Momma looked like she was about to burst with excitement. "Remember! Open the envelope first! Because cards are always a reminder of —"

"—of the love and respect you have for one another..." Davie, Junior and I said in unison.

"Yes, that is correct," Momma smiled slightly at each of us.

"Yes Momma, we remember," Davie goofily remarked.

"Well, I'm glad you all were listening—" She nodded with approval.

Unable to wait any longer, we ripped through those envelopes like they were candy wrappers. Once I got through the white envelope, I saw a white house pictured on the front of the card; it resembled our home only wider. There was a long-curved driveway with a garden on either side. Running on the driveway away from his home was a boy and his dog. The boy smiled gleefully while holding onto a brand-new model plane. Written on top of the card in blue ink was, 'Happy Birthday Young Man!' Every year Momma would write something inside for us individually. So, I flipped it open to read eagerly:

My dear, Jamie!

I cannot believe my two little boys are ten years old today! I know your Daddy would be proud of the young man you are turning into. You have continued to do well in school and have made me prouder than I can explain. I hope you have a wonderful birthday, my sweet boy.

I love you forever, Momma.

I looked up catching Momma's loving eyes watching us intently as she tried desperately not to miss a single moment. She smiled from ear to ear as she watched us read her notes. As Davie and I did every birthday, I passed him my card to read and he passed me his. His card had a picture of a little boy in a baseball uniform holding a baseball bat in one hand and a baseball out for a begging dog in the other. Written across the card said, 'Happy Birthday To A Fine Young Man!'

My Davie!

Happy Birthday to my little boy now grown. You and your brother have grown up so fast. You have been the one to keep me laughing since your Daddy left. Keep making us laugh and making your Daddy and me proud. You are turning into a fine young man and I am so proud of you. Happy Birthday, my always funny boy.

I love you, Momma.

"Thank you, Momma!" I told her sincerely.

"Yeah, thank you, Momma! Now can we open the gifts?" Davie smiled foolishly.

"Yeah, yeah... okay, go ahead and open the gifts one at a time. Jamie, since you opened yours first last year, let Davie go first this time," Momma told me sternly as I reached for my gift.

Sighing dramatically, I pulled my hands back sluggishly.

"Yes! Yes! Gimme! Gimme!" Davie grabbed his present and began opening it without any hesitation. With each rip he made, the louder his laughter grew. Davie was never greedy, but he was extremely passionate when it came to opening his gifts. "A whoopee cushion!" Davie exclaimed holding onto the 'pink, rubbery, and inflatable hell,' as Junior would call it.

'Oh lord,' I thought to myself as I forced a smile across my face. 'This will be going off all night....'

"Thank you! Thank you! Thank you!" Davie yelled before blowing air into it until his face turned all different shades of red.

Davie jumped up from his chair, threw the whoopee cushion on his seat and jumped back on the chair with a big toothy grin across his face. An awful sound of Davie 'breaking wind' came from below him followed by immense laughter. I couldn't help it, I laughed with him. Even Junior cracked a smile watching his youngest brother crack himself up over 'fart sounds.' Davie got up, ran to Momma with his arms wide open and jumped in her welcoming arms.

"OH!" Momma snorted. "Happy Birthday, my darling!"

"Thank you, Momma!" Davie told her again with his arms wrapped tightly around her.

Momma lowered Davie to the ground and looked at him more seriously now, "You are only to use this at home. If I find out you brought that thing to school or put it on the teacher's chair, I promise you, David William Clark, you will have it taken away from you in a second."

"Yes ma'am—I mean no ma'am! I won't take it to school. I promise…" A sly smile appeared across his face, as though he were planning already. "…although—it would be funny—"

"David…"

"But I won't—I won't, I promise," Davie gave her an unpromising smile.

"Alright…Thank you," Momma's eyes lingered on her jokester son. "Now Jamie…it is your turn dear!" Momma sat across from me pulling Davie up in her lap.

Junior slid over my gift so I could reach it quicker, and I started ripping away at the paper. I was so excited to finally lay my hands on my mystery gift. With the war going on, gifts and toys were hard to come by. Goodies and other items around the nation became increasingly scarce. So, for us to even have something to open was a miracle. But there was no way Momma would let us go a birthday without something to unwrap.

Finally, I got to the box underneath the wrapping and I saw a picture of an army plane. I just saw this in town a few weekends back and was fascinated with it. Clearly, Momma took notice. I pulled the gift out of the box as fast as I could, and my mouth dropped wide with amazement. It was an Army plane! Just like the planes used in the war.

"Momma…" I mumbled, trying desperately to form more words. "This is…I can't…I can't beli…Thank you!"

"I thought you might like it. Momma smiled proudly at me.

"But, how much—" I blinked repeatedly questioning her. "Momma…the money—"

"Don't you worry about that." She smiled gracefully. "This is y'all's birthday…it's deserved."

"Thank you!" I told her again.

"Whoa! That is neat!" Davie's eyes were huge with fascination.

I grabbed my new Army aircraft and began running around the living room and dining room, pretending I was flying over Germany, firing ammo onto enemy land, swerving in and out from oncoming planes. I rounded the living room counter and ran with my arms out, straight into Momma, who was now picking up wrapping paper Davie and I threw onto the floor.

"Oh!" Momma laughed, heaving me up into arms. "I am so glad you like it, Jamie!"

"I love it!" I exclaimed, throwing my hand holding the plane in the air. "This has been such a great birthday!"

"Momma, can we just eat some cake now?" Junior asked. "Davie already grabbed a plate."

"Tattle tale." Davie mumbled with his mouth full.

"Yes, yes," Momma sighed. "Get some cake, Jamie… before your brothers eat it all."

We all sat down at the table and enjoyed the chocolate cake. Davie and I were showing off our new gifts to Junior, who looked as though he was being forced to celebrate with us. Momma quickly ran over to the kitchen and pulled out two more envelopes from the drawer. She smiled at us, holding the envelopes behind her back so we couldn't peek at the writing on the front.

"There are two more envelopes for you to open," Momma said with a mischievous look on her face. "Here is the first one... It's from your MeeMaw and Pa. So...open it together."

Davie grabbed the envelope and ripped it open with me by his side waiting eagerly. I saw MeeMaw's familiar handwriting on the front and smiled. They sent us a card with a picture of two boys walking outside with their arms draped over each other's shoulders. On the top of the card was printed writing: 'Happy Birthday to a Well-Matched Pair!' Davie and I laughed together at the card before opening it to read her writing.

Inside was a handwritten message from MeeMaw.

Jamie and Davie!

Happy 10th Birthday you two sweet boys! I wish we were there to join y'all in your celebration! We hope y'all have a wonderful time together celebrating your double-digit birthday! Your Pa and I are so proud of you two boys and everything you have accomplished. We are praying this year brings an end to the chaos overseas and your Daddy comes home! But today live in celebration with those around your table and remain grateful for all we have. We love you boys so much.

Happy Happy Birthday!

Sincerely, MeeMaw and Pa.

Two quarters wrapped in a separate note with Pa's writing fell out of the envelope. The note said:

'A quarter each for my two grandsons. Spend it on yourselves.'

"Momma! Look!" Davie breathed.

"A quarter!" I boasted.

"I see!" She agreed as she read over Pa's note. "Maybe this weekend we can all go to the store so y'all can pick something out? How does that sound? Now, you both need to write them a thank you letter tonight, you hear me?" Momma had on her 'motherly-lecture' face.

"Sounds swell!" Davie shouted while safely putting the quarter in his pants pocket and shooting Junior a threatening stare.

"Now… this second envelope is for all of us, but I thought it would be special if the birthday boys got to open it," Momma said, while trying to get Junior's attention.

She laid the envelope on the table so we could all see the familiar scribbled handwriting on top.

"Daddy!" Davie and I shrieked together in unison.

"Dad!" Junior finally pipped up, reaching out to grab the envelope.

"Whoa, whoa, whoa!" Momma yanked back the envelope. "Someone is finally paying attention."

"Come on, Momma, please? Please let me open it?" Junior begged.

"No sir… It's your little brothers' birthday!" Momma chimed back.

"Aw… Come on…" Junior crossed his arms angrily.

Ignoring Junior, Momma passed us the envelope beaming with excitement. Davie locked eyes with me and nodded, giving me the okay to open and read the letter.

I grabbed the letter with minor hesitation. I had no idea what I would to read or learn in this letter. The only thing I knew for certain was that Daddy was alive… at least from the time he wrote that letter.

I smoothed out the letter, took a deep breath, and began to read his words out loud to my now impatient family. Daddy wrote:

Hi all,
I don't … I don't know where or how to begin this letter. I've tried to write this letter at least a dozen times. Well…here it goes.

On April 22 my unit and I were walking along ████████████████████████████ We all thought we were in the clear. We were laughing... talking about home and our families...when my shoe became untied. I stopped walking and Tommy did too. I bent down to tie my shoe and .... as soon as I bent down a pop went off from far away and Tom—

"No ... No..." I breathed.

I felt the tears begin to burn down my cheeks. I couldn't read anymore. If I read it, that would make it real. And I refused. I couldn't read it. I tossed the letter down onto the table and tried to walk away, but Momma stopped me. Everything was blurred. I couldn't focus on anything around me. My mind began racing with thoughts of panic that I could no longer control. I saw Momma's lips moving, but I couldn't hear the words she spoke. Life was in slow motion. Pressure consumed my body, pulling me back together. Momma's arms tightly embraced me, and the world stopped spinning. Slowly everything came back into focus. My breathing stabilized and my vision cleared.

Junior, who had been emotionless for the past year, was now sobbing uncontrollably with his hands entangled in his hair. Davie was looking at me in disbelief. For the first time in my life, I saw my brother... my baby brother by five minutes, become the older brother. He picked up the letter, stood up, took a deep breath, and continued where I could no longer continue.

—Tommy fell to the ground next to me. I tried to save him. I promise. I pulled him to me to find where he was hurt... I tried. I couldn't... I couldn't save him. I pulled him to the side of the road to protect him and I fired back at whoever was there. My arm... I got hit. My left arm was shot. When I woke up, I was in ████████████████ being cared for...I'm sorry. I know how much he meant to you all...I'm sorry for disappointing you. I'm sorry. I truly am... Dad/Henry

Once Davie finished reading that letter, the tears could not be controlled. Davie fell to the floor crying and screaming out to the world in pain. A pain we had never felt before. A type of pain no one should ever have to experience.

Immediately, Momma dropped her arms from around me to pick Davie up. She tried desperately to comfort him, to end his pain. But...there was no way to end the pain that now consumed him. No one could bring Uncle Tommy back...little Tommy, who is no longer a baby, will never get to know his father. He will never know how truly amazing his father was. He will never throw a ball with his daddy or learn how to swing a bat like Babe Ruth. He will never go fishing with his daddy or simply spend time with him. He will look in the mirror and never realize how much he looked like his daddy. He will never have that reunion at the train station. Instead, little Tommy will say goodbye to his daddy at his funeral looking at only a stone.

'How—How can this world...a world that seemed so great...be this evil?' I cried in my mind. 'How can the world do this to an innocent 4-year-old boy? ...Is there actually a God!?'

On May 7th, 1945—just two weeks before our birthday that year—Germany surrendered to the United States. Uncle Tommy, having survived the entire war with only minor scrapes and injuries, died just fifteen days before war ended. And now Daddy was stuck at a medical facility, somewhere in Europe, being treated for a bullet wound to his arm.

'Where was God in all of this?' I questioned desperately.

"Okay..." Momma began as she wiped the tears from her eyes. "Um...okay...umm, boys we need to...umm... Jun—Junior!"

Junior threw his chair out from below him and stormed out the front door. Each footstep sent an echo throughout the house, symbolizing the anger that filled his body. He left the house without looking back at us. He left us alone as we tried to piece it all together. Momma picked up Davie, who wept uncontrollably on the floor, and ushered us to the couch.

"Stay here..." She told us.

Seconds later, she was out the door to find my grieving brother. We were left sitting there in the quiet of the living room...alone. Grief echoed off the walls. Junior's anger from outside seeped through the walls of our home. I could feel the tension rising with each passing second.

"Daddy got shot..." I whispered, trying anxiously to wrap my head around everything.

"...I know," Davie breathed.

"Uncle Tommy..."

"...I know..." Davie breathed again.

"What..."

"I don't know..." Davie looked at me. His once life filled eyes, were now empty.

I sat paralyzed, absorbed in the silence, staring at our living room that housed so many memories. Memories of Uncle Tommy began flooding my thoughts. I thought of the day when Uncle Tommy brought Joan over to meet our family. The smile on his face was just pure happiness. He had no way of knowing, and neither did we, he would never step foot inside our house again. Our house. Where he taught Davie how to camouflage in with his environment to scare people as a prank. The front yard, where he taught us all how to swing a bat like Babe Ruth. That dinner table was where he would tell us story after story of things he did as a child, things we could have never imagined doing. He was a man who knew how to be professional but how to also enjoy life too. He was a man of honor, a solider, and a friend of anyone he met. I could not believe it had already been a month without his presence in this world. A month without Uncle Tommy being out there somewhere in this world. He was gone forever, and nothing could change that. No amount of tears, anger, or depression would ever bring him back. And, for me, understanding that has been one of the hardest things I have done in my life. When you experience the death of a loved one, a part of your innocence is destroyed. Life is not ordinary; it is a miracle beyond anything. When you can move forward and past all the pain that might try to pull you back into the dark — that too, is a miracle.

The door creaked open and my thoughts were interrupted. The white ghostly face of Junior re-entered followed by Momma. Without making eye contact, he walked into the living room and sat in the chair near us. Momma's eyes followed him until he sat, then her eye fell on us. She looked empty and defeated, as though the world had just slipped out from under her. But then—a sparkle appeared in her eyes.

"Get up," she ordered us with determination.

"Wha..." Davie began before being interrupted.

"Don't argue. Get up and come to the front door," Momma walked straight through the living room, turned into the kitchen, and came out holding her handbag and keys.

We all stared at her, trying to figure out what her next plan might be. But none of us had a clue.

"Don't just stare... I said get up." She said coolly. "We are all going for a drive."

"To where?" Davie questioned.

"You will see," and then she was out the door.

I looked at my brothers for a silence and inconspicuous vote to follow her. Once we agreed, we followed without question. We all piled in the backseat together. None of us wanted the front seat. The front seat was where Momma and Daddy sat, not us kids. And with everything going on, we wanted to hold onto that feeling of childhood innocence just a little bit longer.

None of us spoke as she revved the engine and pulled out of our driveway. She turned right down that all too familiar road. It all took me back to the last afternoon with Daddy—the day before he left.

I reminisced on that moment riding up front in Daddy's car, feeling like I was in trouble. I felt peace in that moment remembering the good times in our life. Back then I thought my life was falling apart. Little did I know; life had not fallen apart just yet. That was actually a good time. A memorable moment in time with my Father. A time when Uncle Tommy was alive.

We pulled down the dirt road and I closed my eyes to take in the smell of the familiar salty river. I listened as the tires left the dirt and rolled onto the grass. The tires slowly pressed against the Earth. I held my breath waiting. Waiting for Momma to fix it all. Waiting for her to take away all the pain we felt. Waiting…for a miracle.

When you are young, you look to your parent or guardian to fix all the bad things in the world. To make everything bad…disappear. But there are some things in this world that your parents can't fix or undo. There are things in this world that just must be. And with that, innocence is damaged — or lost entirely.

"I cannot even imagine…I cannot imagine how difficult this must be for you to understand. No one — especially a child — should ever have to go through this pain. Death is not something that is easy to comprehend at any age, let alone as a child. Youth and innocence are something that should be held onto dearly. But unfortunately, your generation is now surrounded by nothing but death. With all the deaths suffered from this war, children are now fatherless and motherless. Wives and husbands now widowed. And parents...childless. War is neither biased nor forgiving," Momma spoke so softly in the car as though she was trying to be careful not to disrupt the calm that survived outside. "Your father—he won't be the same when he comes home. He will be affected in a way none of us will be able to understand. We will never know the truth of what has happened overseas. He might be distant at first, he might be quiet, and he may not even smile at times. We have all changed since he left, and we all need to be patient with one another when he comes home. So, we all need to write a letter to Joan to tell her how sorry we are to hear of Tommy's passing. We also need to write to little Tommy to tell him how great — how amazing his father was...We need to flood him with stories of his father, stories to help him through the pain he may not understand just yet."

The sound of crickets echoed throughout the river's shore and woods behind us. The sound of the water flowing downstream at dusk made the car feel serene, even in this dark moment in our lives. Neither I nor my brothers looked up from the floorboard, but we were all listening intently as Momma spoke.

"Do any of you have any questions or thoughts you would like to share?" Momma asked.

"What happens..." Davie mumbled. "...what happens when you know...you...you die?" His eyes slowly looked up, desperate for answers.

"Well, our souls leave and go off to heaven. To a place of love, joy, and glory forever. All the pain we feel...leaves," Momma said softly looking in the rearview mirror at Davie.

"So ..." I was surprised hearing my voice come out of me, "Uncle Tommy ... He is ... He is safe now?"

"Yes...he is in peace and away from the war and heartache," Momma's glance turned now to me.

Junior sniffled next to me and adjusted his body as though he was uncomfortable with the subject. His voice eventually broke through, and his eyes finally lifted off the floorboard to meet Momma's. "Do...Do you think Daddy will be home for Christmas this year?"

"I hope so... I really do. I think a beautiful and together Christmas is needed this year," Momma broke her gaze on us and stared out the window into the fading light. I saw something shimmery fall down her cheek. "Remember years ago, before the war, we all came here with your Daddy and Uncle Tommy to fish? Tommy, walked out into the water to cast his line—"

"And he got scared when a tiny fish skimmed his leg," Junior smiled shyly.

"He fell in the water on his butt," I added, smiling now too.

"He scared all the fish away!" Davie laughed.

We all laughed at the memory of Uncle Tommy screaming like a girl with his arms flailing around like a moth until he lost his balance, landing in the water. He stood up, soaked from head to toe, and with a bruised ego afterwards. We had laughed all the way home while Uncle Tommy sat quietly with a smirk on his face that read, 'I will never live this down.'

"Or that time he wanted to teach us how to run bases!" I remembered.

"He hit second base and flipped up in the air and wham!" Davie mimicked with his hands the way Uncle Tommy fell. "—Right down on his back!"

"He laid there for a while..." Junior recalled.

"Yes... while listening to you three and your father fall down laughing at him," Momma interjected, undoubtedly smiling.

We probably stayed out there for an hour, reminiscing on old and memorable moments we had with Uncle Tommy. Remembering him for the good times and not the bad. For a little while we sat in silence, euphoric with the memories that flooded through our minds. But we slowly came back to the realization that the past would never be again. Remembering that Uncle Tommy would not step foot back into our house anymore, hurt. Little Tommy would need to know the man he would never meet. He needs to know that his daddy was a man of honor and courage. A man worth every teardrop and smile created because of him. A man who will only be remembered through memories of a life cut too short.

"Let's go home... okay?" Momma smiled. "When we get home...you can all pile in my bed tonight, if y'all want. If any of you ever needs to talk, I am here. I will always be here. We will make it through this. I love you three more than the world may ever know. To the moon and back."

Momma turned to face us. Her eyes were shimmering with tears. She put her hand out, welcoming ours. Each of us placed our hand out to meet hers. She placed her other hand on top of ours securing our hands in place. Our eyes locked onto hers and hers onto ours.

"Together..." She muttered softly.

We returned home later that night, each of us lost in foggy haze of grief and despair. I remember vividly us walking back through our front door looking at everything we had left behind. Davie's whoopee cushion left on the floor at the very spot where he collapsed in angst. My army plane laid out on the couch where Davie and I had waited as

Momma left to comfort Junior. And a cake remained on the table from a forgotten birthday celebration. A house that was meant for life and love turned into a scene of despair. An eerie presence of both anguish and pain lurked in our house. A house where memories of Uncle Tommy's life will remain.

The next morning continued as normal. School went on like everything was the same. No one else was grieving for the loss of Uncle Tommy. No one knew him like we did. No one cared for him like we did. He was our family, and we were his.

Davie became quiet and reserved. His mind was still trying to comprehend all that had occurred from the night prior. I always felt like that day was the day my brother lost his innocence completely. He was not the same after that. Our tenth birthday was the day the world took away his innocence.

The three of us came home after school to an empty house. I sat down at the dinner table to begin on my homework while my brothers sat around the radio listening for any new information they could find. Davie held tightly onto a paddle ball that a friend from school lent him. The sound of the ball whacking against the paddle bounced off each wall in the house. I heard tires pull up the driveway signaling that Momma was home. Davie jumped up off the floor, turned off the radio, grabbed his books, and started his homework before Momma walked through the door catching him playing with a paddleball. Meanwhile, Junior continued to lay on the ground, unbothered by Momma arrival.

"Hi boys! How was your day?" Momma walked in balancing groceries and mail. "Junior... don't you have schoolwork to work on?"

Davie and I rushed to help Momma put the groceries up, trying to be as helpful as we could. Junior sighed loudly, got to his feet, and sluggishly walked to the dinner table holding his books in his arms. Junior's distance continued to deepen.

"Hey momma... so" I put some groceries down and hugged her hello. "I thought I could help with dinner tonight...if you want."

"Of course, dear." Momma smiled. "I thought we would have meatloaf tonight. How does that sound?"

"Sounds delicious," Davie answered while taking a bite out of an apple he pulled out of the grocery bag.

"Don't ruin your dinner..." Momma said as she pulled the apple out of Davie's hand and put in on the kitchen counter. "So... we got another letter from your father. But I ... I am reading it first, okay?"

All our eyes turned to Momma with shock—two letters in one week. We followed her into the living room like ducks following their mother. Junior's previously sluggish walk turned a little quicker with curiosity. She sat down on the couch and began reading privately.

We monitored each expression she gave trying to infer any information about the direction of the letter. Any slight smile, any twinkle in her eye, any hint of a frown we followed.

'What did the letter say...?' I wondered. 'Is Daddy okay? Is he going to a new location? Is he coming home? What...did he say?' I screamed these thoughts in my head over and over again until finally Momma put the letter down and nodded.

We all reached frantically for the letter at one time, ending with Junior coming out victorious. He took the letter and pushed himself to the other side of the couch. Davie took to Junior's right side to read over his shoulder while I jumped in between Junior and Momma to read with them all.

Daddy wrote:

Hey all,

I realize my last letter... I wrote that yesterday. That I never said Happy Birthday to my twin boys. From Momma's previous letter and pictures, all three of you have grown so much. I am sorry I forgot to wish you Happy Birthday. I hope this reaches you before your big day. I am sorry if it doesn't get there in time. I hope you got something good for y'all's special day. And some very good chocolate cake.

In other news, I am being discharged from the service due to my arm. I don't know when that will mean I will be home, but I am hoping this year. They said possibly October depending on available transportation. War in the Pacific is still happening...so hopefully I will see y'all not too long from now. That would be ideal. When I find out for sure, I will let you know.

Be good and I am sorry again. Happy Birthday, David and James!

Love y'all,

Dad/Henry

"He's... He's coming home!" I exclaimed.

"Momma...he's coming home..." Junior reiterated, as though it didn't seem real.

For once in his life, Davie was speechless. He grabbed the paper from Junior to read it again to himself, as though Junior's spoken words were not real enough. Momma ran her hands in Davie's hair as he sat and digested every single word written.

"And...he said Happy Birthday to his twin boys," Momma reminded us.

"He's coming home..." Davie whispered.

"He's coming home..." Junior said again.

"Alright! Meatloaf to celebrate! Jamie, you wanted to help me, right?" Momma smiled over to me.

"Yes ma'am! Yes ma'am!" I yelled as I jumped up off the couch with great eagerness.

That night was the best night we had had in a very long time. We were all in complete bliss with the thought of seeing Daddy in only a few months. For the first time in years, we each had actual hope. Things began to finally look brighter for our family, and we enjoyed every minute of it all. We sat on the porch for one of the first times in years just listening as the night turned dark. Listening to the crickets chirping, signaling that the moon was now out and shining above the world. We sat in quiet, not wanting to say anything that could ruin the serenity we all felt in that moment.

Momma was the first one to speak.

"Oh! I just remembered—let me grab something!" She exclaimed as she jumped up and ran inside. She searched around the house for a few minutes before returning to the porch with Daddy's guitar in her hands. "I thought we should play a little music. Sitting on the porch isn't the same without a few tunes... am I right?"

We all smiled at each other and back to Momma in complete agreeance with her decision. Music had always been our family's way of decompressing or celebrating prior to the war. Music brings people together and good news, such as this, is always a reason to celebrate together.

Davie jumped up on the bench and belted out, "STAY ALL NIGHT!"

This was Davie's new favorite song to sing. It was a new song by Bob Wills and Davie would listen to it every chance he got. Momma smiled and began strumming a few cords.

Unseen Scars

In full confidence, Davie stood up tall and sang the entire song while tapping his foot on the bench.

We all chimed in and sang together as one; one united family. Life seemed perfect again. An end was finally in sight to this total nightmare, and we would soon become a family of five once more.

That is the weird thing about life. One second everything is great, life is beautiful, and you feel like you are invincible. You look at those around you whom you love and hold dear, and you cannot imagine living a single day without them. But then, the next thing you know, it's all gone. Everything you love and cherish disappears, and it all becomes a faded memory of the past. And nothing you do can fix it.

I looked over at my Momma and brothers and saw the smiles painted across their faces. This moment will forever be locked in my memory. That moment of celebration and love is one that I have held onto for most of my life. The happiness and the hope we all felt radiating from each others' smiles will forever be locked in my heart until the day I eventually leave this earth.

Chapter 6

December 8, 1945

'Only two more days until Daddy comes home,' I must have reminded myself of that a dozen times that day.

Just two more days and we would be picking up Daddy from the train station. It had been four years since we saw him last. Four years of dreaming of the day we would see him, and now it's finally here. Four years of pain and grief, all coming to a long awaited and welcomed end.

Without being asked, Junior, Davie, and I picked up around the house to help Momma out. We wanted the house to look organized and beautiful for Daddy's homecoming. With Momma working hard at her job and at home, we tried to make it as easy for her as possible. We helped with the dishes, laundry and just the general cleaning in the house. We tried to be the best sons that we could be before Daddy came home. We wanted to make it an easy transition for all of us.

Junior came around more. He started to act more like himself since we got the letter with Daddy's return date. It was as though all the burdens on his shoulders had been lifted. Junior had been spending most of his time with friends or working as a paperboy. He tried his best to help Momma pay for groceries and house bills; anything he was able to do. Momma didn't want to take the money from Junior, but there were times when she had no other choice. She would always say: 'a child's responsibility is to be a child.' But then again, extra money was needed on occasion. War time was difficult for families: financially and emotionally. Supplies were hard to come by, especially since factories started supplying primarily for the war overseas. So, any extra money Junior pulled in for our family was appreciated.

Another difference in Junior's life was his first girlfriend, Mary. Whenever Junior would bring Mary by our house, Davie would pretend to throw-up just from the sight of them. Momma would cut her eyes at Davie with the 'don't make me come over there' look.

Junior and Mary were going steady for maybe a month or two before she left him for Robert Jenkins. Robert bought lunch for Mary one afternoon at school, and after that, they were an item. This was Junior's first heartbreak. It upset Momma thinking about all the firsts Daddy had missed over the years. Daddy would have been proud to see Junior go on his first date; it was something every father looked forward to. But unfortunately, Daddy missed it. And Junior dealt with his first heartbreak alone.

Davie and I were ten years old now and still the same kids we were before—only older. Davie, after our birthday, lost a little of his innocence. He laughed and joked around less and less each day, but I guess that was expected. We all suffered a loss that day when we read that letter, and we all processed it whichever way we could at the time. Everyone experiences grief in different ways. Some shut down and block the outside world from coming back in. Others find outside activities and resources to help distract from the pain they are experiencing. There is no right or wrong way to grieve. There is just grief.

I grieved more quietly and privately. I focused on school to help take the pain away after losing Uncle Tommy. He was a role model to each of us. And his death will forever tear a piece of my heart.

With Daddy coming home in just a few more days, our spirits were a little brighter. We all smiled a little more but hidden between those smiles were nerves.

'What would Daddy be like when he came home? Would he be the same carefree man who adored his wife and kids? Or would he be stern and cold to us and our feelings?' I questioned my own self. 'Would he like the men we had become? Or would he be disappointed?'

Prior to Daddy's leaving we were a family of five. After he left, we adjusted and learned to function as a family of four. This was our new normal. It was difficult for me to adjust my state of mind to the new reality that was coming. It's incredible how you can miss something, something that was so normal and natural, but then when it's right in front of you again, it feels almost foreign.

I found myself standing in front of my closet again, just as I did nearly five years ago. Back then I was five years old trying to pick out something to wear to send my father off. Now I'm ten years old, choosing something to wear to pick my father up. To Davie, picking out clothes meant throwing your hand into the closet or dresser and grabbing the first thing you touch. To me it meant finding something that represents who you are. What you wear is the first impression people will make of you. So, I took it seriously. This would be Daddy's first impression of each of us.

After careful consideration, I picked out black slacks and a dark blue sweater. Underneath the sweater I wore a long sleeve white button up collared shirt. I thought this would make me look more mature in Daddy's eyes and maybe Daddy would see me as a man instead of a little boy.

My thoughts were interrupted by Junior singing a Dean Martin song at the top of his lungs. He was in a better mood today than he had been the past few months. Junior ran into our room, changed his shirt, turned around, and smiled at both Davie and me, before leaving.

"What's he on about?" Davie queried.

"I don't know. You think he got Mary back?" I replied.

"Maybe. He had a brown bag in his pocket, did you see it?" Davie pointed out.

"No…? Do you want to find out what it is?" I asked.

"Alright, but it better be good. Better not be something dumb," Davie jumped down off his top bunk, ran to the closet, and threw on a shirt. "Hey… are you…are you nervous about seeing Daddy or is it just me?"

"Umm…yeah… I am…a bit…" I admitted.

"I hope he will be happy to see us…" Davie muttered. "I mean, I haven't made the best marks in school this year…"

"I think he will be happy… It might be a bit of an adjustment but…" I stopped, I thought of Uncle Tommy. I saw his smile in my mind. He was so carefree and optimistic about life.

"But what…?" Davie persisted.

"Sorry—I was just thinking about Uncle Tommy. What do you…or …? How do you think Daddy will handle it or has handled it?" I stumbled through the question trying to find the right words to say but nothing seemed right.

"I don't know… It makes me worried with —"

"JAMES! DAVID! Come downstairs and look at what your brother bought!" Momma yelled from downstairs. Her voice was followed by inaudible sentences, sentences I figured were directed towards Junior.

We ran out of our room finding Junior sitting on the floor of the living room with gift wrap and a brown box. The brown box was about the length of Junior's hand only thinner. The brown bag was crumbled up next to him. I thought it might have been a Christmas gift, but Christmas was not for a few more weeks.

"Boys, look what Junior bought for your daddy!" Momma looked at Junior with pure admiration. "Show them honey."

"Okay. Okay—" Junior began unboxing the gift. "Well, I've been saving up money for the past year or so to buy this—for Dad."

He pulled out a 4-inch brown metal object and flipped out two shiny blades, one longer and one shorter blade. This was probably the neatest thing I had ever seen at that age.

"It's a 2-blade Imperial pocketknife," Junior stood up with a toothy grin.

"Oh boy! Can I see it?" Davie exclaimed; his eyes as wide as can be.

"Yes, just be careful! It's expensive!" Junior snapped.

"I promise! I promise, Junior!" Davie quickly assured him. He held the knife carefully as if he was holding a dollar bill.

I stood next to Davie in complete and utter amazement as he held up the knife examining every detail. At that age, we had never seen anything like it before. Between Davie and I, we had just enough money to make a dollar...not nearly enough to buy expensive gifts like this.

"Daddy will love this!" I reassured Junior. "Where'd you get it from?"

"At Kerry's. It was on sale, so I was finally able to afford it," Junior said with such pride. "I'm going to wrap it up and give it to Daddy as a welcome home gift. I thought... I thought he'd like it."

"Oh, I am sure he will love it! Your Daddy is lucky to have such wonderful sons," Momma wrapped her arm around Junior smiling. "Now! Dinner! It will be ready in half an hour! Wash up quickly!"

She clapped her hands together with excitement and walked off to the kitchen throwing her apron back around her waist. Davie and I remained by Junior's side watching him carefully place the knife back in the box to wrap. This was the closest the three of us had been in an awfully long time. Sitting together and being a part of wrapping Daddy's gift was one of the last great memories I have of that time in our life. Three brothers bonding over a 2-blade knife purchased by our older brother.

Junior wrapped it meticulously. He wanted to ensure he did not cause a tear or an unequal fold in his perfect gift. After he finished wrapping the gift, he hid it carefully in our room. We finished the night with fried chicken and mashed potatoes laughing together as a family. It was a great night. We were all excited and anxious for the Monday to arrive. Momma cleaned the house again that night to ensure the house was flawless for Daddy's arrival. What could be better? Christmas was coming up soon and finally, after four long years...Daddy would be home.

Monday; December 10, 1945

"Jamie! Jamie! Wake up! It's time, get ready!" A voice spoke with much enthusiasm above me.

Once I was able to find my glasses in the fog of my useless vision, I saw Junior staring at me with an undeniable smile across his face.

"Wake up! Wake up, Jamie!" Junior yelled again. "Daddy's train is coming in in just two hours! I'm already dressed...now get up and get dressed. I'll wake up Davie!"

I searched around our bedroom for our clock trying to orient myself to the morning. Across the room my eyes focused in on our clock. I squinted hard until finally seeing the hour hand pointing at the six.

'Damn! It's already six!' I yelled to myself.

I sprung out of bed and grabbed the clothes I had laid out at the end of my bed. Once on my feet, I rushed past Junior who was hanging off our ladder trying to reach Davie. I slammed the bathroom door closed for privacy while I got cleaned up. I rinsed off as fast as I could and put the clothes on that I picked out days prior. I looked at myself in the mirror one time to ensure I was looking stylish and mature enough for the day. I left our bathroom for only a minute as I searched for my shoes in our closet. The last thing I needed to do was fix my hair. I ran back to the bathroom, and—locked!

Davie had snuck in and locked the bathroom door before I could get back in there. He was performing his own personal concert while showering. I banged on the door, hoping to get his attention to let me in.

"Come on Davie open the door!" I banged on the door. "I just need to fix my hair, Dave!" I yelled with my entire body pressed up against the door.

Davie only sang louder, pretending as though he didn't hear me. He was in his own little world. I did everything I could to get his attention, but nothing worked. I was so frustrated with him. I kicked the door one more time while Davie was in his continuous rendition of We Might As Well Forget It by Bob Wills.

"Jamie...come on. You can use our bathroom." Momma stood at the doorway of her bedroom.

She looked stunning as always dressed in her new patriotic dress. A solid blue a-line dress with a red and white stripe running down the center of the dress and on the elbow-length sleeves. Red buttons ran down the center of her dress, parallel with the red and white stripe. A matching blue belt fit around her waist finishing her outfit. She had her hair pinned up with curls under a red fedora hat and her face was made up perfectly. She was smiling like I had never seen her smile before. For the first time in four years, she had on an honest smile. She was happy, genuinely happy. As I walked past her and straight into the bathroom, I smelt an aroma of flowers—but there were none. I shrugged off my curiosity and searched through Momma's bathroom drawers for a comb.

"Here, use your Daddy's," Momma pulled open a drawer on Daddy's side of the counter.

"Oh...thank you," I mumbled as I took the comb from her hand. I held his comb under the faucet to get it wet enough to style my hair. I stared into the mirror to analyze the mop on my head.

My hair used to be light blonde, but over time both Davie's and my hair darkened a little. I wondered then if Daddy would even recognize us. We had changed so much.

I combed my hair down and pushed my bangs off to the side to give me a cool "Cary Grant" look. I felt her eyes on me. I glanced over and found her smiling at me.

"Oh Jamie, your Daddy will be so proud when he sees you, you know that?" she walked over to me, put her hands on my cheeks, and smiled sweetly. That was when I smelt it. The flowers. She smelt like the flowers that I smelt in her room. She'd always smelt good, I guess...but I had never smelt that specific perfume before.

"Yeah—yeah—I hope so," I finally responded.

"He will be..." she smiled at me again before turning to the mirror to check herself one more time for any imperfections. Satisfied with her look, she turned back to me, "Let's go get him."

Once Davie was done with his solo concert and after Momma chased him around upstairs to hurry him up, we all piled in the car. It would be our last time traveling as a family of four. Junior sat up front for the last time, staring out the window with nothing but joy written across his face. At a last-minute decision, he chose to leave the 2-blade imperial knife at home. He tucked it away in the kitchen for a post-dinner gift after we indulged ourselves in lunch. Davie was holding onto the whoopee cushion he got for our birthday, excited to show it off to Daddy.

Momma gently pulled out of the driveway onto the main road that connected us to the city. We drove by tree after tree while on our way out of the countryside. I watched the birds fly around as they welcomed in a new day. Ever since I was a little boy, I preferred watching sunsets. Due to memories sitting out on the porch and spending time together as a family, it was unquestionably my favorite time of the day. But I must admit, there is something magical about watching a new day arrive. Hearing the welcoming messages of songbirds and watching animals run out into the sun to start their day searching for food was breathtaking. But—I'd much rather sleep in.

The city came into view as traffic increased and the number of trees diminished. We found ourselves pulling into the same parking spot as we did a little over four years ago. Memories of that day plowed through my mind. I remembered getting out of the car hearing Uncle Tommy call out for us over the crowd. But this time I knew I would not hear that familiar voice. I would only hear it in my memories from now on.

A crowd had already formed awaiting the trains arrival, and American flags were being waved around everywhere I looked. The morning sun beamed off each white stripe, transforming the scene in front of me into a picture of complete patriotism. It was so moving and motivational for everyone present. It gave us a sense of this is what we were waiting for all these years. This time, tears were not being shed; laughter was being heard. People were not hugging tightly afraid of what tomorrow would bring. They were joyous and living in the moment. Today was not about loss or anger; it was about what we gained and what we won. We all became united as a country. The platform on that morning, radiated nothing but hope.

"Boys! Let's get a welcome home sign for your Daddy. What do y'all think?" Momma shouted as she ushered us through the crowd of waiting families. She led us over to an older gentleman and his wife whom I recognized as Mr. and Mrs. Wilson. Momma greeted them with a smile, "Good morning Hubert, Marge! How about three signs for us please?"

"Of course, Katherine. Ready to see Henry, huh? This town misses those men and even women you know! Yes—yes! Even some women went over there too! Truly remarkable if I say so myself!" Hubert nodded. "Marge, can you get three signs for the Clark men—.75 cents please, Mrs. Clark."

"It's okay Momma. I'll take care of it..." Junior searched his pockets for change. He pulled out three quarters and handed it over to Mr. Wilson whose eyes filled with curiosity.

"Well, well, well. How do you have so much money?" Mr. Wilson questioned while taking Junior's money.

"I've been saving all year, Mr. Wilson. Been tryin' to help my Momma out," Junior blushed.

"Oh, honey, you have grown up so fast. Thank you, sweetheart," Momma put her hand on Junior's head as though trying to fix his already perfect hair. Junior, looking uncomfortable, groaned and rolled his eyes at her words. This only caused Momma to laugh.

"Here you go, dears," Marge came over with the three signs reading, 'WELCOME HOME!' Marge's eyes grew huge with amazement, "My goodness, you three have grown. Junior...you're almost my height already!"

"Well dear, you aren't that tall..." Mr. Wilson winked at us.

Ignoring her husband's remark, Marge continued to study the three of us. "Your father won't believe his eyes when he sees just how grown you three are. Katherine, you should be proud. You raised three good boys."

"Oh, I am. Thank you, Marge." Momma smiled at the Wilsons and politely excused us. "Well boys, we should go take our place before the train arrives. Get our signs ready for Daddy. Have a good day y'all and thank you again!"

"Thank you," Davie and I said to Mr. and Mrs. Wilson.

"Tell Henry hello from us!" Hubert shouted before continuing with their sales to people who were still arriving to the station.

We hurried through the crowd before finally finding an empty spot up close to the tracks. Junior handed us our signs to hold and took his place on the other side of Davie. Momma and Junior stood on either side of us as though we were cattle they didn't want to lose.

Unseen Scars

"Junior!" Davie yelled. "Look, it's Maarryy!" Davie put his hands on his hips and gave kissy faces to Junior for the whole world to see.

"Shut up! David shut up!" Junior hastily shot his eyes over at Davie, then quickly spotted Mary, and then back to the floor.

"Oh Katherine! Hey!" Mrs. Bennett, her voice incredibly high pitched, spoke from behind us. "Oh my, I just love that dress! Aren't you just so excited to see the men? I cannot wait to see my Jack. He left last year when he was only eighteen, you know? Missed his nineteenth birthday but I am so proud of my boy!"

Mrs. Bennett was the gossip queen of Charleston. She was a petite, brunette woman with a sense of class. Her hair was always tightly curled and pushed back to create a frame around her face. She walked with her head held higher than those around her, including her husband, who would typically ignore the rumors his wife would tell. Mrs. Bennett was wearing a yellow-colored shirtwaist dress and a black flowery hat. She knew everything about everyone. And even though Momma participated in the gossip herself, she would complain that Mrs. Bennett 'could not keep a secret.'

Mrs. Bennett's son, Jack, was a star football player in high school. He left in August of last year to help on the European fronts and was now coming home. Mr. Bennett and Daddy worked together at the cigar factory just before the war. Mr. Bennett could not serve due to a previous injury as a teenager, leaving him with a permanent limp. Mrs. Bennett had called it a blessing in disguise.

"Oh, I am extremely excited... The boys are too. It's been four years, so of course you can imagine, we are a little nervous to see him." Momma responded as she put her arm around me. I assumed she was trying to include me in the conversation in hopes of taking some pressure off herself. "Well, Claire — your dress is beautiful!"

"Yes, well I had to wear a color that my Jack will see, you know. This was the brightest thing I could find in my closet. When you go to any event, you know you must wear your best!" Mrs. Bennett must have giggled after every sentence spoken. "Oh, your boys have just grown so much. Henry will be absolutely shocked to see how tall they have become," Mrs. Bennett awkwardly gawked at my brothers and me. "Jerry! Oh Jerry! I'm over here!"

"There you are Claire! Come on we are going to lose our spot. The train should be coming in soon. There is no time for gossip!" Jerry spoke to his wife before offering his hand to Momma. "Nice seeing you, Katherine. Give Henry our love. We will catch up with him and y'all later. We have a family birthday party planned for Jack and want to get him home quickly. Come on now, Claire." He pushed her along while Mrs. Bennett looked frantic as though trying to find one last clever thing to say.

"Oh well, bye-bye dear! It is so nice to see you. Tea this week maybe?" Claire shouted from beyond her husband's arms.

"Of course!" Momma gave her a fake smile then quickly turned to us saying, "That woman can talk to a stop sign."

We three just laughed. We loved watching her get irritated with the gossiping women of the town. Even though she would gossip just as much as they did, she would act as though she would never do such a thing.

We all edged our way closer to the tracks to where the back of the train would be in just a matter of minutes. I felt my nerves creeping up in my body as the anticipation of the arrival of the train grew stronger. Davie and I stood on our tiptoes hoping to get a glimpse of something in the distance, but there was nothing. Not a single shadow of movement heading our way. Not the distant sound of the train coming. Nothing.

The crowd, which was once loud with excitement, began to quiet down to a low hum of whispers. We waited minute after minute with nothing. Nothing to tell us something was coming. Nothing to look for or see. There was nothing. And when there is nothing, the anticipation and hope slowly begin to leave your body. It leaves you with feelings of complete emptiness.

'Maybe we all got the date and time wrong?' I wondered.

Junior and Davie continued to look off into the distance as though they were afraid if they took their eyes off just for a second—they would miss something. Momma's eyes searched the crowd around us as her anxiety and impatience grew inside her.

The silence intensified as a few minutes passed by.

Faintly, beyond view, I finally heard it. A soft hum resonated softly throughout the platform. The hum grew, becoming more and more distinct. A faint whistle came from the same direction leading the crowd to erupt in a cheer that echoed throughout the entire platform. A group of kids broke out from the crowd and ran down the side of the track waving their arms and cheering for the oncoming train. Junior, who hit a slight growth spirt in the summer, lifted Davie so he could see over the stampeding crowd of impatient wives, parents, children, and friends. Momma lifted me up as far as she could while pointing to the dim silhouette of a train moving in our direction. I don't ever remember smiling so hard in my life. The wait was finally over. The days of dreaming of this moment were over. It was over. Daddy was home.

The train drew closer and the signalmen began pushing everyone away from the tracks to make room for the soldiers who would soon get off. Whistles blew and people cheered from every direction. Momma pushed against the crowd with me in her arms. She moved us closer to the front, near the signalmen, followed closely by Junior and Davie. She wanted us to get as close as we could, so we could all look for Daddy. The train grew nearer and smoke filled the platform disrupting our vision while the sound of screeching brakes stabbed at our ears. The train pulled past us and I could see men looking out the windows. Families were whistling and waving at the passing train. Smoke billowed from the train and a high-pitched hiss erupted as the train came to an abrupt stop. Workers emerged from the train to prop the doors open for all the soldiers who were getting ready to come out. Signalmen continued to guard the crowd, struggling to maintain organization.

Momma and Junior let us to the ground so they could hold onto us as the impatient crowd continued to push up against us. Soldier after soldier piled out of the train holding onto duffle bags and tossing them out onto the platform. All the men were wearing the same uniform and the same hat. How would anyone pick their husband or daddy out in all of this? Army green pants with army green jackets and hats made it a crowd full of nothing but green. I started combing through the crowd desperately searching for a familiar face: the face I had been dreaming of for over four years.

'What…what did Daddy look like now? Did he have a beard? Did he have long or short hair?' My mind frantically thought as my eyes met every face that came off that train.

Two children broke free from the signalmen and sprinted to a soldier dressed in green with their arms wide open. The soldier lifted the boy and girl up in his arms and spun them around. Tears were shed at their long-awaited reunion. I realized then that those children were our friends, Margaret and her brother, Ernie. Not far behind them was their mother, whose eyes looked as though they could not believe what they were seeing. It was truly a beautiful moment. Their daddy, just like ours, was one of the few that made it from the beginning of the war to the end.

I realized that many of the people on the platform consisted of new families and friends whose loved one left in the last year or two. Many families who lost loved ones left the city to start a new life. Margaret's family, like ours, was one of the 'lucky ones.'

Desperate for my own family reunion, I continued to search through the swarm of men wearing army green. A man walking aimlessly around the front of the train caught my attention. I could see the desperation in his eyes as he scanned the platform. I studied his face, noticing something familiar about him. There was something about the way his eyebrows narrowed while he searched that reminded me of someone. Someone I had known once. As he stopped to pull off his hat to adjust its position, his blue eyes twinkled in the sun. He scanned the crowd seeming lost as though he was trying to find just one familiar face. I found myself smiling uncontrollably at the man that owned longer and darker hair. I was unable to speak. There were no words to describe how I felt in that moment. Nothing audible would come out of my mouth for my family to hear. My brain was shouting, 'Daddy! Daddy!' but my brain didn't seem to communicate with my mouth. All I could do was stare and point at the man walking toward us dressed in army green.

Davie took notice of my change in posture and behavior. He followed my pointed finger to the strange man walking slowly in our direction.

"DADDY!" Davie shouted while jumping up and down in exhilaration. "Momma! Look! Look! It's him! It's him!"

"It's Daddy!" Junior belted.

"Henry..." Momma breathed quietly before losing her patience completely. "HENRY!"

I saw Daddy's eyes dart around frantically searching for the faces to match the familiar voices he was hearing. He continued to search the crowd of boisterous family members, desperate to find us. I, who was still unable to speak, continued to wave my arms with all the strength I had, hoping, and praying to get his attention.

"HENRY! HENRY!" Momma hollered again. Her hands gripped tightly onto us with fear of potentially losing one of us in the crowd.

His eyes finally found us. Through the crowd of families running and shouting, I could see Daddy's eyes meet ours. His timid walk turned into a sprint. He weaved in and out of everyone passing by. Momma held on to us, keeping us in place as we waited for Daddy to get close enough to reach. Once the distance between us and him shortened, Momma flew around us, crossing that imaginary line laid out by the signalmen, and threw her arms around his neck.

We waited behind. We — Junior, Davie, and I — wanted her to have the first hug. To have that first moment. The night before, we discussed that moment. About how over the last four and a half years, Momma had put us above everything. Her patience, her time off, and her happiness was given to us. She gave everything to ensure we were happy. So, she deserved that moment. For the first time in four and a half years, Momma was put first.

The cries that came from them were sounds that could never be described. They were sobs of relief and grief. She was wrapped in Daddy's arms and Daddy was in hers. It was as though all the turmoil over the past four and a half years had vanished with just a single touch.

They were entwined in each other's arms for a long time without letting each other go. Daddy pulled back from the hug to kiss Momma for the first time. Junior, Davie, and I looked at each other smiling, in awe at their happiness. For once, she was first.

Momma pulled away from Daddy smiling like a teenage girl. And Daddy, he was blushing as though he had just fallen in love with Momma again. They both had identical tears streaming down their faces. It was four and half years of anguish and heartache coming out all at once.

Holding momma close, daddy looked over to us with shock. You could tell he could not believe that we were his sons. His eyes widened as he tried to take in all of differences in us. Differences he didn't expect nor prepare for. Daddy dropped to his knees as though all his strength had left him. The strength he had been holding onto for over four years was gone. His arms opened and the three of us piled in, clinging on as tightly as we could. Daddy had a mixture of laughter and tears as we clung onto him.

For years Daddy had hoped and prayed we would be okay after his departure. But to finally see that his prayers were answered, the emotions became more raw. Junior's face was bursting with excitement, and he was glowing with eagerness to ask him questions about everything and everywhere he had been. Davie could not let go as though he was holding on for dear life, afraid someone would just snatch it all away again. Me, I cried. Every bit of sorrow and anxiety I had ever felt during the last four and half years was now streaming down my face. The feeling of security and fullness I felt back in Daddy's arms was almost indescribable. It felt like nothing could ever go wrong again. And in all honesty, I thought nothing could.

Daddy pulled us apart to get a better look at us: his three sons. He started with Junior first and spoke directly to him.

"Hey there, my mini man. How are you—my goodness...how are you doing? Are you almost an Eagle Scout?" Daddy was tearing up while looking at his now thirteen-year-old son.

"Actually..." Junior took a deep breath before speaking proudly. "I am working now. Making some money for myself and the family. I promised I would be the man of the house and I—I did my best."

"You did a great job... And I am so—I am so proud of you," Daddy smiled as the tears fell uncontrollably. "Alright—Alright, my twin boys. Now let me see if I've still got this...who is who..."

Davie walked up to my side and threw his arm around my shoulder with a goofy smirk across his face.

'Well, he just gave that away,' I thought to myself.

"Ah ha! Yep. Yes sir... you are my Davie," Daddy pointed at Davie smiling with confidence. "And you are my Jamie." He put his hands on our cheeks and smiled in approval.

"They sure have grown, haven't they?" Momma said looking down at us all with pride written across her face.

"I'll say! Junior how tall are you now?" Daddy asked while standing up again.

"Five-three sir," Junior stood tall and proud.

Daddy could not say anything. He just stood there, in awe, taking in the new reality. A faint smile broke through the cloud of sadness that was painted across his face. The realization set in that the last time he saw us we were only five and eight. He tried to hide his feelings, but his emotions were too strong. There was no smile that could hide the truth buried within him.

That truth was simple: regret.

"Well," Momma broke the silence. "Let's head home, okay? And get out of this loud crowd. Do you have everything?"

"Um...yes. Yeah—yeah, I do." Daddy answered her as he picked up his duffle bag and smiled.

I stared at Daddy so dumbly, but I couldn't contain the amount of pride and complete honor I held in calling him my father. Davie and I begged him to allow us to carry his duffle bag back to the car which Daddy willingly agreed to. I held onto one side and Davie onto the other. I saw Daddy crack a smile watching us struggle together carrying it across the platform and off to the parking lot. Together Davie and I hauled his bag into the trunk and hurried to get into the back seat with Junior to be certain we would not miss a single moment with Daddy. He sat quietly in the passenger seat. I watched him prop himself up stiffly holding onto the handle above the window. He slowly started to look around the car, scanning, as though he was on patrol. It felt as though I was the only one who saw this new behavior, but talking with Junior years later, I realized I was not.

"So, Junior has been delivering newspapers in town this whole year. He has been learning the importance of money and how to save it properly. He has become very responsible. Jamie has made perfect marks and has won first place in a boat race at school. He made the quickest boat in his grade. I was so proud. And Davie. Well Davie has gone from getting two to three letters a week from school to now only one a week..."

Momma talked the entire way home. Occasionally, she was interrupted by Junior or Davie who were adding to the discussion. I sat quietly behind Momma's seat enjoying the sight of our complete family of five again.

"Hey Daddy!" Davie giggled. "Do you want to hear a new joke I heard recently?"

"Oh lord, here we go." Junior rolled his eyes. "I don't think Daddy wants to hear one of your child jokes Davie."

"No, it's okay. I would love to hear your new joke, Davie. Go ahead…" Daddy replied, still slowly looking outside the car. It was as though he was expecting something to run out in front of us or something.

"Okay well…" Davie smiled slyly, looking to me then back to Junior. "What did one toilet say to the other?"

I heard Junior sigh as he threw his head in his hands with embarrassment. Daddy relaxed slightly as he looked back at Davie and me without saying anything for a few seconds.

"What did one toilet say to the other, Davie?" Daddy asked curiously.

"YOU LOOK A BIT FLUSHED!" Davie hollered with laughter as he cradled his stomach.

Daddy laughed harder than any one of else in the car. Everyone, except Junior, laughed at the comedy by our very own David William Clark. I watched Daddy's body language relax more as he slowly rested his back into the seat and drop his hand to his side. He looked over at Momma who was still laughing at Davie's joke and slowly reached over to grab her hand on the steering wheel to place her hand on her lap. He gently rubbed her hand and continued to watch her. She glanced over at Daddy momentarily with a look of admiration in her eyes.

The rest of the car ride home included Davie's intellectual revelation, in his own words, on what exactly made a whoopee cushion— whoopee. Davie went on to give not one but many examples on the different sounds one could make with the whoopee cushion. I thought Daddy was going to keel over. I had never seen him laugh so hard before at the humorous remarks of his youngest son.

Junior, completely mortified by the direction Davie had taken the conversation, tried desperately to change the subject. Junior interrupted the laughter to explain his paper route and the best way he had found to throw a newspaper. Daddy, as he had always done, sat patiently trying his best to show interest in all his children equally.

Davie yawned purposefully for Junior to see, wanting him to know how boring he found the conversation. This, of course, led to a disagreement between the two about the concept of a functional joke and how to use jokes in an 'adult' conversation.

As always, they would attempt to throw me into the argument to take someone's side. I took Davie's...as I always did. He was my twin...we stood together in everything. Momma and Daddy sat up front smiling. Both of them purely enjoying the bickering sounds of their three sons in the back seat.

Everything was normal again.

Life finally felt whole as we pulled up the driveway to our old white house. I knew things would not be the same as it was four and a half years prior, but I lived in that bliss for the moment. Nothing could have taken away the happiness we all felt that day. I was so excited to begin where we left off. Life was just getting started for our family and we had the rest of our lives to look forward to.

Well—so I thought.

Chapter 7

We came to a slow stop and parked in the usual spot in front of our garage. Daddy drew in a deep breath as he stared at our home lost in deep thoughts. He had been looking forward to this moment for four and a half years. We all watched him, giving him as much silence and time as he needed to prepare himself for this new reality.

"Ready dear?" Momma asked as she gave him a reassuring smile.

He didn't answer. He just continued to stare at our home transfixed with what seemed to be relief.

My brothers and I got out of the car to wait for Daddy to gather himself. Slowly—and with slight hesitation, Daddy stepped out of the car. As he edged near our house, Junior, Davie, and I rushed to the trunk, each of us eager to unload his sea bag. The three of us argued while struggling to carry his bag from the car to the porch until finally dropping it at the front door. At that point, Daddy had already wandered inside and was now standing in the living room. He stood still, absorbing every detail around him. His expressions flipped between elation and sadness. His mind apparently unable to decide how to truly feel.

He walked over to the wooden railing that lined the stairs. His fingertips feeling for all the imperfections caused by us three boys over the years. A quarter of the way up, he stopped to run his fingers over an indentation caused by Junior and Davie the year before Daddy left for Camp Croft.

Just prior to Daddy's departure, Davie found an old rusty knife while on his way home from school. Thrilled with his discovery, he shared it with Junior and me. Junior teased him saying it wasn't a useful knife and could not cause any actual damage. Davie, of course, disagreed, answering back with a rebuttal. He defended his find, arguing that it could and would cut through just about anything. Junior scoffed with incredulity, so it became a competition in Davie's eyes...

Davie marched over to the stair rail and cut into the railing leaving a small groove just underneath. Daddy walked out of his bedroom just at the right time to find Junior, Davie, and myself staring down at the indentation made in the railing.

Daddy was furious. And the knife—the knife was thrown out, immediately.

The corner of Daddy's lip turned up as he reminisced at the same memory. He looked back up the stairs and continued to the second floor. None of us spoke; allowing him to continue with his inner thoughts. He peeked in our room and our bathroom in complete silence.

It was several minutes before he finally spoke.

"It is exactly the same." His voice was hushed, barely audible from downstairs. And with glossy eyes, he faintly smiled down to us.

"I'm glad you think so," Momma returned his smile. "Well, I am going to get a late lunch prepared. Boys, please take your father's bag upstairs and go outside to the coop and get the eggs. I didn't have time to collect them this morning."

"Okay, Momma," I answered for all of us.

"It's okay, sons, I got it." He made his way back downstairs to pick up his duffle bag. "You three just help out your mother, okay?"

"Alright, Daddy," Junior nodded before breaking off to the back door with Davie right on his heels.

"Are you sure, Henry?" Momma questioned.

"Of course, dear." He smiled sweetly at Momma, patted my shoulder before heading back upstairs pausing once again at the indentation. "I will be down in a little…" his voice less than a whisper.

"Alright…Jamie, go help your brothers out," Momma walked off to the kitchen. "Lunch will be ready soon…country fried steak!"

I smiled in an attempt to hide the uneasiness and uncertainty that rose inside of me.

"What is going on in that head of yours, Jamie?" Momma questioned just as I reached the back door.

"What?" I asked innocently.

"I can tell when something is on your mind…I am your mother. You can't hide anything from me—" Momma whispered. "You can talk to me…"

"Just…" I tried.

Her caring eyes met with mine as her eyebrows scrunched inward. She nodded in encouragement for me to continue.

"Just…is he…is he going to be okay?" I sighed, hoping Daddy would not overhear me through the thin floorboards.

"My dear—your Daddy just needs time for adjustment. And we, as his family, need to show him and give him patience, love, and acceptance. Can you do that?" She whispered back.

"Yes..." I answered honestly.

"Then have faith... okay? It will all work out..." She smiled with honesty while placing her hands on either sides of my cheeks.

"Okay..." I nodded.

"Good—now..." turning her attention back to our lunch and throwing on her apron, "—go help your brothers; lunch will be ready soon. I just need to heat it all up."

The feelings of uneasiness still consumed me. But what could I have said to her? I couldn't lie. The truth was I didn't have faith that things would go back to the way they were before. How could they? So much has happened in the last four and a half years. And Daddy—well, he was not the same, just as I was not the same. We had all changed with each year that passed.

Nonetheless, I turned and left out the back door to find Junior and Davie at the chicken coop searching for and collecting eggs. Neither of them were speaking. They worked in complete silence as they pulled one egg out after another. I grabbed the chicken feed to do my part with the chores when Davie questioned me.

"Where'd you go, Jamie?" Davie inquired.

"Sorry...just taking my time..." I answered.

"Oh, Davie, you know Jamie was inside cryin' to Momma like he always does," Junior snorted without making eye contact with me.

"I was not!" I yelled back.

"Oh, yeah, you were, Jamie. You are always crying to Momma if things don't go how you want," Junior's eyes shot up to mine as he tightly gripped the basket of collected eggs. "So—what were you crying for this time?"

"Come on y'all. Let's just finish this and get inside," Davie, for once, was the mediator.

"Oh, you're right Davie... I am sorry." Junior said with mock sincerity. "I wouldn't want to make Jamie cry again."

I stepped towards him with anger I had only ever felt once before—the night Junior yelled at Momma. Just before I could reach him, Davie stepped in between us.

"Jamie...Jamie...calm down," Davie uttered with angst.

"I—I just..." I began.

"I know... I know...let it go. Okay?" Davie said softly, eager to stop a potential fight.

"Bu—He—Okay—Okay!" I backed down.

"BOYS! Come on in! Lunch is warmed up and the table is almost set!" Momma stuck her head out the kitchen window.

"Saved by our mother..." Junior stepped out of the chicken coop, dropped the basket of eggs in my arms, and purposefully bumped into me.

"Let it go..." Davie gripped my arm.

"Yeah – yeah," I mumbled back.

I stepped back into the kitchen and put the chicken eggs into the sink to wash them off. Davie and Junior shared the laundry room sink to wash up before helping Momma set the table. Momma laid the food out on the table in a decorative manner, ensuring everything was perfect for Daddy.

That was when the thought entered my mind, 'where was Daddy?'

I saw Junior pull out Daddy's present from one of the side table drawers and place it on his seat at the table. He wanted to give it to Daddy when the time was right.

"Henry?" Momma walked over to the stairwell and looked up towards their bedroom. "—lunch is ready, dear."

There was no response. Momma kept her eyes focused upstairs looking for any sign of movement, but there was none.

"—Just come down when you are ready dear." She shuffled back into the kitchen to wait.

My brothers and I sat in our usual spots at the table waiting patiently for Daddy. Davie stared intently at the food, using every last bit of energy he had to refrain from eating. Junior continued looking around, anxiously waiting for Daddy to join us. I listened attentively for any kind of movement upstairs, but there was nothing. There was no shift in the floorboards. There was no sign of anything or anyone residing upstairs.

"Why don't you go upstairs to get him, Jun'?" Davie suggested.

"Just give him some time, boys. This is an adjustment for all of us especially him," Momma sat down at the head of the table.

We must have sat there for close to ten minutes waiting for Daddy. Momma kept looking over at the clock impatiently, but she was too afraid to go upstairs. Davie had his head down on the table, trying to control his stomach from growling too loudly. Junior was holding Daddy's gift in his hands studying every detail of the wrapping lost in thought.

I decided then I should go up and find him. Since Junior wanted to call me a baby, I might as well do something to prove to him that I was not that baby anymore. I stood up and everyone's eyes fell on me.

"I'll go check on him," I told Momma.

"Oh no, honey. It should be me to go check on him," Momma smoothed out the dinner table runner and stood up to make her way over to the stairs before I stopped her.

"No... Momma, let me. I can do it." I said confidently.

"Jam—"

"No. Please…" My eyes were locked on hers. "Please, Momma, let me?"

"Okay…okay…" Momma nodded in agreeance with my request.

I filled my lungs deep with oxygen, calming my nerves down enough to walk past her to the staircase. With my hand gliding over the stair rail, I felt the indentation Daddy stopped on earlier. I closed my eyes tight as precious memories flooded my mind. I knew I needed to control the emotions that consumed me. I reached the second floor and immediately checked their bedroom. I found Daddy's seabag leaning against the wall next to his side of the bed. Nothing was unpacked or moved. It was as though he just left it there and moved on. I hurried towards their bathroom and snuck a simple glance into their opened closet. I assumed he would be shaving, but he wasn't. Their bedroom was just as quiet as the rest of the house.

I left their bedroom and walked past our bathroom slightly peaking in as I made my way to our bedroom. That was when I heard him…

With our door slightly ajar, I could hear faint sounds coming from inside. Faint sounds of soft weeping became noticeable.

I studied the wooden floorboards, ensuring I wouldn't step on any that creaked. Through the many years of sneaking downstairs at night, we each had memorized the floorboards and knew which ones creaked. I slowly peeked my head passed the door frame and into our bedroom.

And there he was, curled up on the floor and gripping onto a photograph of us from before the war.

It was a photo of five-year-old Davie and me standing on the hood of the sedan, eight-year-old Junior leaning on the hood smiling, and a young and happy Momma and Daddy holding each other in their arms, standing at the front of the car. Leaning behind Junior and smiling at Davie and me, was Uncle Tommy. It was a happy photo that brought back so many memories. The photo was taken by Joan, after Daddy and I came back from our talk down by Ashley River the day before Daddy and Uncle Tommy left. The day before all our lives changed, and I understood — Daddy was in agony.

Daddy was sitting with his knees drawn up next to the bunkbeds, gently rocking back and forth crying. I could feel the sorrow in the room. I could almost see the regret and despair that surrounded him as he looked at the picture of happier times with a friend who will forever more be only a memory. What I couldn't do was imagine the pain he must have felt at seeing the happiness in all of us just before it was taken away — or the guilt for being here while Uncle Tommy was gone forever. It had to be a hard truth to accept.

I was about to quietly leave when he began to speak, although it was little more than a whisper, barely audible from the doorway.

"I'm so...I'm so sorry, Tom...I'm sorry—" His words were broken up with gasps of breaths between sobs. "I don't know how...how to get...me together...they...they need you..." He put the photo down, dropped his head into his hands, and began to breathe slow and deep in an attempt to calm himself down. He grasped our bed frame to pull himself up and smooth out his uniform, attempting to hide any signs of weakness from us.

I took a few steps back hoping it would seem as though I had just arrived at the top of the stairs. I didn't want him to know that I had been watching him the entire time.

I gave it another moment before I loudly interrupted him: "Hey Daddy, lunch is ready!"

"Oh, Jamie! Hey— sorry I was...uh...just looking at uh...y'all's room. It looks the same. I'm surprised y'all still sleep in the bunk beds but I guess there isn't that much room in here, huh?" Daddy had his hands on his hips, looking around as though he was trying to act like he had been honestly looking at our room. "You've grown so much... you all have."

"Yeah... well you've grown too," I smiled awkwardly at Daddy, embarrassed by my comment. "I'm still the same though...I guess. Still nerdy and awkward — still the same old sensitive James."

"Listen..." Daddy bent down to my eye level. His tired and weary eyes, full of memories and images that we will never fully fathom, focused onto the innocence of mine. "You stay exactly as you are, okay? There is no better you — than you. Do you understand?"

A dim smile was all that I could give him. Maybe the father I remembered was still there, buried somewhere deep inside, hidden beneath all the grief and heartache. Maybe it was like Momma said, we just needed to give him the time he needs to adjust. Maybe, just maybe, a little faith was all that was necessary.

"Lunch is ready... we had better hurry before Davie eats everything," I grinned.

Daddy chucked a little. "Ah, he hasn't changed either I see...good." Daddy looked down at his watch and tilted his head, "Lunch — at three-thirty in the afternoon, huh?"

"Yeah... I guess it's more a lunch-supper" I smiled.

"Lupper?" Daddy responded casually.

"Yeah...lupper," I couldn't help but laugh. I had missed having these little conversations with him.

"Well, let's head downstairs before we both get in trouble," Daddy straightened up, this time with enthusiasm, and pushed me along to the door with him.

We hurried downstairs to find Momma had covered up the food to try and preserve the heat. Davie had his head back down on the table, as though he was about to collapse from hunger. Junior, who was holding Daddy's present at eye level, quickly shoved the gift back under the table trying to hide it. And Momma, well, she had a smile from ear to ear as she watched us come down the stairs together.

"Sorry, dear." Daddy said apologetically before kissing Momma's cheek. "Jamie and I were having a little chat upstairs. I am sorry if we kept everyone waiting,"

I promptly took my seat next to Davie, who was now sitting up and looking relieved to see Daddy downstairs. Daddy hesitated only slightly before he took the seat directly across from Momma.

"Henry, dear, would you like to say the prayer?" Momma beamed while smoothing her napkin out on her lap.

"Um... it's okay, dear. You — or the boys can say it tonight," he said.

"Okay. Um...well who—"

"I can say it, Momma!" Davie interjected. "I am great at prayer!"

"You!? Since when!?" Junior scoffed.

"I have always been good... Y'all have just never given me a chance to prove it!" Davie was very emphatic.

We all grabbed hands and looked at Davie with uncertainty before he belted out a prayer that, to this day, I still use—the grandkids love it.

Davie closed his eyes tight and declared with confidence, "Dear Lord, I know you put ignorant, annoying people in my life for a reason... but did you have to give me Junior? I'm just asking! Amen!"

Daddy and I found ourselves bent over laughing, our breathing coming in quick gasps between unstoppable giggles. Meanwhile, Momma started her usual, 'David William Clark!' It doesn't matter how old you are, it is never a good thing when your mom, dad, or even your wife uses your middle name. Might as well just go ahead and dig your own grave.

"You are such a –" Junior began.

"LANGUAGE!" Momma bellowed. Trying to determine if she should laugh with her youngest son or defend her eldest, she took a deep and audible breath controlling herself, "David...apologize to your brother, please."

"I am so very sorry for my comment, Junior..." Davie's words dripped with sarcasm as he gave his brother a crooked smile. "Would you mind passing the bread...please?"

"Boys... Henry—you are turning so red, dear." Momma nervously giggled watching him turn different shades of red as his laughter continued.

"I'm so—sorry—I have just—I have—I have really missed this!" Daddy responded through his laughter.

"We've missed you, Henry..." Her smile shined like stars as she stared at Daddy intently.

"Yeah, Daddy—We missed you," I whispered in agreement.

His laughter and smile faded like a whisp of smoke. You could see the anguish return to in his eyes as he looked back at each of us, blinking repeatedly in an attempt to push back the tears.

"I have too...I have too..." the pain in his voice was evident. "Well let's...umm...let's not let the food get cold. Jamie, would you please pass the potatoes."

The remainder of lunch was strangely quiet. None of us truly knew what to say. We sat together eating, but barely making eye contact with one another. Daddy never took his eyes off his plate and finished eating in less than ten minutes. I guessed then that eating quickly was something he picked up from the military.

While the rest of us finished eating, he locked his eyes onto the wall behind Momma. Momma noticed this behavior and would occasionally crack a nervous smile at each of us. It was extremely uncomfortable, and I actually wished for Davie to say something to make us laugh again. Anything that would bring light to the unpleasant moment at hand. Sadly, even Davie had nothing humorous to say.

After continuous silence for close to a half hour, Junior spoke up.

"Daddy...?" he mumbled apprehensively.

"Yes," Daddy responded without removing his eyes from the wall behind Momma.

"Well," Junior began. "I... I, umm, I bought you something and I wanted to give it to you." Slowly, Junior lifted the blue-wrapped box with a little blue bow off his lap. He placed the gift on the table and slid it over to Daddy with an uncertain smile across his face.

Daddy's eyes remained locked on the wall; his body fixed in place. He was with us physically, but his mind appeared to remain lost in memories. Junior's eyes darted between Momma and Daddy as he, too, was unable to see what Daddy was seeing. Silence refilled the room drowning us in apprehension. Davie and I simultaneously whispered 'Daddy' hoping to softly get his attention. I could see disappointment cross Junior's face as he realized Daddy had not noticed the gift.

"Henry..." Momma whispered.

Daddy's eyes remained unmoved.

Momma cautiously stood from her chair and walked towards Daddy. With some trepidation, Momma placed her hand on the back of Daddy's neck and slowly ran her fingers through his hair. Daddy's eyes blinked rapidly as he tried to refocus back to the here and now.

"Henry, dear," Momma's voice remained steady. "Your son bought you a gift, a little welcome home gift."

"What?" Daddy's eyes snapped up to Momma before meeting Junior's gaze. "Oh, thank you, Junior. Thank you."

"Oh...yeah. I mean, yes sir...um...You're welcome..." Junior's words stumbled all over themselves as he desperately searched for what to say next. "I wanted to ... you ... get you something nice to ... to welcome you back home and tell you how pr ...how proud we are of you. I ... I hope you like it."

The left corner of Daddy's lip twitched upwards.

Carefully and with much precision, Daddy began lifting the edges of the wrapping to reveal the object beneath. He was careful not to rip the paper. Once removing the wrapping paper, he neatly folded the paper and placed it at the edge of the table. He turned his attention to the box with the title 'Kerry's Hardware' printed on the top. He opened the end flaps, tipped the box up, and out slid the beautiful 4-inch brown metal knife. His eyes widened and his mouth began to twitch as though fighting back a smile. He seemed unsure of how to respond. He carefully flipped the knife from side to side, studying every detail. His fingers traced over the two blades as he analyzed the quality of each.

"Wha—you?" Daddy started. "You—you bought this for me?"

Junior nodded—unsure of how to respond. He had high expectations of this moment, and it had not gone the way he planned. Daddy looked up to meet Junior's eyes and a genuine smile appeared. The way his lips lifted upward with ease. The way his eyes twinkled with joy. The way his dimples crinkled; it was Daddy. He was back in that moment.

"Thank you. Thank you, Junior. This is absolutely—absolutely beautiful." His eyes blinked back onto the knife. "It's a good quality too; Kerry's? That's the store in town next to the—offi—"

"—post office. Yes, sir. I stopped by after school this week," Junior told him with pride.

"Well...I love it, son. I wish you didn't spend your hard-earned money on me," Daddy's eyes softened. "But... I'll take it." He gave a deep belly laugh, leaning back in his chair relaxed.

The breath I had been holding could finally be released. His familiar laugh brought a sense of relief. At that point, his personality was already fluctuating so frequently that this familiarity was a blessing.

"I had been saving up for a while ... and I — we — Jamie, Davie, and I," Junior nodded at us. "We thought you deserved something nice after — you know — everything."

'Did he say us?' I smiled to myself.

"Us..." Davie whispered to me with bread stuffed in his mouth.

"Yes...us." Junior rolled his eyes. "Jamie and Davie helped me pick it out."

'Was he being sincere or was he trying to earn more points with Daddy this way,' I wondered as I scrunched my face up at Junior.

"Yeah..." Davie swallowed the food he was chewing and happily chimed in. "It's a 2-blade imperial pocketknife! Junior wanted to get just a 1-blade, but don't worry— Jamie and I set him straight."

"No—" Junior's eyes glared over at our smiling brother. "Daddy— He's just foolin'."

"Well, I love it—it's excellent." Daddy stood up and dropped his hand on Junior's head. He slid the knife in his front pocket and gave it a slight tap before picking up his plate, the empty box, and the wrapping paper. He took it over to the kitchen, threw out the box and placed the neatly wrapped paper in the kitchen drawer. We all watched him with curiosity and confusion as he moved through the kitchen without any hesitation. He began washing off his dish and setting it off to the side to dry.

Momma's noticeable sigh pulled our attention back onto her.

"Well... boys, let's pick up our dishes and maybe — Henry — I thought we could sit on the porch for a little while as a family." She walked over to Daddy in the kitchen, reaching around his waist to hold him. "What do you think, Henry?"

I could have sworn I saw Daddy hold his breath as Momma's arm wrapped around him. Initially, he seemed to be unsure of how to respond to her love. It took a moment, but he was able to release his breath and accept her into his arms.

With noticeable uncertainty, he whispered, "of course, dear. That sounds like a great idea. Would you like me to clean the rest of the dishes?"

"No, darling," Momma relaxed. "Let's leave the dishes, sit outside together, and just—relax. We had a late lunch, and the sun will set in the next few hours. Let's just enjoy the sunset together. Maybe—play a little guitar and sing."

"Sounds perfect, dear," Daddy grinned down to Momma. From where I was sitting, the smile almost looked too perfect, practiced. It didn't look real or causal. It was not Daddy's smile. Just like that, he was gone again.

We left our plates and the other dishes inside and moved outside to the porch. Full of glee, Momma pulled out the guitar and met us outside. She was ecstatic having us all together on the porch. This was everything she had dreamed of.

But Daddy—he wouldn't pick up the guitar. He claimed he had forgotten how to play since being in Europe. Momma tried her hardest to sing and get us all involved, but Daddy would not budge. He continued to sit there, quietly, on the swing next to Momma, staring off into nothing. She eventually gave up, leaning the guitar against the front door to join Daddy in silence. We sat all together, consumed in the silence, for an hour, watching as the sun fell into darkness.

Silence is quiet. It is often used as a time to think and clear the mind of any rendering or anxiously unnecessary thoughts. But the silence that surrounded us in that exact moment was loud, as there were no deep and intricate thoughts running through. All that existed were panicked thoughts of the future that awaited our family. For once in my short ten years of life, night became truly dark.

About thirty minutes after the night sky revealed itself, car lights turned into our driveway. I scrutinized the car closely for any details that might reveal who may be inside, but nothing stood out. Through the gleam of the high beams, a silhouette of a man behind the steering wheel caught my attention. The car seemed to be a Buick or Cadillac, but I couldn't be sure.

"Katherine," Daddy stood slowly, edging his way over to the porch stairs for a closer look. "Did you invite anyone over tonight?"

"No, Henry...I didn't. Maybe it's the Bennett's? I know they were hoping to see you at the trai—"

"Junior, get your brothers inside now and hide." His posture was tense...his voice shook with each word. "Katherine, go with them — NOW!" Seemingly panicked, Daddy ducked behind the railing as though shielding himself from gunfire.

Junior jumped off the side railing onto the porch, grabbing hold of Davie and me.

"Get inside," Junior ordered as he pushed us through the door.

Momma, who was visibly shaken by Daddy's change in demeanor, began to study the car in hopes of finding anything familiar.

"Oh, Henry—" Momma began.

"Katherine!" Daddy stressfully peaked over the railing at the car. "Get inside!"

"Henry—Henry! It's Mr. Matthews..." She exclaimed with desperation for him to see reality. "Mr. Matthews, your boss from the Cigar Factory. Remember?"

"Mr. Matthews..." Daddy gasped, out of breath from the delusion. Sweat streamed down his face and his neck as his veins bulged from the rush of blood pulsating throughout his body.

"Yes, Henry. It's Mr. Matthews. Look, he's getting out of his car now. Just look honey. Everything is okay. You are safe... we are all safe." She pleaded with him to see.

Daddy drew in a deep breath and closed his eyes tight. I saw his lips move as he was muttering words that were too low for anyone to hear. He slowly stood keeping his eye on Mr. Matthews as he emerged from his car. Mr. Matthews had aged greatly over the last few years. He was a heavy-set man with thick round glasses. He had begun balding in the front but still managed to keep his jet-black hair around the back. He had a gentle smile and light blue eyes that twinkled from the porch light that shined on him. I watched his smile turned to confusion as he saw the panic in Daddy's eyes. He seemed to immediately understand that Daddy had been alarmed by his unannounced arrival.

"Henry—" Mr. Matthews cleared his throat of nerves. "Welcome home, son! Look at you, you're a—well you're a sight for sore eyes! And, you're a war hero now!" He remained still, waiting for Daddy to speak to ensure recognition.

Unseen Scars

"Oh, um... yes, sir..." Daddy was hesitant at first. "—Good evening, Mr. Matthews. What brings you all the way out here?" Daddy's confidence seemed to grow as he looked back at Momma like a child looking for reassurance.

She nodded slightly as she edged closer to Daddy, placing one hand on his back for comfort, while she held the other out behind her, motioning us to remain inside.

As Momma spoke, her voice unwaveringly calm, "Mr. Matthews, it's been too long. How are you? How is Linda?"

"Linda, oh she is fine, just fine!" Mr. Matthews remained in place. He waited patiently, waiting until Daddy's posture softened. "So — Henry. I was wondering if we could talk privately? I wanted to discuss business wi—well, hey, boys!"

Resisting Junior's attempts to keep him inside, Davie pushed his way through the screen door and onto the porch. Momma shot us a disapproving look for ignoring her instruction.

"Boys?" Momma said as she turned her attention back to Daddy. "Why don't we give your Daddy and Mr. Matthews some privacy. Henry—we'll be inside — safe." Momma spoke softly as she leaned in to kiss his cheek. "You and Mr. Matthews can talk. You will be okay." She said, reassuring him once again.

She stepped away from Daddy and ushered Davie back inside. I stood still behind the screen, looking at Daddy one more time before the door closed. I saw his tension ease as his breathing became more regular.

Instead of joining my brothers' downstairs to wait, I retreated to our bedroom, wanting, and desperately needing to be alone. I picked up the photo Daddy had tossed onto the floor when I found him. My eyes began to burn as tears filled them to the brim with the want to escape. I retreated to my bed holding tightly onto the photo, shutting my eyes for comfort. I was desperate for a glimpse of my memories — our memories — memories of Daddy.

I went back to that moment on the river when it was just him and I. The words he spoke, the bond we held, I will never let go of. I traced my memories back to the Christmases celebrated in the past. Daddy would lay the soles of his shoes in a bag of powdered sugar to make footprints around our home mimicking Santa walking through our house. He wanted to ensure we felt the spirit of Christmas that morning while opening presents.

Images filtered through my mind of waking up to Daddy and Momma dancing in the kitchen while cooking breakfast together. Memories of him sitting with my brothers and me as he taught us about mechanics and hardware. 'Manly things' as he called them. However, now Daddy's smile, once so carefree and effortless, has become strained.

All those memories from the past will remain just that…the past.

In the mist of the thoughts and images that swam throughout my mind, the creaking of the bedroom door interrupted me. My eyes shot open, and I frantically stuffed the photo down by the side of my bed. My eyes glanced towards the door, finding Momma in the doorway. Her smile was soft and welcoming as it always was. There wasn't any hint of judgement in her eyes, only love.

"So…" She gently sat down at the edge of my bed. "What are you thinking about here all alone in the dark?"

"Oh…I…I was…um…" I stuttered uncontrollably as I forced a smile to her. "I was just think…thinking about …you know…um…school."

"About school, huh?" She returned a smile, but I could tell she was undeceived. "What about school exactly?"

"Oh, Arithmetic..." I continued the lie.

"Arithmetic you say?" Her smile remained.

"Yeah, you know. Long division is hard. I was just practicing...in my head," I grinned, unconvincingly.

"Oh, I bet it is difficult. You know what? Personally, I was just thinking about Daddy." Momma admitted.

"Oh, were you?" I sat up quickly, eager to know what was on her mind.

"Yes. You know I was just thinking about the good ole times, you know? When things were, I guess, more normal...before the war." Momma admitted. "I don't know, I guess I'm just reminiscing on old memories."

"Yeah..." I sighed.

"That's not what you happened to be thinking about—along with your math, was it?" Momma's eyes were suspicious.

"No." I tried to lie, but I couldn't. "Well, yeah, I guess...yeah. I don't know, I just miss how it was before the war. Daddy, he's different now. I'm happy he's home—I am—but I don't know, I guess I just wish it weren't such a struggle for him, with whatever he's dealing with, you know?" I admitted. I couldn't keep this to myself any longer.

"I know, Darling," Momma smiled but her eyes were full of sorrow. "I wish the same thing but, unfortunately we can't just flip a switch and fix him. We can't go back in time and undo the past. We need to just give him the time he needs to adjust. They call this shellshock. Within a few weeks, he should be back to normal. Christmas is in a week so let's just try and focus on that. The joy of the holiday. It will be Daddy's first holiday home so that is something to be hopeful about."

"Yeah... you're right..." My eyes focused on the floor as I tried to hide the worry in my eyes. Momma wanted so much to reassure me; I didn't want to let her down. But nothing could have eased my mind in that moment.

"I love you, Jamie. And your Daddy—he loves you too. Don't you ever forget that" she said softly.

"I love you too, Momma," I met her eyes.

"So, I'm going to go downstairs to sit with your brothers so we can be there once your Daddy comes back inside. I do hope you decide to join us." Momma leaned in to kiss the top of my head.

She stood up with grace and left our bedroom leaving the door slightly ajar. Once I knew she was gone, I pulled the photo out and held onto it firmly. I closed my eyes listening to Davie's laughter downstairs. I assumed Daddy was still outside talking with Mr. Matthews. I knew I should probably go downstairs to be with my family, but I couldn't move my body. I just held the photo like I'd never let it go, wanting today to be over with.

After several minutes of thinking and considering my options, I gave up. Tucking the photo back under my pillow, I left to join my family. Walking down the stairway, I could see Junior and Davie sitting on the couch peering out the window.

"What are y'all looking at?" My voice caused them both to jump nearly out of their skins.

"Shhh!" They hissed at me.

"What...?" I demanded.

"Come down here..." Davie whispered.

I squeezed in between them, joining as they looked out the window. Momma had joined the conversation outside. The three of them were talking, but no one was smiling. It appeared as though they were making some sort of deal. Mr. Matthews and Daddy shook hands before Mr. Matthews turned back to his car. Momma and Daddy stood there, watching as Mr. Matthews backed out of the driveway and onto the main road. They remained in the front yard for a few seconds talking. Daddy leaned into Momma, kissing her cheek before coming back inside.

Daddy opened the front door for Momma to enter, then followed closely behind her. Now it was our turn for questions.

"What did Mr. Matthews want, Daddy?" Junior demanded.

"What was that about Daddy?" Davie joined.

"Is everything okay?" I quietly questioned.

His eyes remained locked on the floor, fixed on his thoughts as he walked over to the living room chair. Momma remained near the front door, looking wearily at Daddy as the silence grew louder.

Momma came to the realization that he wasn't going to answer our questions, so she spoke for him. "Mr. Matthews came here to ask Daddy if he would be willing to come back to work."

"Whe—" I stopped myself, wondering if I should even ask.

"—when does he go back?" Davie knowing my thoughts, as twins do, and finished my sentence.

"Tomorrow..." Daddy muttered.

"What? But—you only just got back!" Junior yelled.

"Junior..." Momma interjected, trying to calm down her eldest son.

"No, dear... he has a right to be upset." Daddy finally lifted his eyes off the floor to meet Momma's.

"Why... Why would they do that?" Junior stood up with anger.

"Well, because with the war just ending, we need to focus on production. They need men who are able to work." Daddy's eyes turned to Junior. "I am one of the able men. As I have always been."

"But—But you were shot!" Junior exclaimed; his furry echoed through the house.

"Yes, but compared to others who were injured during the war, my injury was minimal," Daddy's voice never raising. "I am alive and well. There is no excuse for me not to work...I am sorry, son."

"This is ridiculous!" Junior stormed off up the stairs to again barricade himself in our room, as he had done for the last four and a half years.

Daddy flinched to the sound of Junior's shoes stomping on the stairs as though the sound sent memories flying through his mind. Momma was hesitant on stopping Junior but eventually decided it would be best for him to blow off his steam privately. Daddy's eyes followed Junior upstairs and flinched again when our bedroom door was slammed shut.

"Wow..." Davie mouthed.

"Well—I will clean up the kitchen," Daddy faked a smile.

"Dear, I can—" Momma started.

"It's okay... it will be good for me to clean up a little. Let me help... I was unable to help you for so many years. Let me do so now" he stood and held her hands for a moment as he gave her a crooked smile.

Momma stood back and let him clean the kitchen. She sat down at the kitchen table to watch and admire her husband. I glanced over at Davie who was now distracting himself with the whoopee cushion he had pulled from his pocket.

I overreacted quietly to myself as I thought about losing Daddy yet again. Even though he would be home every night, we thought he'd at least have some time off. I needed space...I needed to think. The only place I knew I could go was the fort. So, I quietly stood up and snuck out the front door.

"Where are you going?" Davie whispered.

Ignoring my brother, I ran down the porch stairs and around the side of our house. I ducked out of view of the back door, avoiding being caught by Momma or Daddy. I saw our flock of chickens put themselves up for the night, hiding from any potential danger in the night. I hid away inside the Clark Fortress, decompressing from the events of the day. I hugged onto the blankets left inside, pressed my face against them and cried. I cried for Uncle Tommy and other families who were hurting from the same pain. But most importantly, I cried for my Daddy.

War was a game I would play as a child for fun and entertainment. We'd run around with friends as we pretended to shoot each other with our pea shooters or imaginary guns. If you were hit or caught, we would fall on the ground pretending to die in the most dramatic way. But—we'd always get up. At that age, we never understood the dark reality of those games.

Not one person had ever talked about the psychological damage war can leave on a person. A person who had been so carefree before, becomes a person who can no longer carry a real smile after. I knew and understood that war was necessary at times. But what about the mental and emotional impact war left on those men who served during it?

During those days, after World War II ended, no one worried about the mental impact left on those men. It took years of research and advocation to have a better understanding of those issues. I often wonder how life could have been if we had that understanding back then. Maybe—just maybe—life would have been different. Maybe you would have all known my twin brother. Who knows what could have been? That question remains in my mind to this very day.

The tears and thoughts were unstoppable. I worried about the man inside. I worried for my family. All I had to comfort me in the dark of our fort was the anger and fears that pulsated through my body. I clutched the blanket, drawing it even more snugly around me. I wept louder…wanting just to scream. Scream away the fears that haunted me. Scream away the pain that had been destroying me over the years.

"Hey…you okay?" Davie's voice cut through the night.

I hadn't heard him coming. I had been so lost in my own fears that I failed to listen for anyone who could hear. I didn't want him to hear or see the weakness that had overcome me. I didn't want my brother, or anyone, to see me as weak.

I frantically rubbed away the tears that poured down my face. I took a deep breath, ending up only inhaling the snot from my running nose. I knew it wasn't enough. I knew he would see the truth— he would see the weakness I attempted to conceal.

"Ya…" I gasped in between the tears.

"Jamie…" His voice sounded concerned.

I couldn't speak…I fought against the tears.

"I understand, Jamie… I see it too…" Davie crawled inside, throwing his arm over my shoulders.

"Do you?" I felt alone with my thoughts.

"Yes…of course…He is different. I see it too," Davie whispered. "We hoped and prayed for Daddy to be home…and he's home…in person…but he's not really home yet…is he?"

"No…" I was able to take deep breaths, calming my body down. I exhaled slowly to help me speak clearly. "I think a part of him was left in Europe."

We both looked up at the photo pinned up on the wall, the photo of Daddy in his uniform. The pride in his eyes was undeniable. His strength was irrefutable. And the honor was indisputable. He was meant to be a soldier. He was meant to be a hero. But was he meant to come home?

"It seems that way, but give him time, Jamie. We can't give up on him. He'll be back," Davie looked back at the photo with pride. "He is in there; we just have to give him time to find his way back."

"I guess you're right..." I sighed.

"I know I'm right, that's why you were born first. I had to direct you out." Davie giggled.

"Shut up," We laughed together.

"Yeah..." Davie's laughter faded into seriousness. "I just can't believe they are making him work tomorrow."

"He has had no time off. How can he relax and adjust when the world won't let him?" Rage consumed me again.

"It makes sense—sort of. I know they need to increase production. It's just...I hate it, you know?" Davie sounded heartbroken.

"But like you said...let's just give him time. He will be back. Maybe working will be good for him, you never know," I searched for any positivity I could find. "It might help him to take his mind off of some things, keep him active and feeling valuable to society, you know?"

"I hope...I just hope it doesn't backfire on us." Davie had never been so melancholy before.

"Hope not..." I agreed.

"Well—whatever happens, Jamie, we have each other. We get through everything together," Davie made eye contact with me. "No matter what happens in this world. We will always have each other—and Junior...I guess." Davie scoffed with a slight smile across his face.

"Really now? Do we have to keep him?" I sneered.

"I think so...somehow we are biologically related to him," Davie shrugged.

"How?"

"I don't know... but Momma swears we are all related." Davie continued.

"She could be wrong..." I suggested.

"One could only hope!" Davie added.

We sat together –brother and brother. Laughing and enjoying each other's company in the darkness of our fortress. We discussed life and where we wanted to be in ten years at the age of twenty. We even spoke about girls and if we wanted to get married one day. It was the first time in a long time that Davie and I had actually discussed something other than the war and family problems. We just talked—managing to escape, however briefly, from this new reality.

It was reassuring knowing that we each had similar long-term goals for our future. The only difference was career paths. I knew I wanted to be some kind of businessman when I grew up. Davie thought he would make an excellent comedian or joke shop owner, which I agreed with. He even admitted he wanted to be married one day. I could not imagine either one of us married— it was bizarre to even imagine that at the tender age of ten.

We were just two boys—two brothers— dreaming of a future that wouldn't exist.

"Alright," Davie patted his leg. "Let's go inside and just...just figure it all out together."

"Together..." I smiled.

We locked hands in agreement before crawling out of the fort. Before heading inside, we locked the chicken coop up to keep them safe for the night. I noticed the lights inside had become dimmed.

Davie opened the back door...and there was Daddy. He was sitting patiently, quietly at the now cleaned dinner table— alone.

'Is he waiting for us?' I thought.

"David...James...do you mind sitting down with me to talk." He nodded over to the seats across from him.

My mouth dropped open as I eyed my brother, searching for some kind of mutual agreement to sit with him. Davie had the same look in his eyes.

I nodded making the decision for both of us. We sat down across from him, and I immediately felt the tension of the coming conversation. He remained in his uniform, still unchanged from train station. He was still unable to make himself comfortable...even in his own home.

"So...I know—" clearing his throat, he continued. "I know I may not be the same as I was before. I know you both are probably disappointed in me. And I...I'm sorry. I am honestly trying..." I saw an honest tear fall down his cheek. "Please... don't give up on me just yet."

"We won't, Daddy..." I looked my father in the eyes and promised.

"Yeah...Daddy. We would never give up on you." Davie followed.

Daddy smiled slightly...relieved with our responses. "I love you both..." he whispered.

"We love you too, Daddy," I returned his smile.

"Love you, Daddy," Davie said before asking softly, "Junior?"

"Your Mother is talking with him right now..." Daddy sighed.

"Ah...don't worry about him. It's just how he processes things sometimes..." I reassured him.

"Kind of reminds me of someone I know," Daddy scoffed.

"Who?" Davie and I said together.

"...me..." he replied with a sense of humility.

We remained silent downstairs before heading to bed. We gave Junior and Momma the time needed to handle things privately upstairs. They had a long conversation on appropriate behavior versus inappropriate which Davie and I could clearly hear from the living room. Eventually, Momma opened the door revealing a crying Junior—who, by the looks of it—just wished to be hit rather than to have had to listen to Momma carrying on.

As I got tucked into bed, I pulled out the photo hidden under my pillow to fall asleep with. I felt some hope that things would go back to normal—whatever normal might be. Life, for just a second in time, felt…hopeful. All the worries had momentarily disappeared at the slight possibility of hope. This possibility comforted me and aided me as I drifted off to sleep.

Chapter 8

Christmas came and left, as uneventful as it could be for our family. Davie got a slinky, which was one of the neatest gifts you could receive at that time. He thought it was the best thing in the world as he watched it coil and uncoil down the staircase. He did this a countless number of times throughout the day, each time as delighted and excited as the first. I got a monopoly board game that we all played late into the night. Much to Junior's displeasure, I won. Monopoly, even in our older days, was Junior's and my favorite game to play. We were extremely competitive with games like Monopoly. Davie could care less; his just enjoyed rolling the dice. Junior got a new messenger bag for school and for his paper route. He would repeatedly explain to us how mature and grown he was now that he owned that messenger bag.

We each walked around the house like we were walking on a cloud. Christmas was our favorite holiday to celebrate as a family, and with Daddy home, it felt complete. We made many happy memories that Christmas in 1945; and I'm glad we did.

At this point, Daddy had been home for about two weeks, and it appeared that he was improving. He had his good days, and he still had his bad days, but that's normal for anyone—we allowed him to have his good and bad days and everyone is allowed to have them. Our new concern was his new pastime hobby: drinking.

There were nights when he would not come home until close to midnight. And when he did come home, the majority of the time, he reeked of liquor. Most nights, Junior would wait for him by the oak tree out front. He'd sit with him there and give him water or coffee until he sobered up. We wanted to keep his drinking between us three. We didn't want Momma to know about it since she already had so much more to deal with.

In between the hard moments, there were times that felt like he was on the road to recovery. Like the nights when Daddy would take Momma by her hand and dance with her in the kitchen or on the porch. And the days when Daddy would come home early to take us out to the lake to fish and tell us stories of the war. But, then there were the days when Daddy would lock himself in the bedroom to cry in the dark.

New Years Eve of 1945, in particular, was one of the more difficult days. We stayed up as we always did to listen to the radio as the ball dropped, signaling not just a new year but new beginnings. Davie and I sat on the living room floor to play a game of cards while Junior lay on the couch to read his new favorite book. We were looking forward to the ball dropping all week long, Daddy included. Momma and Daddy watched us from the kitchen as they discussed how much they had both enjoyed the holiday as a complete family.

Everything had been going well until about five minutes before the ball dropped. Momma grabbed the champagne to carry on their old tradition to toast in the New Year. Daddy hadn't been paying attention to her as he was watching Davie and me. Momma opened the bottle and when the cork popped off, the sound— which mimicked a gun shot— echoed off every wall in the house. Daddy sprung from his chair, diving into the nearest corner and pinning his back to the wall. The blood in his face drained instantaneously from the fear and apprehension. His breathing increased as his lungs worked harder to keep up with the adrenaline that was now pumping through his veins. He stared straight at the front door. In that moment, we were not his family. We were strangers.

"Henry..." Momma muttered, trying not to move so as not to frighten him further.

Daddy's hyperventilation continued. I could see the carotid artery in his neck flutter as it pumped blood at a rapid speed. His eyes frantically searched around the room as though he was looking for an exit. The panic in Daddy's eyes increased as he slowly scanned the entire first floor. His breathing became more audible and rapid as though the panic was rising in his body.

Davie, Junior, and I watched everything unfold from the living room; our bodies frozen with confusion. None one of us knew what to say or do.

Finally, the silence was broken by Junior.

"Is he okay...?" Junior asked as he slowly got to his feet.

I saw Daddy's eyes cease scanning as he focused his attention in on Junior, monitoring his every movement.

"Junior...stop moving..." I whispered, maintaining my eye contact on Daddy.

"Wha—" Junior finally realized Daddy's eyes were locked onto him.

"Henry…focus on me. Not Junior…focus on me," Momma stepped slowly in our direction with her arms out in a protective manner.

"STAY BACK!" Daddy bellowed, now looking directly at Momma as she moved to shield us. "Stay—STAY BACK! I'M WARNING YOU!"

"Henry…dear…it is okay. You are alright. You are home… You are safe at home with your family. My name is Katherine…" She pleaded for him to remember. "I am your Katherine…You are safe…"

"Ka—"

"Katherine…" Momma nodded.

"Oh, Katherine…" Daddy's voice lowered to a whisper.

"Yes dear…I am Katherine Clark. Your wife. These are our sons… Junior, Jamie and Davie…" She kept her eyes fixed on Daddy, maintaining the connection.

His posture began to relax. His shoulders that were once tense now dropped with ease. His pale face slowly regained some color as his eyes softened. Noticing his body easing up, Momma gently walked over to him with her arms reached out. She wanted so desperately to bring him comfort. I held my breath as she edged closer to him, afraid to make a sound that might escalate that situation.

"Henry…I love you…We all love you…you are safe…please…" Momma whispered, now only inches away from Daddy.

His breathing relaxed and his weary eyes looked deeply into Momma's eyes. Tears began to fall as the guilt took over. His head fell into his hands, as he seemed to become overwhelmed with regret.

"I'm sorry!" He exclaimed. "I—I'm sorry. I was—I'm so sorry!"

Momma knelt to Daddy's level, maintaining their eye contact. She reached her arms out running her hands through his hair, gently stroking his head. He wept continuously, crying out more apologies and regrets to us. My brothers and I remained in place, still unable to move.

Momma wrapped him in her arms to hold him securely in her embrace, while Daddy began to rock back and forth.

"Henry…Henry…it's okay, love. We are not mad at you, my dear," Momma whispered, comforting him with every tear that fell. "It happens. You are okay…come with me and let's sit on the couch okay… let's relax. Everything is okay."

Momma rose to her feet, holding out her arms to help Daddy balance. His eyes were puffy and his face was flushed from what must be overwhelming emotions racing through his mind.

"Okay… Okay…" He gasped as he tried desperately to control his breathing. His eyes remained locked onto Momma, who kept reassuring him that he was safe. As he shuffled over to the living room couch, his eyes fell onto us. Immediate and instant shame clouded his face. "Boys…oh my boys. I…I'm so sorry…I am so sorry!"

"Sh—shh—shhh" Momma calmed him. "The boys are okay. Here, sit down with me. Junior, back up some to give us space…"

Tears continued to stream down his face at the sight of us. They sat down together; Momma's arms still firmly wrapped around him as though sheltering him from himself.

Not knowing what to say, Junior, Davie, and I remained in place staring at him with our eyes wide. Since he had been home, he had never done something like that. We would occasionally see him drifting off into another world, and come home drunk, but this time he genuinely believed he was physically in another world.

The radio had been playing the entire time off in the background. Cheers for the upcoming year played in the background, which we had all drowned out. Davie and I remained on the floor, paused in a card game that we had both forgotten about.

The man on the radio began to countdown.

"—TEN—NINE—EIGHT—SEVEN—SIX—FIVE—" the carefree and ecstatic radio hosts shouted.

Daddy's sobs continued to echo off the walls.

"—FOUR—THREE—TWO—ONE! HAPPY NEW YEAR!"

We marked the arrival of the New Year, not with cheers of celebratory clapping, but with Daddy's cries. And for the first time in my life there was nothing joyous about the starting of a new year.

"Happy New Year, Henry…" Momma, still holding him, kissed his forehead as the tears slowed down.

"Happy New Year, Momma…" I mumbled. I was hoping to at least make her smile slightly but nothing. All I got from her was eye contact for a slight moment. Her eyes conveying concern and heartbreak for the man she loved.

The night was over after that. Just minutes after the ball dropped, Momma led Daddy upstairs and safely into bed. My brothers and I retired to our room as well. We did not know what to do. My brothers and I didn't speak to one another. Instead of hope this New Year, all that existed was confusion and sorrow as we lay in bed struggling to find peace enough to sleep.

The next day Daddy did not leave the bedroom, and I don't believe he even left his bed. Momma would fix food and take it upstairs for him. Whenever she brought more food up, she'd bring the last plate downstairs, untouched. He wasn't eating. When we asked why he was acting this way, all Momma would say is, "Daddy is sick."

I remember thinking, 'well, I don't remember seeing Daddy sneezing or coughing yesterday, so how could he be sick.' I knew he was sad and upset but he wasn't sick.

I eventually learned that this 'sickness,' was not a common cold or flu, but something a bit more complex. It would take decades for this to even earn a name: depression. Back then, there was no real information on depression. During those years, people, like my mother, simply referred to depression as 'being sick.' So, January 1, 1946, ended up being remarkably similar to the last five New Years— with an absence of Daddy.

Throughout the week, Daddy slowly began to come around. He didn't go into work that week, neither did Momma, both calling in 'sick.' Daddy slowly began leaving their room more, which was an immense step for him. It was a subtle and slow process to get Daddy back on his feet. He began smiling again and talked with us at the dinner table. He even joined us on the porch a few times. I was hoping this would be the turnaround our family needed, but it was just the beginning.

January came and went with continuous highs and lows and no solutions. We came to the understanding that this was just how life would be from here on out. Whenever any of us would mention Uncle Tommy in a causal conversation, Daddy would leave the room to go 'take care of something.' So, we all reminded each other to not mention his name in front of Daddy, giving each other pointed glances and slight kicks when stories turned to anything involving Uncle Tommy. We also learned to be careful when walking around him, avoiding making loud noise or sudden movements that could cause him to go into a panic.

Momma attempted to reach out to Joan multiple times. Each attempt ended in disappointment when there was no response. Momma went into her own slight depression, feeling powerless in her fight to help Daddy. We tried our best to be there for her, but nothing we did could change the fact that Daddy was no longer the same man. It was just something we all had to continue to adjust to.

February came and Daddy's drinking increased more. Days when Daddy didn't indulge in drinks became few and far between. The night before Valentine's Day, Momma had to go out into town to look for Daddy after he failed to come home after work. I don't know where or how she found him. I only remember staying up late, listening to her as she helped him up the stairs and into bed.

By February, his temper slowly increased as well. He had less patience for any of our mess ups or attitudes. Eventually this change led to him demanding Momma quit working. She said she would quit, but she didn't. She continued to work since jobs remained in desperate need of employees. She loved working for Southern Bell. That feeling of being needed and important to something bigger than she was, even though it just was helping connect phone calls, meant everything to her. To her, she was connecting family and friends and giving them the laughter and hope they needed to get through hard times. Being told she was not allowed to work anymore was devastating. So, she developed a plan to continue working. She'd get home just before Daddy, which gave her enough time to prepare dinner. She'd ask my brothers and me to keep it our little secret and hid the money she made in a jar under a loose floorboard in our bedroom. This way Daddy did not see any extra money coming into the house, lessening further suspicion about her.

March came followed by April and still, Daddy did not know about Momma's secret. Their relationship was practically nonexistent. Occasionally he would come home and give her a kiss, but more often than not, he came home drunk and angry. He would yell and scream about things that irritated him: silly things, like a piece of paper on the living room table or shoes at the bottom of the stairs. We became almost robotic in our house. We tried avoiding as much interaction with him as we could. Why would we interact with him? He was not the same and there was no more pretending like he would come back. At this point, we knew he wouldn't, or perhaps he couldn't. This was the new him and we just had to learn how to live with it.

Even amid all his anger, he never laid a hand on any of us. So, I guess you could say we were grateful for that. At night, Momma would call MeeMaw and Pa for family updates; Daddy did not like that. He believed she was calling her 'boyfriend' or 'secret admirer.' Even though Momma would deny it over and over, he didn't believe her. Life, without a doubt, was different, but never in our wildest imagination did we think our future would change so drastically.

One night while Daddy was off on his typical Wednesday night bar adventures, a man from Daddy's work came by our house. He was deployed with Daddy for a year before being sent home due to a leg injury. This injury left him with a permanent limp. He introduced himself to us as Arnold Kane.

Mr. Kane knocked on our front door while Momma was cleaning dishes, and my brothers and I were doing homework. Davie ran to the door with a slight hope to see our drunk but alive father leaning on the porch rail, but he was wrong.

"Good evening... is your mother home?" the stranger said.

"Um...yes. Who are you?" Davie questioned the man.

Momma heard the stranger's voice and ran out of the kitchen without hesitation. She hurried to the front door to pull Davie away from the man.

"Good evening... Can I help you?" Momma pulled Davie behind her. "Davie, go work on your homework please..."

"Yes, ma'am..." Davie stepped back into the living room.

"Oh... I am sorry for intruding ma'am. My name is Arnold Kane. I work with Henry at the Cigar Factory," Mr. Kane responded, his raspy voice echoed through the house.

"Oh Arnold. I have heard so much about you!" Momma offered her hand out to shake his. "What brings you out here? Henry's— he's okay, isn't he?"

"Yes, ma'am. Last I saw him, he was fine," his hand stuck through the doorway to greet Momma. His hand was oil stained and scarred. "Well, I've heard much about you as well. All good things, I promise. I was hoping actually to have a quick word with you — privately."

"Is our father, okay?" Junior stood up tall to question Mr. Kane.

Mr. Kane peered inside meeting Junior's gaze. Mr. Kane was around Daddy's age; he was tall and lean in stature. His light hair was combed neatly in place with expressive dark brown eyes that showed sympathy and understanding.

"Yes, sir... he is okay..." Mr. Kane answered Junior directly.

"Then why are you here so late?" Junior questioned boldly.

"Junior, don't interrogate the man. Sit down and finish your homework, please." Momma demanded before turning her attention back to Mr. Kane. "Of course, Arnold. Let's talk on the porch so my children won't eavesdrop."

The two of them stepped out onto the porch, Momma giving us a threatening look to behave ourselves. The second the door shut, my brothers and I ducked below the picture window, listening carefully for some answers about this private conversation they were having.

"Junior, how can we hear them through the window?" Davie asked.

"Y'all... I understand we each want to hear them but—shouldn't we give them some privacy?" I suggested, already knowing what I said would not be a popular opinion.

"Oh, shut up, Jamie..." Junior snarled. "Come on Davie... open the latch—quietly!" Junior crawled to the window panel farthest away from the front door, hoping not to be too noticeable.

Davie crawled over to join Junior, helped him pop the latch, and lift the window slightly allowing the conversation to be heard more easily. Giving up, I crawled over to my eavesdropping brothers, overcome by the temptation to hear the secret discussion between Mr. Kane and Momma. I peeked over the window seal finding Momma and Mr. Kane sitting on the porch staircase together. They were talking softly; it was as though Momma knew we would be trying to overhear them. The three of us basically stopped breathing to do just that.

"I'm just concerned about him—we're all concerned—at work. He has outbursts, he cries, and has moments when he won't come out of the bathroom," Mr. Kane explained to Momma. "I'm not trying to worry you or make you feel attacked. I just...look—everyone at the factory just wants to make sure you and the boys are okay...that you're safe."

"I understand." Momma said quietly. "He is struggling. It doesn't feel like he's truly come home. Every time I think he's getting better...we take about five steps back. He won't admit anything is wrong or talk to anyone, not that anyone would listen to him anyway. They'd just call him crazy..." Momma whispered to Mr. Kane. "I...I just don't know what to do. I don't want to scare the boys, but I'm worried."

"If you and the boys ever need anything, we— me and all the men from work— we are here for y'all, okay?" Mr. Kane whispered, placing his hand on Momma's shoulder.

"Thank you, Arnold." She sighed with a relief that seemed to come from her toes, as though she were finally getting the last few months' worth of emotions off her chest.

"Oh no—" Junior whispered.

"What...what...?" Davie eager to see what Junior was seeing.

"Daddy...I see Daddy. Look, he's stumbling up the driveway," Junior put his head in his hands.

"What—" Davie and I said squinting into the night.

"Oh no—he's home early tonight..." I said, too afraid to look at Junior.

"This is not good...what do we do?" Junior panicked.

"We...we're not supposed to even be listening..." I reminded.

"I think he sees them—This is not good..." Davie breathed.

"Shhh," Junior hushed. "Listen..."

"Henry...?" Momma whispered standing up quickly, watching Daddy stumble up the driveway.

"MR. KANE!" Daddy slurred loudly. "Well HAY bab—AY! What—What is he doin' here!? Am I walking in on something? What...am I just not good enough for you anymore!"

"Darling...you know you're the only one for me." Momma answered.

"Henry, I came by to see you and ask about how work has been going." Mr. Kane stood, frozen with anxiety.

"Work!? Oh, it is just fantastic! Yes, everything is amazing. I am so glad you asked, Mr. Kane! My best friend is dead! My kids can't even look at me...HELL— they won't even talk to me! And my wife, well, she is obviously in the market for a better husband, and I clearly have interrupted her first date! Should I leave, Katherine... you know...give y'all privacy for your first kiss. Or—should I just go ahead and kill myself to make it all easier for you!" Daddy was shouting, slurring his words together. He was a foot away from Momma and Mr. Kane at this point, swaying unsteadily from what was obviously a large quantity of alcohol coursing through his system.

"Darling...no! NO! I love you! I've always loved you. No one else! Arnold—Mr. Kane – came by to talk with you but you weren't home yet. So, I—" Momma spoke quickly as she tried to explain the situation.

"Henry...go inside and get some coffee in your system. Sleep it off. Tomorrow we—" Mr. Kane's voice steadied.

"NO! You do not get to tell me what to do in my own home! This is not work! This is my house! And at my house, I am in charge! My family! My wife! My kids! My rules!" Daddy was becoming increasingly agitated with each word coming out of his mouth.

"What do we do?" I whispered hastily over to my brothers whose eyes were widening with each passing minute.

"I don't know...do we stay inside?" Davie asked Junior.

"I—" Junior began, but he had no answer.

"You what? Do we, Junior? Do we stay inside?" Davie inquired again concerned, and unsure of what to do while we watched as Daddy got closer and closer to Mr. Kane.

"I don't know...okay? I'm thinking it through," Junior responded flustered.

"Henry...please," Mr. Kane pleaded. "Look, I am truly sorry for coming here and I—I don't mind leaving."

"NO! You leave when I tell you to leave!" Daddy yelled, eyes bulging and spittle flying.

"Henry...look he will just leave...then—then you and I can go ins—"

"No! I am not going anywhere until he understands how to respect another man's property!" Anger seemed to ooze from Daddy's pores.

"What do we do?" I cried out to my brothers.

Davie grabbed my hand as we cowered below the window too afraid to watch. Junior shut his eyes tight, pinned his back to the wall, and resorted to only listening to the scene outside, instead of watching it. Momma began sobbing from the words, and I knew it was only a matter of time before Daddy struck Mr. Kane.

Junior began muttering quietly to himself, "Okay—okay—you can do it—be strong—be strong—"

He took a deep breath before he found the courage to stand. We pleaded with Junior to stay with us, but he wouldn't listen. He had already decided his next course of action, and we weren't going to be able to talk him out of it.

Exhaling slowly, Junior took a step forward, becoming the older brother we needed. Davie and I turned to peer back out the window wanting to see whatever would happen next.

"IF YOU EVER GO NEAR MY WIFE AGAIN, I SWEAR TO GOD—I WILL KILL YOU—YOU HEAR ME!?" Daddy gripped Mr. Kane's collar and shook him, ensuring he understood the threat given.

"HENRY! PLEASE!" Momma begged.

"Daddy—" Junior timidly stepped out onto the porch.

"Baby... Baby..." Tears streamed down Momma's face as she turned to Junior. "Go inside—go to your room, honey—please—Everything is okay out here. Everything is under control!"

"Daddy—" Junior ignored her plead. "Daddy—why are you doing this?"

"Jun—Junior—" Daddy's anger dissipated at the sight of his oldest son. He immediately dropped Mr. Kane from his grip, his eyes shifting from Junior to Mr. Kane. His face filled with horror as he realized what he was doing. "I'm – I'm sorry..."

"Arnold—Arnold, are you okay?" Momma grabbed Mr. Kane, checking for any injuries. "Henry...darling, take deep breaths...sit down, okay. Let's all just sit down..."

"No. I'm going to go home." Mr. Kane said. "I'm leaving. Henry—I'm sorry. I'm gone. Katherine, have a good night." Mr. Kane hobbled hastily to his car, fumbling as he opened the car door and promptly started the engine. Pulling out of our driveway almost faster than he could shut his door, he turned onto the main road and sped off, his tires squealing as they searched for traction.

Davie and I stood up, weakly, hand in hand. We crept to the front door joining Junior.

I peered around Junior and nervously asked, "Daddy…are you okay?"

"I—" Daddy's eyes were wide with confusion and fear, as he slowly came down from the high.

"Henry…" Momma uttered softly.

"Y—Yes… I'm—I'm so—I'm so sorry boys…Oh, Katherine…" Daddy gulped. "I'm so sorry…I didn't—I didn't mean to."

"It's okay…It's okay…co—come sit down…" Momma reached her arms out for Daddy to hold and led him to the porch stairs.

Daddy's legs gave out as soon as he reached the stairs. He cried into her chest unceasingly, hands clutching her waist. She held him in silence, rocking him slowly as his tears of regret soaked her blouse. Momma gently rubbed his back as howls of sorrow worsened with every passing second.

"Everything is okay…" Momma spoke to him quietly. "—we are all okay… We need you, Henry…You are important to us… No one can or will ever replace you…"

"She's right, Daddy…" Davie's small voice sounded from behind me. "We love you…"

"We love you, Daddy…" I added.

"Let's go inside, darling...You need to sleep this off..." Momma continued stroking his back, holding him tight. "I love you... No other man can replace you..."

"I –I love –you –too," Daddy cried out as he gasped for air.

We stood at the doorway...unable to move...unable to breathe. I wanted to reach out and comfort him as he had comforted me when I was young. But I couldn't move. I felt ashamed of myself for not being able to be there for him when he needed us most. But the words he screamed just minutes ago replayed over and over in my mind.

After a few minutes, his wails lessened into hiccups of breath. Momma helped him to his feet, getting him inside and up the stairs. His body shook as silent tears streamed down his face. He gripped the stair rail for support as his weak body climbed. Momma led him into their bedroom, and she closed the door immediately shutting us out. We heard the shower handle squeak as it turned on to rinse the alcohol and memories off Daddy's body.

My brothers and I returned to the couch unsure of where to go or what to do. We just waited there in the silence of the living room, hoping for some sign that everything was okay again.

After the shower turned off, the floorboards creaked as Daddy stumbled off to bed. And then an eerie silence circulated throughout the house. Momma's footsteps ceased to exist. We had no way of knowing where she was.

"I'm going to bed..." Junior spoke with desolation as he stared at his feet.

"Wha—Why—?" Davie hesitated.

"Because...I cannot handle this anymore..." Junior sprung from the couch, pacing frantically while considering his options. "I just have to go to bed. I can't simply sit here and do nothing, and—since I can't do anything about this—I need to go to bed. It's the only way I can handle this. I'm sorry…goodnight." Then he was gone…hurrying up the stairs and straight to our room, shutting the door and hiding away from all that he could see.

Just as his door closed, Momma's door opened. Exhaustion took over her expression as she stood at the top of the staircase. She looked down at us and back at our bedroom in full understanding that Junior shut us out again.

"So," Momma sighed as she slowly made her way downstairs.

She held her head low unable to look us directly in our eyes. With much anguish, Momma sat in between us before dropping her head into her hands breaking down softly. I realized then that it was our turn to be the men of the house. She needed us now more than ever. Davie and I wrapped our arms around her offering her our solace.

Mothers are supposed to keep their children safe from the world around them and protect them from those who want to cause them harm. However, there are times when your mother is the one who needs protection from the world. And tonight, was one of those times.

"Momma, everything will be okay," Davie whispered tenderly.

"We are here for you," I told her. "Junior, Davie, and I—we are all together on this."

"We won't let you fall," Davie encouraged.

"Never," I agreed.

Her pain lessened with a sigh as though remembering she was not alone in the battle ahead. There was some relief and reassurance knowing we were all together during this time as a family.

Momma leaned back revealing her face, red and blotchy. A faint smile appeared on her face breaking through all the heartache. She wrapped her arms around Davie and me, leaning us back into the couch like we were five years old again.

And just like that, Momma put us first again.

"You two are the children...I do the worrying not you," the hint of a smile faded as quickly as it had appeared. Sighing, she continued, "I need to talk to the two of you and your brother tomorrow in private. Your Daddy...probably won't be going to work tomorrow; therefore, I will not be going either. The three of you will still have to go to school tomorrow, but when y'all get home, the four of us need to have a word. Can we do that?"

"Um..." I hesitated, thinking carefully before speaking. "Okay—well, Davie and I will tell Junior on the way to school. Will you need help with Daddy tom—"

"No..." Momma responded promptly.

"Why not?" Davie chimed in. "I mean, I, for one, do not mind staying home from school. Although it would hurt me dearly not being at school, not learning, sitting at a desk—it would be just awful to miss that. But!" Davie smirked. "I will sacrifice it all for you, Mother."

Momma chuckled slightly at Davie's joke and hugged him a little tighter. I couldn't help but laugh with her. It had been months now since she had laughed blissfully. It was doleful when I thought of the last time she laughed, the night before Daddy came home. The night we sang "Stay Up All Night" on the porch as a family. Weird, right? His return was everything to us, and now it's everything we never wanted.

The next morning was abnormally quiet for our house especially for a school day. I lay in bed, silently listening and waiting for any signs of movement throughout the house but heard nothing. The only sounds came from my brothers, who were walking to and from the bathroom as they prepared for school.

Once we were all ready for the day, we proceeded downstairs to grab a bite to eat for breakfast, but there was no food ready. No food prepared, no parents waiting for us; the kitchen was empty. I glanced up at their bedroom, but the door was closed.

Junior didn't hesitate to leave home for school. He walked out the door as quick as he could, avoiding any kind of conversation with Davie and me.

"Ignore him..." Davie sneered. "Let's just go..."

"Sure..."

Grabbing our schoolbooks, we stepped out the front door full of apprehension for the day ahead. I followed behind Davie off in my own world as I reached down to grab my bicycle.

"Have a wonderful day, boys," a familiar voice spoke.

Gasping, I snapped my head up to find Momma quietly rocking in her chair. She had a look of melancholy in her eyes as she stared off into the morning sun sipping her coffee. She waved in our direction, giving us the same fake, painted on smile as the night before.

"You too, Momma!" Davie said skeptically.

"We will see you after school, Momma," I gave her a sly smile confirming our conversation for later.

Momma slightly nodded not paying us much attention.

"Bye, Momma!!" Junior hollered while climbing onto his bicycle.

I can't explain the feeling I had in that exact moment, but there was something very—unsettling—about leaving. I figured I was simply still worried from the night before, which lead me to overlooking that sensation. To this day, I can't help but think; that if only I had listened to myself—I might have been able to help. But I didn't. I left. I pushed the feeling aside, hopped onto my bike, and pedaled off to catch up with my brothers while searching for any reason to stay behind.

I biked fast as I could, catching up with them just in time to hear Davie say, "Momma wants to talk to us today, Junior…without Daddy being around…so when we get home let's meet at Jamies' and my fortress to talk."

"You mean that pile of sticks y'all call a fortress?" Junior rolled his eyes, "sure…I'll be there."

And just like that Junior was gone. Veering off into the woods taking his own path to school, leaving us behind on the main road alone.

Six hours of school felt substantially longer that day probably due to the nagging feeling in my heart that something was wrong at home. I have never been one to believe in superstition; I believe in facts. However, I also believe that the feelings in your heart are real. Instincts that you should listen to and take seriously. Oh, how I wish I had that day.

Davie and I headed home late that afternoon, without Junior. Normally we would meet him halfway home, but that day, we didn't. I wondered then if Davie had a similar feeling to what I had as we left home that morning. We pedaled as fast as we could without saying a word. The closer we got to home, the more worried I felt for Momma.

As we turned onto the road leading to home, the feeling of dread became overwhelming. We turned onto our driveway and we both skidded to a stop, looking up at the eerily quiet house. I was afraid to go inside; afraid to find something I didn't want to see. For the first time in my short life, I was afraid of what my father might have done.

Dropping our bikes on the lawn, we stepped up on the porch and still—no sounds. The only sound came from the floorboards as they creaked under our shifting weight. As we peered through the screen door, with the sunlight behind us making it difficult to see any details inside the house, it dawned on us—the inner door was open. Davie and

I waited another moment, taking a deep breath before pulling the screen door open. 'Please...please ...please, be okay...' I pleaded to myself.

We stepped inside— and I saw what I had been dreading all day. Sitting tearfully, at the top of the staircase was Momma. There was no fake smile on her face. There was no pretending the injuries she had endured weren't there. Her face was pale and there was a look of desperation in her eyes. We saw the devastation of a beaten woman. Her once beautiful pink dress was now rumpled, and wet from the flow of tears that highlighted the dark purple-ish blue shadow over and under her beautiful hazel eyes. Her usually perfectly coiffed hair was now a mess, and she looked as though all hope had been beaten out of her—with red marks, left by angry hands, covering her arms like tattoos.

I couldn't believe what I was seeing. I glanced over to Davie who had an immeasurable look of horror on his face. Her eyes met ours, and she began desperately wiping the tears from her freshly bruised face. She anxiously ran her fingers through her hair in an attempt to tiddy it, but at this point, it was unfixable.

"Hey...Hey...Boys. How was school? What did you learn today?" The fake smile was back on her face as she pulled herself up.

"Are you okay?" Davie muttered; his eyes locked on Momma.

"Yes...Oh, don't you worry about this," Momma walked down the stairs unsteadily, fixing her dress, furtively checking behind her to ensure their bedroom door remained closed. "Your Daddy is sleeping. Where is Junior?"

"He took the long way home again. We didn't see him at the halfway point where we usually meet up." I answered as I glanced over again at Davie. "Momma, are you sure you're alright?"

"Yes, silly. Now, help me move this outside, okay?" She continued with her false smile while grabbing a flowerpot from the kitchen. She turned toward the back door, and we quickly trailed behind without delay.

Following behind her, I scanned the bottom floor in a search of any signs of possible struggle that would indicate what happened—but there was nothing. The house remained in perfect condition.

Momma walked out the back door and straight to the fortress. She looked back at the house, glancing up to the second-floor windows, before crawling inside as best she could.

"Here...This flowerpot would look perfect...just perfect in here!" Momma announced while placing the flowerpot just below Daddy's military photo. "This fortress just needed some pretty flowers; don't you think?"

"Um...yes, I think it does add some life to our Fortress, but—" Davie began.

"Momma, y'all in here—" Junior poked his head into our fortress doorway. "What—What happened...? Did—Daddy?"

"Everything is okay. Come in...squeeze in and make room. Whisper please, okay? Junior, before you crawl in, peek all around to ensure we are alone please." Momma whispered cautiously.

Junior uneasily looked around before crawling in with us. "We're alone," he reassured.

"We need to leave..." Momma began.

"We're moving?" Davie asked.

"No...we, meaning you three and I, need to leave...tonight," Momma's voice was stern.

"Mom—" I tried to speak.

"No...we need to leave." Her eyes met mine. "We are not safe here anymore...you three are my priority. Your safety is everything to me...I cannot risk anything happening to any one of you...so tonight, once Daddy is asleep again—"

"After he drinks...?" Davie asked.

"Yes...after that and when he is asleep. We three— need to leave." Momma whispered with urgency as she stared at each of us, ensuring she had our attention. "Here is the plan...we will go by foot to the train station and take that until we reach Charlotte. From there we will stay somewhere warm before buying a ticket to Raleigh—"

"MeeMaw and Pa? Do they know?" Junior cut in.

"No...I cannot make phone calls," Momma drew in a deep breath; concern filled her eyes. "Once Daddy is asleep, I will turn on the sink in our bathroom three times... you should hear that if you stay quiet enough. I want your bags packed. Take the money out of the jar and conceal it in your belongings. We will need that. Everything should be done by the time he is asleep." Her eyes narrowed in on us, "do you understand me?"

The three of us nodded. We felt too much uneasiness to respond in any other manner at that moment. She gave us a sly smile, trying to reassure us with her plan. I could feel the fear that lived deep within her; fear for us, for herself, and for our future.

I should have listened to my gut feelings and stayed home, to protect my mother—but I failed her.

I had a pretty good idea what had changed today... "He found out you were still working, didn't he?"

"Yes. Your father... is a good man. Never forget that. But sometimes even the good men fall..." A tear escaped and rolled down her cheek.

"Katherine?" a faint voice could be heard coming from the house.

"Okay...smile. Be happy. Act normal. Tonight...we leave," Momma reiterated. "Everything will be okay. Junior, go first; meet him at the front door."

Junior nodded, crawled out, and hurried off toward the front door without a word. Davie, Momma, and I were left inside, waiting for our time to leave.

"Davie and Jamie go run to the edge of the woods and act like you too were playing hide and seek, something. Okay?" Momma told us.

"Now?" I questioned her.

"Go!" She ordered.

Davie moved first while I continued to stare at her. "What about you?" I questioned.

"I will be getting eggs out from the coop," Momma grinned.

"—Junior, have you seen your mother? —" the faint voice spoke again.

"No sir. I just got home...the twins left me..." Junior acted like his same grumpy self.

"... go!" Momma repeated, ushering us out.

I followed Davie off into the woods to hide behind a tree. We peaked around the tree to watch Momma as she crawled out of the fortress and hurried off to the coop, acting as a perfect housewife.

"Alright...our turn." Davie nodded.

"Should we head to the front too?" I asked.

"Just chase me...act like we've been playing all along..." Davie suggested. "Let's go..." He shoved me to start our pretend game.

"GET BACK HERE, DAVIE!" I hollered while chasing him down the side of the house.

"COME AND GET ME THEN!" Davie teased back, running around Daddy's sedan.

I saw Daddy standing on the front porch watching us run, but he was still searching. I could tell he was looking for Momma. Junior must have gone inside already. Easy for him to play the grumpy brother card…no one hardly ever wanted to go near him anyway. While my attention was drawn away from the game, I found myself staring awkwardly at Daddy.

"Hey, Daddy!" I smiled uncomfortably.

"Where is your mother?" Daddy demanded sternly.

"Momma?" I reiterated, unsure how I should answer him.

Thankfully Davie came to the rescue with his scare tactic of jumping on my back and tackling me to the ground. Davie was full of giggles as we landed on the ground.

"Boys…no rough housing now," Momma ordered as she walked down the side of the house smiling at us. "Henry? I thought about breakfast for dinner tonight. Grits and eggs sound okay? The girls gave us a nice amount of eggs today!" Momma held up a full basket of eggs with a beaming smile on her face.

"Um…sure. Sounds great." Daddy answered blandly before turning back to go inside.

"You are a horrible liar, big brother…" Davie whispered smiling.

"And you have gained weight!" I cracked back at him pushing him away.

Davie and I lay on the lawn laughing quietly together while Momma miserably went inside to join Daddy. Davie and I remained on the lawn, wanting so desperately to postpone any of the misery that we knew awaited us once we went inside. Tonight…we were leaving our childhood behind. By tomorrow, Charleston will no longer be our home; we won't have a home. We will be on the run from a man— a man whom I had admired only months earlier. And the little white house that was home to so many beautiful childhood memories, will become nothing but a house from a life that used to be.

Chapter 9

April 29th, 1946

Nighttime came without delay. It's remarkable, isn't it? How all the things in life you dread seem to arrive quickly without a hint of reluctance. Needless to say, that night came sooner than I would have ever been ready for. After dinner my brothers and I left the table to head straight to bed without making a single fuss. Even then, I thought Daddy was suspicious. I mean, he had to be, right? In all our years, we boys had never voluntarily gone to bed early.

Every night, after supper, Daddy would overindulge himself with his favorite drink. Tonight...we prayed he would continue the trend.

A few years prior Davie, Junior, and I received swiss army backpacks as a gift from MeeMaw and Pa. We never had the opportunity to use them until tonight. So, we sat upstairs, packing as much as we could shove into those bags. We packed clothing and objects that would remind us of our home and all good memories. I reached under my pillow pulling out our old family photo to pack with all my belongings.

I continued to fumble around our room searching for items to pack. Things that would remind me of home and bring some light into the dark days that laid ahead. I was content with my selections, feeling confident I had everything I would need. Then I heard Davie above me, clearing his throat.

"Jamie...you gonna bring Winston?" Davie whispered.

I leaned off the side of my bed finding Davie's head peering down at me in the dark.

"Win—oh! Yeah...thanks," I almost forgot our teddy bear. I reached for Winston, who sat in the corner at the end of my bed. I packed him quickly in my bag, near the top, in case of any desperate need of him. I looked back up to Davie asking him the same question. "You're bringing Rufus, right?"

"Of course—just wanted to be sure we both remember," he answered.

"Both of you...lower your voices," Junior snapped at us.

"Sorry..." We whispered together.

"Jamie..." Davie murmured, lower this time for Junior's sake. "I'm bringing this photo of Daddy. You...you didn't want to hold on to it did you?"

Davie held out the photo of Daddy in his uniform that we hung up in our Fortress. It was Davie's favorite. It gave him pride remembering Daddy that way.

"No," I smiled quietly up at him. I knew he would need that photo to remember the good times. "You hold on to it...it's yours."

"Thanks, Jamie..."

I was finally settled on the selections I made for my bag. I lay back in bed enjoying whatever moments I had left in my own bed, in my own room. I had never known anything but this room; I would miss it and the memories that would forever be left inside these four walls.

The awful sound of tape unrolling and screeching ripped me from my thoughts. My eyes shot over to Junior, who was being a hypocrite about the noise and causing a ruckus. He was placing a mixture of money on a long strand of Scotch tape: dollar bills and coins. It appeared he was being strategic, but I didn't understand his goal.

"So, you can make noise, huh?" Davie scoffed.

"What are you doing?" I questioned with confusion.

"Trying to hide the money Momma and I saved. Listen—if Dad catches us...he'll search our bags. This way he won't find the money," Junior explained, seeming proud of himself for thinking of the idea.

"But where—" I began to question but soon understood.

Junior took off his shirt, grabbed the long stand of tape, and began wrapping it tightly around his abdomen. "Now...it'll stay on me, it would make noise in the jar, and this way he won't find it if he searches my bag...clever, right?"

"Well, I'll be...have you always been this ingenious, or is this a new talent you have just discovered?" Davie muttered with complete sarcasm.

Junior flashed a look over at Davie but managed to keep all rude comments to himself. "Are you two all packed up yet?"

"Yes...I think I am...I'm ready to go..." I responded, trying to sound positive and optimistic.

"Davie? Are you ready too?" Junior looked up to Davie.

"Yep," lowering his bag down to me, so I could stuff both of our bags under our bed.

"Alright...if we get caught. We need to come up with a story, any story. Any ideas?" Junior tucked his bag under his bed and put his shirt back on.

"How about—we are just taking a nighttime adventure to the river...Daddy likes the river," Davie suggested while looking down at me over his railing.

"No, no, no...that won't work. Umm—" Junior thought hard.

"Camping...we could say Momma was taking us camping or something..." I thought.

"That—that might work..." Junior agreed.

"Look...let's be honest here... no matter what we say, he isn't going to believe it. And he...he will be unbelievably angry." Davie became uncharacteristically serious. "So, let us all hope we just don't get caught...okay?"

"You're right—I think." Junior seemed surprised by the words coming out of his mouth. He shook his head with wonder, threw on his coat, climbed in bed and continued, "Let's all be quiet and wait for the signal, okay? It's ten thirty already."

The three of us lay back in bed, all uneasy and fearful of what lay ahead. After thirty minutes of lying-in bed wandering endlessly through my thoughts, I heard both the porch and front door close and lock. Footsteps followed, leading up the staircase, stumbling all the way.

"Are you going to bed, dear?" Momma's soft voice carried from downstairs.

"What the hell does it look like I am doing, Katherine? Yes...Yes, dear, I am going to bed. And you...you had better join me too. Member the rule—no phone calls—not a one!" Daddy slurred without any consideration for volume as he spoke.

"Okay, dear...I'll be right behind you—no phone calls, I promise." Momma remained composed.

The three of us lay there in the dark—silent—listening to them moving around in their bedroom. It seemed forever until all movement in the house ceased.

Eleven-thirty ticked on the clock and the only noise left to hear was that of the grasshoppers welcoming the night sky through Junior's window, which he had left ajar. Midnight was drawing closer and closer; then I heard it. The plumbing in the house was signaling that water was flowing through the pipes. This happened three times—slowly—and we knew it was time to initiate our plan to escape from this new reality that was no longer safe.

Junior was the first of us to get up. He grabbed his backpack and signaled us through the dark. Davie dangled his feet off the side of his bed as he searched for the ladder. He was precise, gentle, and conscientious with each step he took. Without making a noise, Davie landed on the floor by my side. We grabbed our coats and backpacks before we met Junior at the door who was waiting patiently for us to gather our belongings. We nodded to Junior too afraid to speak.

Nodding back, Junior opened our bedroom door...careful not to cause any creaking sounds that could echo into our drunk father's ears. Junior put his hand up, signaling us to wait as he stepped around the squeaking floorboards. Thankfully, we already knew which floorboards were the weakest. Junior leaned forward looking down at the stairs before motioning for us to move.

I moved first followed closely by Davie. We matched Junior's footing, step by step as we crept out our bedroom and to the staircase. As we rounded the railing to descend downstairs, we noticed Momma was waiting for us at the bottom. She stood there, bold as ever, holding firmly onto a traveling bag of her own. She wore a coat, with a hat that almost covered her entire face. She held her hand out for Junior, who was already half-way down the staircase. I glanced over to their bedroom door, confirming one more time that Daddy was not lurking around in the dark of their bedroom.

I nodded to Davie, confirming our safety as we continued to move gently down the staircase. I walked carefully as I chose each step I took. Any mistake could end in the downfall of our plan. Momma whispered into Junior's ear, which sent him to the back door to presumedly wait for us. Momma lifted her hand out for us to grab as we neared the end of the staircase. Only a couple more steps down, and we'd be over our first hurdle.

That was when a noise sounded from behind me. It was a long, drawn-out creak which echoed off the walls, causing my lungs to tighten so much, I was unable to breathe.

For a second—a split second—I thought it was Daddy. There was no point to continue because we were caught...already. Then I realized...there was no yelling...no screaming...no anger. I almost couldn't bring myself to look. When I turned around, though, I was grateful to see it was only Davie, cringing as he mouthed, "I'm sorry." He had stepped on a squeaky board by accident.

I felt partially relieved knowing it wasn't Daddy...but then wondered about the potential repercussions of this mistake. I panicked, checking Momma's face for an answer on what the next course of action would be. She maintained her composure, calmly holding her hand out for us to continue. Her face, however, revealed a different story. You could see her anxiety at the possibility of Daddy hearing the noise. She glanced up the stairs to the door of their room as she waved her hand for us to hurry. I grabbed her hand safely making it down. Davie, looking apologetic, slowly made his way down the remaining steps more cautiously than before.

Down…we were all finally down safely. Momma ushered us into the kitchen where Junior waited. None of us spoke, leaving the house still and ominous. We were barely breathing; too afraid a gasp of air could lead to Daddy's rage.

Taking a moment to make sure there were no movements from Daddy, Momma carefully unlocked and opened the back door. Momma looked at each of us with hope and nodded.

We stepped out into the cool night air. Momma signaled for Junior to lead the way, and for Davie and me to follow, as she gently closed the door before it could slam shut. Davie reached for my hand, searching for comfort, his palms clammy from all the angst and anxiety that he felt.

We followed Momma's lead as we hurried behind her along the side of the house. Our plan was to enter the woods as quickly as possible, and to remain out of sight from the house. The trees would screen us from the road, but we could still keep a watch on it to see if anyone came looking for us. We hurried along the far side of Daddy's car, using it to conceal us from the porch.

I could almost see the light at the end of the tunnel. Daddy would wake up in the morning, realize we were all gone, and that he would never see us, be able to hurt our family, or lay another hand on our mother again. He would not lay another hand on our mother again. I longed for the freedom we all deserved. 'We are going to make it,' I privately cheered in my mind. We passed the hood of Daddy's car…we were there. I could taste the freedom…it was right in front of us.

A creaking sound carried itself through the late night air, raising all the hairs on the back of my neck in complete dread. I didn't have to look to know what I would see, but I couldn't resist the compulsion to turn and verify my fears.

The sight of a dark figure sitting quietly in a rocking chair on the porch paralyzed my body. The figure waited…rocking slowly without speaking a word. An orange glow brightened as the figure drew in a breath. The stench of cigar smoke filled my nose and burned my throat, suffocating all the hopes I'd just had.

"Where are y'all off to in such a hurry?" The words were spoken calmly, but none of us responded. We were all too afraid to move, let alone speak. The deep, husky, and all too familiar voice—though still calm—became cold as it reached our ears again. Our escape failed.

'How did he know?' My thoughts raced. 'Was it Davie's misstep that blew our cover? Or was it just a bad plan that only got worse?'

"Anyone of you want to give me an answer?" He ceased rocking and slowly got to his feet, taking measured steps toward the porch rail.

Once he reached it, he leaned out of the shadows, and just as the clouds revealed the full moon revealed his stony face. Finally confirming what we already knew; the threatening shadowy figure— was our father.

"Henry…" Momma barely breathed, unable to find words that would explain our intentions for being outside with our bags. She knew there was not a single excuse for why we were clearly leaving him behind. "We were just— we were—we—"

"—we—we—just—just—" He mocked her. "You were just what? Going out for an evening stroll."

"We were going—" Junior began.

"—to look at stars." Momma jumped in. "I wanted to take them to look at the stars…Davie and Jamie recently learned about the solar system at school, and I thought...I thought I could take them to see the stars tonight..." Despite fear making her tremble, she tried to smile.

"Oh! The stars!" He practically laughed. "I would have loved to see the stars, too. Only problem is—" He walked over to, then down the porch steps, to look up at the night sky. "—it's just a little cloudy tonight. Not many stars that I can see." He had a smug smile on his face when he looked back at us.

"Well, yes—I guess you are right..." Momma's voice shook some as she spoke.

"Am I now?" Daddy grinned.

"Yes, but they...umm...Davie and Jamie were adamant about wanting to go see the stars tonight, to learn...it was their—" Junior said, interrupting himself.

"—Their fault?" Daddy maintained his nonchalant expression. "Oh, well I don't think so."

He held his hands behind his back, maintaining his bland smile remained. His eyes, originally locked onto Momma, now lingered on Davie and me. After careful consideration...he chose mine to look into. He knew I was the weakest of my brothers. Momma protectively stood in front of us...her arms spanned out, covering the three of us.

"Henry, please. It was not the boy's fault..." she pleaded.

"Excuse me, I would like to talk to my son—if you don't mind, Katherine." Daddy glared at her. His words were polite but his tone...sent chills down my spine. "Jamie...Jamie, my boy...What do you have in your bag son?"

"Um...Just some...some things to...to bring to...to look at the stars with..." I stumbled uncontrollably over what to say.

"Well, let me see what you brought..." Daddy smiled but it was more creepy than natural.

I glanced at Momma for some reassurance, and guidance on what I should do. Momma lowered her arms and turned her attention to me. With a gentle nod, I knew this was my signal to allow him to search my bag. Keeping my gaze locked on Momma, I gently pulled off my backpack, my hand holding tightly onto the handle. The palms of my hands began to sweat as fear took over my body. I knew he had seen through the lies being told.

I hesitantly stepped forward, my feeling of nausea increasing with each step. His haughty stare was anything but welcoming. I passed my backpack over to my father, who, at the moment, looked nothing like the photo that was hidden beneath all the clothes. Where my Daddy was a kind and loving man, the man in front of me had nothing but fear and rage in his heart.

Grabbing the bag, he feigned curiosity, leading me to believe he already knew what he'd find. He unzipped my bag as my already uneasy stomach churned even more.

The false smile he had kept plastered across his face faded as he broke our eye contact to peer inside my bag. "Aha! What do we have here? Clothes...lots of clothes, all packed to go look at and study the stars...and—oh—and your teddy bear. Is this to help keep you safe?" Just as quickly as the smile faded, it returned.

"Winston—" I mumbled as I stared blankly at the dirt beneath my feet.

"What was that?" Daddy demanded.

"The teddy bear...his name...his name is Winston..." I stammered, slowly peering back up at the icy blue eyes I had once admired.

"Aww... how about that, Katherine. His name is Winston." Daddy mocked.

"Please, Henry ... we—" Momma began.

"No!" Daddy shrieked, the veins in his neck bulged as anger consumed him. "This is ridiculous! After everything I have done for you... all of you! This is how I am repaid! You try to abandon me! ME! What? I am not good enough for you!?"

"Hen—"

"Do NOT Henry me, Katherine! I am tired of being treated as the bad guy when all I want is to keep our family together!! You are the problem! Not me!" He stopped, drawing in a deep breath. "Boys...inside and upstairs...No one leaves their room tonight. Do you understand?!"

"Yes, sir!" The three of us whispered.

Daddy heaved my bag at me as I turned with my brothers to hurry back inside. Junior and Davie had rushed through the front door when I realized Momma had not moved. She remained in place, standing fearfully in front of Daddy. I held on to the door, refusing to leave her alone...again.

"Momma..." I uttered under my breath.

Daddy glared at me, "Inside now, James... I need to have a word with your mother." He said through tightly clenched teeth.

"Momma..." I whispered again.

"Jamie...it's okay dear," she reassured me.

With every bit of regret my 10-year-old body could hold, I left. I was a coward. Deserting my mother, leaving her outside with him. I was disappointed, both in myself and us. This was our one and only attempt to leave. Now, Daddy would be on edge, expecting and waiting for our next move...whatever that may be.

The three of us lay in the darkness of our bedroom, listening and waiting for any signs of movement outside the house. We didn't have to wait long, as shrieking screams erupted from outside. We knew they came from Momma, but we didn't know what to do. I wanted more than anything to run out and take the blows from Daddy's anger for her. But none of us moved. We lay there—like cowards.

The front door finally opened, and Momma sobbingly walked in followed by Daddy. I sighed with relief to hear her alive, but guilt rose inside me knowing that she had been hurt. We listened as the sound of her footsteps stumbled up the stairs and eventually faded behind their bedroom door. I wanted to run to her, to make her feel better just as she always does for us. But I realized though, she would want us to remain safe, tucked away in our rooms.

Just as I started to feel some small measure of peace, thinking the worst had passed us, the sturdy footsteps of Daddy hitting the stairs reverberated throughout the house. I hoped and prayed he would continue down his path and head for their bedroom…but he didn't.

His footsteps headed to our room just off to the right of the stairs. Our bedroom door creaked to open, and he silently entered our room. He didn't talk; only his footsteps spoke.

He walked through our room, each thumping step sent chills down my spine. He grabbed the chair tucked into the desk and dragged it back across the floor. It seemed he wanted his presence and dominance to be known.

None of us moved.

I could only hear the slow and deep breaths we were all taking as we tried to control the fear each of us felt. He dragged the chair to a stop at the door and sat down. He sat there in the dark, for several minutes, analyzing us for any movement.

"Since I cannot trust any of you in this house…" His voice remained calm, but the tension persisted. "I will sit here all night…to ensure none of you do anything you will regret."

We didn't respond. We didn't move. We continued to lay there in the dark, listening to all the sounds the house made. There was no sleeping that night.

Up until Junior's passing, we would occasionally talk about that night. Talk about anything we could have done differently. Truth is…there was nothing we could have done to predict or prevent the next day. I still blame myself for the events that were soon to follow. I will probably carry that blame with me to my own deathbed. I guess you could call it survivor's guilt.

April 30, 1946

The entire night I just lay there unmoving as Daddy's unwavering glare remained locked onto us. I was afraid if my eyes shut for a momentary rest, I would slip into dreams of the traumatic events of last night or something even more tragic — death. So, I stared up at the bunk bed above while waiting for the moonlight shining in to reveal the day ahead. The sunlight slowly seeped into our room, the rays warning my face. None of us moved, all waiting for permission to stir.

He stood, clearing his throat purposefully, being sure he would have our attention. "It's morning time…" He announced boldly before turning from his chair—that had propped our door open—toward the direction of his bedroom. "Katherine, it's morning time. Wake up!"

"Hurry up y'all…" Junior said as he jumped out of bed for his closet. "We need to get ready for school quickly. Let's—let's not make him angrier…"

"Are we going to school?" I questioned.

"I—I would think so…" Junior thought out loud, unsure himself.

"I don't feel so good…" Davie mumbled from his top bunk.

I climbed our bunk bed ladder to check on him. Davie hardly ever got sick. The last time Davie was unwell was three years ago. So, for Davie to say he didn't feel good—I knew he wasn't joking.

I peeked over the bed rails thinking I would find him in bad condition, and I was right. He was horribly pale, shivering underneath his blankets.

"What's wrong, Davie?" I was concerned by his appearance.

"I don't know...I had a slight sore throat last night. With everything going on—I didn't say anything. But today I just—I just feel so sore and achy all over... can you get Momma...?" Davie asked with his eyes closed tight as he shivered more fiercely.

"Um..." I said nervously, afraid of the possible repercussions of going anywhere near their bedroom. But seeing the seriousness of his condition, I knew I had to do this for him. "Sure, Davie...Yeah—yeah, just hang tight. I'll go get her." I leaped off the ladder and carefully peered out our doorway to Momma and Daddy's room. The door was open, and all was quiet. Looking back over my shoulder, I spotted Junior. I knew he was also unsure if I should go down the hall too. I drew in a deep breath, I sucked up my fears, and crept my way to their room. "Momma..." I mumbled, too frightened to speak at any higher volume.

"Jamie..." Momma mumbled back.

Relief swept over me at the sound of her voice; she's alive! "Momma!" I breathed while peeking inside their bedroom.

Nothing could have prepared me for what I saw. Momma was laying in their bed, an ice pack placed over her now swollen left eye. Old and new bruising indicated the arguments that took place prior, and last night. She looked terrible. The left side of her mouth was swollen and red from the force imposed upon them by Daddy. Her pajama top was covered with the dried tears that were all she had to comfort her in the solitary grief and pain from the night before.

"James..." Daddy's stern voice startled me as he rounded the corner of their bathroom. Half of his face covered in shaving cream. "I told you and your brothers to get up. What are you doing in here?"

"Sorry, sir. Um—Davie—he's sick..." I pointed in the direction of our bedroom as I did my best to add some urgency. "He's really pale in his face and cold. I think he might have a fever."

"Fever?!" Momma sat up in bed, gripping the bed tightly as though the jolt upright made her dizzy. "He felt fine last night, didn't he?"

"He said his throat was a little sore but that was it," I answered back.

"I'll get the thermometer...we may need to call the doctor to come check on him Henry," she stumbled to her feet, dropped the ice pack, and searched for the thermometer.

"We will not be calling the doctor...he is fine," Daddy blocked her with his arm, forcing her to look him in the eyes. "James, go back to your room and wait for us please."

Daddy's demanding gaze forced me to nod in agreement and turn back down the hall toward our bedroom. Junior was impatiently sitting on his bed waiting for me to come back in with information. Davie was audibly shivering now in his bed.

"What happened?" Junior demanded.

"Daddy said to stay here to wait for them to come in here to check on Davie," I responded while climbing back up the ladder to lay eyes on him. "How are you doing, Davie?"

"I'm f-f-fine r-r-really...just a little c-c-cold," He stammered through his clenched teeth.

Thinking quickly, I jumped off the ladder, grabbing sheets off my bed to give him. "Here," I said as I climbed back up to him. "Use this to warm up."

"Th-tha-thank y-you," He stammered again, his teeth chattering uncontrollably. When he reached for my sheets, I saw goosebumps raised all over his arms.

I leaned forward to gauge his temperature with the back of my hand, but before I even touched his skin, I could feel the heat radiating off of him. I knew then, that he had an undeniable fever. Junior sat on his bed staring blankly at the floor looking melancholy. I pulled myself up to sit next to Davie, dangling my legs off the side of the bed. I sat quietly, deep in thought as I replayed the events from the night before.

'How could a family change this suddenly?' I thought, feeling defeated. 'How could we go from a loving and safe family to a family of abuse and instability.'

A hand on my knee pulled me from the depths of my thoughts. It was Momma with her bruised face and swollen lips. She had make-up on in an attempt to cover up the injuries, but it could not cover up the pain inflicted by Daddy. Yet, even with her mangled appearance, her smile still brought comfort to me.

"Jamie, let me get up there and check your brother please," Momma's voice was soft and soothing as always.

"I'm o-o-okay Mo-mo-Momma r-r-really...I ju—" a hackling cough erupted from Davie as he tried to speak.

"Hush you...open it up." She placed the thermometer under his tongue and waited. After some time, she read out loud, "Oh my...101.4...you are sick my baby boy."

"How is he?" Daddy stomped in with a comb in his hand as he brushed his hair back smoothly.

"He has a fever, Darling, 101.4." Momma looked concerned, passing over the thermometer to Daddy for him to read. "He needs a doctor..."

"No...rest and fluids will do fine. If he isn't better by tomorrow, I will consider it." Daddy shot back without a look of concern for his son.

"Okay...well, boys. Go ahead and get ready for school," Momma smiled slightly, brushing off her frustration with her husband.

"School? Oh, they are not going to school today." Daddy said, his tone leaving no room for argument. "Obviously, from recent events, I need to keep an eye on all of you and—"

"Henry...if they don't go to school, people will be concerned and come by the house themselves to check in on us." Momma explained calmly, "Let them go...they will come straight home right after school. Davie will stay home with you and me."

"Well, I have to stop by work but...only for half the day," Daddy was clearly frustrated.

"Why do you need to go to work?" Momma questioned.

"Paperwork...I won't be there long," Daddy looked off out the window for a moment or two. "Fine, fine, fine — school for you two. Katherine and Davie stay here. No doctors, no one can come over, and no funny business. Do not make me regret my decision." He stared hard at Momma, his expression warning her to obey.

"Yes sir..." she nodded with obedience.

"You two—" Daddy pointed at Junior and me. "You both go to school and you come home—nowhere in between. Don't talk to anyone about anything regarding home or last night. If I hear any rumors regarding myself or your mother, your punishment will be severe. Do you understand?"

Junior and I nodded slowly with our eyes wide. We quickly dressed for school with the threats still loud in our minds. Any clothing we could find, we wore. When Junior changed his shirt, I saw that the money was still taped against his skin.

"The tape..." I began to ask aloud.

"Yeah..." Junior interrupted, his eyes darting over to me. "You never know when you need tape in class..." He answered, his facial expression reminding me to be careful with the words I spoke with Daddy still nearby. He could be listening in.

"Alright..." I climbed up to see Davie. "Feel better, brother."

"I w-wi-will...womb m-mate," he smirked. "Have a g-go-good day at school. Please a-annoy the teachers as m-m-much as I w-would if I were the-there."

"No, thank you," I laughed. "But I'll bring back your homework."

"Oh l-lord! P-Please no. Leave t-that at school..." Davie's shivering slowed.

"Fine..." I smiled. "See you after school Davie."

"I'll s-see you!" Davie closed his eyes and pulled the sheets closer to keep him warm.

Junior was waiting at the top of the staircase for me, wanting to stick together on our way to school. I looked back at Davie lying in bed...and that feeling crept inside of me again. The very same feeling I had two days before. A lump in my throat formed, making it difficult to swallow.

'Would I come home to Davie severely beaten like Momma? What do I do?' the fear was overwhelming. I knew I would not be able to stop the wrath of Daddy, but I should be here for them and take some of the anger from Daddy too.

"Jamie..." Junior hissed.

"I'm sorry... just—I have a feeling..." I told him honestly.

"I know... I do too. But we need to do as he says to lessen any more anger...Let's go to school...everything will be okay..." Junior whispered, but a look of concern fell across his face.

"Okay...you're right, I'm coming..." I nodded. I turned back one final time to look at my brother, my best friend. "Davie..."

His eyes opened slightly, "...yeah?"

"I love you...you know that?" I smiled. We, as brothers, never said that kind of stuff. The lovey and mushy stuff. We were 'men', and 'men' were supposed to be tough, not sensitive. But looking back now, I am glad I told him this. I needed him to know that I loved him before I left him with that feeling in my gut that something was going to happen. The only comfort in my heart today is that I told him, 'I love you' before it was too late.

"I love you too, Jamie..." His eyes filled with worry; I thought then, he must have felt it too.

I wanted more than anything to ask him if he had that same feeling, I didn't want him to be worried with my thoughts. So, I waved and told him 'see ya,' before running off with Junior to school.

We walked out the front door finding Momma and Daddy sitting on the porch, deep in a conversation, which Junior and I seemed to interrupt. Momma jumped up to give us a hug and kiss before we left for school while Daddy continued to sit and stare off into the woods. Momma retreated inside presumedly to check in on Davie. We were left on the porch, alone with Daddy. He turned an intimidating stare toward us.

"To school and back... nowhere else. You both understand me?" his voice just as stern as his eyes were steely.

Knowing he was capable of great bodily harm, if not worse, we simultaneously responded, "Yes, sir."

We hurried off the porch, grabbed our bikes to rush off to school before we were late. As I pedaled away, I looked back at that white house with the porch that once held so many warm memories. With each pedal rotation, I felt more and more uneasy about the day ahead of me. I reached the main road that led into the city and stopped momentarily, weighing out my options.

'Should I skip school and watch over the house?' I thought. 'Or should I go to school and ignore the uneasy feeling that is still with me?'

As I looked back at the house, I watched as Daddy stepped out of the front door heading towards his sedan for work. He could have easily looked up and seen me, but his attention was focused elsewhere.

"Jamie…" Junior hissed to get my attention. "Let's go—now."

Sighing, I knew Junior was right. I felt defeated but pushed off the cemented ground and biked towards the city for school. I heard the sedan crank up and watched as it turned onto the main road speeding towards us.

"Get behind me, Jamie!" Junior yelled from ahead.

I pulled my bike over, following closely behind Junior to ensure Daddy had enough space to pass. But he didn't pass us. He sped up only to drive directly behind us. He followed us the entire way down the road. He threatened to keep an eye on us, and he was keeping that promise. I suppose it was his way to be sure we understood his message not to try anything funny.

Once we arrived at the turn that would take us to the school yard, Daddy continued straight leaving us alone. We pulled our bikes up to the bike rack just moments before the school bell was due to ring. I got off my bike, and before I could run off to class Junior grabbed my arm.

"When you get out of class, hurry straight home. Do not wait for me. We need to follow his directions. Go straight home. Davie and you typically get out before me anyway," Junior's eyes were serious. "Promise me, Jamie."

"Okay. I promise, I will go straight home," I answered, the anxiety of being late to class rushed through me.

"No talking about this…Keep everything to yourself," Junior reminded. "Now… let's go." He grabbed my shoulder, pushing me off to my building before running off to his own class.

Throughout the entire class period, I couldn't pay attention. I sat in my chair, staring off out the window deep in thought. I explained to Ms. Robbins, our teacher, that Davie was sick at home and that Davie requested I leave his schoolwork here. She giggled, saying it was a 'good try' on Davie's part, but he would be getting schoolwork at home regardless.

'What would we come home to this time?' I wondered. I imagined coming home to Davie, bruised and damaged. I imagined the furry that Daddy would inflict on them while we were behind school doors.

The bell rang, interrupting my thoughts and signaling the end of school. Before I could walk out the classroom door, Ms. Robbins called me up to her desk to remind me to give Davie the schoolwork from class. I picked up the stack of papers with Davie's name written across the top. I wanted more than anything to tell her about the abuse we had all been suffering at the hands of our own father. I wanted to tell her how afraid I was to go home. I stared into her eyes, mouth opened, trying to pluck up the courage and find those words I so desperately wanted to tell her. But nothing came out.

"Mr. Clark, are you okay?" Ms. Robbins asked concerningly. "I hope you are not getting sick too."

"No ma'am... I'm sorry," I apologized as I realized I was staring rudely at her. "Just—thinking, that's all."

"About what?" Ms. Robbins queried.

Again, wanted more than anything to tell her. To confess my fears. To confess to everything. I felt the words at the tip of my tongue just waiting and wanting to come out. The sound of a vehicle speeding off down the road drew my eyes to the window and distracted my inner desperation.

"My goodness!" Ms. Robbin's stalked off to the window to shut it tightly closed. "Kids these days, they drive around like they own the place. Back in my day, there would not be so much foolishness! Now...Mr. Clark, what were you going to say?"

"Oh—about the homework Ms. Robbins. Fractions are sort of stumping me," I lied to her.

"Oh, Mr. Clark, you are a smart boy. Just work on the homework tonight and tomorrow if you are still having a difficult time, we can work on it after class. Try it yourself first, okay?" She smiled at me. She always reminded me a lot of Momma, tall yet petite with long blonde hair pulled up into a tight bun. She was very proper, a city-type girl, but her smile was calming and comforting—especially when struggling with arithmetic.

"Yes, ma'am. Thank you, Ms. Robbins." I nodded before turning toward the door. I looked back at her one more time, at my last opportunity to potentially save my family, but—I just couldn't do it.

"Of course, Mr. Clark," She smiled softly at me. "I will see you tomorrow!"

"Yes, ma'am...I'll see you tomorrow," I said as I offered a slight smile back at her.

Unseen Scars

I walked out of the school to find my bike still parked next to Junior's. I looked around to find him, but he was nowhere to be found. I checked over at his building, but it was still quiet without a single student in sight. They were usually let out half an hour or so after us, so I knew I needed to begin my ride home…alone. I looked off to the main road a block away which would lead me to our house. Instantly, I felt that same sensation in my stomach again; something was not right, and I knew it.

Then, echoing off in the distance, a faint pop resonated off in the woods. Anxiety hit me like a ton of bricks, and something deep inside told me I needed to get home immediately.

I pedaled as fast as I could and sped off into the unknown.

Chapter 10

Frantically, I pedaled down the main road as the wind blew harshly against my face. My heart was pounding harder and faster than I thought possible. I could feel—no—I knew something was wrong. The car that sped through town flashed in my mind.

'Could that have been Daddy? Did something happen causing him to rush home like that?' I marveled. 'I thought he was going to be home early, why would he be heading home this late?' My mind filled with infinite thoughts and visions of awful ideas of what could be. 'Everything is fine! Everything is fine!' I told myself over and over again. I knew it was a lie but kept trying to convince myself. 'That pop…It sounded like a gunshot…but from where?' It was becoming harder and harder to not give in to my rising sense of panic as these thoughts and ideas whirled through my mind.

I accelerated down the small hill just before turning into our driveway. I came to an abrupt stop as soon as my tires rolled onto the dirt. I looked at the house for anything, any sign that something was off. Daddy's sedan was pulled in near the porch, as though he rushed home and come to an abrupt stop. It only made sense that it was his sedan I heard while talking to Ms. Robbins.

As I slowly advanced down the sandy, rutted driveway towards the house, I was overcome by a sensation of unease and uncertainty of what I might walk into. I could hear yelling inside the house. I could not understand what was being said, but I knew the voices belonged to Momma and Daddy. I tossed my bike onto the grass, and as I got closer to the porch, the yelling inside finally became comprehensible.

"HENRY, PLEASE—PLEASE STOP!" Momma shrieked.

"This is how it has to be, Katherine! I have explained this to you already," Daddy was calm while Momma was hysterical.

"NO, HENRY! IT—IT DOESN'T HAVE TO BE LIKE THIS! I'M SO—SORRY! MY BABY! OH, MY BABY!" She cried.

"I told you to stay home! I told you not to use the phone! You caused this! THIS IS YOUR FAULT, NOT MINE! If you—If you would have just obeyed me!" Daddy hollered, the anger and rage radiating through the screen and across the porch, making me flinch. "CHRIST, KATHERINE—I WANT US TO STAY TOGETHER! YOU CLEARLY DON'T!"

I carefully crept up to the porch steps, trying my best to avoid making too much noise. I needed to find Davie. I needed more than anything to question him on the argument and what it pertained to. I needed to hear his side of the story.

Momma continued to groan and whimper uncontrollably. The front door was open, leaving only the screen door as a barrier between me and them, and I slowed my steps as I peered in. I could see the silhouette of Daddy pacing in the kitchen waving something in his hand. Momma was on the floor; her arms spread out as though she were covering something, but I couldn't see what.

'Did he hit her with whatever he's got in his hand?' I pondered to myself as I tried to evaluate the situation.

I pulled the door open, revealing more clearly a scene no one could, or ever should, be prepared for, and my heart sank. I held my breath as I tried to comprehend what I was seeing. There was blood pooling under Momma, staining her clothes. In the pool of blood off to her side lay a tiny hand stretched out as though reaching for help.

Momma leaned up, revealing his face. He appeared peaceful as though he was in a deep sleep. Momma held him, cradling his body as though she was desperately trying to will him back to life. She stroked his all too familiar dark blonde hair, sobbing uncontrollably. His glasses lay off to the side, although it's not like he needed them now.

Davie was gone, shot in the chest by our father, who stared down at the scene below without any hint of remorse. The revolver was still in his hand. He gripped the handle tightly as rage seemed to surge throughout his entire body. The screen door latched shut, drawing their attention towards me.

"RUN, JAMIE! RUN!" Momma shouted instantly, her voice urgent and her face full of fresh terror.

Daddy, his face showing no emotion, raised the gun and pointed it at me—then pulled the trigger. The bullet shattered the window adjacent to the door. I felt shards of glass penetrate the side of my face. My mind was lost in a blended fog of confusion and fear. My legs took me up the staircase, running for safety of their own volition. Then my legs, again acting on their own, carried me towards our bathroom.

Screaming, which I believe belonged to my mother, erupted from behind me—then ended with a howling and a final pop. My heart sank with the understanding that she was gone; forever. My ears rang from the deafening sound of the revolver as I stumbled into the bathroom, climbed into the hamper, and concealed myself beneath several day's worth of dirty laundry. I hoped and prayed that he would not think to look in here. I closed my eyes, trying desperately to control my breathing so as to not give away my hiding spot.

His footsteps stomped up the stairs, anger reverberating with each step. His attention seemed set on our bathroom.

'He must have heard my footsteps in here,' my anxiety spoke.

"Jamie…come out please. Come on, son…all you need to do is come out and we can talk this through," Daddy whispered in a spine-chilling tone. He ripped open the cabinet doors beneath the sink, hoping to find me cowering inside. "Jamie…where are you?"

He stepped meticulously around the bathroom, each step well-thought-out. He neared the hamper where I hid, and my breath stilled. The lid to the hamper opened suddenly and to this day, I'm amazed I didn't jump. I was too scared to inhale or even exhale. The risk of being found was too high and I knew I had to be quiet. All he had to do was reach one hand down just beneath the dirty shirts and pants and he'd find me.

But his hand didn't search any further. He had stopped moving and his breathing quietened, as though he was listening or waiting for a something. I listened too, waiting for what I felt was the inevitable.

Then I heard it; the sound he seemed to have been waiting for.

The sound of bottles being smashed into pieces stole his attention, abruptly causing him to turn on the spot and charge out the bathroom door.

"Boys!" He shrieked. Vibrations traveled throughout the house as the floorboards received the force of his heavy stride. He stomped through the kitchen and out the back door, slamming it shut, leaving the house in utter silence. I was left frozen beneath the clothes, as fear immobilized my body leaving me alone with my thoughts.

The sound of a door creaking open caught my attention. Soft footsteps scurried up the stairs and into the bathroom with me. The footsteps carried a familiar voice with them, "Jamie...Jamie...where are you? We have to go."

It was Junior!

Hope released my body from immobilization, and I found my way to the surface. A determined and wide-eyed Junior rushed over to me and helped me out of the hamper. He grabbed my clammy hands and without hesitation, led me into our bedroom, where he shut the door, locked it, and grabbed the chair at his desk to position it under the doorknob in an attempt to keep Daddy out.

"Grab your backpack. We have to go," Junior struggled to maintain his calm. The little boy inside him was gone, leaving a mature man in his place.

"How...we're trapped, Junior!" I whispered desperately as I grabbed hold of my backpack.

"No, we are not," he reached into our closet, pulling out a long rope. "If Cub Scouts taught me anything, it was to be prepared." Junior pushed his bed into the corner of our room nearest to the window. He bent down and tied a bowline knot—the king of knots I might add—around the bed post. "Look out the window, do you see him?" Junior demanded.

I peeked out and saw Daddy was staring at the fragments of beer bottles thrown for nothing more than a distraction. He appeared to be analyzing the sounds he heard, piecing together the events that occurred. Daddy stood and turned slowly, staring back at the house intently before cocking the hammer back of his revolver and walking into our house, seemingly intent on finishing what he started.

"Now! Now, he's heading back in..." I whispered just as the backdoor opened with fury. I looped my arms through the straps on my backpack, trying to ready myself for anything.

As Daddy opened the back door, Junior pushed open the window, tossing out the rope. Thunderous footsteps made their way through the living room heading for the staircase.

"Climb..." Junior hissed.

"Wait!" I whispered.

"No! Jamie—now!" Junior argued.

I ran to Davie's backpack, ripped open the zipper, and pulled out Rufus along with Davie's favorite photo of our father. I couldn't leave either behind. Daddy attempted the doorknob before realizing it was locked. Screaming, he threw his fists against the door, enraged. With my backpack on, the photo safely in my pocket, and Rufus tightly in my hand, I climbed out the window. I looked up seeing Junior hanging over the edge of the window letting himself down. Daddy's screaming intensified as taunting threats were directed toward us. He had realized Junior was home. He had realized everything.

I lowered myself down, swinging in front of the kitchen window while gripping onto Rufus as tightly as possible without losing grasp. Peering in through the kitchen window, I saw Momma's battered body sprawled out on the floor, arm stretched out. From the position of her body, it seemed as though she was shot as she ran in my direction.

Grief circulated throughout my body, reaching my eyes, and causing tears of anguish to form. With every ounce of my being, I forced the feelings to the back of my mind, focusing on our escape. I dropped myself to the ground. Junior was not far behind. He didn't look as he passed the kitchen window and dropped to the ground beside me. The banging and door rattling continued on our bedroom door. Junior grabbed my hand and pulled me through our back yard.

"We will go through the woods so he can't see us...we'll stay off the main road," Junior breathed hastily while running through the late afternoon sun that dappled through the trees.

With our hands tightly entwined, we sprinted diagonally through our backyard with the edge of the woods in sight. Our intensity increased with our strides, desperate to get to the safe cover of the woods. Daddy would soon break down the weak and feeble bedroom door. When he did, he would see the direction we took, unless we were hidden in the protection of the woods.

We had just entered the tree line when the sounds of the locked door bursting open followed by multiple and distant pops could be heard. Junior continued to pull me through the woods, but a little slower, both of us trying not to step on any twigs that might snap.

"URGGGGG! BOYS!!" Our father's voice echoed through the woods, penetrating our ears and sending chills through every nerve my body owned.

"Keep—running—" Junior breathed.

"To—where?" I gasped back, trying my best to speak clearly.

"Po—Police," Junior huffed. "Run..."

Anxiety flowed through us as we hurried through the trees, desperate to get to the police station. We had to tell them—needed to tell them—what had just happened. We were far enough off the road not to be readily seen but close enough to hear any vehicles passing by.

An engine revved furiously off behind us. I broke out into a cold sweat, and I knew that engine belonged to Daddy's sedan. We continued to run until we reached the road perpendicular to the main road that led to our home. Just before crossing out of the shadows of the woods, we stopped abruptly. Breathing heavily, Junior put his hand up for me to remain still, as he edged beyond the trees to scan our surroundings for any sign of danger. His hand dropped, signaling me to move closer. As I neared him, Junior gripped my hand to pull me closer.

Whispering, he continued to scan our surroundings. "Listen…the police station is just beyond that building…we need to be quick," His eyes anxiously searched the streets for any movement. He pointed off to the alley ahead of us. "We're gonna run into that alley, it will lead us to the police station…okay?"

I nodded, as I was unable to formulate any coherent words.

With our hands gripped together and no car lights or sounds to be seen or heard. It was time. We rushed across the street as fast as our legs could take us. It felt like a horror movie or a scary dream; when you run as fast as you can, yet you are still just as far from the destination as when you started.

It felt just like that; impossible.

I felt eyes watching us. I felt like someone was running behind us, tracking us, and wanting to grab hold of us. Horrific memories of the popping gunfire replayed in my ears as the shelter from the woods slipped away leaving us completely exposed.

My body relaxed slightly as the shadows of the alleyway concealed us. So far, we had remained unseen. And together, we slowly inched down the alleyway toward the police station. Every sound seemed to be amplified due to the walls around us, increasing my anxiety.

As we neared the end of the alleyway, Junior pulled me behind him. His body stood in front of me with strength. He stood in a protective manner I had never seen before tonight.

'It could not be this simple to escape from him. It could not be this easy and simple, could it?' I asked myself as we edged toward the corner.

Junior peered around the side of the alley for less than a second before pulling back promptly, pressing himself against the wall of the alley. I followed his lead, trusting him completely.

"What?" I whispered.

"Dad…" He mouthed back, too afraid to speak.

A car door slammed hard enough to cause the vehicle to rattle. The wail of a seriously heartbroken and desperate man eruped from the direction of the front of the police station. A wail that was entirely fabricated.

"HELP! HELP! MY FAMILY—MY FAMILY IS DEAD!" He yelled as he clumsily climbed the stairs of the police station. The front door was flung open. and the concocted weeping became muffled, signaling to us that he was inside.

"Come on…" Junior grabbed my hand.

Crouching, we dashed across the street, through the parking lot and down the alleyway bordering the police station. We pressed up against the wall of the building, each of us on the side of a cracked window. We tried to hear everything that was discussed inside.

It appeared that Daddy had all the officers' attention. They were all out in the main lobby, listening to and absorbing every detail of the lies he spoke regarding the events that had led him to the police station.

"I worked l-late this afternoon. I t-took the long way home stopping by the lake t-to just clear my head. Oh, I shouldn't have! I should have just gone straight home! Why didn't I just go straight home?!" He fell on the floor of the lobby in tears.

"Mr. Clark—calm down! Please try to explain to us what happened so we can help..." An officer spoke calmly.

"Well, I-I heard distant gunshots and thought it was strange. Immediately, I-I got in my car to head home. And w-when I got there—" The howling resumed to tell his erroneous story. "The front door was kicked in and my wife—my wife—she was dead. My boy! Oh, my boy! He was already gone! Both shot..." The groaning seemed realistic; they all believed him. "My other boys—their bikes were out front—I searched inside and out for them but they are gone! Their room showed signs of a struggle and there were bullet holes in the wall. And m-my b-boys are missing!"

"Mr. Clark...Mr. Clark...calm down...did you see any tire tracks on the dirt outside of your home?" One officer inquired.

"What? — I don't know. I was panicked when I saw the door, I forgot to check..." Daddy's crying halted, and anxiety took over. "Y-you don't think I-I missed the man w-when he left with my boys?"

"It's okay, Mr. Clark...we are going to send a unit out to your house now and another unit out to search for the boys. Do you have any recent photos of the boys?" The same officer questioned.

"Um, y-yes I do!" Daddy responded, hope entering his voice. The officers may have thought it was hope that they would find his sons, but I was pretty sure it was hope caused by the fact they all seemed to believe him.

Junior bent down below the window and pulled me down the alley away from all the chaos inside.

"What...where...where are we going?" I asked. He just continued to drag me down the road. "Junior?" He gave me no response. "Junior!"

He suddenly stopped. "Listen to me...", he said with urgency as he pushed me against the wall. "If you want to go into that police station—

then go! I am getting out of here. He is turning everything around. Acting like someone else did this and he will probably end up trying to blame it on you and me. He wants us dead. And will probably kill us…if we don't get out of here! We need to go!"

"But…Davie…Momma—" Tears started to slide down my face as the images I witnessed earlier flooded my mind.

"Davie and Momma are dead!" Junior let out a deep sigh. "And we are not…" the tone in his voice softening. "We need to stay that way."

We could hear the officers begin hustling outside. Some prepared themselves for a search by foot, while others were getting in their cars. Our home was now a crime scene.

Daddy's voice broke through the ruckus of men, "I'll head back to the house with you, Sargent!" His voice was no longer shaky with concocted anxiety but filled with strength. And why wouldn't it be? He could have won an award for his acting.

"Alright…" Junior whispered, to avoid being overheard. "Here's the plan…We run north to the train tracks. We will hide out there until morning and take the train to Charlotte—"

"Momma's plan…" I remembered.

"Yes…" Junior responded anxiously. The officers' voices drew closer as they entered the woods to begin their search. "We need to go… Keep your head down."

Grabbing my hand again, he led us through the city, trying to stay off the main roads, running behind buildings to avoid being seen by any passersby. We moved beyond all the stores we had shopped at throughout our childhood, all memories of which were being left behind in a cloud of chaos and confusion. Sneaking behind buildings and hiding from people who were out and about, we had to avoid being spotted while making our way to the train station in order to keep

Daddy clueless as to our plans. Charleston was normally a peaceful city, but thanks to Daddy, we were leaving it behind in complete and utter turmoil.

An untold number of minutes passed, and we found ourselves one building behind the parking lot that led out to the train crossing. We were almost there and the relief I felt was undoubtedly present. Men were out working on the tracks. They were checking the train carefully as though searching for something. Off to the right of the crossing, a patrol car pulled into the parking lot. Junior's anxiety level was now, without a doubt, elevated and quite evident. We remained still, intently listening to the men and officers' talk. The officers' tone was sharp, as though his nerves were on edge.

"Nothing…you found nothing in the cars…" The officer questioned the men while looking into the boxcars close by.

"No, sir. Are you going to tell us what all of this is about?" One worker asked. "What are we looking for exactly?"

"Um…well, you and the rest of the town will find out eventually…" The officer's tone changed with concern. "Mrs. Clark… you know of her?"

"Of course, I do. Henry Clark's wife…sweet woman. What happened?" The men gathered around, listening to every detail.

"Well, she and her son were murdered by someone. Their other two boys—Junior, and Jamie— are missing. Evidence suggests they were taken." The officer recited the blatant lies our father told him. The men gasped, clearly horrified by the story. Some of the men repeated the information as though they could not believe what their ears were hearing. "I was hoping they escaped and were hiding out here, but…I guess not. You are free to move the train if you need to."

"I—I can't believe it. Who—who would do such a thing?" One of the workers pondered.

"Yes, well...We will be questioning people in town tomorrow...I need to get back to helping with the search. Have a good evening you hear..." The officers left, off to announce to everyone—including Daddy—that we were not found by the train. Daddy would be lost trying to find us now.

"Alright, men..." One of the workers clapped his hands. "I know this is sad news and all, but we have to get going. We have a delivery to make in Charlotte by tomorra' so...get the train ready!" He said before turning around to head back inside the ticket booth.

"Jamie...we have to get on that train..." Junior turned to me with determination.

"How...?"

"Um..." Junior scanned the situation again. "I got it. Follow me."

We crept silently along the backside of buildings until reaching the street directly across from the woods that surrounded the end of the tracks. Junior grabbed my hand while looking intently from side to side, making sure no one was watching or coming from either direction. Once he confirmed that the area around us was clear and the rail workers were walking up the side of the train paying no attention to the back, we ran across the street hand in hand to the woods for better cover.

The engine slowly warmed up and the smoke began to rise; this was our chance. Junior tightened his grasp on my hand to keep me at his pace while we shot down the side of the train desperately searching for an open compartment. The train's whistle blew, signaling the train would soon move. I moved faster, lengthening my stride to keep up with my brother.

Every compartment that passed was closed. The rail workers up ahead jumped in for the impending journey while Junior and I still frantically searched for an opening. The train began to move quicker. Junior picked up his pace, pulling me along behind him. My feet stumbled as I tried to keep up, my hand still gripped firmly onto Rufus.

'Where is an opening?!' I desperately thought.

"We need to run, Jamie!" Junior hollered.

"I'm—I'm trying!" I yelled back in between attempts at catching my breath.

Six compartments down, there appeared to be an opened door wide enough for us to jump in unnoticed.

"There! There it is!" Junior pointed.

Junior pulled me up to him and over toward the opening. He pulled my hand up to the railing beside the compartment for me to grasp hold of. Still running, he helped hoist me up into the boxcar. Rufus's arm slipped through my fingers. I reached for him, desperate to keep him with us. I needed him...I needed him with me on this journey.

"RUFUS!" I shrieked, hanging off the doorway.

"LEAVE IT! GET ON!" Junior screamed back.

Struggling to get my legs over the side, I reached my other hand inside the compartment, clutching onto the metal handle to pull myself in. With all the strength I had left, I heaved my legs over the side. I rolled inside gasping for breath, relieved to have made it.

Beneath me, I felt the rumble of the train picking up speed.

'Junior!' I screamed at myself. I had been so relieved, I forgot about my brother!

I got to my unstable feet and stumbled over to the compartment door. Junior was sprinting to just keep up with the train; he was determined to make it on. I held out my arm, but he ignored it. He forced himself to go faster and, with all his might, jumped into the compartment.

Just as mine were, his legs dangled off the side as the wind from the train's forward motion tried its best to throw him out, but Junior held on tight. I leaned down and grabbed my brother's belt, pulling him with all my might into the train with me.

"Oof!" Junior let out a sigh of relief as he rolled safely into the compartment.

"Are you okay?! Jun—Are you okay?!" I questioned him as I checked him for any injuries he may have sustained.

"Yeah—Yeah—" He exhaled; keeping his eyes shut while he took slow and deep breaths. "We—made it..."

"We did!" I sat with my legs sprawled out in relief. I watched the Charleston trees flash by the open door—Rufus. I thought quietly to myself, 'How could I have dropped him? How could I have failed?' I knew I should have felt blessed to have made it on safely, but I was devastated not to have a piece of my brother with me. Our teddy bears had never been apart in all our years...Now Rufus—like Davie—was just a memory of our past.

"Let's—Let's umm—" Junior looked around the compartment as he thought. "Let's sit down in that corner and just—sit until we arrive in Charlotte." Poor Junior, was still trying to catch his breath.

"Okay..." I stumbled to my feet as my legs tried to give out. Junior reached for me, grabbing my arms to stabilize me before I fell over. My legs were shaking from what happened at home, escaping the house, hurling ourselves into a train, and the effort involved in all of it. As they were about to give out, Junior reached for me, grabbing my arms before I fell over.

He walked with me over to the far end of the compartment, where I slid down to the floor in disgust and anguish. I loathed myself for letting go of Rufus. I let Davie down. Even in death, I had let him down.

The compartment was eerily quiet even with the late afternoon sun beaming in. We pulled off our heavy backpacks, letting out deep sighs of relief while the boxcar rattled and the sound of rushing wind filling the empty compartment.

Neither of us spoke. Not that it mattered. There was nothing we could say, no small talk or joke, that would make anything better or bring Momma and Davie back.

My mind began to wander off to the now dismal memory of my brother, my twin…my best friend. How was it that one second he's alive and the next, he is just a memory? How does that happen? It's as though his life meant nothing. He was only ten years old… He had so much life left to live. We were supposed to grow old together and create new and exciting memories together. Now, every birthday I celebrate, I'll celebrate alone. I had never celebrated a birthday alone. And Momma—Momma won't ever hold me again. She won't be able to watch us grow up, get married or have children of our own. Their lives were over, forever leaving Junior and me alone in this big world—scared and on the run from the man we believed would always be our protector.

How could our father decide their lives were no longer valuable enough to spare? He was supposed to be the man we looked up to, now he was the man who would haunt our dreams. Tears once again collected and spilled over at the vivid recollections of Davie and Momma. Our innocence forever gone; both Junior and I had to be strong. We could not afford to be childish ever again if we wanted to survive.

"Jamie…" Junior said while streams of tears rolled down his cheeks, the calamity of the day finally setting in.

"Yes…" I softly replied, trying to control the tears that continued to pore out.

"Our family is dead…" The reality of the situation suddenly seemed to hit him. "We have no home…"

"Yeah…" I responded monotoned. "Well—technically, home is where your loved ones are…"

"And?" Junior scoffed, looking out the compartment door at the sun slowly starting to set.

"Well… MeeMaw and Pa always said we had a home there…I guess that'll be our new home now." I told him, with the last remaining ounce of positivity I had. "We are just far from it…"

Junior looked at me, eyes red from crying and anguish. "Far from home…"

"Exactly…we'll get there. Take the train to Charlotte and we will figure out our way to Raleigh. We have some money for food. We will be okay…" I spoke with as much enthusiasm as I could muster, doing what I could to take on the big brother role for him, even if for just a moment.

"You're not so bad you know…" Junior smiled, placing his arm back around me.

I was shocked to hear those words leave his mouth. For years I had dreamed of the day Junior would like…actually like … me. Instead of being forced to because of our questionable genetic relations.

I took advantage of the moment. "You're not so bad yourself!"

"Well…" Junior shrugged. "Shall we sing a song in honor of Momma and Davie?"

"You, sing?" Astonished by his suggestion.

"Yeah...why not? It might speed up this train ride," Junior gestured in an attempt to act like the neat big brother again. "What was Davie's favorite song again?"

"Stay All Night!" Warm memories overjoyed me as I reminisced for a moment of Momma stumming Daddy's guitar as Davie jumped up on the bench singing with pure confidence. These memories of a past, that now hurt so much to think about, were all we had left of that white house in the country.

And together, Junior and I sang in unison, "You ought to see my blue-eyed Sally..."

We sang together, laughing and bonding at old memories that would forever connect us. We even reminisced on recollections of Daddy.

"Remember when—before the war—Daddy would go way too far into Christmas!" Junior laughed so free and pure, almost childish despite all that had occurred. "Pretending to be Santa Claus!"

"Yes! He'd stomp powder into the house making it look like Santa Claus had been inside to give us our gifts!" My mind flickered to the memories as I joined him in the laughter.

"I didn't have it in me to tell him I didn't believe in Santa any more...he was so in love with the holiday and spirit of it all...I just couldn't tell him..." Junior's laughter faded as he thought of this confession.

"You stopped believing when you were seven years old?" I was astonished.

"Well...yeah. I overheard them talking about it and then found the gifts hidden away under their sink..." Junior admitted. "It wasn't the best of hiding spots but hey...that was what they chose. Momma made me promise not to tell you and Davie that Santa wasn't real...why—when did you stop believing?"

"Well—" I was unsure of how to answer his question, but I figured I'd be honest. "—just now."

"Really...?" Junior shot me a look of utter disbelief. "Well...I'm sorry for ruining it all for you."

"No...I...I guess I had an idea last Christmas when the powdered footprints disappeared..." I smiled dimly, as a rush of awful memories of Daddy flooded back.

"Yeah...I guess that would be a huge giveaway." Junior's smile was full of sorrow from what I could only guess were memories and thoughts similar to the ones that I had. "Momma did a good job keeping the house up and running while he was gone, didn't she?"

"Yeah, she did..." My mood lifted picturing her comforting smile. "She tried to keep every holiday the same while Daddy was gone...she really was a good mom..."

"A great mom..." Junior agreed. "And Davie...well, he was—" Junior stumbled while finding an accurate description of him.

"One of a kind?" I added while smiling foolishly.

"Definitely!" Junior approved. "He was a good brother...it definitely won't be the same without his quirky personality...or wonderful sense of humor."

"No..." I grinned though my heart felt heavy at the thought. "It won't be the same..."

We rested in silence. Sitting in place while privately ruminating on memories and dwelling upon our own individual feelings. We didn't need to talk to be together at the moment. For once in our lives, Junior and I finally agreed on something.

Unseen Scars

Our individual differences did not compete with the immense amount of love and gratitude we felt for one another. All our past arguments and disagreements did not matter anymore. All that mattered was that we survived, we escaped, and we needed each other to make it to Raleigh to set the story right. This was not a random crime. Momma and Davie were not murdered by some random stranger. They were murdered by the very person who vowed to protect us, who taught me how to change a tire at the age of five, who promised to be there for us. The person I dreamt of growing up to be—once upon a time.

We were all we had left. Two brothers on the road to uncertainty.

Chapter 11

The darkness was overwhelming…I was covered, my vision shielded. I was surrounded by a woman. Her arms were stretched out in an attempt to conceal me. She was pleading with someone. It sounded like a man. I looked up to see who she was yelling at, but I couldn't see around her. She was protecting me, keeping me safe from the threatening stranger above us. I looked closely, checking for any details that could reveal the identity of the woman, but the darkness hid her face.

"STAND ASIDE, KATHERINE!" The strange man spoke.

'Mom? Momma?' I was tormented with the thought.

"NO PLEASE! PLEASE!" Momma's voice was easily recognizable.

The shadows cleared out revealing her long blonde hair and hazel eyes that I had known my entire life. It was Momma. I looked at her dress—it was covered in red. Blood? I searched around me. I needed to know where the blood came from. My eyes glanced to the left. I could see his hand stretched out, lying there motionless. The side of Davie's face that I could see, looked peaceful as though he was in a deep sleep.

But I knew he was gone. I scanned the area, desperately trying to figure out where I was. I saw the familiar light blue couch and I realized I was home. Someone had attempted to run upstairs to flee from the horror but failed to get past the first step. That someone appeared to be a young boy. All that was visible was his hand, dangling over the edge of the stairway, a brown messenger bag dropped on the floor. It was Junior's favorite gift from last Christmas. That boy was Junior.

'How? How was Junior dead?!' I screamed inside my head. 'We escaped! We—We were on a train to Charlotte. How—How could he have died? When did he die?'

"STEP AWAY, KATHERINE! GIVE HIM TO ME! IT'S HIS TURN!" The stranger's voice intensified, sending chills down my spine. "HE IS THE LAST ONE!"

"HENRY! HENRY! PLEASE! He's just –He's just a boy!" She pleaded.

'Dad?' I was shocked. 'Daddy was the strange man...'

I looked up, pushing past Momma's arms that refused to stop desperately cradling me. I had to see. I had to know. I had to face him. I had to face the truth. Pushing through her fighting arms, I found myself face to face with a revolver. The man's dark and shadowy image suddenly became crystal clear, I recognized the thick dark hair and light blue eyes—it was my father.

Without any hint of remorse, he pressed the revolver against my forehead and smiled ever so contentedly. I shut my eyes, trying to push the image away as though that would make it all disappear. Momma's wailing filled the house before a loud snap pinged in my ears. My body became lighter, as though I was being pulled away through some type of portal. I swung my arms out, fighting against the unknown. Swirls of different shades of darkness filled my vision as I frantically fought against this unknown feeling. I didn't want to die. I couldn't die. I haven't lived yet! How could a child die? How could it end like this?

"Jamie?"

A familiar voice broke through the spiral of visions that surrounded me. A familiar voice I had heard my entire life.

"Jamie?"

Junior? Could it really be Junior? He was alive! Are we home? Are we safe? Had this all been a dream?

"Jamie! JAMIE!" Junior repeated. "Jamie! Wake up!"

Someone held a tight grip on my arm, shaking me frantically reeling me back into reality. My eyes shot open, and I was back. Back in the train compartment, bouncing through the countryside far from Charleston. My face flushed with sweat dripping off my forehead. I pulled myself up too quickly off the floor. Lightheadedness took over my balance, so I leaned against the boxcar wall, fumbling my glasses onto my face. Gradually my vision focused, revealing Junior kneeling in front of me.

'He's alive...I'm alive...We're alive!' I thought with great jubilation. 'Oh, thank goodness it was a dream!'

"Jamie! Talk to me, are you okay?" Junior was looking at me with concern filled eyes.

"Yes—yes, sorry—bad dream," I stared blankly at him, focusing on controlling my breathing and re-grounding myself. "It was just a dream."

Junior's tense stance eased at the sound of my voice but still lingered with curiosity. "About what? You—You were screaming..."

"I was?" I cracked a soft smile of embarrassment.

"Yes..." His tone was full of trepidation.

"Well—I—I had a dream we were back at the house...Davie was dead...you were dead...and Momma was shielding me. But I got out of Momma's arms and Daddy—he—he shot me..." I stammered through the recollections of my dream as freshly formed tears streamed down my cheeks.

"It's okay...we're safe—we're both safe. He can't get us here," Junior smiled trying to comfort me. "He has no idea where we are actually. I think, brother—I think we may have fooled him."

"He shot me, Junior..." I mumbled.

"It was a dream...just a dream..." His voice was soft.

Drawing in a deep breath, I nodded, accepting his comfort. "I'm sorry if I woke you."

"No, you didn't," Junior stood up to stretch. "I haven't slept...been busy...thinking you know."

"Oh..." I pulled myself upright. "Hey—you still have the money on you right?"

"Yep..." Junior lifted his shirt, revealing the money taped onto his abdomen. "Probably should take it off now, huh?"

"Probably," I nodded.

"Yeah...pass me the jar. It's in my bag," Junior lifted off his shirt and began lifting the tape off.

I grabbed his bag, still shaking from my nightmare, and searched inside the main zipper for the jar. "Where in your bag?"

"Should be at the bottom," Junior answered while unwrapping the first layer of tape.

I searched the entire bag, from top to bottom hunting for the jar. My hand glided over an object covered in clothing. He had wrapped the jar in a shirt, hiding it from anyone who would peer in.

'Smart,' I complemented him in my mind as I pulled out the shirt and unwrapped the jar. "Here ya' go."

He bent down with the long strand of clear tape with money scattered randomly it. Junior pulled off seven or eight one-dollar bills, a few two-dollar bills, a handful of five-dollar bills, and several ten-dollar bills, along with some change.

"HA! We're rich!" Junior hollered with a smile that spread from one ear to the other. He neatly stacked the bills together before placing them back into the jar.

He threw me the jar of money and I stared at it all in complete and utter fascination. I had never seen so many bills in my entire young childhood life. The quarters, dimes, nickels, and pennies he pulled off, clanged into the jar bringing music to our ears.

We talked for a time until it was morning. We discussed everything we would buy if we had our own money. Junior said he'd buy himself a boat. A boat he'd be able to sail away in, to enjoy the tranquility while catching all the best fish in the lake. He lay back against the wall of the compartment, describing what his dream boat will look like. Back in those days, there was a boat called the Buzzards Bay 14. Oh, it was a beauty! We saw it in a magazine at a street corner on the way home from school one day. Junior swore up and down he was going to figure out a way to buy it. It would be a long time before he was able to buy his first boat, but that's the dream boat he dreamed of at thirteen. Momma suggested that he name his boat The Katherine. And he did, eventually.

***

It was just past dawn when the train began to slow down. The high-pitched whistle sounded, signaling that the destination had been reached. Charlotte was nearing, leaving us both eager and anxious for our next move.

"Change your shirt, Jamie," Junior ordered while packing up the jar of money, pushing a few bills in his pocket and searching for a button up to throw on.

"Why?" I questioned as I searched through my bag for a clean button-up and hat to wear.

"Just in case...you know?" He justified as he put on his light blue button-up shirt. He combed his hair with his fingers and threw on a brown cap.

I found a dark green button-up and quickly put it on. Throwing on my worn black cap, I was ready for whatever lay ahead. I thought of Momma, and how she had wanted me to throw out that black cap. The thought brought a smile to my face.

I quickly packed up my bag, safely securing Winston, ensuring no possibility of losing him. I threw my bag on my back and checked my front pocket for the photo of Daddy, preparing myself for the run. Junior was over by the compartment door looking out at the station where we were preparing to stop, planning our next move.

"Listen—when we stop, we will wait for all the workers to calm down out there. We will hide in the corner on this side of the compartment. Nothing is in here, so they won't need to unload anything out of here." Junior explained to me while pushing me over to the corner as the train slowed down to a gradual stop. "Keep quiet..."

We stood in the dark corner of the compartment, listening to men in the distance yelling at one another. Some of them were giving out directions, and others voiced their complaints regarding their job. Voices of two men drew closer. They were discussing an issue that sounded crucial from their tone. I listened intently, trying to pick up on what exactly they were discussing. Their voices drew nearer and became more audible from our hiding place.

"I'm just saying, Marvin...I wouldn't be surprised if it came out that, that old man Simmons did this..." One man said.

"Oh, come on, you know the father is hiding something..." The second man responded.

"Please, Simmons is a creeper. He sits outside his house and watches all the kids and women walk by. He's a creep—I'm tellin' ya!" The first man carried on.

"I don't know, Barry; something was just not right with Henry last time I saw him. He's not the same man he was before he left..." Junior and I looked at each other in disbelief; others had noticed his change too. "I'm friends with a few guys from his work; they always talk about him and his outbursts. Something isn't right with his story either. I don't know, Barry—I'm just worried about those boys...I hope they're okay..."

"They probably already found them...they're kids. They're probably just out goofing off in their woods or hiding because they were scared," The first man, Barry, continued.

Their voice stopped at our compartment and one of them pushed the door open further. Junior's arm drew around me, shielding me in case they jumped inside.

"It's empty, Barry. Come on, it's break time!" Marvin yelled at Barry, trying to speed up their inspection.

"Just some jam and biscuits on the track, Marv. Nothing to be too excited about." Barry lamented as they continued down the track to do their quick inspection of the train.

Junior peered out of the compartment as their voices became more distant. Once he confirmed the area was clear, he motioned me forward. He jumped out of the compartment first, then turned to assist me. Together we climbed up a gravel hill to put distance between us and the tracks. Once we reached the top, Junior pushed me down into the bushes so we could scan the parking lot nearby while remaining hidden.

We had never been to Charlotte before, and we had no idea what our next move should be.

"I have no idea where to go..." Junior professed.

"How about we just go up to the ticket booth and ask if there is a train leaving for Raleigh soon?" I suggested.

"Um...yeah I guess that will work. Come on...stand here and wait for me with our bags, okay?" Junior helped me up to walk with me over to an oak tree nearby.

"I—I—I'll go..."

"What?" Junior asked, stunned.

"Let me... please. I can do it! I promise." I grinned childishly to him. I wanted to do something, something imperative for our journey ahead. Besides, to only have Junior recuse me the entire time...that would be embarrassing. "Plus— you look too much like Daddy. The men on the track might recognize you..."

"Yeah...okay—yeah, guess you're right. But don't give them our real name if they ask. Say your mom asked you to come out here to check...okay?" Junior brushed off my shirt and fixed my hat to ensure I looked ready to talk to the ticket booth man. "And here...take some money. I'll give you ten dollars."

"Wow..." I was child again, staring in fascination at the dollar bills, completely enthralled with the green paper. I looked up at my older brother with a keen smile on my face as I shoved the bills proudly in my pocket.

"Don't you spend it all you hear..." Junior warned me.

"I won't, I won't... it's just—it's so neat, isn't it?" I asked.

"Yeah it is..." Junior smirked as he gestured me to move on. "Now go!"

I tossed my bag next to the oak tree with Junior's, gazing around the tree towards the ticket booth. Building my confidence, I drew in a deep breath, fixed my hat, and stepped out from my hiding spot, eyes set on the booth. I noticed a man inside sitting on his chair staring off into the distance. He was a plump man with a dark green vest, white button-up and a high cap, with 'Charlotte' written on it. His black hair was combed snugly inside the hat, giving him a professional and intimidating looking, especially for a ten-year-old boy. I slowly ambled towards him, my nerves building up.

"Can I help you with anything young man?" The man peered over the counter at me.

Until he spoke, I hadn't realized that I was standing there, staring vacantly at him. I quickly scanned his vest for his name tag, which read 'Charles.'

"Oh, good afternoon, sir—" I cleared my throat before continuing. "I was wondering when the next train was leaving for Raleigh?"

"Raleigh, huh?" Charles put on his glasses, studying me closely before pulling out a program looking for the printed schedule for the week. "Well then—let me check for you."

"Thank you, sir." I spoke with as much confidence as I could muster up, realizing only after that I spoke only loud enough for me to hear.

"Raleigh—Raleigh—Raleigh—Hmm, what is a young man like yourself doing heading up to Raleigh all alone for?" He peered his eyes over his glasses to look at me with question.

"Um...Well, I'm not going to Raleigh alone. I'm going with my Momma and little brother. I just pulled the short straw and got sent to find out the times and buy us tickets..." I embellished my lie with a convincing eye roll.

"Uh-huh...and what's your name, boy? I ain't never seen you around these parts of town before..." Putting the schedule down, his eyes narrowed, intensifying his stare as though he could see through the lies as I spoke.

If I knew anything about this town, it was that everyone here would know everyone who resided here including all their personal business. Nothing done in a town like this was a secret, and the town's main gossip ladies made sure of that. Understanding this, I panicked privately while conjuring up a name to give Charles.

This led me to the only name I could come up with on the spot.

"Williams...sir." I blurted out.

"Williams... I don't know a 'Williams' family with sons around here. The only Williams I know has only one little girl, no boys." Wariness took over his expression.

I will not repeat the words I thought to myself very loudly in that moment, but I had learned them from Daddy while he'd work on his sedan. I searched for the only explanation I could come up with for why our fictitious family was there.

"Well...we're new in town," I gave him a panicky toothy grin. "We just moved in this week...from out of town."

"Ahh...and already y'all are going out of town?" He interrogated me further.

"Yes, sir. Just got news that my grandmother is sick. So, sir, if you can please tell me when the next train for Raleigh is leaving" I was a bit short with him as I spoke, not wanting to stay on the subject any longer than necessary.

"Okay—um, let me see here," Charles returned to the printed schedule. "It says the next train out is –"

"Charlie!" A dark man wearing overalls with worn white button-up and a cap with grungy hair poking out the sides, interrupted our conversation. "The boys and I were just wonderin', when are your boys going to load up the train for our next stop?"

"It's break time, Marvin…my men will get to your boys when they get to ya!" Charles, who was completely peeved, shouted back to the man.

'Marvin…Marv…he must be the man Junior, and I overheard talking to his friend Barry,' I thought. 'Please—please, don't recognize me.'

"Ah…good afternoon, young man! Is Charlie here givin' you a hard time about getting a ticket?" Marvin leaned against the ticket counter with his arms crossed. "Hey…you look familiar. Do I know you?"

"Um…no sir. My family and I just moved here from Columbus." I responded, unable to hold eye contact as I lied.

"South Carolina, huh?" Marvin contemplated.

"Um…yes sir." I nodded marginally.

"Anyways… Mr. Williams…the next train leaving for Raleigh, North Carolina is on Friday at noon." Charles leaned over the counter, peering over his glasses at me again. "Will that be okay with you and your—umm—family?"

"Yes, sir, how much for two tickets?" I queried while pulling the dollar bills out.

"Two?" He was desperate to catch me in a lie. "Is your brother not going with you now?"

"Oh, you're right...I apologize, I forgot him...I try to forget him sometimes," I gave him an awkward grin, hoping he would continue to fall for the lies. "Um—three tickets, please."

"Alright...well, that will be $1.46 please," Charles gave a sly and mistrustful smile.

"Okay..." I counted to two dollars before eagerly handing him the money.

Nodding, Charles passed me the tickets with a speculative smile plastered across his face. I knew right then there was no way he believed me. But I think there was a quiet understanding to agree and just move on. Before turning away, I nodded to Marvin, my expression full of pride for succeeding.

Three steps away from the booth, Charles' voice stopped me abruptly.

"Boy! What—what was your first name again?" He leaned back into his chair with an expression full of suspicion.

I mentally fumbled through all the names I had heard while growing up.

'What name do I use? Henry...no...Arnold...no....' I became flustered. I knew my hesitation was noticeable and unusual for a casual conversation. So, with noticeable panic in my voice, I blurted out a name that I thought would work.

"Johnnie!" I was too excited with my response. "My name is Johnnie..."

"Johnnie..." Charles' eyes narrowed while smiling. "Johnnie Williams. Well then—it's nice to meet you, Mr. Johnnie Williams."

"It's nice to meet y'all too," I nodded at the pair of them.

With the tickets clasped in my hand, I hurried through the parking lot to the building that sat parallel to the oak tree where Junior waited.

I knew once I stepped away from that ticket booth that I could not return to the oak tree. If Charles continued to watch me—which I felt certain he would—he had to watch me walk near the city. So, once I was hidden from the view of the ticket booth, I waved to the nearby oak tree to catch Junior's attention.

Junior caught my gesture and gave me a 'what are you doing' look. Throwing his backpack on before grabbing mine, he began to casually walk across the parking lot. He nonchalantly nodded to all those he passed by, doing his best to blend in and not bring attention to himself. Once he was shielded by the building, he threw my bag down at my feet and gave me a look of complete and utter confusion.

"What the hell was that all about?" He demanded to know. "Did you at least get the tickets?"

"Yes!" I exclaimed, as I pulled out the tickets to Raleigh from my pocket. "See! I told you I'd get them."

"Why did you buy three?" Junior was confused.

"Oh…um the guy—the ticket seller was onto me. Said he hadn't seen me around town before. He wanted to know my name and why I wanted the tickets…" I explained to him everything that had just transpired. How in a desperate panic, I chose the name Johnnie Williams as my cover story, to which Junior rolled his eyes.

"You gave him our grandfather's name?" Junior said in disbelief and without empathy.

"Well—I—I couldn't think of nothin' else, okay? So that's what I said. My name was Johnnie Williams. And you'll need a first name too. If you had a better idea, then you should have told me what name to use before I went down there. But you didn't!" I defended myself with a confidence I had only discovered once before. I was angry…incensed for the derisive attitude he pushed off on me.

"Alright. Alright." Junior stepped back as he was caught off guard by my defense. "Well, good job then — good job getting us the tickets." He grabbed my bag for me as he looked around the area as if he were searching for an answer to an unspoken question.

"What?" I asked.

"Why don't we umm...Why don't we find someplace we can stay tonight?" We ambled aimlessly down the alley together. "We will just have to change your story up a little bit...maybe even give us different names—not that yours were bad—but so that no one begins to connect our stories together in this town."

"Alright—alright," I shrugged agreeingly. "Where should we go?"

"I don't know..." Junior sighed as he took his hat off and ran his hands through his hair. "Let's just—Let's just continue on this way—away from that ticket man, how about that?"

Junior and I shuffled along the alleyway to the conjoining sidewalk that led out into the city. As we rounded the corner out onto the sidewalk, we puffed out our chests and lengthened our strides, strolling through the city with confidence. We needed everyone here to believe that we belonged there.

We had been walking around for quite a while, when my stomach began to rumble with pain, reminding me that I had not eaten since yesterday afternoon. And just by glancing over at Junior, I could tell he was thinking the same thing. He gripped his stomach while he scanned our new surroundings.

The smell of hamburgers slowly took over my attention. The closer we got to the city, the thicker the smell became. Eagerly we both scanned the immediate area, searching for the source.

"Look!" I pointed excitedly at a restaurant across the street from us. "The Diamond Soda Grill, can we eat there, Junior? Can we?"

"Shh...don't use my real name! While we are in the restaurant, I will be Jerry. Jerry...umm...I don't know—how about Collins. Jerry Collins." Junior nodded with a grin, pleased with himself for coming up with a name on the spot. "And you, you will be Lewis Collins. Do you like that?"

"Lewis...alright. I can do it!" I beamed back up at my brother, proud of how well we had managed to work together thus far. "So...Jerry, would you like to eat there?"

"Oh, yes. So very much, Lewis. Let us walk on across the street for a splendid lunch, shall we?" Junior smirked, wrapping his arm around my shoulders.

Together, arm in arm, we strolled off towards the smell that dazed our minds and ached our bellies. Before that day, Momma had cooked most of our meals. She would always say she wanted her boys to grow up eating home-cooked meals provided by her, and no one else. It was expensive for a family of five to eat out, and going out to dinner was not something we really did as a family. So, this was pretty much Junior's and my first trip to a restaurant.

Walking into that restaurant...we felt like kings. We had money in our pocket and adrenaline pumping through our systems; nothing could stop us. Not only had we barely escaped the grips of death by our father and his revolver, but we were about to fool an entire city with false identities. If only Davie could have seen us, he'd have been so jealous.

The restaurant didn't look like much on the outside; a little grungy and run down—but the inside was a completely different story. The walls were, green and tan, the two colors separated by brown trim. Greenish blue booths with tan tables between the seats completed the restaurant's color scheme. There was even a bar at the back where people could sit if they were alone or in a hurry. It was unlike anything we had ever seen before. The smell and sound of the grill sizzling up burgers intensified. I felt my stomach cramp with the want and need for something to eat.

Interfering in the daydreams of burgers and hotdogs was a slim woman dressed in solid white with a notepad in her pocket and pen in her hand. Her thick brown hair was slightly curled and pinned back into a bun. She graciously welcomed us into the restaurant.

"Good afternoon gentlemen. How many are in your party?" Asked the woman, whose badge indicated her name was Betty.

"Um…two please," Junior answered with uncertainty of what to do and how to behave but followed her lead.

"Two it is!" She picked up two menus at the hostess stand near us. "Follow me please!"

Before following behind her, Junior and I looked to each other for reassurance. Betty looked back at us, as though she was studying our every movement. As we passed by tables, I noticed customers with wandering and judging eyes. I knew it probably had to do with our tired eyes and traveling bags strapped to our backs. And instead of being in school, we were—well, there.

I began noticing the curious eyes of an older couple sitting across the restaurant from us. They were close to MeeMaw and Pa's age. The woman was whispering something to the man, never taking her eyes off of us. I turned my back to them as I took my place at the table. Even with my back turned, I could feel their eyes locked onto us and I could tell Junior noticed too.

"So…" Betty subtly brought our attention back onto her while pulling out her notepad. "What can I get started for you two?"

"Um…" I gazed over the menu.

"I'm sorry, ma'am, but we ain't never been here before." Junior confessed to her.

"Well…" Betty's eyes lifted from the notepad to meet ours. "I can get you something to drink to start. Maybe a water, some pop, tea, or coffee if that is what you boys are into."

"Oh, I'll have some Coca-Cola please!" Junior gave her a toothy grin.

"The same please!" I joined him.

"Okay then…" She raised her eyebrows at us while smirking. "When I come back with the drinks, I'll be asking you what you would like to eat. Our burgers and hotdogs are listed on the back of the menu. I recommend y'all read that over while I am gone."

"Thank you, Betty," Junior's cheeks turned different shades of red as he smiled at her.

Betty turned away towards the bar and Junior and I watched. I'll admit it, she was unbelievably attractive, especially to two young boys like us. But Junior…Junior was in love with her from that moment on. Thirteen-year-old boys, you know?

Junior left to use the restroom, and I waited behind with our bags. I had my eyes on the older couple across the room who still seemed to find us interesting. I tried to avoid bringing more attention to us, but I couldn't help but look back at them.

'What did they want?' I wondered to myself.

I felt my feet begin to tap with anxiety beneath me as I waited for Junior to return. He was probably only gone for a minute, but it felt like more. When he returned, I was up on my feet, separating myself from the meandering eyes that were attached to me.

Turning down the hallway, I followed behind two men who were also going into the restroom. They had come from the bar and seemed to be good friends. I had always hated using public restrooms so, I selected the urinal farthest from them to maintain some privacy. From their loud voices, I couldn't help but listen in on their conversation.

"Still can't believe what happened out in Charleston, can you?" one of men said.

"No...it's unbelievable. Wife and son dead. Two boys still missing, and now the father..." the other responded. "I bet he had something to do with it..."

'What? How do they now?' I screamed in my head. 'How could they possibly know about my family?'

"You think so, huh? It does make sense. The radio said his automobile was gone, along with him later that night. Only after they declared the boys were in fact missing..." the first man continued.

"I wonder where those boys went off to..." the second man responded.

"Who knows? At this point, I think they are better off staying away from it all...just hope the father doesn't find them before anyone else does..." the first man shook his head woefully as he walked over to wash his hands.

"Yeah..." the second man joined him by the sinks. "Wonder where the father went off to as well..."

"Hmm...Yeah...Right? He could be anywhere." the first man sighed. "Anyway, John, we should leave. Let's tip that gorgeous Betty and head on back to work..."

Their eyes fell on me, bringing me to the realization that I was standing behind them, staring.

"Well, hello there, son..." the first man broke the silence.

They were both around Daddy's age with hair as dark as his. They wore clothes that made me believe they worked in some factory nearby. Their stained hands solidified that guess.

"...do you need anything?" the second man questioned me.

I gaped back at them in silence, afraid of them somehow recognizing me from their story.

"Don't be scared, son...we're leavin'..." the second man continued.

"And before you leave... you best tip Ms. Betty!" the first man smirked while they walked out the bathroom door. "She's the best waitress in all of Charlotte."

I remained in place, staring blankly at the closed door. My mind frantically thought about the conversation I had just heard. My mind racing with anxiety, leaving me off balanced and unsteady. I tried to control my breathing, but I found it difficult to even breathe.

'Daddy knew—He knew...But how did he know? We—we left Charleston unnoticed, right?' Panic and anxiety took control of my every breath. 'How? How? How could he have known? Where did he go? Could he be coming here? Is he already here? I – I have to tell Junior!'

I rushed over to the sink, cleaned up and left the restroom. I exited the hallway to find Junior sipping casually on some pop. From the look on his face, I could tell he didn't have a worry in the world. I took my seat back at the table across from him and instantly felt heat from the older couple's eyes. I paced my movements trying to hide the panic that I knew radiated off me. Junior's eyes studied me and my body language.

"What happened to you?" His voice remained quiet, but the concern was evident.

"Jun—Jerry...Jerry..." I corrected myself. "We need to leave..."

"What? No. She's coming over now to get our order. Isn't she pretty?" Junior was mesmerized.

"Jun—"

"Well, boys...have we decided?" Betty questioned, as she sped her way through the aisle towards us.

"Yes, ma'am!" Junior's cheeks regained the red tinge from before. "I'll have a cheeseburger; medium well, and fries, please."

"Yes, sir!" Betty wrote it down on her note pad, grabbing his menu. "What about you little man?"

"Umm—same thing, please," I said, handing her my menu while looking back to Junior.

"Yes sirs. Two cheeseburgers on the way," Betty smiled as she took my offered menu, went back to the bar, and passed our order over to the kitchen.

"What is up with you?" Junior demanded.

"Daddy...he left Charleston," I whispered, slowly peering around to ensure no one was listening in.

"What are you talking about?" Junior pushed himself back in the booth, his mouth agape.

"When I was in the restroom, I overheard two men talking about something they heard on the radio. About a murder of a mother and her son in Charleston," I spoke softly to make sure my words stayed between us. Junior leaned in now, absorbing every word I spoke.

I told him every detail about the conversation I overheard in the restroom. Then I told him how one of the men mentioned a belief that Daddy could be responsible. I knew at this point I had Junior's full attention, as his eyes widened with every detail. We never thought that news from Charleston would travel this far or fast. We definitely didn't expect Daddy would disappear along with us.

"Okay...okay..." Junior muttered.

"What do we do? The train won't leave until Friday. We don't know anyone here...and where can we stay?" My mouth began fumbling through sentences as my mind attempted to organize all the thoughts that entered it. "Jun—J—Jerry...what if Daddy comes here? To Charlotte?"

"Shush!" Junior hissed. "Do you want everyone to hear us? Listen—first, we will eat. Second, we will find a place to spend the night. Third, we will keep an eye out for him. There is no way he would know to come to Charlotte. How could he figure that out? No one saw us leave Charleston."

"You're right...I guess I'm just worried..." I was honest. "Daddy...he's—trained. I just think...I don't know. I feel like he could find us easily if he wanted."

"He can't. There is no way. No one saw us get on that train," Junior thought back, going over every step we made that night to get to Charlotte.

"Jun—Jerry...that older couple keeps looking at us..." I mentioned to him, tilting my head towards the still staring couple. "...have you noticed?"

"Yeah...I've noticed them too..." Junior sighed, his eyes glancing over to them.

"Jun—what if they know?" My face flushed with worry.

"I—" Junior began before Betty interrupted us with two plates of delicious cheeseburgers and fries.

"Anything else?" Betty smiled.

"No, ma'am," Junior's mouth watered from the sight of the cheeseburgers.

"Ketchup?" I asked, my stomach growling with joy.

"Of course," Betty snatched a ketchup bottle from a nearby empty table. "Enjoy boys."

"Okay—we will eat first...then we plan our next steps..." his eyes never moving off his plate. "Deal?"

"Deal!" I agreed.

We indulged ourselves with the delicious cheeseburgers and all the fries, ignoring every problem that lay ahead of us that we had assumed we escaped from. So, we tried to enjoy each other's company inside a restaurant that made us feel like we were home and safe again.

We cleaned off our plates, consuming every crumb available. Betty came around the corner, she must have been watching us finish our plates from the bar. Junior took a five-dollar-bill out of his pocket with an obnoxious toothy grin placed across his face.

"This should cover it!" He handed over the bill to Betty.

"My, my, my...where did you two get this money?" Betty gasped; her eyes were wide with wonder.

"Oh...um... I just— saved my money from many Christmases," Junior lied horribly.

"Yeah...we have lots of grandparents..." I added, mentally kicking myself once the words left my mouth.

"Now listen," Betty bent down deepening her eye contact with us. "I don't know who either of you are...and I know most people in this town. But, if I find out y'all have been stealing from the people around here, I promise I will report y'all to the police..."

"No, ma'am, we're not..." Junior said, practically begged her to believe us. "I promise."

"What's your names then?" She stood straight, crossing her arms as she questioned us.

"Collins...Jerry Collins," Junior remembered.

"And I'm Lewis!" I tried to act casual and normal. Looking back, I realize I was acting neither casual nor normal.

"Okay…Jerry and…Lewis. What are you two doing in this town?" She eyed us, looking for any signs of deviations in our story.

"Well…" Junior looked over to me with a crooked smile. "We are on an adventure. You know like Huckleberry Finn. We're on an adventure to find gold."

"Fine…" Betty sighed, snatching the five-dollar bill from Junior's hand while we laughed. "I'll be back with the change."

"No need…you can keep it!" Junior stood up and I followed his lead.

I scanned the restaurant, searching for the older couple who took notice of us. But they were gone. They must have left sometime while we were engrossed in the food and conversation with Betty.

"Thanks for the food, Betty. Have a good afternoon, ma'am." Junior threw his backpack on and tipped his cap to her as he said goodbye.

"Have a wonderful day!" I followed Junior's lead, tipped my hat to her, and left, following close behind him.

Before I had overheard the conversation between the two men inside the restroom, we both had begun to feel slightly invincible as though there was nothing that could stop us from our final goal. We were beginning to feel safe, as we honestly believed we had escaped smoothly and unnoticed from Charleston. Now, however, that feeling of safety slowly diminished. I watched as Junior attempted to compose himself as best as he could to seem undaunted and self-assured. And together, we sauntered out of the restaurant with an attitude as if we knew exactly where we were going. Though, the obvious truth was we hadn't the slightest idea.

"Jun—Junior—" I spoke quietly to Junior, remaining unheard by anyone passing by. I knew we needed to remain anonymous, but I was so desperate for something of a plan. "So—where are we going to stay for the night?"

"Um...maybe we can find a hotel or somewhere we can stay," Junior commented as his eyes scanned around for any nearby listeners. "Let's just keep walking around till we find one...I don't want to draw any more attention to ourselves then we already have. We are two strange boys looking for somewhere to stay without a parent present..."

"Yeah...you are right..." I agreed as I tried to keep up with Junior's pace.

We wandered past them all, pretending to window shop as we actually searched for a place to stay. That was when we found it—a tiny brick shop tucked away between a clothing retailer and a market. Above the red door was a ragged old banner reading, 'David's Toys and Joke Shop.' The name stopped Junior and me like running into a wall. What were the odds that a store in a strange town we had never been to before would have the same name as our late brother?

Without the slightest bit of hesitation, Junior and I entered the store in desperate need of a laugh. And this store seemed like just the place we needed, now more than ever.

Opening the front door, the bells that hung on the door handle chimed, welcoming our arrival. A thick aroma of lit cigars surrounded us as the door closed.

"Welcome to David's Toys and Joke Shop!" A man's voice hollered at us from the back of the store. "Let us know if we can help find you anything."

Rows of shelves towered over us containing every joke toy and game anyone could ever think of ranging from monopoly to slinkees, whoopee cushions to silly putty, trains, and dolls. Toys were laid out everywhere in the store, positioned for children to easily pick up. Model airplanes and helicopters were hanging from the ceiling above us. Hanging out of some of the aircrafts were toy soldiers with parachutes attached to their backs. The open parachutes were hooked up to the ceiling, giving the illusion that they were parachuting down to the ground.

Gazing through the rows of the organized mess of toys, I saw a portion of the register in the back of the store. I searched for the owner of the voice but found nothing.

"Jamie..." Junior nudged my arm. "Look, isn't this what Davie was talking about a few weeks ago?"

I followed Junior's pointing finger to a tiny yellow and blue box located in the corner of the store. As I got closer, I read what was printed across the bottom of the box: Crown Trick Ink. I immediately began laughing at the sight of the toy as I reminisced on the conversation Davie and I had about it.

Davie mentioned wanting to buy trick ink to take to school to put on Mary Ray Elder's dress. He had a slight crush on her and, instead of admitting his feelings, he pulled tricks on her to gain her attention. He honestly believed she would fall for him after all the pranks he'd played, but each one would typically just result in his having to stay late to write, "I will not play pranks on Mary Ray Elder," repeatedly on the teacher's board.

I grinned from ear to ear as I stared at that little box on the shelf.

"It is!" I finally replied. "How much is it? We should buy it...don't you think? You know—just to have it around. Even—even though Davie can't use it...we can buy it and have it for him...in his memory?"

"Sure…" He picked the box off the shelf and tossed it to me. "It's yours. Boy, this sure is a nice store. Davie would have loved it. There is nothin' like this back home, you know."

"Momma would have had to pull Davie out of here if we had this back home," I remarked as I continued to stand there gawking at the immense amount of toys piled on top of each other.

We wandered through the aisles in complete awe of the store. Under a picture book was a gun handle sticking out. I realized almost instantly it was a cap pistol. Davie and I would always play with pea shooters, which was sort of the same thing. But cap pistols… Cap pistols were much higher end and realistic compared to the pea shooters.

"Jamie…come on," Junior nudged me along after realizing that he might have to drag me out of there. "We need to get going…"

"Okay okay…" I placed the cap pistol back where I found it and stood back up.

I took my place at Junior's side as we walked through the toy store. A clearing opened, allowing me to see through the clutter which revealed a register sitting on the counter. Behind the register was an elderly man sitting down staring at his newspaper through the glasses that were placed gently at the brim of his nose. I noticed almost immediately the familiarity in his eyes. I knew I had seen him once before, but I couldn't place where.

Being young and naïve as I once was, I didn't question the warning that crept inside. I pushed the feelings away and walked up to register with my brother to buy the Trick Ink. The heavy-set older man wore overalls with a white button-up shirt beneath it. He had white hair around the sides of his head and an obvious bald spot. As we drew closer, the smell of cigars grew stronger. He looked up at us through the glasses still propped up on his nose. His light blue eyes were outlined by rectangular glasses.

That's when the memory came flooding back to me, the restaurant. Images of the older man and woman, who had been so avidly staring at Junior and me in the diner, popped in my head. My inner alarm system finally woke up, causing me to feel a sense of panic, rendering me unable to speak or move.

Junior nudged me unsure of why I was stuck in place. The strange man smiled softly at me, put the newspaper down, and waited. I knew he recognized me too. Without speaking to either of us, he stood up, walked over to the stairway hidden off to the left of the cash register and yelled up at someone.

"Edith, dear." He looked up as he hollered up to the second floor. "We have customers dear." He turned back around to us and shrugged, "women."

A woman's voice broke the silence from upstairs as she argued that he 'shouldn't need her help to simply check out a customer.' She continued mumbling incoherent sentences upstairs. Her aggravation with her husband was undeniable as her footsteps echoed downstairs.

The man sat back down in his chair at the register, picked up his newspaper, smiled, and continued where he left off. Moments later a woman with long grey hair, which was loosely pulled up into a bun, hurried down the stairs wearing a green knee-length dress with short sleeves and a well-used white apron around her waist. Her light brown eyes seemed frustrated and flustered with the man until they met with ours.

"Oh—well hello, dears…" giving us a welcoming smile, she rushed over to the register checking for our selected item.

Just like the older man, I knew straightaway that this was the older woman who had stared so intently at us at the restaurant. My eyes shifted to the floor, avoiding eye contact hopefully any possibility of her recognizing us.

"Edith, this is—did I hear you both correctly over there, Junior and Jamie, is it?" The older man smiled; his eyes remained glued to the newspaper.

'He overheard us talking. He knows our real names. What if Daddy came to town?' my thoughts raced.

With my eyes remaining down, I glanced over at Junior. His facial expression matched my own feelings: shocked and afraid. Junior lifted his eyes to the older man while the woman, Edith, looked to her husband, beaming at his comment.

"I thought so…oh, Walter…I just knew it—Ohh… I just knew it," she muttered as she nervously smoothed out her apron and dress. "Stay here…" Edith promptly moved past the register, past Junior and me, and straight to the front door, where she fumbled with the open sign before turning it over to signal to any possible customers that they were now closed for the day.

I looked over to Junior, hoping he would at least look as though he had a plan, but I could tell he was just as confused and unnerved as me. The man had not removed his eyes from his newspaper. He was still lost in the story that he was reading, or he was simply choosing to ignore the situation in front of him.

"I knew from the first moment I saw you boys walk into that diner. Oh, I told Walt. I told him… 'those boys are not from around here.' I thought, 'is it just a coincidence that the day we hear on the radio of the events that occurred in South Carolina and the man in question was on the run, that two unknown boys enter our town?'" Edith talked fast, faster than Junior and I had ever heard, as she locked every lock that lined the door, and closed the blinds to the windows blocking all the light that shined through. "Walt told me that I was over analyzing the situation, but I told him. Oh, I was sure that I was right and look at me. I was right. That is one thing you boys will learn one day; the woman is always right." She casually strolled back over to us and picked up the Trick Ink. "Follow me, please—Walt, you can stop pretending that you are reading that paper."

"I'm sorry, ma'am... I think there might be some confusion. You see, my name is Jerry, and this is—" Junior began.

"Oh, stop pretending boys. You both are safe...no need to hide from us," Edith glanced back at us with a gentle smile.

We remained in place. Unsure of what we should do. Unsure of who we could trust in this unfamiliar town.

"Please, boys...you can trust us." Honesty glimmered in her eyes and an inexplicable feeling of safety pulled me toward her. "Everything will be okay...just follow me..." She turned her back to us and disappeared up the stairs.

"Better listen to her, boys, or she'll just keep naggin' ya." Walt groaned as he slowly got to his feet. "And I would know..." He folded the newspaper and stuffed it in his back pocket as he made his way up the staircase.

"Jun—what do we do?" I whispered to Junior whose eyes were fixed on the staircase.

"I don't know...what do you think?"

"Me...umm—well, part of me wants to run and the other part...trusts them..." I muttered.

"Yeah..." Junior breathed.

"What do we have to lose?" I suggested.

"Everything..." Junior replied. "Life..."

"Yeah...but..."

"Okay...then—let's go..." Junior turned to me, his eyes finding mine. "...if anything happens, I want you to run. Don't worry about me...you just run...if it comes to that."

"To where? The doors are locked..." I scanned the bottom floor, searching for a quick exit if need be.

"Hide then...anything..." Junior grabbed my arms. "Just...if anything happens...leave me behind...do you understand?"

"We're fine, Jun—everything will be okay..." I think I tried to convince myself more than him.

"Just promise me..." Junior persisted. "We stick together...don't leave my side up there...but if I say run...you run. Tell me you understand?"

"Yes..." I answered, concern was obvious in my tone.

"Alright...take my hand..." Junior held out his hand for me to grab.

We crept up the stairs slowly, not knowing if we were about to walk into danger or safety. I remembered questioning our decisions. We were entrusting strangers—opening ourselves up to being completely vulnerable to them.

There are many times in my life when I have wished to go back and redo some of the events in my life. For example, I wish I could go back to that tragic day and stay home with Momma and Davie...to be there for them. I wish I could go back and tell myself to enjoy the little things in life rather than focus so much on the negativity. But that isn't possible. You must move forward with life to fully learn from the past rather than dwell upon it. However, the one thing Junior and I would always agree on was regretting that lack of trust we had in them.

At this point in our lives, we had experienced so much heartbreak that trust became difficult to earn. It was only after our time with Edith and Walt that we learned of all the good that was hidden away in this world. We knew we were lucky to be alive, but we were even luckier that we found those two angels. They were willing to sacrifice themselves for two strange boys; boys they had never met until today. As we made our way up those stairs, we had no idea that these two people would forever leave a mark in our hearts and souls. They changed our lives forever.

Chapter 12

Hand in hand, we climbed up the dark and narrow staircase. Our ears focused on the mumbles of Edith and Walt above us. Framed photos decorated the walls with the same cluttered fashion as the rest of the store. Memories from the past of a young couple who appeared deeply in love and shared their life together. Soon, a baby boy appeared in their photos, a child who seemed to become the center of their world. A photo of a toddler with blonde hair and deep dimples, gripping tightly onto a teddy bear, caught my eye.

Inside the various frames, the young boy carried a blissful and toothy smile, a smile that made it clear to see that he carried the ability to brighten up an entire room. Even in the black and white photos, I could tell the boy had light colored eyes that were undoubtedly full of an innocence that only a child could carry. His deep dimples showed off a personality that was trapped, and frozen within the frame. His blonde hair fell softly over his forehead and was neatly combed down for the photo. There were many photos of this boy throughout his young years. Photos and memories from newborn to about the age of ten carried us up the staircase. Family snapshots and recollections incased in frames that would be forever sealed in the past.

We reached a point where the photos of the young boy ended. It appeared that the memories ended once the boy reached a certain age, as there were no more photographs to recollect the past.

Up to a dozen family photos of the boy adorned the wall before his school photo ended the decorations nearly halfway up the stairs. The rest of the wall remained blank as it led to a well-lit room where I assumed they lived. From the sounds of dishware clattering and water running through the pipes to the sink, I assumed Edith was preparing food of some sort.

We cautiously stepped inside. Peering around Junior, my eyes immediately found Walt sitting on their dusky green couch with his attention back on his newspaper. Meanwhile, Edith rambled on about pointless topics while preparing what looked to be dinner. We remained just inside the door. They evidently lived in a small disorganized upstairs apartment with only a sitting room and kitchen that had only a few doors, that led into what I assumed would be even more disordered rooms.

Above the door nearest to the kitchen was a wooden plaque with writing etched onto it reading: 'David's Room.' The blue eyed and blonde-haired boy from the photos popped into my mind as I read the sign. I wondered if that room belonged to him. I wanted desperately to know the answers to the questions I had, but my voice seemed to be absent in that moment.

"Dears… come in, come in. Would you like something cold? Tea maybe?" She asked as she stirred a pot on the stove.

"Um… sure," Junior said with a polite whisper. "Thank you. Yes, ma'am."

"Edith—you've scared them. These boys have no idea who we are or what our intentions might be." Walt's eyes peered over his newspaper to his wife. "They are smart boys, not dumb."

"Oh...well..." Edith promptly wiped her hands off on her apron and moved near us. "Please... Please, boys...won't you sit down. We will explain everything, I promise."

Junior reviewed the situation in his head before peering over to me to nod which gave me the okay to take a seat at their way too small table. I took the seat closest to the kitchen, allowing me easy access to view the apartment and Walt's movements. He seemed to have no interest in us or his wife's nervous movements. I scanned the room taking notice of all the papers scattered throughout the living room. Every surface contained a spread of papers that contained no apparent organization pattern just like their shop downstairs.

Laying on the old raggedy couch were maps and what seemed to be reports with notes written on them. Walt was sitting on the couch as though he had no idea that he was sitting on papers. He was too involved in the newspaper to care about his surroundings. Past him and tucked neatly into the back corner of the apartment was a radio placed near a clock that indicated it was now three o'clock in the afternoon.

Directly across from the distressed couch was portrait-sized photo displaying a family of three. On one side of the photo was a well-dressed woman with beautiful long chestnut brown hair and her makeup perfect, just as Momma's had always been. On the other side was a man whose appearance indicated he was both proud and confident. He had short blonde hair and glasses outlining the blue eyes that resembled the eyes of the little blonde headed boy sitting on his lap, both with smiles beaming from ear to ear. They were carbon copies of each other.

'Who was that little boy?' I thought to myself.

Edith interrupted my thoughts as she sat down to my right with a tray that was almost the same size as the table. The tray was filled with iced teas for us all, prompting Walt to stand up from the couch and join us. He took the seat across from me, removed an iced tea from the tray, and sipped it. Again, I looked to Junior for a nod of approval before following Walt's movements.

"Augh!" I gagged, immediately spitting the drink back into the cup as I made a face of complete disapproval.

Junior chuckled at my disgusted reaction while he took a sip from his glass of his iced tea, which he enjoyed.

"Oh, honey…" Edith smiled as she put her hand on my arm. "I am so sorry. You must be a sweet tea drinker."

"Oh—Um…yes ma'am…" I mumbled, too embarrassed to make direct eye contact.

"Oh, well you are just like my little David." Edith smiled gently at me. "I'll grab the sugar for you…"

Walt released his gaze from his newspaper to quickly study his wife as though he was astounded at the mention of the name David. She pulled out the sugar from the cabinet and came back with a spoon to allow me to add as much sugar as I wanted. Junior watched me as I dumped sugar into my drink, and he slowly shook his head with displeasure.

I finally looked up to Edith and took notice of the age lines that marked her face. I wondered 'what from her past has haunted her, forever leaving lines on her face as reminders.'

"So…you, two. Here is our explanation…This morning, when Walt and I first woke up, we turned on the radio as we do every morning while getting ready for our day." She looked at us ensuring she had eye contact with both me and Junior. "The radio reported the events that occurred in Charleston yesterday late afternoon. They talked of two boys who disappeared shortly after the shootings and that they remained missing. Their names we're Henry Clark, Jr., and James Clark. The radio also mentioned that the father, Henry, vanished after police began searching the parents' bedroom. They asked if anyone saw a man fitting their description to notify police. Now, typically we would have lunch at home but today, well today Walt mentioned the idea of going to The Diamond Soda Grill. I agreed and that is when you two boys walked in. I told Walt at that very moment that I didn't recognize either of you. We know practically everyone here, seeing as how we have been here so long. Walt mentioned you might be traveling with, or visiting family, but I thought how odd it was that just that morning the news coverage discussed two missing boys and the next thing—two boys show up in our town. So, I told Walt I thought you might just be those missing boys. He, on the other hand, did not seem to agree at the time. But then you walked into our shop...curious don't you think?"

"Um...I guess so. But –" Junior attempted to cover up our story but was quickly interrupted.

"Walt heard you two use the names, 'Junior' and 'Jamie.' So...there is not much room for you to wiggle out of this." Edith smiled; she knew she had won.

Silence grew louder as Junior froze in place.

"We...umm..." Junior muttered.

"Yes...dear?" Edith encouraged.

But Junior could not find the words that would counter her rather spot-on speculation.

"Okay..." I blurted out, not able to handle the stress anymore. "You're right... We are the boys from Charleston...I am Jamie or James, and this is Junior."

"We—We umm— lived there with our Mom, Dad, and brother. That was until yesterday. Um—you see..." Junior told them the entire story. He left no details out of the unfortunate and horrific events that occurred the day prior.

Finally, Walt laid down the newspaper as the words Junior spoke grabbed his attention. Walt's eyes spoke volumes, as he could hardly believe the words spoken by a mere thirteen-year-old boy.

Junior continued, "—we escaped...out our bedroom window. Hopped onto a train and came here...we found out at the diner that he has left Charleston. He isn't on the run...he's looking for us. We are trying to get to our grandparents' house in Raleigh... but the train doesn't leave until Friday—"

"—Friday ...no, a train left this afternoon for Raleigh...Who told you Friday?" Walt demanded.

Junior's eyes shot over to me at Walt's words. I looked desperately from Walt to Junior and back again.

"The man...he told me. The ticket man..." I fumbled as I tried to remember his name. "Um...Charles, I think..."

"Charles Murray...Oh, Walt, do you think he suspected them?" Edith became concerned.

"It would appear..." Walt crossed his arms across his chest. "He knows you two were lying. He is trying to keep y'all here longer to find the lies within your story, whatever story you gave him, then call the police or—"

"No! He can't...please..." Junior pleaded. "We can't...Our father— he told the police a different story. He's—he's very manipulative and good at lying. We're only trying to reach our grandparents' home in Raleigh. It's the only home we have left...please..."

"Well, the report didn't say they suspected their father, Walt..." Edith said with uneasiness. "It just said they wanted people to look out for him and the boys for further questions..."

"Yeah..." Sighing, Walt stood up from his chair with one hand still gripping the newspaper and the other rubbing the side of his face in thought. "Okay—how about this? You boys can stay here...but you stay out of sight until Friday. Maybe Murray will forget that the two of you are here. We will take you two to the train station on Friday to ensure you get on safely...get y'all to Raleigh as soon as we can..."

"Really?" I asked, astounded by his generosity.

"Of course! That is a perfect idea, Walt." Edith said, before reiterating, "But do exactly what he said, you two just stay out of view...stay away from the windows," Edith sighed. "It will be nice having you two here for a few days."

"Thank you...my brother and I really appreciate it..." Junior told them with complete sincerity. "But—"

"—No "buts" about it!" Edith pointed her finger at Junior and me. "We will have it no other way..."

Giving up on the argument he prepared, Junior sighed revealing a soft smile, "Okay—thank you."

"You two are welcome...I am sorry for your loss." Walt took back his seat, his eyes weary as he spoke. "—Honestly, I can't imagine what the two of you have been through...".

"Thank you..." Junior whispered.

"...ma'am..." I whispered to Edith.

"You can call me Edith, dear," she smiled back at me.

"...Edith...right. Um..." I hesitated unsure if I would be stepping over a line with my question, but I was desperate to settle my own curiosity. "Who is David?"

"Oh, well..." she looked up at the ceiling to draw in a calming breath before breathing out, "my David."

Walt cleared his throat, and he glanced at the dining room table looking as though he wished to just disappear from the conversation. I thought then I had definitely crossed a line with them, and I momentarily considered changing the subject of the conversation until Edith spoke again.

"David—David was our little boy, around your age..." Edith nodded at me as her eyes began to water up with memories. "Thirty-four years ago, our beautiful son David left early one morning. David was what they called a newsie...he sold newspapers on the street for money. I never wanted him to sell papers, but he wanted to. He still went to school, of course, but not like he should have. Well...this one morning he woke up late for his newspaper sales. He washed up fast, kissed me good-bye and left telling me he wanted eggs, potatoes, and bacon for dinner that night. Then—he was gone. Walt was downstairs at the time opening our general store; we owned a general store before our joke shop. Anyway, he was opening it up for the day, so he saw David last. David ran through the store. I can still remember what he was wearing. He had on his favorite black knickers, grey knee-high socks with his worn black shoes, white collared shirt, and black suspenders. He had his Charlotte Daily Observer newspaper bag across his body for his morning job before school began..."

"He yelled... 'Bye, Pa... love you!' and he was gone. Out the front door and hurrying down the street to pick up the papers he needed to sell..." Walt whispered looking over at Edith for strength as he spoke.

"We didn't realize something had possibly happened until dusk came. David wasn't home, and that was not like him. He always came home on time... he was ten years old... afraid of the dark like most little boys. So, we naturally became worried. Walt went out to search the neighborhoods nearby while I stayed here just in case he came home. Since we lived above our store and on a street away from the neighborhoods, David had to go into the neighborhoods down the road a little way to even see his friends..." Edith and Walt looked into each other's eyes as they recalled their story, both gaining strength from each other to finish.

"I searched everywhere for him... I went to his best friend Robert's house. They were newsies together at the Charlotte Daily Observer. Robert told me that David never—he never came to pick up the papers that morning. He never made it to school that morning...From our store to the Observer where the boys picked up the papers...something awful must have happened," Walt shook his head at the word "awful" as though the word scared him more than he cared to admit.

"Walt went to the police station and reported David missing... but they believed David was out with friends or possibly even ran away. We told them no—no, David was afraid of the dark and always stayed near his home, especially at dark. He told him that Robert said David never made it to the Observer that morning, which was where he was headed."

"They said David lied to us..." Walt's voice grew angry as old memories became fresh.

"They wouldn't dispatch a unit until it had been 24 hours since David was last seen..." Edith continued.

"You waited?" Junior quietly asked.

"No...we searched. Oh, we searched everywhere. The train tracks...the woods bordering town...nothing. No one had seen him...it was as though he disappeared into thin air. People cannot just disappear like that...Someone knew something...Someone saw something...And, oh, people here still know..." a cold tone grew within Edith's voice, a maternal protectiveness I had ever only seen in my own mother.

"Did anyone come forward with any information at all?" I desperately asked.

"Charles Murray..." Walt growled.

"The ticket man?" I was confused.

"The very same..." Walt's eyes narrowed with rage.

"Charles was a butcher at the time and only worked a few buildings down from us—" Edith added.

"He was also a drunk—" Walt snarled to Edith.

"—Charles told us the following day, once the police decided they would actually look into David's disappearance, that he had seen David walking on the sidewalk where the Diamond Soda Grill stands today. The night before, when we searched alone...Charles said he didn't even remember our David and forgot we even had a son. Walt and I both, obviously, found that odd...but the police didn't, and excused him stating it had been the alcohol that fogged his memory. Later that year, Charles switched career paths to become the Charlotte ticket seller at the train stop, strange switch from butcher. But the police did not seem to find that odd either. Over the years, Walt and I began to suspect Murray took our boy that morning and buried him somewhere along those train tracks...We know he did. So, all the papers scattered all over our home... are all the reports of David's case. His missing fliers and maps of this town throughout the years. Our life has been dedicated to doing anything and everything we can to bring David home. Thirty-four years have passed since David was lost to us—since his last birthday cake, his last Christmas celebration, and his last home-cooked meal. All these years, he has been out there—somewhere.

"David loved jokes and pranks; he was fun like that. So, ten years after that day, Walt changed the downstairs from a general store into a joke shop in honor of David. We have left David's room the same. We haven't changed it, even though if he came home today, he'd be a forty-four-year-old man. Can you believe it? I have a forty-four-year-old son." Tears from the pain of their past dropped uncontrollably as she spoke. "Our life has never moved on since January 6, 1912. We have aged yes but our lives are stuck. Stuck on that day that changed us forever. Every day I think how different our lives would be if I had stopped him that day from walking out that door. When I close my eyes today, I can still see him walking out that door with his smile and dimples so deep with happiness. For years, I would have dreams of him; of his tears and voice crying out for me and begging to come back home. But—no one has ever come forward regarding David's disappearance...and no bo—I'm sorry—I'm sorry...his body has never been located. Walt...he rereads the newspapers that covered David's disappearance. He reads them over and over every morning searching for something that will give us the answers. Our hope is that one day we will find something in these scattered papers and maps that will give us the answers we need. I know we might sound crazy but—he's...umm—he's—"

"Our son..." Walt whispered; his heartbroken gaze glued to his wife.

"Yes—he is and he's still our baby... it's our job to take care of him...we're his parents. Even though he isn't here, he is still our responsibility." Edith breathed back the tears that were now trickling, rather than cascading down her cheeks. "It's been thirty-four years...and David is still missing."

"Our little brother...Jamie's twin...his name was David. We called him Davie. He was a jokester too. That's why your store caught our attention. It felt like some strange sign from Davie...and I guess—I guess we were right." Junior's voice was genuine as he spoke. "I'm sorry about your son...you two aren't crazy. You do what you can for your family...to protect them..."

Edith didn't respond with words, but with a simple smile which was answer enough. For the couple who had seemed to keep only to themselves in this town, they seemed grateful for this small moment of understanding. It was a conversation of complete empathy between two different generations. Each one of us at that table had lived through something terrible; something that was only imaginable in a nightmare.

We remained together in silence while we drank our tea, each of us in deep thought. It was amazing at how simple it was to enjoy the company of two people who could relate to the immense heartache and loss we had experienced.

Edith stood up from the table and wandered into the living room bringing back a flyer to us. On the top of the paper, I could make out the word 'Missing.'

"This was the first flyer we released during our search for David..." Edith slid the flyer across the table for us both to read.

Missing

David Matthew Cole

January 6, 1912

10-year-old David disappeared from Charlotte, NC

while walking to the Charlotte Daily Observer. If

you have any information on the disappearance of David, please notify law enforcement.

REWARD
$500

Printed at the center of the flyer was the school photo of David with his big dimply smile that radiated even from the paper. I couldn't help but feel bad for the boy I never knew. He was forever frozen at the age of ten and eternally stuck on a flyer that begged anyone for any information. His parents remained just as stuck as he was. They had never moved forward since that day and, and how could they? I felt sorry for the Cole family and for the first time since the day our own world changed, I stopped feeling sorry for myself.

Even with the pain, Edith smiled gently at us. But deep within her eyes, I saw the unimaginable sadness she fought. She left the table for the stove to continue cooking what seemed like some sort of soup for dinner. The smell of her cooking brought me mentally back to our little white house in Charleston. I closed my eyes tight allowing me to see my memories more vividly. Momma was there, standing in the kitchen as she cooked without a single worry. In my mind I could see her turn to look at me with her beautiful smile that I will forever miss.

I couldn't help myself from smiling at the images in my mind. Opening my eyes, I glanced over at Walt who continued to stare down at the flyer. Tears swam in his eyes as he stared at the photo of his son. I could tell from Junior's torn expression that he was not sure what to say or do. To be honest, I wasn't either. What can you say to parents who are still trapped in time, replaying the events in their mind leading to the disappearance of their one and only child? I imagine it would be similar for someone trying to talk to us after the events we had just experienced. There is no amount of kind and sincere words that could bring any comfort to anyone who has gone through this sort of tragedy—just as there isn't any amount of time that can make these tragedies easier to live with. Regret and doubt join forces with grief and make the attempts to move forward that much more difficult. There are so many ifs and buts that are thought every day leading to that doubt and probable separation of parents and families who have endured such a loss. But Edith and Walt managed to stay together through it all. They managed to put those fears behind them in the past and put their son ahead as their sole priority. That amount of strength and courage was inspirational. And, as I grew up, I often thought back on them and the courage they displayed. It was only when I had children of my own that I realized just how much strength they truly had.

The silence in the kitchen and the overwhelming thoughts that flooded through my mind were interrupted by Walt standing up from the table.

"Follow me…" he demanded; his eyes remained fixed on the flyer. He turned and walked towards the room directly next to the refrigerator. This was the room where the wooden plaque rested above the door reading, 'David's Room.' We followed him with slight hesitation. "Now…this was David's room. We've—we have never changed it. Come on in…"

He opened the door, slowly revealing a small and quiet room that remained in the year 1912. His bed was partially made, showing that he was in a hurry to leave just as Edith had recalled. Newspapers he had not been able to sell lay on the floor showing he took after his parents' ideas and methods of organization. A small twin bed with untidy plain white sheets sat in the right-hand corner near the window. His wooden dresser, which was across from his bed, still had clothes sticking out after being forced shut by the rushed boy who had lived in here. Posters were taped up on the wall of Little Nemo, a character created by Winsor McCay. I had never seen Little Nemo, but I remember hearing Momma and Daddy talking about the cartoon when I was younger. Slingshots were nailed onto the walls, used for decorations. Above his bed, on the wall, were headlines and stories from newspapers he had sold taped as a collage.

I read some of the headlines: "Harvey Drops Wilson/ Editor of Harper's Weekly Breaks with his Protégé/ Many Rumors Flying About/ Col. Henry Watterson Said To Be Party To The Breach—A Sensational Situation." Another printed cutout said "Charlotte, N.C. Monday Morning, December 25, 1911." His room was homey and personalized to David.

"He was such an amazing newsboy. He...he would play this trick on people... He would say to people 'please, please, this is my last paper I need to sell it to get paid...please if I don't get paid this morning, we won't be able to afford dinner tonight.' They would give in, of course, and buy the paper. Then he'd run over to his stash of papers to continue to sell them!" Walt laughed at the memory of his only son. "David made twenty-five cents for half a day of work...that was all we would let him work. We wanted him to go to school too, to get an education. He deserved the best...that boy deserved everything life offered..."

Walt rested his hands on his hips while talking about memories of his only child. Tears began to stream down his face, yet a smile appeared through the sorrow. He shook his head as he walked over to David's bed, bent down, and pulled out an old teddy bear.

"Oh, David..." Walt chuckled. "David never picked up his room even when we asked him to. This was the stuffed bear my mother gave him a few months after he was born...when he was two-years old he finally gave it a name: Theodore." Walt put the teddy bear back under the bed where David had left it and walked over to the closet at the end of his bed. "This...David made." He pulled out a wooden sled with 'David's' painted on the top. "He liked to make things...it was his passion even at the young age of six. He wanted to know how everything worked, but especially toys. He loved the idea that simple objects could bring so much joy and happiness to people. He loved making things that assisted him in pranking friends and family. His best creation was something he called the wooden board. He got a wooden board from my store and managed to attach little wheels onto the bottom of it. You could ride it...slowly...but you could ride it. He liked to take it to school and to pick up his newspapers. He was so proud of that board...he took it with him that day...we never found that either..."

"What do you think happened...?" Junior whispered.

"Me?" Walt asked for clarification.

"Yes...You said it yourself. You've done a lot of research into his disappearance...what do you think happened?" Junior asked again.

"Well, I think...I think Murray saw an opportunity when David rode by. I think he lured him into the shop before the owner got there that morning, and I think he hurt him. I think he took the job as the ticket seller to watch the spot where he buried David. I think he buried David there—in the dead of the night—the very day he disappeared." Walt held onto the sled while talking, unable to look at us. "I know David is probably not alive...but I want David to be found and buried properly. Not left somewhere like he meant nothing...He deserves someone to fight for justice on his behalf, for whatever may have happened to him."

"Have you told the police that theory?" I asked.

"Yes—" Walt whispered.

"And?" Junior questioned.

"They told me Murray is a respected man in this community with no negative comments from any other resident here and to accuse him of such an act would be an insult to his name..." Walt looked up at us smiling unsteadily. He did not smile with any sign of happiness but with a look of a regrettable understanding that this, unfortunately, was what it was.

"They haven't even listened to you!?" Junior roared, becoming increasingly angry with the lack of concern from the community. "I mean, have they even looked!?"

"My boy...it has been thirty-four years..." he smiled again. "...of that same frustration you now feel. However, being frustrated and angry won't bring anything or anyone back."

"But—"

"Believe me, I understand that feeling...that trapped and desolate feeling—" Walt tried to explain.

"Why can't the police take the side of the victim!? Why do they take the side of the ones responsible!?" Junior asked loudly, tears filling his eyes. He took a deep breath before the tears that struggled to stay in broke free. "Why does life have to be so unfair?"

Walt leaned the sled back against the wall of the closet and grabbed Junior, pulling him into his chest. He held Junior tight as gut-wrenching sobs tore through the room. Edith hurried in to see what had happened. Concern lingered in her eyes at the sight of her husband and Junior, and she put her arms around me. My own tears were forming, but I was determined not to let them fall. Junior's legs collapsed out from under him and Walt was right there to catch him. All the anguish and ferocity Junior tried to keep inside no longer could be contained. Junior's forced strength gave out, and Walt remained by his side through his surrender to devastation in the middle of his son's bedroom.

"It's okay...it's okay, son..." Walt's arms tightened their grip around Junior. "You are okay...do you understand me? You are safe here...and you are understood..."

Junior's wails continued without a pause. He gasped from breaths in between the sobs.

"sh—shhh, slow down, slow down..." Walt whispered. "Slow breaths, slow breaths..."

"Jamie...come in here with me okay..." Edith murmured in my ear. "Let's give your brother some time..."

"But—" I began to say as she led me to the doorway. I took one more look back at Junior, who continued to be racked with heart wrenching sobs.

"Let's give him a moment...he'll be okay," Edith sympathetically smiled down at me. "Would you like to help me with dinner?"

"Um...I guess so...but I should be there for Jun—" I tried resisting her, but she wouldn't let me budge.

"Jamie...he is okay. This is good for him—and Walt. Junior needs to feel protected...especially after what you both experienced. Let him be thirteen for a moment...let him be a child, and let Walt be the protector." She put her hand on my cheek just as Momma used to. "Come help me with dinner?"

"Okay..." I gave in, nodding and following her willingly into the kitchen.

"So..." Edith passed me carrots to chop. "Do you like to cook?"

"My Momma..." my chin began to tremble at the name. "I used to help her cook...it was our time together I guess...Junior would read books, go out with friends, or work and Da—Davie would wait for the food to be done so he could eat it."

Edith laughed as she added pasta noodles to the broth. "I swear your twin brother and my David were the same! He would eat everything I made and stand by the kitchen for any scraps I would have for him to nibble on."

"Sounds like Davie too!" I giggled as I thought of the memories of my brother. "You would have liked him and Momma, even Daddy. He wasn't always like this you know..."

"Can you tell me what he was like before?" Edith inquired as she stirred in the chopped onions and celery.

"Amazing..." an honest smile crossed my face as I remembered the man I had once admired. "He would dance with Momma around the house, help us with our homework, teach us about tools and fixing things, played the guitar and sang with us. Every Christmas he'd powder up the bottom of his boots and make it seem as though Santa walked through our house...he was the best father I could have asked for...until he wasn't anymore."

"So, what caused all of this?" She asked as she scooped up the chopped carrots I just finished.

"He left for Germany...early in the war. He left with his best friend...family to us...Tommy—Uncle Tommy. His girl found out they were expecting a baby a month after they left for training. Well, on April 22—just fifteen days before the war ended—Uncle Tommy was shot and killed in front of Daddy. He hasn't been the same ever since. He came home distant, cold, and just scared. He had his good moments...he was still there deep within himself. But it seemed that whenever a part of him came back, more parts would easily slip away. He started getting protective and controlling over everything Momma was doing. That's when the anger worsened, and the abuse started. Momma tried to escape with us...but he caught us. One of the last things I heard him say before he...before he shot Momma...was 'I want us to stay together.' Next thing I knew, Davie was dead, Momma was screaming for me to run, and Daddy tried to shoot me. Broke the window next to me instead. That's why I have these scratches on my face. Anyway—I heard him shoot Momma as I hid, thinking Junior wasn't home yet—but he was. He distracted Daddy by throwing bottles at the house. As Daddy ran outside to investigate, Junior ran inside to get me. We went to our bedroom window and ran into the woods. At first, we went to the police station, but he beat us there. We tried to get to the police station, but he beat us there. We overheard him lying to the police, saying he came home and found Davie and Momma like that—acting all bereft that some madman had killed his wife and son, and stolen his other two beloved boys." After a deep and heavy sigh, I concluded the story by softly saying, "The police—they believed it."

"Oh, honey...no child should have to go through that..." Edith swiped at her eyes, but the tears fell anyway.

"No...but it happened. Truth is Junior and I were never close. Not until now anyway..." I sniffled quietly as my tears kept threatening to spill over.

"Siblings never get along at a certain age...hard times and age help strengthen that bond..." She reassured me. "No matter what happens in the future...never give up hope that good people exist. There is more good than bad in this world...but it will take time to understand that..."

"How do you two do it? I mean... how do you search for him every day?" I asked, my voice steady with wonder.

"He is our only child...he looked to us for protection and security...that was our job." Her bottom lip trembled with sadness.

"Walt...has been the strongest of the two of us. David's room became more of a sacred place...a place where I would just go in and just...be—"

"He sounded like a neat kid...someone I'd be friends with for sure," I grinned enthusiastically at her, trying my best to cheer her up some.

"Yeah..." a smile broke through as she continued to stir the soup. "He was a great kid...a beautiful smile and such a bright future ahead of him."

"I'll say..." I gasped. "Look at all his inventions he had created. No telling what he could have come up with in time!"

"Yes! He had quite the imagination that's for sure...Never knew what he would bring home..." She ceased stirring, staring off out the small window above their sink lost in thoughts I wish I could hear. "David was taken too soon...before he barely had the chance to really live. Before he could accomplish all the things he wanted to achieve. There are so many times—more than half I'd say—where, I just wish I could trade places with him...give him life and I'll take the unknown. I would do just about anything to hold him in my arms again. He used to love to sit in my lap and be held. He loved life. But life has moved on without skipping a single beat, as though nothing sinister had ever occurred. And the damage you feel within is not visible to those on the outside."

An abrupt but soft clearing of the throat behind us caught our attention. Walt was making his entrance into the kitchen with Junior by his side, Walt's arm wrapped tightly around Junior's shoulder. Junior's eyes were sunken and bloodshot as though all the anguish and despair had drained out of him, leaving him empty.

"Oh, boys...dinner is just about ready with the help of Mr. Jamie here." She grinned down at me; her eyes still teary.

"Excellent! Jamie, thank you for assisting my wife." Walt nodded kindly.

Giving him a slight nod back, I turned my attention onto Junior.

"Junior, are you okay?" Edith wiped off her hands on her apron and walked over to my distraught brother. Edith placed her hands on his cheeks, unknowingly mimicking Momma's comforting techniques.

"Yes, ma'am..." Junior mumbled, his eyes drifting to the floor. "I'm sorry for—umm—I'm sorry for that..."

"Oh, you are more than fine sweetheart and more than allowed to have those moments...especially with us..." Her voice was gentle, maternal towards him.

Junior's eyes met hers with weariness. He nodded slightly before being pulled into a tight embrace by Edith. She longed for him to feel safe there with them and to be able to feel like a child once again, a child without the weight of the world on his shoulders. And Junior, of all people, deserved that.

"Well...Edith and I will prepare the table if you two would like to get washed up. The bathroom is in the corner over there. Alright?" Walt patted Junior's shoulder and gave me a slight smile before making his way into the kitchen.

Agreeing, Junior and I walked through the living room, careful not to step on the flyers, reports or maps laid out on the floor. As we reached the rugged and scratched up door in the corner of the living room closest to the window, I glanced out onto the alleyway behind the store. An old black truck with wooden rails, which I figured belonged to the Coles, was parked out back behind their building. Pausing momentarily to view the truck, I remembered Edith's remarks regarding keeping away from the windows, so I moved instantly. I followed behind Junior into their disorganized bathroom, and we took turns using the sink to wash off. Junior went first and washed off his face.

"Jamie…I'm sorry…" Junior calmly told me as he dried off his face.

"For what?" I questioned.

"Not being better…before…when you needed me most. I was supposed to be the man of the house for you and Davie and I-I failed." Junior's eyes became soft with regret. "I just want you to know that I truly am sorry."

"You were the best you could have been. We didn't expect any outstanding greatness from you. We only expected you to be you, and you did that. Don't apologize for being a brother," I grinned reassuringly at him.

He returned a sincere smile, and not long after, we were back with the Cole's. We enjoyed our first homecooked meal with them and we enjoyed the conversations we shared. They asked both of us what we wanted to be when we grew up and what we dreamed of. They wanted to know each of us for who we were. So, we told them about Momma and Davie, of course. Junior went on and on about the home-cooked meals Momma would make and the memories we had of sitting on the porch as a family. We told them about Daddy and how he used to be with us. We didn't want people to see him as an evil person because that wasn't who he was. He was just damaged, as were many men who came home from the war with broken dreams and sad memories. Our father was not a good man anymore, but the Daddy we both knew and loved…was. And once this was all over, that was the Henry Clark we wanted people to know. The man who was once an amazing husband and father who loved his family.

And as for us? We were fortunate to be where we were. To be with two people who wanted to be free from the past that haunted their dreams—just as we did. We were safe now. Finally, safe. How long that safety would shield us from what lurked in the shadows was unknown.

Chapter 13

Junior gave me the couch that night while he slept on some sheets made up on the floor surrounded by papers dedicated to young David Cole. As the night consumed us, my nightmares returned pulling me back into the afternoon prior, when all our dreams died. I found myself staring down the barrel again. As the trigger was pulled my eyes shot open in desperation. I found myself lying face down on the couch, drenched in sweat as my mind swarmed and heart raced with overwhelming panic.

My vision was clouded as my glasses were lost in the fog that surrounded me. The smell of eggs and bacon filled my senses easing my anxiety and bringing me back to reality. Dishes clanged together signaling someone was in the kitchen cooking at a fast pace. The smell reminded me of the many mornings we had back home. These memories comforted my heart reminding me of the security we finally had.

Today was Thursday, May 2 and there was now just one more day until the train left for Raleigh. After that, we'd be safe with MeeMaw and Pa. They would take us in the second they saw us and wouldn't hesitate to believe our story. Since that horrible afternoon, it had become so hard for us to truly trust anyone. But trusting Edith and Walt was so simple.

The door diagonal to me, which I assumed to be their bedroom, opened. I recognized the voice as belonging to Walt.

"The police are talking about the Clarks again..." He whispered to Edith, hoping not to wake us.

I closed my eyes tight to pretend as though I was still lost in sleep. I wanted to hear their conversation as they thought they were unheard.

"What are they saying?" Edith quietly moved through the living room over to her husband.

"They still have not located their father and obviously neither of the boys. They aren't declaring whether they believe Mr. Clark is a suspect. All they have said was to notify the police if anyone sees Mr. Clark, Junior, or Jamie. And that if anyone in the local area has any information, please notify police as well. Also, there are no suspects to be named at the time..." Walt sighed as his hands fell to his side in disappointment. "Do you think the police really believe Mr. Clark's story? Shouldn't we tell the police about the boys?"

"I don't know what they believe, dear...I want to call them also and tell them that the boys are safe, but I think we need to listen to the boys...they were there, and they know the situation they are in more than we do..." She sighed with uncertainty.

"But...you're right," concern filled his sigh. "I need to teach Junior how to use our truck outback. Just in case you know. It's good for him to know. He should know how to drive, how to get away from something. And I want to give them our gun for their trip—"

"—Gun? Walter, they are only young boys..." she spoke in disbelief.

"They are boys who unfortunately have had to grow up too quickly. When they leave tomorrow, they will be in danger," he responded quickly. "I will not leave another child defenseless—not again."

"How do you know their father suspects they are heading to Raleigh?" She was becoming increasingly frustrated.

"Where else would the boys go? Their last living relatives live in Raleigh. I'd go to Raleigh too to find them." The tone of his whispers increased with tension.

"Okay...Okay...but you need to talk to them about how to use that thing properly. Breakfast is ready, are you?" Edith sauntered off; each step echoed with aggravation.

"I love you," he whispered, to which she simply mumbled inaudible words back at him. I heard him quietly chuckle at his wife's attitude before turning back into his room to get ready.

Once I realized neither of them was near me, I shifted my body in Junior's direction. I wanted to check to see if he was awake and possibly overheard their conversation as well. Opening my eyes only slightly, I glanced down at the floor to find Junior with his mouth opened and snoring softly. He hadn't heard anything they said. Junior was one who could sleep through just about anything back then; it was truly a gift.

"Good Morning, Jamie," Edith's voice grabbed my attention.

"Oh! Um...good morning," I responded, realizing how obvious I looked leaning over the side of the couch.

"Do you want some breakfast?" She asked me as she poured the eggs into a serving bowl.

"Oh—Yes, ma'am. Can I help with anything?" rubbing my eyes and stretching to pretend as though I had just woken up.

"Oh, no, dear. You just come over here and pick out what you'd like to eat...let your brother rest some more," Edith pulled the sizzling bacon off from the skillet onto a serving plate, further enriching the smell in the room. "Is milk okay?"

I stepped around Junior to fold my blanket politely leaving it on the couch. I hoped that the more I moved around, the better chance I had at disturbing Junior to wake him from his sleep. I had to tell him about what I overheard Walt saying. But he did nothing. There was no movement or any signs that Junior was stirring. Frustrated, I looked back up at Edith remembering her question. "Um...yes, ma'am, it's my favorite."

"It was my David's favorite too. He could chug an entire bottle of milk if you'd let him," she remembered as she poured me a cup and passed over an empty plate. "I put some bread in the toaster. I figured you would like some along with your breakfast."

"Thank you so much, Mrs. Cole," I beamed as I filled my plate with scrambled eggs and a few pieces of bacon. "Any news this morning from the radio? Have they found him yet?" I desperately tried to subtly push her for answers.

"Oh, actually, I'm not quite sure. We will have to check with Walt—Walt! Look who just woke up!" Edith smoothly changed the subject. I'm sure talking about the subject made her uncomfortable especially without Walt present.

"Well, good morning, son. I hope you and Junior slept well!" Walt was dressed up nice. He had on black pants and a long-sleeved red and grey striped shirt with his suspenders. Walt walked over to Edith and me in the kitchen to help himself to some breakfast. He looked over to Junior who was beginning to stir in his sleep.

"Good morning, sir. I did…Junior always sleeps well," I scoffed at the sight of my brother.

"Does he now? I do think I saw some drool dripping from his mouth," Walt teased causing me to laugh.

"Oh, let the poor boy sleep!" Edith hushed at us while she continued to flip bacon on the skillet. "Walt, can you get the toast out of the toaster and put it on that big plate please and thank you."

"Edith, where are we going to put all of this food?" Walt trifled with her as he kissed her cheek. "There isn't much room on the table you know."

Sighing forcefully Edith looked back to me, "Jamie, toast?"

"Yes, ma'am. Thank you!" Grabbing the two pieces of toast from him, I indulged myself in the breakfast she had prepared.

Junior's stirring became noticeable as he began shifting around on the floor. I knew Junior needed sleep; it was his first night sleeping since being on the road. But I was relieved to see him waking from his dreams. I wanted so desperately to tell him about the conversation I had overheard that morning.

I saw his face twist as his eyes adjusted to the light shining through the windows. His arms stretched out as his body began waking up and preparing for the day that lay ahead. His hair was flattened out on one side and sticking up on the other.

"Well, good morning!" Edith exclaimed with enthusiasm as we all watched Junior slowly wake himself up.

"Huh…" Junior groaned, his eyes blinking in adjustment.

"Morning, Junior! Get over here and have some breakfast! She is a real neat cook!" I told him as I continued to shove my face full of bacon and eggs.

Junior stretched out one last time before picking himself up off the floor while rubbing his eyes to clear his sleepy vision. Junior picked up the used blankets sprawled out on the floor and left them on the couch before stumbling over to the kitchen. Edith beamed with joy as she passed him an empty plate for him to fill up. Junior's tired eyes lit up at the sight of bacon sizzling on the plate and he rubbed his belly with immediate hunger. He quickly filled up his plate before taking his seat at the kitchen table with Walt and me.

"Thank you, Mrs. Cole," Junior smiled, just before he stuffed his mouth full of eggs.

"Call me Edith, dear, and it's no problem. It is nice to cook for someone other than Walt and me," Edith laughed as she grabbed her own plate of food to join us at the table.

"How'd you sleep?" Walt asked in between bites.

"Good. Really good actually." Junior admitted. "Thank you again for having us here. The train was not very comfortable."

"I wouldn't think it would be..." she chuckled.

"So...did the radio say anything this morning about...um...our dad?" I asked with some obvious hesitation.

"Well—yes, actually—" Walt set down his fork and knife while he cleared his throat. "—They still have not found him, and they requested that if anyone has information to please notify law enforcement immediately. And—" His eyes glanced over to Edith before completing his thought, "—and there are no suspects named at this time."

"No suspects...seriously?" Junior's voice developed an edge of anger.

"I guess they did believe Daddy's story." I muttered in utter disbelief.

"How could they believe him?" Junior dropped the fork onto his plate causing a clattering sound to echo throughout the house.

"Remember... the police are going off whatever evidence they have," Edith's voice was neutral, as though she was trying desperately to bring out some understanding of their actions. "People in power have a way of manipulating other people in order to get what they want. We just have to stay one step ahead."

"Which is why I thought today I could teach you, Junior, how to drive," Walt suggested.

"Me?" Junior said with astonishment.

"Yes sir, you," Walt gave a toothy grin back. "You need to know how to drive...So after breakfast get washed up, and we will practice a little before the shop opens at ten."

"Okay! Thank you!" Junior immediately began filling up his mouth full of food with much excitement to start his training.

"Whoa there, son...slow down! We don't need you to choke on breakfast now," Walt snorted with laughter.

"Mmhmm—" Junior smirked while nodding to Walt.

Edith and I giggled as we watched them together. Walt was excited to teach a young boy how to drive. Junior was acting as sort of a surrogate son for Walt as he wanted and needed to have his son back, just as Junior longed to have that father figure again. This was therapeutic for them both. They needed one another, just as I needed Edith as a mother figure. Each of us in that moment had a "something" we each longed for, family.

Following breakfast, Walt excused himself downstairs to prepare the store for opening in an hour. Junior and I assisted Edith with the dishes, cleaning up the kitchen and dinner table while Walt belted out a chorus downstairs. Edith had a look of admiration while listening to him sing completely out of tune.

"What song is he singing?" I asked curiously as I watched Edith's cheeks turn different shades of pink.

"Because" her smile radiated as distant memories filled her mind. "It's our song. Walt sings it to me every morning while he prepares the store."

I listened closely to hear the lyrics he sang. It was about God making someone, and cherishing them through light, and darkness, and time. "That's sweet..." I told Edith while thinking of the days when Daddy would sing to Momma. He would sing her love songs, and they would sing together. "Daddy used to do that too...before."

"But that was a long time ago, Jamie," Junior said with a note of sadness. He dried off the last plate before heading in the direction of the bathroom, "Mrs. Cole?" He queried, "would it be okay if I washed up quickly?"

"Of course, dear. Do you need some fresh clothes?" Edith questioned.

"No, ma'am, we have some extra clothes in our bags," he grinned embarrassingly as he picked up his packed bag. "Thank you, though, I won't be long."

"Take your time, dear," she told him. "Thank you both for helping me clean up the kitchen."

"Thank you for breakfast," I smiled earnestly at her.

"Yes, thank you; it was delicious." Junior said with sincerity before closing the bathroom door.

I sat back down on the couch with thoughts overwhelmingly circulating in my mind. I will admit, I had a problem with over analyzing situations. At that age I contained so much apprehension regarding situations that were completely out of my control. I would make myself so tense with anxiety that I am surprised I had not given myself a stomach ulcer.

So, while I sat in the living room alone as Edith finished up the kitchen, thoughts and visions took over my inner self. I began to worry compulsively about stepping aboard the train tomorrow afternoon. My imagination concocted visions of Daddy aboard the same train as us, making my heart race. I noticed my respirations increasing as my anxiety took over almost completely

When I close my eyes at the end of each day, would nightmares of Daddy always take over? Was I to be reminded every night of the evil that had invaded his mind? How is it that someone who was once so wonderful, so pure, and so honest, could change so drastically?

In an attempt to switch the subject of my thinking, I found myself looking at the family photo that hung on the wall. I studied each of their contagious smiles which was so transmittable to anyone who could have seen them. The innocence in young David's eyes was completely and utterly surreal. He reminded me so much of our Davie, a soul that could never know any type of evil.

I stared at the photo and realized the pure happiness that this home had once contained. Until someone with much malice and evil stepped over the line and altered their fate by taking away the glue that had molded their family into what they once were—happy.

"That photo was taken in 1908, a day after David's sixth birthday. He was so excited to turn six years old; he was so proud of himself," Edith's voice broke my stare, and I found her staring at the photo with me from the edge of the kitchen. I watched a solemn tear run down her cheek as she looked up with me. She continued to voice out loud the thoughts held inside, "he looked just like Walt, and, oh, did Walt love that. The day David was born, that was all he would talk about. He told everyone he met how proud he was to be the father of a boy he knew was destined to change the future. Life, of course, had other plans. He was an angel, and we were blessed to have him for those ten years. Selfishly I just wish God had given us more time with him..."

Quietness grew as I was left with no words that would surely be enough to take away her pain.

"I have always loved this photo..." She mumbled, her eyes remaining locked onto the memory trapped in print.

"It is a beautiful picture of the three of you," I tried so desperately to suppress the feelings of the grief that I contained in my heart. I thought of Junior and how he always looked like Daddy's twin; similarly, to David Cole's resemblance to Walt. The longer we stayed here, the more connections I found between our family and theirs. This only caused it to become harder for me to hide my emotions.

"It's okay to cry, Jamie," Edith sat to my left opening her arm for my comfort.

Her voice was so soft and gentle, eerily similar to Momma's. The tears I strained to keep in slowly became free.

"I'm okay," my voice broke. "I guess, I-I'm still—"

"—In shock? That is okay...I understand that feeling all too well," her arms tightened their grip around me, her thumb stroking my arm. "The day David left...it took me a whole week before I would let out just a single tear. The shock and anger at everything left me shattered. It left me feeling nothing. You are entitled to take your time to grieve your loss, because they impacted your life...not mine. No one has the right to judge the way you chose to grieve...I just hope that once you are with your grandparents, and Junior and you settle in with them, you will be able to find some peace."

I felt my chin begin to tremble as my tears increased their speed down my face. Until she mentioned it, I hadn't realized that I had not shed many tears. I had become so focused on escaping that putting up a barrier between Junior and myself against the outside world caused me to not properly grieve. I guess it had not yet felt real to me. I still felt like I could return home to a house full of love and security.

I continued to sit there and stare off at their family photo as the tears kept clouding my vision. Edith's arm remained locked around me and her head rested on mine as she slowly rocked me. I felt the deep and surreal pain of losing my mother tear at my heart. I felt panicked as I searched for air between my sobs, but the air wasn't enough to get rid of the pain. Her soft voice comforted me as she shushed my tears with acceptance.

The bathroom door opened, and steam seeped out from Junior's bath. I frantically wiped the tears from under my eyes in an attempt to hide the pain I felt from Junior. I didn't want him to see the weakness I still contained. I wanted him to believe that I had grown, matured since our days at home.

"Ready for my lessons," Junior smiled cockily with his hair combed and fresh clothes on. I figured this learning to drive endeavor would eventually get to his head.

"Yes, you are." Edith's laughter filled the room. "Hurry on downstairs, I expect Walt is waiting for you."

"Yes, ma'am. Thank you!" Junior started for the front door until he stopped almost abruptly to look at me. "Jamie...are you okay?"

"Of course, Jun, have fun," I smiled reassuringly at him. "Don't wreck his truck you hear!"

Uncertainty lingered in his eyes unsure if he should leave me. His eyes met Edith's and she must have given him the okay signal because soon he gave me a slight smile before throwing on his black jacket.

"I would never Jamie! I'm a professional!" He carried along with the joke before winking at me as he turned for the door to run downstairs for his lesson.

"Now, you!" Edith turned to me; her hands rested on either side of my cheeks wiping off any remaining tears as a mother would do. "You need to learn how to read a map…"

"A map? But we're taking the train from here to Raleigh. And I'm sure once we get there, we will find our way to MeeMaw and Pa's house." I tried to reassure her and ease her mind in wanting to help.

"Yes, I know that dear…but if something happens on y'all's trip, I want to be sure you know how to get to Raleigh or get back to us…" Her tone became very serious, leading me into believing she had thought long and hard about this. "Do you understand?"

"Yes, ma'am…" I nodded.

"Good… get washed up and meet me downstairs, okay?" Edith stood up to take her apron off and walked to the door to join Walt and Junior downstairs.

The door came to a quick close and for the first time since that night… I was left alone. The silence that filled the room was almost a nightmare. Before then I didn't mind being alone. Being alone was my time to think and dive into a world strictly of my own imagination. It was my time to "get away" from the world around me. But now…the thoughts that filled my mind scared me. Silence had, once again, become too loud.

I grabbed my bag and pulled out the clean clothes that had been packed in tightly the night of our attempted escape. Tightly packed beneath the dirty clothes I had worn the previous night was Winston. A tear slipped from my control once again as memories of Davie swarm through my mind. Since our birth Davie and I had held tightly onto these teddy bears; and since then, those bears had never been apart. This was the first time in ten years that Davie and I, or the bears, had ever been separated, but this separation would be permanent. I gripped tightly onto Winston as though I was a little boy all over again. I wanted to feel the same comfort and support it had given me as a young boy. I wanted to feel as close as I could to my late mother and brother. I would have given anything for them to be with us today, safe and away from all danger. Life forces you to move forward and you must do everything you can to not dwell on the past.

I knew then that I didn't want to live in a house full of photos and reports scattered on the floor regarding Davie and Momma. I knew we needed to get to MeeMaw and Pa's house to continue living the life we should have all been able to. I wanted to live on to become the man my mother raised me to be and I wanted to live freely for Davie. I wanted to enjoy life to its fullest extent and laugh at the small things rather than focus negatively on them. I needed to begin living a little like Davie.

My tears ceased as I rubbed and dried my tear-stained eyes. I inhaled deeply in an attempt to relax since I had been hyperventilating with the panic and deep sadness I had been feeling. I looked at Winston and held him tightly before tucking him back into my backpack to keep him safe.

I grabbed my backpack and made my way to the bathroom. I peeked out the window near the bathroom just in time to see Junior pull the car forward only to come to a rough stop as he hit a metal trashcan after stalling out. I couldn't help but crack a smile at the sight of him leaning his head out of the window with a look of complete embarrassment.

"Professional—huh—" I laughed to myself.

I only took about fifteen minutes to get washed up and dressed for the day that lay ahead. I bolted to the door that led down to their store, excited to watch Junior drive some more. As I opened the door, I stopped almost immediately when an all too familiar voice from downstairs found my ears. The confidence in the deep and husky voice echoed into the stairway leading up to the Cole's home and I knew instantly who was speaking. I leaned as far left as the door frame would allow me, to get a slight glimpse of Edith standing at the register while her hands fidgeted in front of her. Her voice was uneasy with obvious nerves as she spoke, and I could tell she knew without a doubt who the man was too.

Holding my breath, I listened closely to hear the conversation below.

"So, I haven't seen you before. Did you just arrive in our town?" Edith questioned.

"Yes, ma'am...on business. I was talking to Mr. Murray near the tracks, and he told me that y'all had the best toy shop in town," the man's voice remained strong with confidence. "I thought to myself, 'well I will just have to stop by and see what is so great about it.' My youngest boy is a big jokester, and I thought he would love it if I picked him up something from here. His birthday is coming up, so it's perfect timing."

"Oh, how special...well, what is he interested in specifically?" Edith desperately tried to relax her quivering voice.

Unseen Scars

"Many things...he loved this whoopee cushion he got one year...and loved his peashooter...he is turning eleven May 21st," the man told her.

"Oh, how precious. Eleven years old...he's growing up, huh?" Edith smiled.

"Oh, yes. He is growing up quickly," his voice grew slightly cold as though he was becoming irritated with her respectful hospitality.

I turned quietly on the tips of my toes to step back into the apartment. I shut the door gently, hoping to avoid making any accidental noises. I tiptoed over to the back window where I was able to see Walt and Junior practicing in the truck. I glanced over at the clock learning that it was only ten minutes past ten, meaning that the store had only been open for ten minutes. He must have been outside, lurking in the shadows waiting for it to open. I hadn't been able to see the man's face, but I knew from the voice and the story of his son, it was my father. He found us. And Murray directed him right in our direction. I knew I had to prevent Junior from entering through the back door and walking into a trap planned by our father.

I pulled the window open and spotted them immediately. Walt had his arm around Junior as a father would, and they both had proud smiles across their faces.

"I told you it wasn't too hard!" Walt belted out with pride. "You are a professional driver now!"

They were heading to the back door, and I knew I had to stop them.

"Junior!" I called down to them as loud as I could without drawing attention to them or me. "Walt! Junior!" I called again.

Junior's eyes found me, and his face lit up with joy and pride. "Jamie! I did it Ja—"

"SHHH! Dad...Dad is here!" I whispered as panic pulsated through my blood stream.

I watched Junior's face turn white as a sheet as he froze in place, his eyes wide with shock. "Dad..." he mouthed back to me as he turned a look of utter panic towards Walt."

Walt grabbed Junior's arm and rushed him back into the security of the truck. His voice was deep and his tone direct, "Stay in here, stay down...and do not get out until I come back to get you!" I watched Junior drop to the floorboard of the truck out of sight. Walt turned to look up at me and quietly, but urgently stated, "hide in our closet. Do not come out. We will come get you."

I nodded at Walt before he walked up to the back door, composing himself. I turned away from the window, grabbed Junior's and my backpacks, then quickly but carefully walked into their bedroom, and closed the door quietly. I scanned the room around me and saw two doors on the side of the room. One of the doors had been opened revealing their bathroom inside. The other door was closed.

Carefully, I walked on my tiptoes over to the one that was closed, which opened to reveal a full closet with clothes that hung in disarray. I threw Junior's and my bags in the corner and ducked down beneath the hanging clothes. Stretching my fingers below the door, I pulled it to a close with a soft click. I sat with my knees pulled into my chest in the darkness of the closet, as my level of anxiety increased, my lungs tightening in fear with each passing minute. The same feelings of complete despair that I felt while hiding inside our dirty clothes hamper, rushed back inside me.

I rocked my body back and forth with my eyes shut while muttering words of encouragement to myself. The closet space began to shrink in size as time continued to pass. Echoing through my memory were the screams let out from Momma and heavy footsteps sounding throughout our home. All the safety and security we had both gained while being with Walt and Edith disappeared in an instant. Fear burned down my cheeks in the form of tears, as the tension became more than overwhelming. The air inside the closet seemed to become limited, making it difficult to simply breathe as my thoughts were the only thing keeping me company.

Off in the near distance, I heard footsteps rushing up the staircase and the apartment door swing open. I closed my eyes tighter than before as the memories replayed in my mind of waiting inside our hamper.

'He couldn't have known I was up here...' I thought frantically to myself. 'I'm going to die...I'm going to die...'

The footsteps grew closer, and I tried desperately to control my breathing, but no amount of focus could quieten my breaths down. The door to Edith and Walt's bedroom opened abruptly and the footsteps hurried swiftly over to where I was hiding.

'He found me! He found me!' I screamed in my mind as my body began shaking with sure panic.

The door to the closet was thrown open, and my eyes remained closed as I braced for my end. The nightmares of staring into the barrel of my fate were soon to become my reality. I waited in complete disquiet for my end to come crashing down when her voice broke through my pain.

"Oh, honey!" Edith's voice was calming yet tense. "It's okay...he is gone...he is gone..."

My eyes shot open, but still my vision was clouded by the tears that swam in my eyes. I saw the outline of her body and her loosely tied up grey hair. Her light brown eyes that had been so comforting the past day came into focus. At the sight of Edith, my breathing slowly began to relax allowing me to finally feel my lungs open with the air it was so desperate for. Edith reached her arms into the closet and wrapped her arms around me to pull me in tightly.

"Jamie, you are safe now...you both are safe..." she whispered in my ear before kissing my forehead with her maternal instincts, as though protecting her own child.

The panic came rushing back just as fast as it had left as I thought of Junior.

"Jun—Junior!" my voice sounded broken, as though it was desperately trying to be heard.

"Junior is okay...Walt went to get him out of the truck..." She put her hands around my face, helping me focus and steady my breathing yet again. More footsteps pounded on the stairs and my heart raced once more. Taking notice of my sudden change, Edith whispered, "it's okay...it's okay...it's only Walt and Junior..."

"Jamie! Jamie!" Junior's desperate voice echoed through the living room. "Jamie!" He rounded the doorway with Walt following closely behind him.

"Junior!" I called out to him, desperate for him to see me.

"Jamie..." Junior swiftly crossed their bedroom and dropped to his knees as Edith welcomed him into her embrace.

"Are you okay?" He asked.

"Yeah...are you?" I breathed in between my breaths.

"How...how did he find us?" Junior exclaimed with fright as he looked from Walt back to Edith.

"I...I don't know..." Walt's eyes were locked onto Edith as he too searched for lost answers.

"Um...okay—well, boys...let's go out to the living room, okay?" Edith, who was still on her knees, stood up and put her hand out for me to grab. "Everything is okay. Trust me..."

With uncertainty, I reached carefully out to grab Edith's hand as Junior smiled reassuringly at me. He put his hand out for me to grab along with hers, and they both helped me up and off the floor. Walt picked up our bags while Edith and Junior escorted me slowly out of the bedroom and over to the living room couch.

"I heard him—I heard him talk about Davie—as—as though Davie was still alive..." I stumbled through my sentence. "I heard him—he talked about Murray...Murray must have told him we were here..."

"I agree...there's no other way he would have known to look here..." sadness resonated in Edith's voice.

"He talked about Davie?" Junior questioned as he dropped to my side on the couch.

"Yeah...he told Edith Davies' birthday was coming up and that he'd be turning eleven..." I couldn't look at him and I knew if I did, I'd see the same empty expression I felt. "He talked about the whoopie cushion, Junior...he talked about our peashooters...he talked about Davie."

"What do we do...?" Junior muttered softly.

"...In the morning, Edith and I will drive you two to Raleigh...we aren't letting either of you on that train alone..." Walt's voice was calm. "We will leave early tomorrow morning...okay?"

"It's a far drive..." Junior mentioned.

"It'll take most of the day...but we'd rather make sure you both get there safely...especially with your father in town—" Edith sat down at the tiny kitchen table, her eyes focused on Junior and me.

"—should we call the police?" I asked, unsure of what we should do.

"I don't know...it's up to you boys...if he is hanging around Charles Murray then I'm not sure anything will be done..." Walt's hands were on his hips thinking intently about the next few steps. "He doesn't know you two are here...and he left without a fuss after buying a cap gun."

"A cap gun?" I questioned.

"Yeah...he said thank you for being genuine and that he loved our toy store...then he left..." Walt answered with some hesitation.

"Did he mention Momma?" Junior solemnly whispered.

"No..." Edith spoke. "He didn't mention anyone but Davie..."

"So...We will leave early in the morning before the sun comes up and get to Raleigh by late afternoon or early evening." Junior walked himself through the plans.

"Yes...okay so I'm going back down to the store to continue on as though it was a normal day...I locked the store back up to come up here. You both stay up here with Edith..." Walt began walking to the door but then quickly turned back around, his glasses slid to the brim of his nose. "Junior, do you have any questions on the pickup?"

"No, sir!" Junior smiled. "Thanks to you, I think I got it!"

"Good," Walt grinned slightly. "If any of you need anything, let me know."

He left again, closing the door tightly before leaving to go down to the store. I heard the doorbell jingle, signaling the store was reopening. Edith was quiet after he left, unsure of what she should say to us. I guess I understood that. I wouldn't know what to say to someone who was going through something I couldn't understand either. Edith was a fixer. All she wanted to do was fix and care for those around her, especially us. She related with us more than I think anyone could understand during those times. We needed one another more than we knew.

"I need to go over the map with the two of you..." Edith stood up to face us, her tone becoming increasingly serious and direct. "You both need to know how to get to Raleigh...if something were to happen—if we're—you need to know how to get to Raleigh."

"But—" I began.

"You need to know—do you understand me?" Edith repeated.

"Yes," Junior replied looking at me and then back to Edith, "yes, ma'am, we understand."

"Yes, ma'am." I agreed.

Edith nodded and walked off towards their bedroom. We heard her in their bedroom going through more paperwork and drawers searching for what I could only assume was the map.

"Junior..." I whispered hoping Edith wouldn't overhear me. "I don't want Daddy to hurt them..."

"I know..." he whispered back with concern. "I was thinking...we need to leave here...before he hurts them...you know—"

"But—" I stopped to think about our options, but there were none. "Where do we go Junior? Everywhere...everywhere we go he finds us. What if we get them—"

"No!" Junior's eyes shot over toward Edith and Walt's bedroom. His voice lowered to a whisper. "Nothing will happen to them...tonight once they're asleep, we will take their truck and drive it to Raleigh by ourselves—"

"How?" I looked at him with uncertainty. "You have only driven the pickup one time before...and how are we going to—"

"Edith will show us how to get there with a map…" Junior was moving his hands with every word, and I could tell he had given this plan much thought in just a short time. "We will take the map and once they are asleep, we will sneak out the back. We will get out of town before they or Dad even know. It'll be simple…"

"But—"

"Jamie, are you in this with me, or not?" Junior's eyes narrowed in on me.

I looked over to Edith and Walt's bedroom, listening as she continued rummaging through her things. I thought for a moment of our options and realized there was no other choice.

"Okay…I'm in," I agreed.

"Here it is!" Edith beamed as she walked out of their bedroom waving around the map. "I knew I had it in there somewhere! Alright, now—" She sat down at the table, ushering us to join her as she opened the map up wide enough for us all to see.

She immediately began describing all the roadways we would take on our trip tomorrow morning. Junior kept his eyes glued to the map taking in every detail and trying hard to memorize everything she said. I felt guilty for not sharing our new plans with Edith, but she couldn't know.

What would they think when they woke up tomorrow morning to find us gone? What would they think when they found their only truck stolen by the kids they trusted? They'd been so good to us, and now we were putting on fake smiles only to plan our own escape that will hopefully keep them safe.

Chapter 14

We spent the entire day with Edith upstairs while Walt continued to work in their store as though it was just a normal day. After spending an hour or so studying the roadways leading to Raleigh, we all decided on playing Monopoly to pass some more time. We watched Edith closely as she placed the map inside the cabinet located directly above the sink. I glanced over to Junior and he, too, had his eyes on the location of the map.

For the remainder of the day, we played Monopoly together, and Edith made sandwiches for us around noontime for lunch. Meanwhile, Junior bought just about every single house on the board. Usually, I won at Monopoly. But today, I couldn't focus on buying houses and charging people for landing on my property like he could. Junior won that time. And boy did he let me know when he won. Each time I would land on his property, he would announce loudly to Edith and me that I owed him some money. Edith seemed to just enjoy the company and laughter of two young children.

"So, why didn't you and Walt have any other children after David?" Junior asked without any thought or consideration with his question.

"Oh," Edith was taken back. Her eyes darted to the table, avoid our wandering eyes. "Um—"

"It's okay...you don't have to answer that...my brother was just being nosy," I tried to excuse my insensitive brother.

"I was not—" Junior blurted. "I was just wondering—"

"Ha! You landed on Atlantic Ave!" I exclaimed, hoping to change the subject, "which means you owe me exactly $110 dollars, please!"

"Ugh!" Junior exclaimed as he pulled out his money from the stack of play money hidden behind him. He hid the fake cash in fear that I would somehow steal the money he had accumulated throughout the game. "Fine, here. One hundred and TEN dollars!"

"Thank you!" I swept the money out of his hand with a cocky smile intended for him.

"Well..." Edith's voice broke through our silent glare at one another. "If you must know...we had David at a young age...eighteen. We married in October after school and nine months later, David was here. Our fourth of July baby! But after David...we could not seem to have any other children." Edith's expression changed to despair as she thought back to those times. "I had four miscarriages before we gave up. David was the only one...and ten years later we lost him."

"I'm sorry..." Junior whispered.

"Oh, it's okay," Edith smiled falsely. "We learned to just get over it, get on with life and just enjoy our boy for the time we had him...and now we are trying to remain understanding of the many things life throws at you. So... that is why we never had any more children; it just was not possible for us. We were, and are, content with that."

"I'm sorry too," I whispered, my eyes solemnly looking at only Edith.

"It's okay..." Edith smiled. "I know in my heart that David is gone... I felt that way the day after that first night. As a mother, you just know when your child is hurt or in any pain. That connection is strong, and I knew my David was gone; that connection I felt with him...broke. I know he is above us all now, watching us and protecting us... and I know in my heart where he is."

"The railroad..." I mumbled; her eyes connected with mine.

"Yes..." Edith shook her head, "If they would just dig...they would find him...and I would have pe—peace knowing he was home..." a single tear slipped from her eye.

"Knowing exactly where he was..." Junior spoke up.

"Exactly..." Edith wiped the tear. "Having a spot dedicated to his beautiful life and his beautiful name: David Matthew Cole."

"I can understand that..." I smiled sincerely at her while I rolled the dice to continue our game.

"Ah HA!" Edith shouted. "You landed on my land now!"

"Okay, okay!" I surrendered. "How much do I owe you?"

"Whitechapel Road...sixty dollars please, sir!" Edith smiled holding the card that claimed her possession of the road.

We continued playing monopoly, laughing, and talking about our memories and dreams for the remainder of the day until the sun began to set. It remained just the three of us, while Walt sat downstairs welcoming customers in and out. I didn't think they would have many customers, but to my surprise they were fairly busy throughout the day. Edith said the only reason their store made it through the war was because, during those hard times, people needed a laugh; she was right. Their store provided some light and hope when things became dark.

Kids could come in to play with the toys and games, while their mothers were working at various jobs throughout town. Edith explained that parents would come into their store asking what toy their child enjoyed most when they came in to visit. Walt and Edith had a talent for knowing each child by name, and they assisted their already busy mothers in finding the perfect gift for their children. Their store was a staple in Charlotte, and it was all because of a boy we never had the opportunity to meet.

Around seven o'clock, Edith pulled out the left-over soup from the night before to warm it up. The store didn't close until the sun was down, when most kids and parents were home for the night. Walt came upstairs occasionally throughout the day to check in on us, but he mostly spent his day downstairs reading his newspapers and enjoying the customers who came through. Edith fixed us bowls of the left-over chicken noodle soup for dinner. While she wanted to wait for Walt to close the store up before eating dinner, she let us go ahead. By seven-thirty Junior and I had already demolished our bowls and were mentally preparing for our journey at midnight.

"Edith..." Junior called out. "I was thinking of putting the map in my backpack...you know just to be sure we have it packed securely before the morning. Is that okay with you?"

"Of course!" Edith replied while helping me pack up the Monopoly board still laying on the floor. "Why don't you two put your bags by the backdoor downstairs. It'll make leaving in the morning a little bit quicker."

"Okay, you don't think Walt would mind us going downstairs for a second?" Junior asked while reaching up into the cabinet, pulling out the map of North Carolina where Edith had circled Raleigh and marked the roads to take.

"No...he should be locking the doors any minute now," she smiled.

I threw in the last pieces of the wooden placeholders used for the game into the box before Edith closed the lid to stack it on the kitchen table. I rushed over to the couch to help Junior as he grabbed our bags. Junior tossed me mine and I quickly peaked inside to ensure Winston was securely packed.

'He's there—He's there—' I reassured myself.

Not having been downstairs but only the one time when we first got there, I followed behind Junior for direction. Edith followed behind me telling us the story of when they first purchased their 1929 Model A pickup parked out back. She said when they bought that pickup, they felt like they finally made it financially in this world. It was not just a truck to them; it was a lifelong investment.

We found Walt sitting in the same chair he had been in when we met him. His blue eyes grew wide from behind the frames at the sight of us coming down the stairs.

"Edith... boys..." He stood up immediately in disbelief. "I thought we agreed you were both to stay upstairs until we leave tomorrow!"

"Oh, Walt, relax, they are just putting their bags by the back door for tomorrow. Besides, the store is closing soon anyway," Edith put her arm around Walt who tried desperately to relax and remain calm, but the anxiety in his eyes was evident.

He was irate with his wife's decision to bring us downstairs but kept his comments to himself. I followed behind Junior, who ignored Walt's remarks and made a sharp left once he stepped down into the store. I tried my best to avoid eye contact with the panicked Walt, but his eyes were hard to miss. I smiled blankly at him as I followed Junior into a nook that led to their back door.

The nook was hidden from view of the register and crammed tight with books, papers, hats, and coats. Junior found a spot under an old wooden bench by the door for us to store our backpacks. Junior pointed to a hook next to the door where two metal keys were hanging.

"Well boys, did you find a spot for your bags?" Edith joined us with a polite smile across her face. She looked around the nook seeming slightly embarrassed by the cluttered mess. "Sorry...I know we are a tad—disorganized."

"We found a place for them," I pointed at our bags that were tucked away under the bench.

"Excellent!" Edith turned sharply on her toes to look back in Walt's direction and whispered to us, "let's head back upstairs before Walt loses it with each of us."

Junior and I looked at each other and smiled quietly.

Just before we were to walk out of the nook, we heard the bells jingle at the front door. Without a moment of hesitation, Edith put her arms around us as though guarding us from the unknown. I could hear the slow and firm footsteps of what sounded like an adult walking through the store. Edith remained quiet, refusing to speak aloud to us or to Walt. Eventually, Walt's voice sounded from the register questioning the stranger who had entered.

"Well, good evening again, sir. We are just about to close our store for the night. Is there anything else I could help you find before we closed for the day?" Walt's voice remained relaxed and calm as I traced his footsteps around the register.

"No...actually I'm looking for someone..." the stranger's voice was deep and husky, the same voice from this morning. "Well...two people...actually...two children..."

"Oh," Walt's tone changed. "Who exactly are you looking for?"

"One of the two carries the name Henry, but prefers to be called Junior," The man's tone grew deeper as his footsteps drew closer. "The other one has the name James...but prefers the name Jamie...I'd just like to have a word with them...if you don't mind...sir."

"I have never heard of those children before," Walt's voice never faltered as he responded. "Are they new here in town?"

"You could say that, yes..." The man answered quickly.

Edith turned sharply to us, her hands on each of our cheeks and her eyes steady and direct. Her voice was lower than a whisper, "grab your bags, the keys, and leave..."

"No..." I mouthed; my eyes began to swell with tears and my voice thankfully failed. "Not without you..."

"It'll be okay..." She wiped the tears from our eyes. "It will all be okay... now go..."

Junior didn't wait any longer. He turned sharply on his toes, grabbing our bags and the keys hanging off the hook. He was tearful but determined just the same. Edith opened the door quietly and pushed us out into the alleyway. Junior moved hurriedly over to the truck and threw our bags in the front seat before turning around to find me. I remained frozen in the dimly lit alleyway looking desperately at Edith as my vision blurred with tears that now fell. She reached into the front pocket of her dress and pulled out a revolver.

"Take this...use it if you need it...only if you need it..." Edith smiled slightly through the tears that trickled quickly down her cheeks. "We love you both...now, don't look back..."

"No—" It felt as though I was losing my mother all over again.

Junior's footsteps ran up behind me, pulling and guiding me to the truck. Edith smiled...smiled without any hint of fear. She smiled with a love that we carried for years.

She closed the backdoor and turned the lock, now barricading herself and Walt inside the store they built from the ground up. They had no escape—

Junior continued to pull, push, and force me into the truck. Our backpacks thrown onto the floorboards trapped my feet from moving any further. I couldn't find the strength to push myself into the passenger seat as my mind wandered frantically inside the store we were leaving behind. It was then I found myself wanting and hoping for a quick death to end our journey. Wanting to take the place of the innocent people we were leaving to an undoubtably dire fate.

It was Junior who found the strength for both of us. He showed no signs of hesitation. He continued to shove me, forcing my body to move with greater force until I finally landed into my place as the passenger. Junior took his position as the driver slamming the door shut. His hands shook nervously as he attempted to jam the keys into the ignition.

Watching as my brother failed over and over to throw the keys into the ignition, I found the voice inside me. Drawing in a deep breath I bellowed, "hurry!" at my fumbling brother.

After several more attempts to shove the keys in the ignition, he finally succeed. The engine started and Junior's face glowed with considerable relief, when two horrifying loud pops came from the direction of the shop. We knew in that moment that death now lay on the floors of the store that was meant for so much life.

I found myself staring blankly in utter disbelief at Junior who had been quietly reciting the steps for starting the truck. He knew we could not afford the seconds it would cost us if we stalled.

Taking in a deep breath, Junior pumped the clutch and shifted the truck into gear. The truck started out rough originally, with sharp jolts, but it eventually smoothed out as he shifted for a second time. The truck picked up speed driving down the alleyway and I got onto my knees to look back at the store in the distance. Through the darkness, I was able to make out movement near the back door of the store. From what my vision allowed; it seemed as though the door was opened abruptly as a shadowy figure rushed out onto the middle of the alleyway. The man raised his arm and I knew what was about to happened.

"Duck!" I dropped my head below the window as I yelled at Junior, who responded almost immediately.

Junior slid down so his head would be covered by the seat, but his hands retained the sturdy grip on the wheel. Two pops sounded again, and bullets burst through the glass in the small back window and through to the windshield.

More pops followed the first. Junior and I found ourselves screaming as bullets ricocheted off the bed of the truck.

"Drive! Drive!" I yelled as I gripped the seat below me tightly.

"I'm tryin'! I'm tryin'!" Junior hollered.

He peered slightly over the steering wheel to be sure we were still heading in the right direction. Junior turned the truck to the right as he pulled sharply out onto the main road leading to the highway. The force of the turn threw me onto the floorboard.

The firing ceased. Junior pulled himself back up in the driver's seat, holding tightly onto the steering wheel as he mumbled inaudibly to himself while shifting into the next gear to pick up more speed.

"Jamie? Jamie?" Junior called out while looking frantically behind us and back to the road. "Are you—are you okay?"

"Yeah...yeah...I'm alright..." I mumbled dazedly, pulling myself back up to the seat. I did my best to wipe off as much glass from the seat as I could when I took notice of the back window. There was hardly any glass left.

"Is anyone following us?" Junior asked with desperation.

Scanning the dark road behind us, I could tell instantly—we were alone.

"No...no, Junior, wh—"

"Good, okay—Jamie, get the map out and tell me how to get to Raleigh," he desperately breathed.

I grabbed Junior's bag, threw my hand inside to feel for the map with my fingertips and found it in a matter of seconds. I tried to adjust my eyes quickly to the darkness so I could read off the directions for my brother. I anxiously tried to pinpoint where we were according to the map, but my eyes would not focus long enough on one thing to figure out what to tell him. I stammered as I tried to find any helpful words, but nothing came out. All my mind could see or focus on was Edith's face as she shut the door.

'Why didn't she come with us?' I thought angrily to myself while my eyes stared blankly at the map. 'Why—why?'

"JAMIE!" Junior shouted while driving as quickly but steadily as he could through unfamiliar roads. "Anything? Anything would be helpful right now!"

"I'm sorry! I ca-I can't," I stuttered anxiously.

"It's fine..." Junior breathed. "Look for State Highway 27...I'm taking that!"

"State Highway 27?" I questioned as my eyes were still fighting to focus.

"Yes!" Junior screamed. "State Highway 27... hold on—"

"I'm looking!" I shrieked back as my eyes finally found the road he asked for. "Okay, okay! It leads us east and across a river, eventually connecting to Highway 64 to Raleigh!"

"Perfect..." Junior mumbled, his mouth barely moving as he spoke with his eyes remaining fixated on the dark road ahead.

Once again, we were on our own, and I was becoming dismally doubtful that things would end okay for us. It all seemed hopelessly pointless.

"Junior..." my eyes fixed in a gaze staring down at the floorboard.

"I know...I know..." he breathed deeply while studying the road intently.

"Junior—"

"Yes!" Junior slammed his hand on the steering wheel. "I know, Jamie! We were leaving tonight to protect them...we were trying to protect them...we were try—trying to protect them..."

"How did he—"

"Probably that slick bastard Murray!" Junior hollered as his head turned sharply in my direction.

"Junior—" I was shocked at the abruptness in his voice.

"What?" He questioned loudly. "What would you like me to call him? A gentleman? Well Jamie, he isn't. He is an awful person who deserves to be in jail or worse! Because of him, Edith and Walt...Edit—"

Junior couldn't finish the thought. His eyes glazed over with tears that he seemed to have no control over. He was furious. I thought I had seen Junior enraged before but never like this. His hands were gripped so tightly around the steering wheel that his knuckles became pale. I didn't know what to say to him. He was right, the reason we were leaving at midnight tonight was to prevent this from being their fate. We did not want to be the reasons they were in danger. Daddy was after Junior and me, no one else. No one else should have been in danger because of us. The loss of Walt and Edith was now the catalyst that drove a new anger and determination in Junior.

"Once this is over," Junior's tone lightened as he spoke this time. "Once we are safe and all of this is over, if that ever happens, we're going back to Charlotte to find them."

"But Junior, I don't think they—"

"We will find them, and we will tell police about the evidence they collected regarding David's abduction," Junior explained. "We will help David get the justice he deserves and bring him home...okay? We will do this, for Walt and Edith."

"Deal," I smiled over at my brother through the darkness.

A sense of pride came over me. Pride in how mature he had become over the course of only a few days. He wasn't thinking solely about himself anymore. Finally, Junior became the man of the family he had set out to be. He became the protector and leader at the tender age of only thirteen.

"Junior—" I started thinking about the logistics of this trip and the gas it would take us. "—will we have enough gas for the whole trip?"

"Walt said he had a few gas cans in the back...he said he was going to fill them up before tomorrow morning," Junior explained intently. "I don't know if he did or not...it should only take three and a half to four hours to get there."

"Wait...Jun—" I hadn't even considered that we didn't have an address to MeeMaw and Pa's home until then. All I could remember was they owned a farm, but we had never been there, and I had never listened to any additional details given. "Where do MeeMaw and Pa live? I know they live on a farm but where?"

"Check my bag...in the front pocket there should be a torn paper," he nodded in the direction of his bag on the floorboard.

I reached in the front pocket of his bag and immediately found the paper he described. It was a paper torn out from Momma's address book. Scrawled on the paper with Momma's all too familiar handwriting was the address of MeeMaw and Pa.

Johnnie and Vera Williams

10 Wheatstone Ln

Raleigh, North Carolina

"How?" I pondered, stunned by the unnoticed cleverness of my older brother.

"Not me—" Junior confessed. "Momma gave it to me the night we tried to leave all together. Once I made it down the stairway, she passed it to me before she sent me to the back door."

"Really?" I was in shock.

"Yep..." Junior smiled at me with pride. "Smart of her though...but it makes me question if that was how Daddy knew we were leaving. Maybe he found the page torn out of the book."

"But if he did, don't you think he would have asked for it when he caught us?" I wondered.

"Maybe, or maybe he just questioned Momma about it once we were back in our rooms. He may not have thought she'd pass it to me..." Junior speculated.

"I didn't even know she passed it to you!" I laughed.

"Well, I'm sorry," he grinned. "I honestly forgot I even had it on me. So much has happened, I didn't remember until you mentioned it."

"Well, that was smart of you and Momma..." I said with much relief. We had a truck; we had money and now we had an address of our final destination. "I hope Daddy isn't following us...this truck isn't hard to spot with all the bullet holes in it."

"That is why we aren't going to stop much," Junior's eyes focused on the road. "I'm driving 45 miles per hour. Walt said this truck gets about 10 to 15 miles per gallon and it's about 150 miles to Raleigh. So, I calculated that we'd only use about half a tank... So, Walt said he was gonna fill up some gas cans and throw them in the back of the truck. Do you see them?"

I turned back to look in the bed and saw three gas cans laying down flat. Thankfully, the bullets that ricocheted off the truck missed the gas cans, and a smile grew on my face. We had something for the road ahead.

"Yep! They're back there! I don't know if there all filled though..." I sat back down, looking out at the road ahead.

"Well...we only have a little less than half a tank now..." Junior thought out loud. "And if those cans back there aren't filled...we're gonna need to find gas somewhere."

"Junior...if we have to stop to get gas, we will catch people's attention. You know...with bullet holes and two children driving..." I gestured with my hands.

"You're right...you're right," Junior sighed, thinking desperately for a solution.

"We could —" I began but the words I was about to say just didn't seem right coming from me. Junior took notice of my hesitation.

"What? We could what, Jamie?" He egged me to continue.

"Steal...from other people's gas cans...from homes along the way...only if we need to." I suggested as my eyes fixed onto my feet. "Or — steal from people's cars a-along the way..."

"Siphoning?" Junior asked.

"Yeah..." I whispered. "Bad idea?"

"Bad?!" Junior exclaimed. "It's genius! That way we aren't spotted by anyone in the towns as we pass through. We'll just need to find a hose, but I think we could find one on the way. Jamie you're a genius!"

"Yeah?" I was shocked by his response.

"Yes!" He exclaimed again. "You know what? I think I've raised you right!"

"Learned from the best!" I grinned over at Junior.

"Jamie..." Junior whispered with sincerity. "I want to apologize for being rude to you—you know, while you were growing up. You didn't deserve that, especially when we were all dealing with Daddy being gone. And then again as we dealt with him being home — so distant...but home—"

"It's okay," I reassured him. "You're my brother. Besides, if you were nice to us back then we would have thought you were sick or something."

"Yeah—" Junior chuckled. "I guess so...Well, I'm sorry nonetheless..."

"All forgiven," I reassured him.

"You're my little brother and I shouldn't have called you all of those things," he admitted. "Nor should I have told you to grow up. I really am—"

"Oh Junior, you and I both know I was, and still am, sensitive. And unfortunately, I'd say we both need to grow up now," I gestured towards the road. "It's not really like we have a choice, is it."

"Yeah..." His laughter held some nervousness. "I guess you're right..."

"Momma would be proud of us, you know?" I whispered. "If she could see us right now, you and me getting along and working together. She'd be proud."

"Yeah...and Davie would probably fake throw up multiple times at the sight of us!" Junior snickered.

"And make some ridiculous joke causing us all to laugh," I continued.

Junior and I continued in laugher. Laughter at the memories of Davie and the moments that could have been. But that wasn't our reality. Our reality consisted of the dark and empty road to absolute uncertainty that lay ahead of us. We were desperate to get to Raleigh, and to finally feel safe again.

So, as we continued down the highway headed towards Raleigh in silence, I couldn't help but think about Walt and Edith. I thought of how unfair their lives had been. How they had to suffer the ultimate price because of us two kids. If they had not opened their home to us, they'd be safe and unharmed right now. They would have continued their lives in search of answers and hard evidence that would support their speculation concerning the disappearance of their own son— speculation that could have eventually led to the recovery of their one and only child.

I longed for them to have peace even in their death. To give them the burial of their precious child. A burial plot that will have his name forever etched onto stone. And I knew that between Junior and I, we could do that. We could bring their missing child home and end the mystery that haunted the Cole's for decades.

But for now, we were just two brothers on the road, driving past endless fields in the dark, with nothing but three gas cans, two bags, a revolver, an address, and each other for company.

Chapter 15

Not a single truck or car came into sight as we traveled northeast. It was just Junior and me, the night sky, an old truck, and enough silence to last a lifetime. We had only been driving for a little less than an hour although there was no way to truly tell. There was no clock, radio, or GPS as there is nowadays. We had to figure it out as we drove, with only the starlight to guide us along the way.

The total darkness and stillness of the night caused my overactive mind to nearly spin out of control. With each passing tree, I could see Edith's smile. Even through everything she suffered, she never lost her smile. As the silence continued without wavering, Davie's infectious laughter filled my heart. It was that infectious laughter that defined him and kept us all smiling during those difficult years of the war. A cold breeze blew, and my eyes shut automatically remembering the comforting and warm embrace Momma provided whenever any of us felt alone or defeated. She offered us the comfort we all needed whenever we needed it. It was because of that love she instilled in us that gave us the ability to even work together. And finally, the fresh smell of pine circulated around the cab of the truck, and I remembered the permeating aroma of Walt's cigars. It reminded me of the times when Uncle Tommy and Daddy would smoke together out on our porch. Momma would leave them outside when they brought out the cigars claiming that the smell would linger in her hair for weeks after.

All these memories of our loved ones gone too soon continued to flow through my mind and would have probably continued if not for Junior. His voice broke through the silence that had dominated the cab with a comment purely intended for mere small talk.

"It's beautiful out here..." He mumbled. "Don't you think?"

"Yeah—it's very...calm out here." I pulled myself up and stuck my head out the window to feel the breeze blow through my hair. "You can see all the stars in the sky out here. I wonder what time it is?"

"Well, I think we've been on the road for about forty minutes..." Junior looked intently at the fuel gauge. "Jamie...look at the next sign so we can figure out where we are on that map."

"Um...okay, hold on—" I looked closely for a sign but there was nothing. It was so dark out with only a rare amount of light luminating the area. The wind created a howling sound as it blew through the cab.

After a few minutes of searching for anything that would give me an idea of where we were located, a sign appeared in the near distance. As it grew closer, I squinted to make out the printed words. Even with glasses, my vision still was not perfect.

"Badin...?" I questioned my own vision. "Badin Lake?"

"A lake?" Junior reiterated.

I checked closely on the map and found almost immediately where we were. We were soon to hit a curve in the highway that would lead us to a bridge that would carry us over Badin Lake and into Asheboro.

I relayed the information I had gathered over to Junior and he nodded with understanding remaining concentrated on the road.

The road began to curve alongside Badin Lake, just as I had said. The dimly lit headlights revealed a grove of trees off to the right side of the road. Junior slowed the truck and pulled off the road carefully towards the grove of the trees. Once the truck was concealed from the road, Junior cut the engine and lights off, immersing us in complete darkness.

"Stay in here," Junior whispered to me as he stepped out into the night.

Not wanting to be left alone in the sickening stillness of the cab, I jumped up to join him. Being alone was not much comfort to me anymore, as it had once been. I popped the latch of the passenger side door and jumped out to join my brother at the bed of the truck.

"I asked you to stay in the truck…" Junior sighed at the sight of me.

"I—I just want to help," I begged. "Please! I should at least know how to fill up the gas tank. Please, Junior."

"Fine—only one can is filled anyways…the rest are empty…" Junior softly kicked the emptied cans. "Okay then… carry this can for me."

I grabbed the filled can from his hand and waited for him to jump off the truck and onto the ground. I followed behind him closely around the truck and to the front of the cab.

"Okay—Jamie, I'll help hoist you onto the hood of the truck," he gave me directions. "You see that metal cylinder just in front of the windshield?"

"Yeah—"

"Screw the cap off and that is where you'll pour the gasoline in…" he explained softly. "Do you understand?"

"I think so—"

"Yes or no, Jamie?"

"Yes—Yes sir! I understand…I can do this…" I said out loud, trying to convince my own self.

Junior positioned his hands low for me to step onto.

"Come on, Jamie," he encouraged. "I'll hoist you up."

Stepping one foot onto his hand and my left hand holding onto the hood, he lifted me, hoisting me onto the hood.

"Perfect!" Junior cheered. "Now…unscrew the cylinder and pour it in!"

Carefully I poured the gas in and prided myself by not spilling a single drop. Daddy taught all three of us how to take care of automobiles, but Junior and Davie were more hands on than I. I enjoyed watching and learning everything I could more than the actual doing. So, as I helped Junior with even the simplest of tasks, I took more pride in myself than others would have.

"Nice job, Jamie," Junior congratulated me as he helped me down to the ground.

Walking back to the bed of the truck, I felt a little cocky as I threw the empty can into the bed. Junior walked over to the tailgate and pulled it down to ensure all three cans were secured in the bed before driving off again.

It was then that he stopped, fixing his eyes onto something he could see inside the bed. Without saying a word to me, he jumped up into the bed of the truck and bent down to pick something up. Slowly Junior stood holding onto a long clear hose.

"Where did this come from?" Junior asked me.

"I—don't know," I replied.

"Jamie…we can use this!" Junior hollered.

"We can?"

"Yes, Jamie! You're the one who thought of the idea!" He rolled his eyes.

"For siphoning!" I remembered.

"This is excellent, Jamie...there shouldn't be any problems getting gas now," Junior smiled brightly at me. "Hold onto this, Jamie...and don't lose this. This will be your job, okay?"

I grabbed the hose from Junior as he jumped off the back of the truck with a sharp smile across his face. He threw the tailgate back up into place and threw his arm over my shoulders as we walked back to the cab to continue our journey.

There was still not the slightest activity on the road in front of us. The road remained dark and empty. Junior cranked up the truck without a single problem, as though he had done this multiple times before. I could tell he was starting to get a little big headed with his driving abilities.

We followed the curve in the road leading to a bridge that carried us over Badin Lake. The narrow bridge was bumpy with many inconsistencies the entire way across. You could tell the road had not been maintained. Looking out in the direction of the lake, I couldn't even see the outline of the water. All that was visible to our eyes was the road just ahead being illuminated by the truck's dim head lights.

We made our way across to the other side of the lake, and an outline of an old white house with a darker roof appeared. The house was not too far away from the lake. Like our home back in Charleston, there was a darker and rustic garage detached from the home. Parked just out front were a couple of old sedans.

First thing that came to my mind—was gas.

I didn't even have to point this thought out to Junior for him to understand. Just as I began to think of the amount of gas in each of those vehicles, Junior pulled the truck over behind an oak tree away from the lake but still hidden from view of the house and the road. Junior silenced the truck and flicked the lights off quickly.

"Stay here—"

"No—" I protested. "I'm going with you!"

"Keep your voice down..." Junior shot at me. "We need gas...they have to have lots. From their vehicle and inside that garage. Remember how many cans Momma and Daddy kept?"

"Close to ten—"

"Exactly!" His eyes narrowed. "Jamie, I need you here...if you came with me, it would just distract me. I'd be worried the entire time about you being caught. No one will see you from here...you'll be safe."

"But I can't drive—"

"It's easy, Jamie listen," Junior mimicked how to turn the ignition as he tried desperately for me to understand. "Turn the fuel on, there is a valve here at the bottom...make sure the truck is in neutral by moving it around to ensure you aren't in gear...the spark needs to be up all the way and the throttle down a little...alright...so look Jamie...look at my feet. This is a footrest...this is the gas...and the little silver button in the far back is the starter...so, once the key is in the ignition, throttle is down and spark is up, you're ready. At the same time... you need to press on the starter and pull the spark down...got that? This is the parking brake...you'll release this—"

He continued to explain how to start this truck and I tried desperately to keep up with him, but I couldn't. My mind was flooding with thoughts of Junior getting caught or attacked by some sort of lake creature. Everything Junior told me went in one ear and out the other. I tried to look as though I was keeping up with his explanation by nodding occasionally and saying 'got it' throughout his demonstration just to keep him talking.

"—now the gears are in an H pattern...so up to the left is reverse. You'll have the clutch in, which is here," he pointed to the left side of the floor under the steering wheel. "Slowly release the clutch as you press on the gas as you reverse out from behind the tree. Straight down is first gear, release the gas and press in the clutch again, and do that again. Up diagonal right is second gear...and down again...third. And that—well, that's it—it's quite simple..."

Junior looked up at me with a smile of encouragement as he waited for me to give a response. I had no idea what to tell him. I struggled to find the words; I then decided my best option was to say with believable enthusiasm, 'got it!'

"Look, you probably won't even need to drive this..." Junior became optimistic. "Just trust me...stay here and keep your voice down and stay out of sight, got it?"

"—but"

"Jamie...please," Junior begged.

"—okay"

Junior grabbed the hose next to him on the seat and hugged me tight before slapping my back and slipping out the door. I watch him from the silence of the truck jump quietly into the bed to grab the three empty cans. He crept through the trees in the night towards the quiet farmhouse that had only a single porch light revealing the home. The garage was about fifty yards from the truck, and I sat uneasily as I watched Junior's every move. He kept his body close to the ground to remain hidden from any person who might look out the window from the second floor.

He made it!

Junior reached the first car, a sedan, which held a strong resemblance to the Ford we owned back home. He knelt behind the front right tire as he uncurled the hose he held in his hands. He positioned the three cans to his side preparing for a quick transfer once the flow began. I saw the outline of Junior's body peer over the hood of the car to ensure he was in the clear. So far, the house remained quiet.

Junior stepped onto the tire, pushing himself up onto the hood to unscrew the gas cap. Just as he got himself up to the top of the sedan, a deep and pugnacious bark erupted disrupting the quietness of the night. My heart leapt into my throat as I scanned the area for the source of the bark. I saw Junior pull his legs up on top of the hood of the sedan, just as a tall, muscular, white dog with a curled tail charged at him from the porch. The dog didn't jump up onto the truck, though it wouldn't have had any trouble reaching Junior. Instead, it positioned itself with its back to the garage and facing the cowering Junior. The dog's front legs braced themselves as if for a possible attack. The barking ceased but even from our truck, I could hear a low menacing growl. My body dropped in the seat, leaving only my eyes visible.

Junior slowly repositioned himself into a sitting position on the hood of the sedan, his legs tightly pulled into his body as he showed his hands, appearing as though he was surrendering himself to the dog.

The windows on the second floor glowed with light as the owners awoke from the alert given by their guard dog. I began hyperventilating as the situation continued to intensify. I found my hand gripped tightly around the handle of the door, preparing myself to sacrifice my life for the safety of my remaining brother.

Just as I released the latch to the door, the dog who once had a predatory stance, relaxed. The dog's tail began to wag with sudden enthusiasm. I scanned the area around Junior to find the source of the dog's newfound tranquility but saw nothing. Junior slowly slid down to the front of the sedan and the dog walked cheerfully over to him, accepting Junior as a friend. Junior rubbed the dog's head and the dog seemed to enjoy it. He had made an ally with the dog.

Suddenly, the front door burst open to reveal a man in a white shirt and beige pants with one suspender hooked on, while the other one hung freely to his side. Gripped fiercely in his hands was a shotgun.

"Nellie!?" The man bellowed. "Whatcha see, girl!"

The dog named Nellie turned her head in the direction of her owner and then quickly back to Junior. She let off a high-pitched whine before running off to her owner. I saw Junior take the given opportunity to pull himself under the truck, avoiding too much noise or notice to himself. With the grass around the car being long and unkept, he was hidden decently.

One of the gas cans fell over while the other two remained upright. The owner didn't hesitate; he fired a bullet into the air as a warning shot for his unexpected guest before making his way out onto the property to search with Nellie by his side. The man crept slowly over to the garage where he had seen Nellie standing.

'Pull the gas cans in, Junior, pull the cans in!' I yelled in my head hysterically as I watched the man pass the front of the truck.

I pulled myself up and over into the driver's seat. My hands shook fiercely at the wheel while I gripped the key in front of the ignition. I thought intently about the options that were in front of me. I could continue to hide out here in the truck until the man passed by Junior and hopefully returned inside. Or I could reverse this truck out of the trees and onto the road to fool the man into thinking the intruder had escaped. I wanted so desperately to run, to save the day, but my body wouldn't move. I was frozen in that truck, unable to decide and unable to help.

'I'm a sissy...I'm nothing but a sissy,' I cried to myself, in my head. 'How could I stand by while my brother was in danger? I would never be like Junior; a risk taker, a protector, or a leader...I would never amount to anything!'

Opening my eyes, I looked back at the scene by the sedan and noticed immediately that the gas cans were gone, and the man was now standing with his shotgun lowered in front of the sedan that was concealing Junior. He looked hopeless as he scanned his property in search of the person or object that caught his dog's attention. But there was nothing for him to see. Our truck and Junior were hidden from view and the gas cans were gone.

Nellie was no longer interested in Junior but focused solely on her owner while he stood there in silence. After a few minutes he turned to retreat inside his home, ending his search. My body relaxed as the man moved further away from Junior. Once he reached the porch, he turned to look one last time at his property, still unsure of what he heard. Nellie obediently followed him up to the porch with her mouth open and tail wagging. He patted her head before withdrawing into his home. The downstairs lights turned off and soon the second floor turned dark. The porch lights still luminated the driveway just enough to see Nellie run back over to Junior who was now crawling out from his hiding spot. Nellie wagged her tail at the sight of her new friend.

Nellie was one of the largest dogs I had ever seen. She sat upon Junior's command; her eyes were fixed on him. I was amazed by his ability to communicate with this dog seemingly so easily. As Nellie sat patiently, Junior bent down to pick up the gas cans and hose to finish the job. He turned in my direction to give me a sign that all was okay.

Junior leaped back onto the hood of the sedan and returned to business. He finished unscrewing the gas cap, shoved the hose into the hole and slid off the hood. Grabbing the empty gas cans, he positioned one of them so the gas would fall easily into the can. By putting his mouth to the hose, he began siphoning the gas. The process of siphoning went by quicker than I had anticipated; in no time he was done with both cans. Not long after he grabbed the second can, he pulled out the hose, picked up the cans and ran back through the property to our truck with Nellie following closely behind. I decided to remain in the truck to prevent her from becoming defensive and possibly waking up her owner again.

Junior placed the cans in the bed of the truck and walked swiftly to the passenger door to speak to me.

"I got those two cans filled up—each can is about 5 gallons each..." Junior was out of breath. "I'm going back...I'm going to check the garage to see if there is another vehicle inside...try to fill up the last can...just in case we need it. I'll be back—"

"Don't leave..." I begged him.

"I'll be back, Jamie," he smiled. "I promise, now stay here."

I nodded, unable to speak as Junior jumped back out of the truck and darted into the dark with Nellie still by his side. He reached the garage and crept in through the garage door. He and Nellie entered, and they were gone from my sight, leaving me alone again with nothing but the darkness and leaving my mind to, of course, become overrun with thoughts of complete turmoil. I thought about how neat Davie would have thought Junior was right then and there. I thought about how proud Momma would have been to see her two boys working together for once rather than working apart. Funny how it took our life turning upside down to realize that we actually meant something to each other.

Minutes after he went inside the garage, Junior came out struggling but holding four cans in his arms and the hose hanging out his back pocket. I had never felt such pride in my brother before, we now had six full gas cans. Junior reached our truck, dumped the new gas cans into the bed of the truck and ran by the window with his finger up as though saying, 'one minute.' Nellie's tongue was hanging out of her mouth with excitement as she chased Junior through the yard. Junior seemed to be enjoying her company as well. And just as fast as he went into the garage, he was out with another four cans and a toothy smile that could be seen for miles.

He placed the two of the cans into the bed of the truck before heading to the hood with the other two cans. He place one gas can on the hood and pulled himself up to get to the gas tank. He poured the two cans into the tank perfectly, filling up the truck without a single spill.

Placing the two empty cans in the bed, he opened the driver's side door with pride written across his forehead.

"We did it!" Junior smiled as he tossed the hose onto the floorboard.

"We?" I grinned. "You did it…not me."

"You are always helping by just being alive…" he smirked. "We have ten cans full of gas…think that's enough?"

"Definitely," I beamed back at him.

Next to Junior breathing just as heavily was Nellie. She was even more gorgeous up close. Her white furred face with black ears and snout gave deeper definitions to her features. She had a demeanor of strength and dominance but a personality of loyalty and faithfulness. She licked Junior's hand as though asking him if they would run again. Junior laughed at her and patted her head, which she seemed to enjoy.

"Jamie…meet Nellie," Junior smiled proudly.

"Hi Nellie," I beamed as I moved over for her to sniff my hand before patting her head.

"Alright so… we have ten full cans. Five almost six gallons in each, so about fifty gallons total," Junior closed his eyes tightly as he intently calculated the amount of gallons we had total. "We will have plenty of gas to get to Raleigh and more…just in case we need it. Are you ready?"

"I think so…" I answered, enjoying Nellie's company.

"Alright…let me take her back," Junior smirked looking down at Nellie. "Come on Nellie, let's go!"

Nellie's eyes shot up to Junior and followed him closely across the yard back to the truck. Junior made her sit before he patted her head saying say goodbye. She licked him across his face to say her own goodbye. Junior turned in my direction and sprinted across the yard leaving Nellie behind. This was one of the best and most positive encounters we had had with anyone or anything since we began this journey. Not that Edith and Walt were negative or awful encounters…no. But because of us they lost their lives, making the entire experience negative and us full of guilt. But Nellie…Nellie was the first one we had met since the day we left Charleston that didn't die as a result of our being there. This moment was needed and almost therapeutic for the both of us.

Junior made it back to the truck with pride in his eyes, and it was refreshing seeing Junior this way again. He jumped into the driver's seat and sang out in cheer as he started the truck with such ease. Watching Junior, I knew I could not have done that. Junior threw the vehicle in reverse, backed out from behind the tree, and pulled out onto the road. He stopped briefly to look at Nellie and the house one final time before leaving.

"One day, Jamie...I'm going to get myself a house just like that," he said grinning with pride. "A nice house on the lake where I can fish any day and any time!"

"With a big farm dog like her?" I asked.

"Yes...just like her!" Junior agreed.

"I want a big porch...just like we had back home," I reminisced on our Charleston home.

"I do too," Junior agreed. "A wrap-around porch."

"You think we will get there one day?" I questioned, thinking about what slim chances we had at having a happy and normal life.

I watched Junior's smile fade slowly before he turned his head towards me. I could see the concern in his eyes thinking of the comment I made. I could tell he was actively thinking about what he could possibly say to comfort my thoughts. Like I said before, Junior was never good at showing his feelings before all of this happened. It took escaping death multiple times for him to begin to see and think of things differently.

"I promise you..." Junior whispered softly shifted his gaze back to the road. "I will not let anything happen to you. He will not touch you or hurt you ever again. No one will. As long as I am alive, I won't let anything happen to you..."

I nodded quietly, and taking in a deep breath before speaking, "I wish I could be more help. I wish I weren't—afraid of everything...Davie could hav—"

"Davie would be proud of you...and so would Momma," Junior interrupted. "You are ten years old...you shouldn't be—we shouldn't be expected to do any of this. But you...you are my little brother and my responsibility. You have nothing to be ashamed of, okay?"

A tear slipped through my lashes and ran down my cheek, "I was wrong about you before; I use to think you didn't care about me or Davie."

"I don't—" Junior responded quickly, "did I say that?" he winked at me, reassuring me that it was merely a joke. "Alright, let's get going, Jamie...we've got grandparents to see!"

We continued down the dark and thankfully still empty road. At this point we had to have been on our journey for close to two hours, which made me think it was around ten o'clock. Since we now had our own gas in the back of the truck, it eliminated so much extra time we would spend trying to find gas on the road. We were lucky to come across that house on the lake. We were even more lucky be alive, let alone find a house that had filled and ready gas cans. I guess if you live so far out in the country, you need to have extra gas on hand in case of long and unexpected trips. Fortunate for us, but when the owner woke up the next morning missing jerrycans, he might not feel the same way.

I sat with the map in my hands doing all that I could in aiding us in an easy and smooth drive. Since I had no idea how to drive the truck, my job and sole responsibility became giving out directions for our trip. I studied that map, guaranteeing that I knew every roadway, and each turn we would take to reach MeeMaw and Pa's house. We both were obviously exhausted by this point, but we had no choice. We needed to get there. If we pulled off to the side of the road to sleep only to continue our journey tomorrow, we would allow Daddy ample time to catch up with us. Who knew, he could have been following us the entire time with his lights off. What if the entire time we were driving, and working desperately to stay ahead, he was lurking in the shadows behind us, watching.

Junior mostly took everything as it was and continued to do what he needed to do to ensure we both survived.

Me? I couldn't get it out of my head the change that came over Daddy. How could a man, a man we had all looked up to, commit a crime such as this? That question is simple if you think about it from today's understanding; but back then there was no such thing as Post Traumatic Stress Disorder or Psychosis. Daddy should have been seen by a professional, he should have been talked to or listened to. But this world was just too busy to take a moment to worry about the mental state of all the men who came home from war. War is sometimes necessary, but it is still damaging to the ones who are sent. We should have been there for him to ensure the stability of his mental state during those first few months after coming home. But even if we did, would he have listened? Would we have been able to make a difference in him if we had known then what we all know now? It is often thought about, but it is a question that can never truly be answered. All we can do now is learn from the mistakes made then, and make sure that every man or woman who comes home today is given a chance to be heard.

So, as we continued down the road trying, desperately to find some hope and a reason to continue, we joked and recalled old memories of Charleston. Memories of our childhood that were joyous; of Daddy smiling and joking with us every chance he had, of mornings that started with the rhythmic knocks from Uncle Tommy as he joined us for breakfast with his never-ending stories and forever humorous jokes, of Momma's laughter when Daddy would surprise her with flowers throughout the week, and of the way Davie saw the beauty and humor in each and every situation. Remembering that we had a remarkable upbringing up until the war. We tried and wanted to remember the man our father was, not who he is.

Unseen Scars

Our father was a war hero and to this day remains my hero. Regardless of the man he became following the war, he will always be the man who was there cheering me on when I took my first steps in this world. And even though he became the monster in my nightmares each night, I will never forget the man he once was.

Chapter 16

It took an additional two and a half hours on the road until we finally made it onto Highway 64 through Pittsboro and almost into Cary. We did not need to stop for gas but planned on stopping one more time before driving into Raleigh. We weren't running on fumes or anything, but Junior explained to me that we needed to be sure we had plenty of gas, just in case it was "urgently needed." As we edged closer to Raleigh, my mind began to explore the idea of where we would go if this did not work out as planned.

'Where else was there to go?' I thought silently to myself.

I didn't know of any other family members nearby or even afar. Apart from MeeMaw and Pa, there were no other blood relatives that were still alive today. Daddy's parents had passed away many years prior, and Momma and Daddy were only children, so we never had any uncles or aunts, or even cousins. The closest thing we had to an uncle was Uncle Tommy and, unfortunately, he was no longer with us. Thinking of Uncle Tommy brought me back to Joan, whom I hadn't thought of in some time. We had not even the slightest idea of where she could possibly be. I toyed with the idea of searching for her if all else failed; but then there was the fear of putting her and Little Tommy in danger. I could not bring myself to even contemplate doing that to them. I didn't want to put MeeMaw and Pa at risk either, but there just did not seem to be any other alternative than to show up on their doorstep in the middle of the night. I knew they would want us to come to them. I knew they would do just about anything to protect us, even if it did put them into danger.

Junior began to slow the truck down to a stop off to the side of the road. There were no trees to hide behind with this stop, but we only needed to top the tank off.

"This will be just a quick stop," Junior reminded me.

I followed him around to the bed of the truck to help if needed. Junior grabbed only one can to top us off for the last thirty minutes or so of our trip. I was so relieved to think we were almost done with our journey and hopefully to our safety. I couldn't wait to see MeeMaw and Pa again and I trusted they knew exactly what we should do. They knew who Daddy was—the good man he was before he became a monster.

An image popped into my head before I could stop it. I cringed as I visualized Daddy pointing his gun at MeeMaw and Pa, and I imagined their cries as he removed them from this world. My body shuttered at that horrific thought.

'That will not happen this time,' I told myself. 'That will not happen...'

Junior brought me back to our current reality by shouting my name. His voice cut through the cold air like a knife.

"Jamie!?" Junior shouted. "Hurry up! Let's get going!"

"Oh! Sorry, Jun—" I was so lost in thought that I hadn't realized Junior had already filled up the tank, tossed the empty can into the bed, and was now waiting impatiently at the driver's door.

I hurried back to the passenger-side door and quickly jumped in. We were in a hurry to get back on the road and toward MeeMaw and Pa's. It was still dark, and we still had no idea where Daddy was or what he was planning.

The corners of Junior's lips lifted into a smile as I got myself settled in the passenger seat. I had, yet again, become too distracted in my own head to focus on anything else. Yes, I was a bit of a worrier back then and still am today. I guess some things never change.

"Tired?" Junior asked as he pulled the truck back out onto the highway.

"Just thinking...Not tired actually," I answered honestly. "Are you?"

"A little...but I'm okay," Junior shrugged, his eyes fixated on the road ahead. "Just desperate to get there and be done with this..."

"Yeah..." I sighed looking over at Junior as he drove on. "What do you think MeeMaw and Pa will do when we get there?"

"They'll probably make us tell them every single detail of what has happened from the beginning." Junior expressed; his eyes remaining focused intently on the road. "After that...I don't know to be honest with you. I would hope that...it would—" his voice broke off as though he was trying to catch the tears that were attempting to escape. Junior gripped the steering wheel tighter and took a deep breath before continuing. "—I wish that it would all just go back to normal; That we would drive up and Momma and Davie would be sitting on the front porch with MeeMaw and Pa. Davie would be laughing and telling us that we won. That this was all a game to force you and me to get along better — to learn more about each other and appreciate each other more. Momma would hug us, proud that we succeeded. And ... Daddy would walk out onto the porch — as Daddy. Not whoever this is, but as our Daddy — the way I want to remember him. That — that is what I wish would happen when we get there..."

"I wish that too..." I answered softly.

"It isn't fair..." the tone of Junior's voice raised slightly as he continued to try and control his feelings. "How is it that we are the family going through this, you know? We were all so happy...I know you and I didn't exactly see eye-to-eye most days, but regardless. We were a happy family. Momma and Daddy loved each other and were happy. Daddy loved us. It just doesn't make any sense."

"Daddy still loves us Junior. I know it doesn't feel that way. Especially when—"

"—when he's firing bullets at you as you're driving away in a truck?" He interrupted.

"Yes," I replied looking deeply at my brother who so desperately continued to try and hide the emotions he held inside. "But Junior, Daddy does love us. He is just sick. He is sick—"

"How does he love us, Jamie?" Junior's eyes shot over to me in dire need for answers. "Please tell me, because right now...I feel as though my father wants to murder me..."

"He is mentally sick...I heard him...that day." I closed my eyes recalling the words that were said just before I stepped foot in our home. I could see, hear, and feel it all over again. I fought back the urge to cry, not wanting to give in to the depression and anger I had been forced to suppress. Junior waited silently and patiently for me to speak. "He said he wanted us all to be together..."

"What?" Junior, who had returned to watching the road, looked over at me again, before turning back to the road. "How does that make any sense?"

"It doesn't. Junior, he is sick…in his head," I tried to explain to him exactly what I witnessed that day with words that would make it easier for him to understand. Back then, I had never even heard of the word psychosis, and there weren't many—if any—conversations regarding mental health, but I understood Daddy's logic. "He thinks the only way for us to be together is in death…"

"In death? But then…" the pieces to the puzzle began to connect in his mind. "He's going to…"

I didn't know how to say the words that were too dark for young boys to speak. At the tender age of ten years, how could I tell my brother that our father planned on ending his own life as well? I couldn't. All I could do was hang my head and say, "Yes."

I remained quiet in the passenger seat, and eventually I returned to watching the white lines on the road speed past our truck. Junior remained deep in thought and continued to stare straight ahead while digesting this new piece of information. Junior had believed that Daddy performed these acts of true evil because he did not want us as his family anymore — That Daddy had grown too tired and frustrated to continue dealing with us and our baggage. This new detail changed some things for Junior. He didn't look back over to me, nor did he speak. Just as I did, he struggled with the truth. The truth being that as far as our father was concerned, the only way we could remain together as a family — was in death.

Thus, the reason for the chase was to end our lives allowing him to peacefully end his own. He couldn't leave this world until he knew for sure we would be on the other side waiting with Momma and Davie. In

Daddy's mind, this was perfectly logical. Our escaping—not once, but twice—kept putting a dent in his plan. Junior and I both realized that this would never end until he and I were gone — or Daddy was. He would not stop until we were all dead.

From the day Daddy left for the army, Junior's way of coping was through anger and tears, eventually leading to utter silence. His silence was not for any harsh or malicious reason, but because he needed that time to genuinely think things through. All my life, I have been the type of person who needs to talk about any concerns or new understandings out loud to fully process and comprehend a situation. Davie ... well ... Davie would always laugh his way through things. He was, by far, the most carefree of us Clark boys.

I used to argue with Junior, push him to talk. It was what I needed, not him. All it accomplished was increased tension between us. Throughout our journey together, we learned to accept the differences between us and respect them instead.

So, I gave him the silence he longed for in that moment, to process the new details in the privacy of his own mind.

After a while, Junior composed himself and glanced over to me. I continued to gaze out the window, lost in my own thoughts, but could feel his eyes return to me a second and third time.

"So..." his voice was low, almost a whisper. "...this is not going to be easy to end, is it?"

"I don't believe so..." I replied.

"Well—we can do this, Jamie," He had a hint of faint optimism in his tone, as though he had practiced saying this in his head multiple times.

"Can we?"

"Yes." His tone strengthened. "I don't see any outcome though, that will lead us to returning to that old white house with Daddy."

"I know—"

"To be honest with you, Jamie, I don't see a way to get out of this leaving Daddy alive..." Junior's tone softened again. "I can't see how this will end positively."

"We have to try..." I pleaded. "He is still our father, regardless—"

"Regardless?! He murdered our family...Edith and Walt—" Junior desperately tried to remain calm but failed. "How can you even say that?"

"Because he is sick..." I wanted him to understand, but he didn't see things as I saw them.

"No, Jamie...Dad is crazy..." Junior scoffed. "He is crazy, bottom-line."

"Regardless—Junior—we need to wait until we see MeeMaw and Pa." I said, in an unsuccessful attempt to change the subject from Junior's obvious plot of murder.

"Do you still have that gun Edith handed you before we left?" He asked.

"Y-yes," I reached down below my seat where I hid it out of sight as we got out onto the road. I didn't feel comfortable holding onto the revolver, and I felt more uncomfortable realizing Junior planned on using it against Daddy. "But, Junior, maybe we can talk—"

"No!" Junior was undeniably enraged now. "There is no talking to him. There is no pleading with him. There is only defending ourselves against him. He won't stop until we are gone. I don't know how you feel, Jamie, but I plan on having a future..."

"Well, I do too, but—"

"—but nothing! This is the only way..." Junior's eyes became sincere again, as though he began to understand that this was harder for me to grasp than for himself. "Look, I will do it—you won't have to. You can stay hidden."

"All I am saying is let's just wait for MeeMaw and Pa...discuss this with them," my tone changed as I was increasingly desperate for him to hear me out.

"What if Daddy is already there when we arrive?" Junior pointed out.

"Then—we keep driving," I suggested warily.

"To where exactly?" He glanced at me impatiently. "No, Jamie—this ends now. No more discussions about it."

I didn't fight him, I didn't even respond. I allowed us to be engulfed again in the silence of the night. Junior was set on his plan and there was no sense in arguing further with him. Once he made up his mind, there was not much that could persuade him against it.

Besides, I knew that once we arrived at MeeMaw and Pa's house, they could talk him down. They would be able to convince him of a different course of action that wouldn't lead to a duel between father and son.

After another twenty minutes of driving, we turned down Wheatstone Lane feeling both increasingly anxious and undeniably hopeful. We both searched urgently for number 10, that housed the remainder of our family, the last living relatives who, we hoped, would provide an end to this seemingly never-ending nightmare.

At last, we spotted a black mailbox perched on a wooden pole with the number 10 painted on the side. It was placed on the edge of the road next to a long driveway that led to a dark home partially hidden away from the road. It was a quaint two-story white home, like ours, but with a blue roof that was visible even in the darkness of the night sky. There was a worn red brick chimney centered perfectly on the front of the house, with a porch that was smaller than ours and had no railing. A deep brown front door was outlined by a shade of red that matched the chimney. Three steps, made from the same brick as the chimney, led up to the porch in front of the door. Immediately next to the front door were three lovely rectangular windows with blue shutters. The only light that radiated from the home was the small light next to the front door.

In the distance, off to the left of the home was an old barn with a single light revealing the shadowy outline of a tall horse behind what looked like a wooden fence. Similar to our home, close by their pasture, was a chicken coop where I assumed the chickens had put themselves up for the night, away from any danger that lurked in the nearby woods. They had a simple garage offset from the home with colors similar to the color scheme of their house. There was only one car parked in front of the garage. It was a simple car, which was impossible to make out in the darkness of the night. I was starting to breathe a little easier when I realized the car parked there was not the sedan from home. But then again, for all I knew, Daddy could have stolen a new car while on the run.

Junior and I were hesitant as we pulled into their driveway. Ifs and buts were going through my mind faster than anything else had in my entire ten years of life and I noticed my hand gripped the revolver tighter as my anxiety increased. Junior came to a sharp stop a quarter of the way down the driveway and quickly turned the headlights off.

"What—" I whispered warily.

"I'm not parking here—" Junior threw the truck in reverse and backed us out onto the road.

Unseen Scars

He continued down past their driveway until my view of the house was obstructed with trees that lined the road. Junior slowed down again as he pulled in between two trees blocking the view of our truck from both the road and the house. He slowed the truck to a stop and cut the engine.

"This way if he comes...he won't see our truck..." Junior whispered.

"Hopefully..."

"This will work..." His blue eyes found me in the dark. "We will walk up to the house, knock on the door...and just see what happens."

"Junior, what if he is already in there..." I looked nervously over at the house I had been so desperate to see.

"You have the gun—"

"No!" I interrupted.

"Then give me the gun and you can knock on the door..." Junior snapped back at me.

"But—"

"No!" Junior's voice rose with tension. "Listen...I need you to grow up right now. Push back every insecurity, every opinion, and every difference we have. If you want to live...we need to work together. It has to be this way. So, give me the gun and you go knock on the door."

I couldn't answer him, I knew he was right. He'd been right about everything so far on this trip, how could I not trust him now? So, with much reservation, I gave him the revolver. I knew I would not have it in me to pull the trigger if it came down to that.

"I'll knock," I mostly told myself as I handed over the revolver.

"Okay," Junior nodded as he took the gun from my hand. "Now once you knock, I want you to come back to me and look out for me from behind. I will keep my eye on the house...understand?"

My voice was not strong enough to answer through the trepidation that consumed me. Junior took note of this.

"I need you to answer. I need to be sure that you understand me," he pushed me to speak.

"I—" I began, while desperately pushing back the memories of pain, heartbreak, and agony that tried to take over my mind. "I understand, Junior—I understand."

"Okay...let's go," Junior hopped out of the driver's side with the revolver grasped firmly in his right hand.

Junior made his way around the front of the truck as he scanned our surroundings for any signs of danger, but there was nothing. All that could be heard were the distant crickets that announced to the world that nighttime had come.

We walked steadily, side by side, across the yard toward the dimly lit white house. My nerves became more on edge, the closer we got to the house. I tried to think of ways to possibly get out of this. I came up with an idea of how Junior and I could live in the middle of the woods in a tiny tent. We could survive with limited supplies, staying far enough away from the city but close enough to occasionally run in for errands. In that moment, it seemed like a logical idea. If I had any extra strength inside of me, I would have spoken up, but I kept as quiet as the night while we stepped closer and closer into the unknown.

After what felt like a lifetime of walking, we found ourselves staring point blank at the porch door. A cool breeze blew ever so gently, causing the hairs on the back of my neck to rise. The child in me still wanted to run away, but the new, more grown up, ten-year-old me remained in place. Junior was waiting eagerly for me to build up the courage he was so confident I had and step up onto the porch and knock on the door — but there was nothing. I felt five years old again, desperate to run into my momma's arms for comfort and safety or hide under my bed sheets to get away from the monsters that I was certain lived under my bed.

Junior's arms wrapped around me from behind in a tight embrace. He rested his chin on my shoulder and I could feel his breath brush against my cheek. I realized then that I had been holding my own breath. His tight arms reminded me to breathe again.

"You can do this—" Junior murmured with a softness in his voice.

I nodded in response, took in a deep breath of fresh air, and stepped towards the porch. My hands gripped around the handle of the screen door and pulled it open leaving just the porch door in plain sight.

With another breath I raised my hand to the door, tightened my hand into a fist, and knocked strongly on the door a few times before turning back down the porch to Junior's side. I kept my eyes on the yard behind us looking intently for any movement in the dark, an additional car hidden behind the trees, or sounds that indicated any unwanted person was nearby.

Junior's body tensed next to me as he whispered, "someone peaked through the window curtains on my left."

Swallowing back my fear, I stuck to my job as Junior's eyes from behind. I knew he was counting on me to remain strong, and I could not fail him.

I didn't need Junior to tell me someone was unlocking the front door. The sound of a struggling key was audible for anyone to here. Junior raised his arms with the gun pointing directly at the door as he prepared for another trick. We became almost certain that it was Daddy who would answer.

The struggling key found its way into the slot, freeing the door from the latch and allowing it to open slowly until coming to a creaking end.

I heard Junior take a quick breath, holding himself down for the unknown, waiting, and ready for anything.

"Junior...Jamie?" A man's voice whispered out with hast. His voice was familiar, even at a whisper.

"Show yourself..." Junior replied, fear evident in his trembling voice.

"Junior...is it really you?" The man spoke again while opening the creaking door more. "Jamie? You both are okay..." Relief was evident in his voice as though he honestly believed we had been hurt or maybe even dead.

I turned to see who the man was when I noticed Junior lowering his gun. I recognized the thinning blonde and grey hair, thick grey mustache, and the kind eyes behind round glasses. Smiles of relief took over our faces, and joy filled our hearts as the sight of Pa became more real by the second. We were finally home.

I recognized the woman's voice from behind Pa. Her voice was anxious, but there was melancholy in her tone. She called out our names in a questionable manner, as though she couldn't believe the words Pa had spoken. I recognized the short and plump older woman as she pushed past Pa. Her brown hair held tightly in a bun with more noticeable grey hair since the last time we'd seen her.

Her face lit up at the sight of Junior and me.

"Boys!" She shrieked, her voice echoing throughout the night.

"Vera—" Pa's shushed her. "Keep your voice down...there is no telling who is listening—"

"Junior—" MeeMaw's eyes locked onto the revolver still gripped firmly in Junior's hand and she slowly reached out toward him. "Give me the gun, dear—everything is okay. We, nor anyone else, is going to hurt you—okay."

Her tawny-colored eyes full of sincerity and honesty met with Junior's uneasy gaze. She walked gently towards Junior with her arm extended, palm up, and he reluctantly handed her the revolver. As soon as the revolver left Junior's grasp, MeeMaw wrapped her arms tightly around Junior. He collapsed into her embrace as relief and overwhelming happiness took over. She tossed the revolver off to the side and extended her arms to pull me into their hug.

"Oh, boys!" MeeMaw breathed in exclamation. "Boys—We have been so worried..."

"Vera!" Pa hissed from the doorway. "Get them inside now...do you want us all to get killed!"

"Come on, boys—let's get inside and get out of sight," she quickly wiped the tears from her eyes before retrieving the gun and ushering us inside their dimly lit home.

We walked up the steps past our anxious Pa, who was scanning their property for any signs of immediate danger. We stepped through their front door, and I grabbed hold of Junior's hand. Normally, this would be something he would object to, but tonight, he seemed to welcome it. We stood in the center of their living room, off to the right of the doorway coming in. A maroon couch was pushed securely against the wall, and a dark green lounge chair with a footrest was to its left, facing the fireplace on the front wall of the room. A medium-sized table rested at the center of the room covered in numerous family photos. The windows had been securely locked and were shielded by heavy curtains that were closed, preventing any passerby from seeing in.

Pa immediately turned and closed the door behind us, locking the single bolt over the handle, then sliding a thick piece of lumber through two handles that had been bolted to the wall on either side of the door.

From the looks of the house and their makeshift barricade, they seemed to have been expecting someone.

Pa glanced over at us and nodded slightly before turning away into what I assumed would be the kitchen. There was a dark wooden table big enough for four nestled against the wall where the three windows were. It was a sunroom, with plenty of windows to bring a relaxing view of their land. Pa was gone for only a minute as he rummaged through things in the other room.

"He is just checking the back-door lock," MeeMaw noted after noticing the curiosity in our eyes. "Boys—please have a seat and try to relax a little, okay?"

Neither Junior nor I moved. We continued to stare at MeeMaw with uncertainty over the decision to come here. Putting them in danger was the last thing we wanted. Now, after seeing that they expected us to get to them made us feel responsible for whatever the future lay out in front of them.

"It's okay, boys," she spoke again, calmness radiating from her. She walked up to us, gently wrapped her arms around us, and led us to the couch. "I can't imagine what the two of you have been through...but you are safe with us. We will get all of this sorted out; we promise."

"Have y'all—" My whisper broke off into silence as I thought back to the past few days.

Junior, whose hand was still holding onto mine, finished my thoughts. "Have y'all heard anything?"

"Yes..." MeeMaw's eyes filled with sorrow; sorrow only a mother who has lost a child would understand. "We got a call from the police that –that next day. They told us about your Mother and Dav—Davie. They explained that you two were not there when they arrived to investigate. They described the story Henry gave and that—"

"His fabricated story—" Pa interrupted with obvious anger as he returned from the back of the house. "Back door is locked and secured, Vera. I didn't see anything outside, and the animals are not acting different. I think we're okay..."

"I thought we would be. I was just explaining the past few days to the boys," MeeMaw spoke to Pa.

"No—" Pa interjected. His stance changed; his arms crossed his chest and his eyes were directly on Junior and me. "We need to know your story...the right story. Not some fabricated bu—"

"Johnnie!"

Pa held himself back from the profanity and continued calmly, "I only want you to tell us what really happened...please."

"If you can, boys," MeeMaw corrected him, her eyes beaming with sympathy. "I can't begin to understand how difficult it must be for you two to relive everything, we ju—" MeeMaw caught herself just before her voice cracked with grief. She regained herself and spoke with new confidence, "—we just want to know what happened to our daughter and our beautiful grandson."

"Please..." Pa begged. His face filled with a combination of concern and curiosity, tinged with grief.

"Well—" Junior squeezed my hand a bit for security.

I felt his hand grip tighter around mine as he searched for support and I gave him a slight smile of encouragement to help him find the strength to tell our story, yet again.

Closing his eyes and taking in a deep breath, Junior told them everything starting with New Years Eve of 1946 and our father's moment of complete panic when Momma popped open the champagne bottle. As he continued through the time we came home to find Momma bruised up and broken hearted, MeeMaw became tearful, and I wondered if maybe he shouldn't have told her about that moment. I thought perhaps I should have taken control of the story telling, and kept to only the main details, omitting any additional information that might be too hard for them to hear. However, they needed to hear it, all of it, in order to understand everything that had happened.

They dabbed at fresh tears as he described the warmness Walt and Edith gave us. How Walt stopped everything to teach Junior how to drive a truck and how Edith spent her afternoon going over, in detail, the map that would lead us to them. Junior struggled as he described our last moments in Charlotte and the way he felt as we drove hastily away while Daddy opened fire on us. We even told them about stealing gas along the way. I thought they might lecture us about how stealing was wrong, but if anything, they seemed proud of us.

We sat in silence after Junior concluded our story. I kept looking at the floor, unwilling to look up and see the heartbreak that was surly visible on their faces.

Pa spoke, finally ending the silence.

"We need to take them to the police station, Vera—"

"No!" Junior protested.

"Well, honey, we need to sort out the story with the police," MeeMaw attempted to explain.

"But—" Junior tried.

"No, Junior...they need to know you two are safe, and they need to know there is a dangerous man out there!" Pa's anxiety led him to begin pacing up and down past the fireplace. His voice was eager for us to understand. "They need to know – the world needs to hear what he did to his beautiful family."

"He's just sick," I whispered.

"What was that dear?" MeeMaw asked me softly.

"He's sick—in his mind," my gaze finally lifted to find hers. "He is sick in his mind—"

"No, Jamie...he is insane...absolutely crazy—" Pa disputed.

"No! This isn't Daddy!" I shouted, frantic for them all to see what I saw. "You of all people should know who the real Henry Gene Clark is! This is not him! He left for the army and the war as Daddy and came back as someone else. Whatever happened over there...the death of Uncle Tommy...all of the death he witnessed...that created this man. He's in there somewhere—he just can't find himself anymore."

"Oh, dear," MeeMaw looked at me with sympathy, as though she felt bad for me and my rationale. But I didn't care. I knew I was right.

"Dear, boy," She placed her hands on my cheeks, "If that is what you believe...then that is what you believe. But we must put an end to this. Your grandfather is right; we need to go to the police station. We need to tell them what we know. We will stay with you both the entire time...nothing bad will happen to either of you...okay?"

I didn't refute her, and Junior joined me as we stared blankly into MeeMaw's eyes.

"Do you trust us?" MeeMaw asked.

"Yes but—" Junior whispered.

"But? You both trust us...correct?" MeeMaw asked again, this time looking at me.

"Yes, ma'am, we trust you both...." I answered for Junior and myself.

"Then...let's go," MeeMaw stood up and held her hands out for us to grab onto for extra support and safety.

Pa hurried over to the cupboard under the stairs which was place horizontally at the back of the house. He pulled out a shotgun and dumped shells in his pockets. He stopped us at the door and motioned us to wait as he checked the front yard for any sign of Daddy.

Once Pa gave us the signal for 'all-clear,' MeeMaw rushed both Junior and me, one on each side of her, down the porch stairs and out to their garage where their old car sat. We piled into the back seat as Pa took the driver's seat. My mind began flooding with panic of the possible consequences for following through with this plan. I began weighing the pros and cons to myself as Pa drove through the darkness of the country and into the closest law enforcement available—the Sheriff's Office. I stared out the window but did not watch closely for directions or landmarks I could possibly need later. My eyes were fixed, but my mind was venturing to endless thoughts and possibilities that could take place in the next few hours.

We sat out front of the Sheriff's Office for what felt like an eternity as we took a moment of calm. That peaceful and serene moment prior to a storm is called the calm before the storm. That term was most accurate for tonight—and that storm was called Daddy.

I can't tell you that I was entirely ready to get out of the car that night. What I can tell you is that there is only so much you can do to prepare for the inevitable. So, when Pa turned to us, we did not hesitate. We were ready. As ready as we could be for the unknown that would come our way.

And just like that we were pulling ourselves up and out of the car towards the Sheriff's Office. To men who had never seen such evil prior to our arrival.

Chapter 17

"Hey there, Johnnie! Well, Ms. Vera, I must say Clara loved the casserole you made last week!" a man in a sheriff's uniform greeted us as he sat behind the front desk. "She's done nothing but talk about it ever since."

"Oh good! Well, I'll just have to bring her the recipe then." MeeMaw blushed.

"Johnnie! Whatca doin' out this way this late of night?" Another man in uniform spoke while coming out of the back office with a cup of coffee in his hand.

"Actually, Floyd ..." Pa stepped out from in front of Junior and me.

Junior and I looked around the small sheriff's office. The space was disorganized with papers scattered on desks and cups of both freshly poured and old coffee on every surface. It was easy to see they were not accustomed to much activity in this small town. The two middle-aged men in uniform looked down at my brother and me with expressions of astonishment and confusion. They knew who we were without asking, or us saying anything. They just couldn't believe it.

"Is this—" the greeting officer said.

"Yes—" MeeMaw whispered.

"We need your help, Floyd." Pa's voice was steady with determination. "Their father is coming, and I don't know when—"

"Have you boys seen him recently?" Floyd asked.

I looked up at my brother, whose anxiety level could not be more obvious in his body language.

"Um..." Junior looked for the words within. "Earlier today...w-we were in Charlotte you see—"

"Charlotte?" The man who was standing in the back office questioned. "Isn't that where they had the—"

"Yes..." Floyd cut him off quickly, obviously trying to keep certain information a secret. "Continue."

"Well..." Junior started again, "we were in Charlotte for only a few days you see. We met a couple who took us in, and they lent us their truck and a road map—"

"Walter and Edith Cole—" I added, as their faces flashed into my memory.

Junior's eyes met mine with sorrow. Taking in a deep breath, he continued our story for the second time.

"Our plan was to leave early in the morning, all together," Junior struggled to find the words that would describe the fatal end of Walt and Edith. "But—our Dad—he–found us. He came in before their store closed. Edith rushed us out the back door with the truck keys—She stayed behind with Walt. Jamie and I—we—we got away in their truck—we heard two shots go off inside the store. That was followed by more gunfire directed toward us as we were driving away. We made it out of the alley way and all the way up here..."

Again, MeeMaw could not hold back the tears that began to flow freely down her cheeks. She slowly moved behind us, wrapping her arms around us for comfort and support. I knew the truth Junior spoke had been too much for her to bear. This was too much for anyone to bear. I didn't want MeeMaw or Pa to feel the pain we had felt, or deal with the weight of guilt and grief for not seeing this before it was too late.

Looking back as a grandparent myself, I now understand. They had no choice. We were their pride...their responsibility and now their only remaining family. And for anything to happen to us would destroy their entire emotional state. They would fight for us and for our safety forever.

"Did he follow after you two?" the man behind the front desk, spoke up with a little too much eagerness.

"We don't know..." Junior whispered.

"We got onto the highway without any sight of him," I told them. "The entire drive here, there was nothing..."

"So, you both have no idea what car he was driving or where he went?" Floyd questioned us.

"No, sir—" Junior answered shortly.

"Floyd—what do we do?" Pa asked despairingly.

The room was silent as we waited patiently for the men in charge to answer the question or come up with a plan. Nothing like this had ever happened in Raleigh before, and I could tell neither of them had any clue what to say, or how to say it.

"Well—we can call the State Police, can't we, Floyd?" The front desk man asked.

"I guess so, Kenny—" Floyd responded, not hiding the solemnness in his voice. "But we have nothing to go on...No idea what he is driving, not even the slightest idea where he is heading. He could be headed here—but he might not. He might head off somewhere else—"

"But wouldn't he—"

"I don't know, Ken—" Floyd placed his hands on his hips and began to look around the office as though searching for something that would spark any idea; but there was nothing. "Let us see what we can do on this end of things; why don't y'all just head on back home. If you see or suspect anything, call here at the station and we will get there as fast as we can."

"That's it?" Pa's voice started out quiet and controlled but quickly became agitated. "How is that all you can do!? How am I supposed to tuck my grandsons in tonight and tell them everything will be okay!?"

"Johnnie—" MeeMaw muttered.

"No, Vera! They will be the reason we all end up murdered!" Pa stepped forward aggressively toward Floyd who took a step back. "Floyd—there must be something you can do for us. I'll do anything to make sure my grandsons and my wife are safe—please—".

"Johnnie, all I can do is what I am telling you—" Floyd clarified calmly, doing his best to maintain control over the situation. "Unfortunately, we have nothing to work with—"

"But—" Pa began.

"Johnnie, did you see anything suspicious?" Kenny urged, doing his best to take some of the pressure off Floyd.

"Well—no, but—"

"If you see anything—call us," Kenny reiterated. "We will be there as soon as we can, we promise."

"I promise, Johnnie—I won't let anything happen to your family," Floyd's eyes were honest as he spoke directly to Pa.

Pa reluctantly changed his demeanor, giving in to their promise of safety as he realized that he would not win their argument. He knew at that moment that he would be the one solely in charge of our security.

"Johnnie—I think we should head home," MeeMaw spoke faintly as she edged near him to further calm him down. "We will keep an eye out for anything suspicious as they have mentioned; and as soon as anything unusual happens, they will come when we call."

The office became still again, no one knowing what to say or do for a moment. Floyd and Kenny merely seemed thankful that Pa's conduct had settled, and nothing more had come from his outburst. MeeMaw held back, waiting for Pa to speak, feeling trepidation after the tense situation that had just unfolded. Junior and I seemed rooted in one spot, too afraid to move and cause even more of a disturbance.

"Fine—" Pa said as he spun angrily toward the door, signifying his anger and disgust with the Sheriff in a nonverbal manner. "Vera, Junior, Jamie...let's go."

"Johnnie—call us please—" Floyd spoke one last time as Pa's hand touched the door handle.

Pa stopped abruptly and without turning to look back at the men he said coldly, "yeah—just hope you get there in time."

Then he was out the door, holding it just long enough for Junior to catch it so MeeMaw and I could walk through. I looked back before the door closed, making eye contact with Floyd and Kenny one last time before they were gone from view.

We piled into the car, each one of us feeling as though there was no hope remaining. If the sheriff's office couldn't help us, then who could? We were alone. Wondering where in the world Daddy was and what he was planning next.

I watched as the buildings of the city turned into woods. With each passing tree, the knot in my stomach grew bigger and bigger. I realized that even with a phone call, there was no way the Sheriff would make it to us on time. There were just too many places out here where Daddy could conceal himself. Even a police dog would have a difficult time finding him out here in the total darkness.

"Boys, put your heads down and out of sight," Pa whispered without looking back.

Before ducking down concealing ourselves on the floorboards, I saw that we were nearing their home. I felt the car turn down the dirt road that was their driveway, the tires rolling over the small rocks and imperfections as I tried to hang on. Pa stopped the car in a not-so-gentle manner, making the brakes squeak. There was total stillness. None of us moved from our position.

In a low voice, Pa gave us instructions. "Wait here…no one is to leave this car without my permission. Junior and Jamie keep down until instructed otherwise, do you understand?"

"Yes, sir—" Junior, barely audible, responded.

I heard the sound of a shotgun being loaded and prepared for any danger that may come our way. Pa unlatched the door and stepped out into the night. He left us to search the house to be sure we were not walking into a trap. MeeMaw sat still, staring straight ahead. I looked over at Junior, and he gave me a slight smile, as though trying to reassure or calm me. I sought to give him an honest smile back, but all I could muster was something obviously fake and forced.

We continued to sit there, the three of us, waiting for any sign that the area around us was safe and secure. I glanced up at MeeMaw to look for any visible sign from her expressions that would reveal a possibility of what was happening outside, but there was nothing. All I could do was cower on the floorboard of her car waiting for instructions to be given.

Just as we were starting to worry about Pa, without moving in her seat, MeeMaw spoke very softly to us. "Don't respond. Just listen. He is coming back. Get ready to move quickly out of the car and get into the house."

I braced myself to lift and move as told, while Junior did the same. It may be clear inside the house, and the immediate surroundings, but there was no telling who could be watching us from the woods, or what weapons they may have.

The car door next to me opened and Pa stood there continually scanning everything surrounding us. "Let's go, inside quickly. Vera, help him."

MeeMaw had Junior's door open in seconds, and they each held their hands out to help us get out and not stumble. I did my best to avoid bumping into anything that would cause me to fall and waste the valuable time we had to move.

Once I was out of the car and steady on my feet, I grabbed Pa's hand tighter. He rushed me through the front yard without pausing. I glanced up only momentarily to ensure nothing seemed out of place, but everything seemed to be as it should.

All four of us reached the house without any incident. Neither Pa nor MeeMaw had spoken since we stepped out of the car. They were nervous and rightfully so. We were the children, and we were their responsibility now. Their job was to protect us from any evil acts that may come our way. The most eminent evil was our father, and they had no way of knowing if Daddy was watching us from a concealed spot as he lurked in the shadows.

"Okay, boys." Pa finally spoke. He was still holding the shotgun in one hand, but it was pointed at the floor. "You'll both sleep upstairs on the floor in our room. Your MeeMaw will stay with the two of you. I will stay down here for the night."

"Can't I stay with you?" Junior asked.

"No," Pa stated rather emphatically. "You and Jamie both need to stay upstairs. At least until daytime. It is too dark outside, and I can't tell if anyone is out there. We need to make as little movement and sound as possible from now on in this house."

"Are you boys hungry?" MeeMaw asked kindly.

"No, ma'am," I responded. "I think we are just ready to sleep after our long drive…"

"Thank you though, MeeMaw," Junior added.

"Alright, well…let me show you upstairs," MeeMaw headed toward the stairs which were toward the back of the house and ran parallel to the fireplace. "Grab your bags and follow me."

Junior moved first, picking up both his and mine. Pa appeared to be distracted. When I looked closer at the object trapped in his gaze, I saw it was an old photo of the day Momma and Daddy brought Davie and me home. Junior was being held in Daddy's arms with a huge smile across his face, proud to be a big brother. Davie and I were tucked securely in each of Momma's arms, while she and Daddy smiled at each other, completely in love with the little family they had created. I looked back at Pa, saw a small tear on his cheek, and knew his mind must be flooded with memories of not just us but his little girl, his only child, his daughter.

"Pa?" I whispered, watching as he turned his head to look at me. "Can we take some of these photos upstairs to look at before we go to sleep?"

"Oh, well..." Pa looked over at MeeMaw as though he was silently asking her to answer the question. "Um—"

"Jamie, pick out some of those pictures, then you, Junior, and I can go through some of them while you get ready for bed," MeeMaw smiled politely.

"Okay—" I quietly gathered up some of the photos that had been scattered out on the center table and hurried past Pa without looking at him.

I followed closely behind Junior up the narrow wooden stairs. Like Edith and Walt's stairway wall, MeeMaw and Pa's wall was decorated with photos—Momma as a baby, a child, and a young adult; photos of Momma and Daddy's wedding, followed by pictures of Junior, Davie, and me. Unlike Edith and Walt's though, the photos didn't end abruptly. They continued, signifying that their daughter's life continued into adulthood. The only indication of her death was the grief that lingered on their faces.

Upstairs and to the immediate right was a room that I guessed belonged to Momma's childhood. The door was ajar, showing a small twin bed hugging the corner with a bedside table by its side. On the table was a bible in front of a picture frame with a picture of a young couple happily placed inside. A box of tissues was on the bed, which I assumed were MeeMaw or Pa's. Any parent, when hearing the news of the death of their child, would naturally retreat towards the comfort of their child's old bedroom to feel the serenity it may contain.

Straight off from the stairs was the washroom, which I assumed the three of them had once shared. Momma always said the reason our home had a second washroom was because children never want to share it with a parent. Seeing their old living situation up close, I could tell she might have been the one truly pushing for that extra space.

MeeMaw turned left which headed to their bedroom on the front of the home. These windows, too, had curtains concealing us from anyone who looked from the outside. In the center of their room was a full-size bed.

MeeMaw made her way over to the closet to pull out blankets and pillows for us to sleep on tonight. I glanced over at the clock and saw that it was now one-thirty in the morning.

"So, you both will sleep on this side, closest to the window," MeeMaw tossed the blankets on the floor nearest to the window. "In case someone comes through that bedroom door tonight, you won't be quickly spotted. If your father comes in tonight...hide in the closet. Do you understand me?"

"Yes, ma'am," Junior and I answered in unison.

"Alright...enough unpleasantness for the moment—" MeeMaw smiled brightly while sitting in the middle of the bed. "Let's look at those photos."

Junior tossed the backpacks on the floor as we both piled up on the bed to join her. She put her arms around us, welcoming us into the safety of her embrace. I tossed all the photos down onto the bed and picked up the one of Davie and me soon after we were born.

"Oh, this one!" MeeMaw's voice was pure happiness. "This one is your grandpa's favorite. This was the day your Momma came home with you and your brother. Oh, was your Daddy proud. We got the long-distance call from the hospital that the two of you were born. Oh, the joy! We had no idea she was carrying two. From her letters, she said she was bigger than she had been with Junior, but there was no way to tell. So, when your Daddy called announcing that we had two new grandsons...oh your Pa! He just about screamed with joy. Everyone we saw that day, he had to tell them about his new grandsons David and

James. And, of course, he would also tell them about his three-year-old grandson Junior who could already say half of the alphabet.

"That day, Pa and I got tickets for the next day down to Charleston. We just had to be there to see the first twins in our family and, of course, to see you, Junior. So, that is when I went to the store to buy y'all's teddy bears: Winston and Rufus. We wanted to give you two a gift that you could keep throughout your childhood. Something matching that would forever unite the two of you."

"And those bears are still around to this day..." Junior said with sarcasm.

"They are...I brought Winston with me—I—I lost—Rufus..." I didn't even try to hide the tears that flooded down my face as I thought how for the first time since May 22nd, 1935, the teddy bears were separated.

"It's okay, sweetheart, we will get Davie's bear back..." MeeMaw tightened her arms around me, comforting me with love.

"Don't worry about it, Jamie..." Junior whispered. "Come on, let's look at some more photos."

Junior picked out a photo on the top of the pile. It was a beautiful photo of a young couple dressed for the evening. The young man was the spitting image of Junior, and the girl looked youthful and beautiful. They looked deeply in love and in awe of one another. The young man had his arm wrapped around her waist and she had her hand on his chest. They were young and they looked as though nothing in the world mattered except each other.

"This was—your Momma and Daddy—" MeeMaw said with slight hesitation.

I couldn't imagine how difficult it was for her to look at those pictures — not after everything she had learned about what happened. Such a tragic love story, and it happened to her baby girl.

"They were in love from the beginning. Everyone in their school knew they would be wed one day. It was inevitable. Pa and I could tell from the moment we met Henry that he would be the one for her," MeeMaw reminisced softly. "All Katherine would do was talk about him. Since she was a little girl, she had this obsession with Charleston. I think it was because of a dear friend of ours who had lived there once before. He'd tell stories of the ocean and family life; it got her to daydreaming. From that moment on, she wanted to live in Charleston.

"Henry wanted to live wherever Katherine wanted to live. He just wanted to be with her. Nothing else mattered. This picture was taken prior to their high school dance. They were such a cute couple. At the end of that year, just after they graduated, Henry proposed. Your Pa cried all night because he knew she'd move to her dream home in Charleston."

"And her dream porch," Junior smiled.

"Yes, oh, she thought our porch was too 'small' for a family," MeeMaw chuckled quietly. "I remember when they purchased that home in Charleston. One of the first things she did was write to me about the beautiful porch they had and how her dream was to teach her children how to walk on that porch."

Junior and I couldn't help but laugh together because that was exactly what she did. All three of us had learned to walk on that porch with Momma and Daddy right there cheering us on. Once Momma had a plan, she stuck by it and everyone around her did as well.

"What was —Daddy—like back then?" Junior questioned. He seemed to find it difficult to even say 'Daddy.'

"He was a good boy!" MeeMaw's voice increased with excitement. "He was smart, sweet, and head strong. He was ready for the world and ready to explore it all with your Momma by his side."

"They were in love?" I asked, even though I knew the answer.

"Yes—more than ever then and even now…" MeeMaw responded, her voice becoming solemn with old memories.

"Even now?" Junior queried.

"Yes—I believe so—" She sighed. "I believe he still loves her; he just loves her so much; he was afraid to lose her—"

"But he did lose her! We all lost her!" Anger immediately overwhelmed Junior.

"Shh!" I hushed at him. I knew this subject was touchy for him, but he needed to understand there was a time and place for outbursts.

"I understand, honey." She turned her attention to Junior, not fully realizing how touchy Junior was to this subject. "What your Daddy did was absolutely horrific…but I think in his mind he believes she can't leave him or be away from him if she's gone."

Footsteps pounded up the staircase leaving the three of us frozen with our eyes glued to the door. I expected Daddy to rush into the room, shooting at us with his eyes blazing red with insanity.

It was only Pa.

"What are y'all screaming about? I told you all to be quiet up here. What is all the fuss about?" Pa demanded.

"I am sorry, dear," her voice becoming soothing and calming. "We just got a little excited discussing the pictures. Everything is okay, and we will be quiet; I am sorry, dear."

"I'm sorry, Pa," Junior whispered embarrassingly.

"Yeah, we're sorry," I followed.

"Where is the truck y'all drove here?" Pa asked as his aggravation subsided.

"I parked it a little further down in the grove of trees," Junior pointed in the general direction.

"Okay," Pa nodded. "Y'all have anything in there y'all need?"

"No, sir. We brought everything inside," Junior answered.

"Pa," my voice was timid. "What was your favorite memory of Momma when she was young?"

He was caught off guard and his eyes misted over as thoughts of his beloved daughter swirled in his head. But this was not the time for that. He shifted his weight from one leg to the other while looking at the floor.

"I believe I might just have to think on that a bit ... so many good memories." He attempted to control his emotions as he spoke, "I'll tell you tomorrow... okay?" Pa knelt at the end of the bed to see us each eye to eye. "Now, MeeMaw told you to hide in the closet if anything happens tonight, correct?"

"Yes, sir," Junior responded while I simply nodded.

"Okay..." Pa stood up. "MeeMaw will call the Sheriff's Office and you two will remain quiet in the closet."

We both nodded again understanding the commands given to us. Pa left to go downstairs and continue his night guarding the bottom floor, pacing from window to window, doing his best to ensure the safety of his family that slept upstairs. MeeMaw, Junior, and I continued to look through some photos before falling asleep in MeeMaw's arms. The last thing I remembered was looking at a photo of Junior holding up a fish he caught years ago, with me and Davie standing on either side of him, smiling blissfully. After that, I had fallen into a deep and well-needed sleep. Lost in cheerful dreams of warm summer days fishing at our river without a single problem in the world.

An hour later, I was awakened by a voice whispering in my ear.

"Jamie—Jamie, wake up."

"Wha—" I mumbled.

"Shh—get up," the voice said again.

My eyes blinked heavily as they adjusted to the room around me trying to make out the blur of a shadowy figure in front of me. I searched through the dark for my glasses, frantic for some assistance with my vision. The shadowy figure grabbed the glasses and pushed them onto my face. Instantly my vision cleared as the blurriness settled. Junior was knelt over me; his eyes filled with uneasiness. I was laying on the floor, stuck between the window and the bed. MeeMaw must have laid me down here after I fell asleep.

My senses slowly awakened allowing me to hear the world around me. MeeMaw was on the phone speaking with someone with a firm calmness in her voice. There was a slight sense of urgency in her tone.

"—yes, he is walking up to the house right now," she told the person on the other line.

"What's happening?" I rubbed my eyes and asked groggily. My eyes found the clock, 'three in the morning—' I read to myself.

"He's here—" Junior whispered.

"Boys—in the closet," MeeMaw ordered.

Gathering myself, I stood up on my unsteady feet. Instantly Junior wrapped his arm around me, steadying me at his side. MeeMaw was standing with her back to the bedroom door still on the phone. Her body swayed from one side to the other with pure anxiety. Junior pulled me with him in the direction of the closet when a sound echoed through the house vibrating the walls surrounding us.

—boom, boom, boom—

Mine and Junior's bodies froze, paralyzed with fear. Daddy was here. He found us…again.

Chapter 18

MeeMaw hung up the phone with the Sheriff's Office and paced frantically up and down the room. She didn't speak immediately, but I knew from her expression—she too was afraid. We all knew this was bound to happen, but I don't think we had prepared for it at all. The possibility turning into a reality came quicker than any of us were ready for.

After a few seconds of silently collecting herself and her thoughts, MeeMaw spoke with haste. "Boys—into the closet—"

"Is the Sheriff on his way?" Junior questioned, his arms still locked around me as though he was guarding me.

"Yes, he said they were on their way…" she said with some doubt.

"They won't get here in time…" I realized as the banging on the door downstairs continued.

"Don't you worry…just stay put…" worry filled her eyes as she attempted to reassure us.

MeeMaw lead us to the closet and promptly shut the door, leaving us alone in the darkness of the small, clammy space. Our vision was impacted by the lack of light and the dangling of shirts and pants that were on hangers. As we sat there in the dark, we took in all the sounds that crept inside and outside of the house. Junior's arms increased their hold around me. I could feel the terror coming off him in nearly visible waves as I tried desperately to control my breathing so the sounds from downstairs could reach our ears without difficulty.

I was able to eventually steady my anxiety, allowing me to focus my attention on what I heard around us. I was able to track MeeMaw's footsteps as they trailed away down the hall towards the top of the staircase and came to a stop. By the sound of her footsteps halting, I presumed she was peering down to the living room.

The house grew quiet, as the banging at the door ceased momentarily. Junior and I held our breath at the new silence, waiting for something more to happen.

"Johnnie!" Daddy's familiar deep-toned voice echoed through the house, raising every hair on my body. He continued with his voice remaining strong and controlled, as though he knew he had the power. "Vera! I know you are in there also! Why don't y'all open up the door so we can discuss this as adults?"

I assumed that Pa was hesitant on an appropriate response due to the noticeable silence. MeeMaw, following Pa's lead, remained silent and in one place. There was not a single sound of movement in the house or outside.

In the midst of the silence, a loud and destructive sound erupted sending vibrations throughout the house. Fear gripped us. Daddy was back to banging on the door. The makeshift lock became the only thing keeping Daddy out.

"JOHNNIE!" Daddy bellowed as he continued to crash into the door with undeniable aggression.

Pa's only response to him was racking his shotgun.

"I know you have my boys inside there!" Daddy continued as he antagonistically banged on the door. "I saw the truck parked outside…hidden! You thought that I wouldn't have seen that? Do you seriously doubt my ability to track? I knew their every move!"

Pa's and MeeMaw's silence continued inside the house.

"Alright—alright…listen here, Mr. Williams —if you just give me my boys, I'll be on my merry way and I will never bother you ever again. I –I solemnly promise."

The silence grew with each passing second. I tightened my grasp on Junior's arm, wanting so much to scream. I wanted to scream all my frustrations away. I wanted to scream until all my breath was gone. But I couldn't. All I could do was remain in place and wait for the inevitable, because waiting until someone shook me awake from this seemingly never-ending nightmare was too much to hope for.

"Look—I just want to talk to them—I just want them safe. Just the same as you. Just –please—give me my boys so my family can be together!" The wails from Daddy became increasingly emotional with each word.

Even as his aggravation intensified, Pa refused to give him an answer. Pa refused to speak with him or give him anything he requested. He stood there with patience, his gun poised and ready.

"Fine!" Daddy said after realizing the silence from inside was not going to change. "I'll be back then…I'll be back—don't you worry!"

Junior and I remained still as stone.

MeeMaw and Pa remained quiet. Each holding their positions while waiting for any sign that Daddy was truly gone. Any sign that the current nightmare was over. Any sign that we would be safe if we let our guard down. We all waited for that sign, but it never came.

Instead, the sudden and hellacious sound of splintering wood resonated viciously throughout the house as the back door frame was ripped apart, and the door itself was torn from its hinges. I heard Junior behind me whimper as he and everyone else understood that the nightmare was not over. Daddy, enraged and delusional, had assaulted and destroyed the back door.

"Henry! You have no right to enter our home!" Pa's voice remained firm as he waited for Daddy to storm around the corner.

Remembering the layout of the home, I knew Daddy remained invisible from the back door as Pa was waiting in the living room, shotgun at the ready. There was only one way for Daddy to get to Pa. And Pa had only one corner to guard. There was no hiding or sneaking up on one another.

"I have no right? I—have no right!? You are the one who is keeping my children from me!" Daddy kicked the remnants of the door frame in, to further announce his entrance into the home.

"Henry…I know what you have been through, and I know you are dealing with a lot…but this…this is not how you handle it," Pa desperately attempted to talk Daddy down. "Your wife and son are dead…you killed them. You can't change that, but you can change this! Just leave… we will act like this never happened!"

"Katherine and David are not dead! They are both waiting for me!" Daddy shrieked. "Just give me back my bo—".

A loud boom echoed through the house, abruptly cutting off Daddy's sentence. Pa had fired his gun at Daddy, who I could only imagine had attempted to turn the corner that led into the living room.

"Johnnie!" MeeMaw wailed from the top of the stairs; she, too, was unsure of all that was occurring.

"Henry – I'm warning you—LEAVE!" Pa sounded strong and determined. The fear he must have felt seemed to become nonexistent, replaced with the courage to protect his family.

"And I told you, Mr. Williams, to hand over my boys!" Daddy hollered, sounding enraged and unwounded.

Junior placed his hand calmly over my mouth muffling the rapid breathing I had not realized I had started. I was too anxious and too concerned about the situation occurring downstairs that I had forgotten to maintain my own silence.

"Stay calm—stay calm—" Junior reminded me.

The silence returned, causing an unnerving feeling to creep once again throughout the house. Daddy was not making a sound as he likely planned his next move. Pa seemed just as hesitant, probably avoiding saying or doing anything else that might increase Daddy's anger. I'm pretty sure Pa was just hoping to hold him off until the Sheriff came and there was more gun power against our father.

The top of the staircase creaked as MeeMaw shifted her weight to get a glimpse of what was happening. She, too, had been hesitant to move too much and cause any more tension, but her curiosity won over.

"Henry—" Pa's voice, still calm and controlled, interrupted the silence.

A loud bang filled the house and left painful ringing in my ears. As my head began to spin, I closed my eyes and clung onto Junior's arm to keep myself here — to keep my mind in the present rather than the past. But it just wasn't enough. Images of Davie's body, sprawled out on the floor, began to flood into my mind. The haunting screams from Momma filled my ears. Tears from these memories, that I could and would never forget, poured endlessly down my cheeks.

Pa's screams sliced through my memories pulling me away from the past and into the present. Junior's loud gasp and tightened grip kept me from falling back into my own head full of heartbreaking memories of recent events.

"Johnnie!" MeeMaw's wails carried through the house. She screamed for her now wounded husband. I heard the creaks from the stairs as she hurried down to Pa who was suffering greatly.

"No—" I heard Pa's weak voice warn MeeMaw. "Vera stay—sta—stay there," He desperately tried to convince her to remain hidden, but she couldn't stand aside while her husband lay there in a pool of his own blood.

"Oh, Johnnie," her voice much softer now but still audible to our ears.

"I told you to give me my children!" Daddy's hostile voice returned, only this time more confident in his plan. "Now…where are my boys?"

I felt Junior's weight shift from behind me as he stood up quickly, and with such haste, it caused me to fall deeper into the closet. Junior ran from the closet, focusing his attention forward. I stretched my arm towards him, desperate for him to stop.

"Don't leave me—" I begged as the tears continued to burn down my cheeks.

"I won't—I'll be back—" Junior's smile was an act, an attempt to reassure me, yet again. "Stay here—I love you, Jamie—Never forget that…"

My vocal cords were paralyzed at the thought of being alone again and listening to the sounds of my family being annihilated. I sat on the closet floor, crying behind the coats and pants that smelled of MeeMaw and Pa. I listened as Junior's footsteps moved hastily down the hall towards the danger of the downstairs.

"Oh—looks like one of my boys knows his Daddy is here—" Daddy announced with sarcasm.

Junior moving down the hallway was loud enough for those below to hear.

"No—" Pa groaned.

"No—stay upstairs!" MeeMaw screamed desperately as my brother continued without hesitation into danger.

How could I sit here as my family died? How would I even make it in this world if I lived and they died? Junior and I—we were supposed to stay together. We were going to make it out of this—together. I searched my soul and decided, if he wouldn't make it, neither would I.

I finally found the courage I had been searching for over the past ten years.

And with that courage, I pulled myself up and out of the closet, into the dimly lit bedroom. As I was about to hurry out of the room, I saw a glisten of silver under the bed. I reached down and realized it was the revolver given to us by Walt. MeeMaw had left it. She left unarmed. Pa was wounded and Junior—Junior left with no defense. It was up to me to help them. It was up to me to stop Daddy's wrath. It was up to me; the weak ten-year-old little boy from Charleston, South Carolina.

Grabbing the revolver, I was filled with a simultaneous sensation of anxiety and power. A power I didn't want to use, but as I cocked the hammer back, I realized that this was my moment, the moment I would become the man in charge.

I walked slowly down the hall urgently trying to control my breathing and the emotions that burned inside. I focused my attention on what was happening downstairs, to prepare myself as I forged together a plan of how I was to shoot the man that provided me life.

"Daddy—" Junior, whose voice was little more than a whisper, spoke. "—please—"

"Well, hello there son…" Daddy's voice was cold; there was no sign of the loving father we had once known. "I've missed you—"

"Daddy—why are you doing this?" Junior whispered. "Momma—she loved you."

"Your mother?" Daddy reiterated. "She—she was the one who wanted to leave me, to leave us!"

"No—Daddy—no, she loved you," Junior explained again. "Davie—he was innocent. He didn't do anything to deserve that."

"And I am trying to bring us all back together. I am trying to keep us all together!" Daddy screamed as the psychosis remained intact. "They—they are waiting for us—they are waiting—"

"No—Daddy – they are dead," Junior tried to explain.

"They are at peace—and you will be too—" Daddy ran his fingers through his hair.

I crept down the staircase peeking out at the scene that I had only been imagining in my mind. Daddy was pointing the gun directly at Junior, and the anger I felt inside surfaced. Junior had his eyes closed tight while mouthing something I assumed to be a prayer. MeeMaw was crying over Pa who was still hanging on to life as he did his best to remain focused on the scene that surrounded him. Images of the pain and agony on the faces of those whom I loved so dearly gave me more strength than I knew I had.

"Don't," I was surprised to hear my own voice as my arm raised the revolver to point directly at Daddy. "Back away from my family…"

"Jamie!" Daddy's eyes, crazed with delusion, met mine. "Happy Birthday son… I have missed you…so much!"

"Daddy, why are you doing this?" I kept the gun steady as I lowered myself slowly down the stairs and onto the floor. "We love you…you need help…we can get you help…"

"Help? The only help I need is for you and Junior to join me, your mother and Davie…" Daddy moved his gun to face me. "Join me, Jamie…"

"No, Daddy…Uncle Tommy, he wouldn't want this," I fought the lump in my throat and pushed back the overwhelming urge I felt to run away and hide. "—We were happy, we can still be happy."

"How?" Tears flooded in Daddy's eyes as he fought to hold them back. "How…how can we be happy?"

"We have each other. Junior, you, and I. We have each other," I tried to talk Daddy down, to bring him back to the reality he had been away from for so long. "Let's leave…we three together, okay…leave as a family of three. We will be happy. We can still find the happiness we once had."

"You think so?" Daddy's eyes started to show some glimmer of hope.

I could see him thinking about the idea of being happy again as a family. Daddy lowered his gun slightly. He was coming back. Reality and lucidity began to fill his lost eyes with the familiar shade of blue that once comforted me for years prior to the war.

Off in the distance, sirens were faintly heard and slowly increasing in volume. I knew my time was up. The clarity would shift back to delusional rage, and I had only a second to decide my course of action. My finger lingered on the trigger as I thought back to all the harm and damage he had done to our family. All the tears that had been shed because of the actions he committed. I thought about Momma and everything her short life had taught me. Her message about love and commitment that still resonates with me to this day. I thought of all these things in less time than it takes to blink. And I knew.

I knew I wouldn't be able to pull the trigger. I knew I would die. I knew I would let my family down, and we would be killed. I spared a glance over to Junior and saw that he understood the brief moment of Daddy's fragile lucidity would soon diminish, leaving us to contend with the killer that resided deep within.

"You—you called the Sheriff on me—" Daddy's eyes tore to the front door as the red and blue lights were barley noticeable around the edges of the drapes. "You turned me in—How could you? You said we would be happy—"

"We will be—" I pleaded.

"No—No –you are lying!" Daddy raised the gun back up pointing it directly at me.

My finger sat on the trigger, and I knew I could not and would not pull it. My time on this earth was coming to an end, and I was sure I would soon see Momma and Davie as I left this world behind.

I closed my eyes, hoping that when I opened them, Momma and Davie would be smiling at me — or at the very least, that I would wake up from this horrific and seemingly never-ending nightmare. Another boom exploded in the room, the sound causing the ringing already in my ears to double in strength. Believing I must have died, opening my eyes, I expected to see the lights of heaven welcoming me to an eternity of bliss, but — I was wrong.

What I saw instead was my father wounded on the living room floor. Shot by my dying grandfather, who was being held in my grandmother's arms. His final sacrifice for the safety of his family. His final gift to us. He may not have been able to save his daughter and grandson, but with MeeMaw helping position him up so he could take the shot, he saved us. Pa could now leave us and be at peace, knowing that he had stopped the evil from taking the remainder of his family.

Daddy was struggling to catch his breath. The buckshot left several smaller holes in his chest, shredding his lungs. Instead of filling with air, they were filling with blood. We knew he only had a few moments left on this earth.

Junior and I rushed to his side, pushing aside the gun he had once threatened us with. The man we feared was now leaving but so was the possibility of the man we once loved ever coming back. He'll be gone, never to return, but the memories we had would live with us forever.

We held his hand and looked into his eyes as lucidity reentered. He was frantic, desperately trying to form words.

"I-I'm sorry—" Daddy breathed.

"Shh...save your breath," Junior whispered, his voice trembling with despair.

"It's okay Daddy—" my voice was barely audible.

"F-F-Forgive...me." He said to us as his eyes blinked rapidly trying to focus.

"We forgive you—we forgive you—" I reassured him.

Junior was no longer able to speak. Due to his emotions, all that came out was muffled and incomprehensible muttering.

"I-I...l-love—" Daddy breathed one final time before his clear blue eyes closed forever.

Junior and I bowed our heads as we unleashed the cascade of tears we had fought back. All that mattered to us was being with Daddy during his final moments, saying our last goodbye to the man we had once longed to be just like.

"What's this?" Junior mumbled.

"What—"

Out of Daddy's pocket fell the 2-blade imperial pocketknife that had been gifted to him by his first-born son. Junior gripped the knife and touched his forehead to Daddy's. Junior squeezed his eyes lids shut in hopes his tears would end, but there was no such end in sight. Junior's shuddering breathing continued.

A few minutes must have passed before we were able to finally turn our attention over to Pa. To the man who became our protector against the man who once was. We left Daddy's side and clutched MeeMaw, whose sobs were only broken up as she gasped for air. She rocked him slowly with her arms wrapped firmly around her now late husband.

After only a moment, MeeMaw relaxed her hold on Pa and pulled us into her arms, where we leaned on each other for support — something we needed now more than ever as we became a family of three, and it would be just us from now on.

A loud bang vibrated from the front door as the Sheriff and his deputies finally reached our home. The makeshift lock Pa made kept them out and we were too lost in grief to assist them inside. Maybe if they had done their job quickly enough, Pa would still be here. Maybe Daddy would have found the help he needed while in prison instead of through death. Maybe we would be a family of four rather than three. As far as we were concerned, it was no one else's fault but theirs. We kept our focus locked onto the loss that filled the room with us. To the loss of two great men, one of whom was already lost, simply wanting to be found.

The Sheriff and his deputies eventually made their way in through the back door that had already been reduced to kindling wood.

"Vera! Johnnie! Boys!" Floyd yelled through the dark as he scanned the living room with his flashlight, blinding us in the process.

They had entered the room with their guns drawn but holstered them as they observed the scene. Two men — good men — were now dead because of their lack of urgency. I knew they didn't believe us when we went to them earlier in the night. There was no call to the State Police, and the look on each of their faces showed every ounce of guilt they carried. There was nothing they could say or do that would take the pain away from us. Not now. There was nothing any of us could do.

I have forgotten, and don't care to remember, the details of what happened next. My mind was too flooded with images of death and pain that I had seen in the past week to focus on any small specifics from the remainder of the morning. The grief of our new life began to set in as the loss of our loved ones overwhelmed us. For a ten-year-old, this was too much to comprehend.

I kept my head tucked into MeeMaw as I searched for the comfort I longed for in that moment. She held us tight within her embrace for the remainder of the morning and all the way to the Sheriff's office. Even for our questionings, we remained by her side. We were MeeMaw's priority just as she was ours.

The deputies found Rufus tucked away in the car stolen by Daddy during his journey to find us. Junior and I decided then that he must have gone back to the train station in search of any evidence that could have explained our quick and unnoticed escape. It was the discovery of Rufus that led him to Charlotte.

I reunited Rufus and Winston once again and kept them with me as we stayed at the Sheriff's office that morning, and into the afternoon, while we answered all of the questions they had prepared for us. MeeMaw, Junior, and I remained huddled up together, refusing to become separated. They took Daddy and Pa's bodies out of the home to prepare them for examination and eventual burial. Floyd promised MeeMaw that he and Kenny would clean and repair any damages caused to the home, which all seemed so insignificant to us then. Our lives were now forever changed and would never go back to normal. And MeeMaw, well, she was now tasked with the unimaginable job of preparing for not just one but four funerals. Junior and I knew the emotional toll it would have on her, so we tried to be there for her in any way we could, although it was just as difficult for us too. Since Momma's and Davie's deaths, neither of us had any time to grieve properly. In order to survive, Junior and I had to accept their untimely demise and move on quite quickly.

Floyd had to make a long-distance call to Charleston to request the transfer of Momma's and Davie's remains to prepare for burial. They deserved to be buried the proper way in the family plot that waited for them in Raleigh.

MeeMaw discussed with us if we would prefer to bury Daddy near Momma or to just bury him near his parents. Privately, Junior and I discussed our options and what would be best for our family. I thought we would have different opinions on the subject, but we didn't. We both decided the best idea would be to bury Daddy near Momma. We decided that this was the most appropriate decision to make. To bury him near her but not next to her like they had initially planned.

Our decision was based on knowing how much Momma had loved Daddy. Even that night we had all attempted to escape, she only did that to ensure the safety of her children. She knew he was not well, that he was lost, still stuck in the world he had hoped to leave behind in Europe. And that was not entirely Daddy's fault. The lack of understanding of mental health during that time led to the downfall of our Father. But at the end of the day, he was our father, and we were and always have been his children.

The flash of clarity that my brother and I saw in him during those final moments led us to the decision we made. The damaged side of him had unfortunately won, but the father we knew was still in there. I was afraid MeeMaw wouldn't agree with or understand our final decision, but she seemed comforted by the idea.

We learned later that MeeMaw and Pa had received a detailed letter from Momma the week prior to her death explaining everything Daddy had become. She explained how she wanted to escape the house with us to allow us to have a happy life with them. She wanted to continue to be there for Daddy, but we were her priority. Our safety was her one and only concern. Before they could figure out a way to help, they received a long-distance call from the Charleston Police reporting her and Davie's deaths as well as our strange disappearances. Since that phone call, MeeMaw and Pa had debated on going out to look for us or to allow us to find them. MeeMaw wanted more than anything to leave home and search, but Pa decided it would be better to wait. He believed we would be able to find our way home to them.

"Jamie—Junior—?" Floyd called out to us from his office. "Can I have a word, please?"

I looked over at my brother who gave me the same look of uncertainty. MeeMaw nudged us and nodded for us to go on ahead. This would be the first time we had left her side since the incident.

'What could they want now?' I thought. 'Hadn't we answered all their questions?'

Junior and I stood up together, grabbed each other's hand for support, and made our way to the office of the Sheriff in charge.

"Yes, sir?" Junior quietly asked.

"I just received a call from Charlotte regarding Walter and Edith Cole," Floyd took off the glasses that outlined his dark brown eyes. The lines on his face reflected worry. "They were preparing to bury them when the lead detective found a note written by Mrs. Cole."

"A note?" I asked, my eyes darting over to Junior with unease.

"Yes—" Floyd nodded. "It looks as though prior to her death she wrote out a note. The note read: 'Junior and Jamie Clark know the truth. Find them and the truth will be known. DMC.' What does this mean?"

Junior didn't answer; I felt his eyes lingering on me. Astonishment had silenced him as Floyd read the note aloud. The final request of Edith Cole. She wanted and needed us to solve the mysterious disappearance of David in their absence. She knew they were not walking out of the shop alive once Daddy stepped inside. She knew her time was limited. So, in an act of desperation, she scrawled out her last message for the world. And I knew what she needed us to do.

"It's time to bring David Matthew Cole home," I smiled to Floyd.

Chapter 19

Today was May 4th, only two days since we had last seen Walt and Edith. Only two days—It's unreal how the passage of time feels altered when you're swallowed by, and locked into, so much grief. Just two days ago we were with Walt and Edith in their home, planning out our drive to Raleigh. Just two days ago — Walt, Edith and Pa were alive.

And today, we were aboard a train with MeeMaw and Floyd heading back to Charlotte. Back to the home of Walt and Edith Cole.

We spent much of the trip telling MeeMaw the story of David Cole and his parents' mission to bring him home with the justice he deserved so much. She teared up as we spoke of the similarities between David Cole and our own Davie. Their love of jokes and their equal adoration of life. Their similarities had been so uncanny; but as far as Junior and I were concerned, it was an honest blessing. If we hadn't seen their store sign, would we have even met them? And what would have happened to us?

"Boys," Floyd leaned over to speak with us. "We are almost there. When we do get there, we must stop by Mr. and Mrs. Cole's home first to meet with the Charlotte police. They have some questions for you regarding the Cole's theories, proof, and details regarding their passing. Are you both okay with talking to them?"

"Yes, sir," Junior spoke for us. "We will do whatever is necessary."

"Okay—" Floyd smiled faintly.

I knew the kindness and compassion he portrayed came primarily from the guilt he continued to feel. Guilt stemming from his lack of urgency to protect our family.

"We should be there soon..." he continued. "They will be stopping the train just before the station. They should be preparing for the dig which will take place in a few hours...I hope we are right about the location."

"We are..." Junior responded.

"Have they talked yet with Mr. Murray?" I questioned Floyd as I shifted closer to MeeMaw like a magnet. Noticing my body language, MeeMaw wrapped her arm around me, drawing me in closer, servicing all my insecurities.

"Yes...he—he will be at the station," Floyd answered careful with his wording as his eyes watched me carefully. "They have been speaking with people within the community gathering any information or evidence they can regarding his recent and past behavior."

"Has anyone said anything revealing?" Junior interrogated without hesitation.

"One man...Robert McClennan...he has been telling police about certain behaviors he noticed as a child regarding Murray. He stated that Murray would stand and stare at the boys every morning as they picked up their newspapers. Another man claims that he actually had an incident with Murray in 1911. When Murray walked up to him and a few other boys holding up a photo of a dog he had claimed he lost.

When he stepped forward to look at the photo Murray was holding, he claims Murray grabbed him and attempted to pull him into his car. Fortunately, the boy, and the others he was with at the time, screamed so loud it scared him away," Floyd recalled as he looked from Junior, to MeeMaw and back to me. "They could never one hundred percent identify the man as Murray back then—"

"Really? Because Walt told us the police claimed there was not a single soul in Charlotte who had a negative thing to say about him...I'm assuming they didn't truly investigate as they claimed they did." Junior's voice displayed anger.

"I was not there to know for sure...but it seems as though—from what they have told us, Murray was looked at for several incidents in town such as stalking, peeping, and wandering around homes, schools, and playgrounds..." Floyd's voice remained calm as he now spoke directly to Junior. "Now—also from what I have heard...Murray had a close friend who was in the police department at the time...I'm not saying that the man helped keep him out of trouble. But—it is possible that there was some—assistance—in that way."

"It wouldn't be a surprise if there was," Junior retorted.

"That is just awful..." MeeMaw whispered as her arms tightened around me. "I can't imagine just how much those poor parents suffered for all of these years...and to die so tragically before learning the truth..."

"Well, hopefully we find out some answers today..." Floyd sat up straight, turning his attention to the window. "...and hopefully, we will be able to bury the Coles together as a—complete—family."

None of us spoke following his comment. We were all too individually subdued deep within our own personal thoughts and imagination to pay attention to each other. MeeMaw, already heartbroken about the passing of her daughter, grandson, and husband, now dealt with the thoughts of a little boy buried and forgotten under cold dirt. Junior remained quiet as he too gathered his thoughts and controlled the anger that tended to overwhelm him. I looked out the window, out at the city that was slowly coming into view. Memories of our time here consumed me, eating at The Diamond Soda Grill as brothers Jerry and Lewis Collins as we tried to conceal our true identities and wandering around town, walking into a store where we'd find safety and housing with strangers who later became more like a family to us. And now, Junior and I were on our way back to Charlotte, not for protection, but to bring David home to a proper burial site where his family would forever stay together.

The loud screeching from the wheels of the train pulled me away from the deep thoughts that left me dejected. The whistle blew, signaling that the train would be coming to a stop soon. MeeMaw closed her eyes tight and began to brace herself in her seat as the train quickly began to slow down. I reached for her hand, offering comfort as the trained rattled to a stop. Her weary tawney-colored eyes met with mine and the wrinkles around her eyes came alive as she smiled down at me.

Finally, the train jolted to a complete stop just before the crossing. I could see a crowd of people further up ahead, some watching the train and others presumably waiting patiently for orders to begin the dig.

"Ready?" Junior asked.

I took a deep breath as I looked across to my brother whose eyes were narrowed and steady, "Ready..." I nodded in agreement.

Junior followed quietly behind Floyd while I waited as MeeMaw grabbed her bags. As we stepped outside onto the gravel, the rays from the sun met my face as it welcomed me back to Charlotte. On the platform, policemen eagerly gathered around with hired diggers. A few spectators were waiting with their cameras pointed at my brother and me, as they longed for a proper photo opportunity which would later be labelled as the 'Grief Stricken Children Arriving to Unearth the Horrors Buried Beneath the Soil.'

MeeMaw's warm breath brushed against my cheek as she whispered in my ear, "It's okay, dear, keep your head held high."

She must have noticed the anxiety that burned inside of me as flashes from cameras began to surround us. All the voices that had been humming throughout the station came to a sudden stop as the officers' and diggers' eyes found us. The spotlight was on us as everyone at the station had their eyes fixed upon the remainder of my family. They watched us intently while we walked up the slight hill that led us to the station as we followed closely behind Floyd who was now shaking hands with a man introduced to us as Eugene Clayton.

"Junior..." I pushed myself forward to his side.

"What?"

"He's here..." I said as I stared back at the eyes which were locked onto me. "Murray..."

Junior turned his attention to the ticket station where Charles Murray stood between two officers; his dark and intent eyes were locked onto us. He was being requestioned by officers regarding the abduction and disappearance of David Cole in 1912, and I could tell by his demeanor that he was not pleased with this new interest in the case and at the resurfacing of our faces in town.

"Keep your eyes straight..." Junior warned. "Do not look at him...We are safe. We will meet with officers at the house and then come back here for the digging."

"I hope they arrest him..." I admitted as I broke the eye contact with Murray. "Do you think he will try to get away?"

"I –I don't –I—hope not—"

"Alright boys, Mrs. Williams, after you," Officer Clayton ushered us into a patrol car parked at the back of the lot.

Junior, MeeMaw, and I piled into the back seat together as Floyd took the front seat. I gazed out the window as we drove through the city. We drove past The Diamond Soda Grill where our story here had begun, and Betty was there standing outside. She had been one of the first people we had met in this city apart from Murray.

As we drove by the restaurant, I knew that soon we'd be driving up to David's Toys and Joke Shop. I began wondering if this would actually become too much for Junior and me emotionally. Was all this happening too suddenly? It had not even been one week since most of our family members died plus the devastating loss of Edith and Walt. And now, we were about to walk into the home of the two people who took us in as their own while asking for nothing in return. They were without a doubt two of the most selfless people I had ever known. I just hoped I would remain strong enough to carry out their mission and bring them some peace, to repay them for their love and affection for us.

"And here we are…" Officer Clayton mumbled as he gently pulled the patrol car over to a stop right outside their home.

I looked up and out the window at the store that stood there untouched as though life had never moved forward. Deep inside, I felt the knots in my stomach tighten. I looked up at their store and felt nothing but regret and guilt. Guilty that we even stopped at this store and regretful that we included them in our journey. If it were not for us, they would be alive today to share their own story. Instead, we were getting ready to answer questions about not only the murders of Edith and Walter Cole but the disappearance of their only son, David.

Officer Clayton assisted Junior and me out of the car while Floyd opened the door for MeeMaw. She quickly made her way to our side to be sure she did not miss any question or comment directed towards us.

As we stepped into that familiar disorganized store, I felt the lingering knot make its way up to my throat as my anxiety level started to skyrocket. My eyes focused on the shelves of untidy joke products that had originally lured us deeper into the store just days before. My mind began to fade back in time to when we found Walt sitting at the cash register waiting for our arrival. It was as though they knew we would eventually make our way to them. However, this time—entering their store—was different. This time we found ourselves in a store crowded with officers gathered in a circle waiting for us. And the place where Walt once stood was now blocked off as a crime scene. Every investigator turned and met our uneasy gazes. All of them had questions they knew only we could answer.

"Alright, men, this here is Junior and Jamie and this is their grandmother, Mrs. Vera Williams. Now she is allowing us to question the boys; however, she is requesting that they only be questioned with her present," Officer Clayton announced to the men who began hovering around us like vultures. "Everyone understand?"

All the officers indicated their agreement in unison, staring at us as Junior and I stared back. All we were to them was a thrilling story and new possible headlines for the town's newspaper. To us this was our life. Somehow the unfortunate tale of the Clark and Cole families became the town's primary source of media coverage. Everyone in the country would soon know our family's name. And instead of positive and happy thoughts, horror would cross people's minds when our name would be discussed. And now we are unearthing more mysteries and horror that this town did not even know existed just beneath the surface.

'Is this what my brother and I were now?' I thought to myself. 'Just boys who seemed to attract nothing but unfortunate luck. And that is what people across the country will begin to think as well.'

"Jamie…Junior…this here is Detective Peter O'Conner. Peter has some questions for you regarding David Cole…" Officer Clayton explained as Peter, who held his head high with pride, walked forward firmly holding onto his notepad.

"Hello, boys…I first want to offer you three our condolences," Peter's voice was sincere as he spoke to us and his eyes were steady with focus looking from Junior to MeeMaw and finally to me. "Our question for you two is mainly regarding the Cole Family. As you both know, David Cole disappeared from our streets January 6, 1912; he was only ten years old. At the time of his disappearance, our officers believed David had just run off with friends or simply had gotten lost. Our officers never imagined someone would have taken a child off our streets without anyone noticing or seeing anything. It was unimaginable to us all at the time and quite frankly, even now. We have continued the search for David—"

"No, you hav—" Junior began.

"—Junior!" MeeMaw hushed as she rested her hand on Junior's shoulder.

"—how—however, not as well as we should have, I guess." Peter hesitantly looked off to Officer Clayton who nodded encouragingly for Peter to continue. "As events from the past few days have unfolded, we have learned some interesting thoughts and theories into his mysterious disappearance. One of them being in the interest of Charles Murray. Now we have police with Mr. Murray as we speak, reinterviewing him and looking back at transcribed interviews with him from the past. We have found and reviewed some of the writings left here by the Cole's giving us some insight to their side of the story. However, we would like to know more before continuing with our search by the tracks. We are halting transportation for this search; and before we continue with our plan, we need to know as much as we can. Between the two of you…can you tell us what the Coles entrusted with you?"

I looked up to Junior, waiting for him to answer the questioning men. His eyes were pointed down to the ground while he shifted his weight from one foot to the other, as though he was calming down the anger that raged once again inside of him. I thought about responding for us, but I didn't know what to say. I did not know where I would begin the story told to us. My mind shifted to memories that took place just up those stairs behind the officers. I remember Walt's words as he trusted us with his thoughts about David's abduction. And just the thought of Charles Murray waiting for David to ride by his store to only lure him inside the store with the sole intention of causing harm to him caused tears to swell in my eyes. Charles Murray taking away the light and joy of two parent's lives for a sinister purpose. My mind wandered back to the train station and the secrets that lay just beneath the surface. The anger Junior felt began to burn inside of me. These officers were soon going to take the investigative credit. Credit that should have been given solely to Walt and Edith. And before I could brush up the courage to speak to the men, Junior's voice broke through the wall of silence that separated us from them.

"Walter and Edith Cole told us the entire story of David's disappearance starting from the morning he woke up and walked out that door…" Junior pointed at the door from which, thirty-four years ago, David had walked out, excited, and ready for a new day. "The last thing Walt heard his son say was 'Bye, Pa, love you.' His last request for dinner was eggs, potatoes, and bacon. But he never got that. Instead, he rode his own invention, the wooden board with wheels, down the street towards the Meat Shop where Murray worked as a butcher. Somehow Murray lured David inside the store as he opened for the day. He murdered him and later that night or sometime before he started his job at the ticket booth, he buried him near those tracks. He buried him there so every day he could watch the spot and relive the murder he got away with."

"What was their evidence of this?" Peter replied.

"Oh, well, I thought your search for David had continued…if you have no other evidence to go by…why are you questioning their theory at all?" Junior took a step forward, sounding more like a man than just a thirteen-year-old boy. "Take this theory and search…if it is wrong, then it's wrong and we continue to search. But if it is right, you could bury a family together today. You have a chance to make a difference. You have a chance to solve a case that has been open since 1912—1912! That is thirty-four years of questions and wondering…end this now. Approve the search. We should be at the train station rather than here…"

"I understand that…Junior—" Peter began before Junior cut him off again.

"Henry—my name is Henry to you. Only my family or close friends can call me Junior. You are neither…and I refuse to be called Junior and made to feel like a stupid, arrogant child," Junior told them sternly. "My brother and I have gone through more than anyone in this room has. Now…speak to me as a person…a man rather than a child. My innocence is gone… treat me like it."

Unseen Scars

"Okay—umm—yes, sir. Henry then..." Peter's eyes showed every bit of feelings he felt. They were soft, as though he just began to understand this was not just paperwork...this was a life that we were discussing. A life that was cut short and in effect ruined two more lives. He thought carefully about the next words he'd speak, "Henry...I just need to know their evidence and then we can move out to the train station and bring an end to this. I was not a sheriff or investigator back in 1912...and I am terribly sorry about the lack of motivation to search. However, the policies and paperwork involved forces me to ask this question. If you can... either one of you ... tell me about the evidence gathered by the Clark's...we can continue from here to the station, what do you say?"

I looked up at Junior...or Henry...however he preferred me to call him at that point, and waited for him to decided what to say. I was afraid to ruin the tough-guy attitude, so I tried my best to puff out my almost eleven-year-old chest and tighten my jaw hoping to portray a strong man. Looking back on that, I probably just looked ridiculous.

"Well...the first night David was missing, Walt combed the streets looking for him, while Edith stayed back here anxiously hoping he would come through those doors. But he didn't—obviously," Junior's tone never wavered. "Walt asked Murray if he had seen anything that day, to which Murray claimed he was never aware that they even had a child. He claims he had never heard of David Cole before. But Murray did. The Coles bought meat from that store frequently, and David sometimes would run or ride down there to pick up meat for their dinner. Well, when y'all interviewed him the following day...his story changed. He claimed he saw David walking on the sidewalk near the Diamond Soda Grill. Y'all blamed that slip up on his alcohol consumption. But Walt said he seemed perfectly sober to him the night before... Also—David Cole was riding his board that morning...not walking. He would have ridden that board all the way to The Observer to show his friends what he made... I know this...well because it is what I would have done. It is what every ten-eleven-twelve-year-old boy would have done in the same given situation. That board has never been found...and I guarantee...if you search Murray's possessions, he will still have David's board. That could have been his token from his murder. That or it is buried with David. Now...let us get back to the train station..."

Junior turned on his heel quickly heading towards the front door just before Floyd, who had kept so quiet in the corner we had almost forgotten he was still with us, stopped him.

"Wait a second Ju—Henry..." Floyd grabbed Junior by the shoulders. "They have more things to tell you both...and this...you'll want to hear this..."

"What—" his voice echoed with frustration.

"Well, umm, who is going over the other matter with the bo — the young men here?" Officer Clayton asked the now not so eager officers.

"Umm—that—that'll be me..." A tall and thin blonde-haired man raised his hand slowly in the air from the corner near the register. He walked forward slowly, his eyes never meeting ours.

I must admit, at this moment, I truly believed that I had been contributing to the 'tough-guy' persona. But with my small and slim appearance...I was not at all intimidating.

"Ah—Roger..." Officer Clayton lifted his arm to introduce the blonde-headed officer. "Roger has the details on the Cole's final request."

"Final what?" Junior asked.

"Umm—their request..." Roger's eyes briefly met Junior's gaze, before returning to the note pad containing the information he would soon read. "Upon search of the house, as part of our investigation into the double murders of Walter and Edith Cole, we came across two notes. One note leading us to you two bo—men; you two men. And the other...a will—"

"A will? A will to do what?" I so innocently asked.

"A will—you create one stating who you'd like to have your things or what you would like to happen to your things...in any circumstance that you tragically— pass..." MeeMaw explained to me as she hung her arm tightly around my shoulders.

"Oh—"

"Yes—well—we uncovered Mr. and Mrs. Cole's will...it honestly was not difficult to find. It was left on Mr. Cole's bedside table," Roger boasted with pride. "The letter reads as follows:

The Last Will and Testament
Of
Walter David Cole and Edith Virginia Beckham Cole

I, Walter D. Cole and Edith V. H. Cole, of Charlotte, North Carolina, being of sound mind, declare this to be our Last Will and Testament, hereby revoking all prior Wills and codicils made by us.

I. Personal Representative

We appoint Henry Gene Clark II and James Lee Clark as Personal Representatives of our Last Will and Testament. In the event of death, resignation, removal, incapacity, refusal or inability of Henry Gene Clark II or James Lee Clark to serve as our Personal Representative, then I appoint their grandparents

Johnnie Williams and Vera Williams of Raleigh, North Carolina to serve as Successor Personal Representative.

II. Payment of Debts and Expenses

We direct that our just debts, funeral expenses, and expenses of illness be first paid from our estate.

III. Deposition of Property

We direct that our residuary estate be distributed evenly between both Henry Gene Clark II and James Lee Clark. If one of these children is deceased, our shares will go to the remaining child. If both children are deceased, these shares shall be distributed evenly to Johnnie Williams and Vera Williams. If one of them is to not survive, our shares will go to the surviving one. If neither survive, our residuary estate shall be given to the railroad system for further development for safer travels.

In Witness Whereof, I have hereunto set my hand this May day of 2nd, 1946 in Charlotte, North Carolina.

Witness Signature: <u>Robert G. McClennan</u>"

"Any questions?" Officer Clayton smiled with pride.

"Umm—yes...what—so exactly what does that mean?" Junior questioned the officer.

"It means that they have left everything...to you." Roger smiled proudly. "Everything in here is yours...it is your decision what happens to the joke shop and their home upstairs. Their remaining money...is yours—evenly distributed, of course. But nonetheless, you two have a big decision to make."

"Oh my..." MeeMaw breathed. "How much is that exactly?"

"We aren't sure...you will have to discuss that with the bank." Officer Clayton commented.

"And...the—house..." MeeMaw questioned.

"It is the boys' decision what is to happen to it and the shop once they are of age..." Office Clayton responded.

"Who –who is Robert McClennan?" I asked quietly.

"Robert—Robert McClennan was David Cole's close friend before he vanished," Officer Clayton explained. "He remained close with the Coles after David disappeared. He must have come by the other day to authorize this noting the date..."

I looked over at Junior in disbelief. I couldn't believe that they would leave this—all of this—for us. A few days ago, we were nothing to them. We were just two lost boys looking desperately for a place to stay for a few nights. We never intended on becoming close to anyone on our journey to Raleigh; it just happened.

"One final thing..." Floyd's voice was hesitant. "Officer Masen...the floor is yours."

"Good afternoon, gentlemen..." Officer Masen walked with more confidence than the others. His broad shoulders announced power with each stride he took. "I am here to collect a statement regarding the evening of May 2nd. Any details of the events that led to the – unfortunate—passing of Walter and Edith Cole."

"Well—we spent the day playing Monopoly together—Edith, Junior, and I—" I recalled. "But—early that morning Daddy showed up here talking with Edith...nothing more than a conversation. So, we, Edith and Walt included, decided that early the following morning we would leave before sunrise. The remainder of the day we spent with Edith upstairs learning how to read a map and really just mentally preparing for the following morning. Junior and I - we decided—that we would sneak out that night once Edith and Walt went to sleep. We—we di—" My voice trailed off into a subtle silence. I could not finish my thought without my emotions taking over me entirely. My eyes gradually met with the floor as I attempted to forget about the questioning eyes that remained on me.

"—We didn't want to put them at danger…at risk…so we decided to leave without them, hoping to spare them," Junior took over my thoughts. "—But—unfortunately…Daddy returned early that night just before the store closed. Jamie and I had come down here with Edith just before he walked in through these doors…"

"Edith—she told us to leave—" the tears became more than I could control. Everything about that night was still just as vivid as the moment it occurred.

Junior continued to tell the crowd of curious officers about our narrow escape in full detail. He told them how Daddy fired live rounds at our truck as we fled away from the now quiet and lifeless home of the Cole's. How we heard the echoing sound of the gunfire that ended their beautiful lives. You could see the pain deep within the officers' eyes as they patiently and respectfully listened to our story. None of them interrupted us. None of them redirected the conversation with specific questions. They continued to eagerly jot down on their notepads careful not to miss a single detail spoken.

I saw tears run down their cheeks as they began to realize that this story was not a fabrication, or some story created by an author; this was our real-life story.

Around one o'clock in the afternoon we made our way back to the train station. We were escorted through Charlotte by two patrol cars. I couldn't help but notice heads turning our way as we passed by. I felt as though our life was now on display and the entire world was tuning in just to get a glimpse of it. I didn't know what any of this meant for our lives going forward.

Thoughts clouded my mind: 'Would anyone sit with us at school? Would anyone hire us to work for them? And would anyone ever marry someone with a past like ours?' So many uncertainties crossed my mind as images of buildings and people flashed by.

Soon the car came to a stop, forcing my vision to refocus on the present as sounds of people chattering and arguing broke through. I hurried out onto the platform joining my brother and grandmother. MeeMaw quickly grabbed both Junior's and my hands to be sure she would not lose either one of us in the mist of all the commotion.

I searched the crowd frantically for sight of Murray. I wanted to be sure he was watching as his thirty-four-year-old secret was being unearthed at the hands of two young boys. I continued scanning from one unfamiliar face to the next, there was no sign of the plump man with black greasy hair. Every face my eyes met was unfamiliar. 'Where is he?' I thought frantically to myself. 'He has to still be here! There is no way they would let him go! Would they? No, they couldn't. They just couldn't—'

I almost gave up my search for him when I heard a loud gasp from the onlookers. A storm of people gathered in front of us looking eagerly at something or someone near the ticket booth. I looked over at Junior who was standing on the tips of his toes desperately trying to see over the adult barricade. There was no way to see anything through them.

"Junior…" I pulled on his arm to get his attention. "Lift me on your shoulders!"

"What?" Junior yelled forcing himself to be heard over the yelling and shouting of citizens around us.

"LIFT ME UP!" I shrieked back.

"Oh…" Junior, realizing my plan, bent down low enough for me to climb on his shoulders.

MeeMaw, who was unable to see as well, helped hoist me onto my brother's shoulders and to secure me as he steadied his feet and stood up tall. Finally, I was just above the crowd and high enough to see what was happening. And there he was; Charles Murray handcuffed and being led away to a patrol car parked out on the street. Cameramen ran up and down the street desperate for the perfect shot for the headline in the paper.

'Was it a confession that led to his arrest?' I wondered.

The digging had not yet begun so what was it that led to his arrest? I watched as the heavy-set man still dressed in his green vest and white button-up was pushed into the patrol car headfirst. He was too much of a coward to look back at the onlookers, too ashamed of his capture and too ashamed of the truth that would soon be discovered.

"Jamie!" Junior shouted up at me. "JAMIE! What do you see?"

"It's Murray! He's—he's being arrested!" I told him, still having a difficult time believing it myself.

"He's what?" MeeMaw shrieked below me. "He's—oh...Floyd! Floyd!"

Junior dropped me to my feet unable to hold me up any longer. We hurried off after MeeMaw as she pushed her way through the crowd to get Floyd who was in deep conversation with Officer Clayton.

"Floyd!" MeeMaw bellowed again, this time catching Floyd's eye.

"Ah! Mrs. Williams!" Floyd smiled brightly before catching the glare of our now determined MeeMaw.

"Now, Floyd. I have been patient with everything you and your men have thrown in our direction...but this...I and the boys deserve an answer right now," MeeMaw waved her finger at Floyd reminding me of Momma.

"Yes, ma'am..." Floyd quickly gathered himself. "Let us move on over by the tracks to discuss this..."

We followed Floyd, Officer Clayton, and two other officers we had not yet met, back through the crowd to a secluded spot just off the tracks. The crowd of onlookers and diggers were too distracted with the arrest of Murray to notice us.

"We sent a few officers out to Murray's home and...you were right, Jun—Henry..." Officer Clayton remarked, proudly looking down at Junior. "They searched his home and hidden in his closet was –what did you call it? A wooden board? Anyway, engraved on the inside of the board was 'David Matthew Cole.' So they brought it down here and showed Murray."

"We thought he'd put up a fight." One of the officers commented.

"He didn't!" The other officer said with astonishment.

"He admitted to the whole thing!" Floyd smiled proudly. "Isn't that fantastic? That along with testimonies from other men in this community...he'll be put away without any issue—"

"Did he state where he buried him?" Junior pressed them for more information.

"Yes...he did," Floyd smiled.

"Well!" I bawled.

"Under that oak tree...just off to side of the tracks..." Officer Clayton revealed. "Jay...Terrance...gather the diggers. Let's bring that little boy home."

It all seemed so surreal to me. After thirty-four years, David Cole would be home. The diggers began their dig under the oak tree, the very same one Junior and I stood under our first few minutes here. We had stood there so innocently, not knowing that just below the dirt lay a little boy named David who had been lost and forgotten by his town.

It was not long before one of the men halted the work. Out of the ground they pulled a worn and tattered white button-up shirt. A sense of relief hit me as they pulled his clothes out of the ground. I felt Edith and Walt in that moment as we recovered their beloved little boy. The clothes and shoes he was last seen in were all buried with him in that cold shallow grave. His bones were exhumed; and, for the first time in thirty-four years, warmth from the sun beamed down onto him. I don't think there was a dry eye in the crowd. Even the diggers had to take pauses while they dug to process what was happening. The lost boy that the town would only talk about as a scary story just to terrify the new younger generation was real. He wasn't just a story. He was real. He wasn't just a flyer or a number or even an old case file. He was a real ten-year-old boy who had dreams and a life stolen away from him…similar to our own Davie.

We found out later that day the entire horror story of David Cole. He did, as Walt and Edith believed, ride by the meat store where Murray was opening the store early for the day. When David rode by on his way to The Observer, Murray stopped him. David walked back to Murray to hear what Murray had to say. Murray lured him inside promising he would show him how to cut meat like a butcher. David walked into the store voluntarily, but what happened after that was far from voluntary. Murray admitted to trapping David in the meat locker before assaulting and murdering him. He hid his body inside the locker before burying him out by the oak tree. He took the job as the ticket clerk for reasons we knew: to watch and remember his 'perfect' crime as he called it.

At last, on this quiet early evening on May 4th of 1946, the Cole family was reunited and now forever together. The town was appalled and horrified after hearing the gripping confession made by a man

Unseen Scars

whom a majority of them seemed to trust. Feeling guilty for the treatment each of them had given to the Coles since 1912, the entire town decided to show their regret and apologies by attending their funeral. Fake tears were spilled as the preacher discussed the amazing life led by Edith and Walt. These people barely knew the Coles. After David's abduction, the Coles became the city's outcasts. The only people who continued to genuinely care for their family was Robert McClennan. He stood with Junior, MeeMaw, and me as they lowered not only Edith and Walt but David into the ground.

I felt proud of what Junior and I had accomplished together. Not only did we manage to survive, just the two of us, but we helped bring closure to a case police had labeled as cold. And now the Cole Family was finally together again, forever. Edith and Walt were now resting in peace with David by their sides.

All that remained was the burial of our own family back in Raleigh. But for now, this chapter of our life was closed. We found comfort in knowing that home may not be a location but rather a feeling of comfort and security within the people you surround yourself with. Love is what makes up a family. Love is what we all must hold onto.

And because of that love, Junior and I had a lifetime to look forward to.

Epilogue

"...And here we all are now, seventy-three years later, gathered around celebrating and remembering the life of my big brother...my protector. He was more than this gravestone will ever reveal, and he was more than just a 'poor' Alzheimer's patient. For all of those who only knew him during his – 'forgetful' years—you really missed out on a man who was truly a once-in-a-lifetime man. He was a man who put his family first regardless of the consequences that would follow. He was a man who knew the importance of family and cherished the memories made. Junior was forced to grow up at the age of thirteen and from then on never once complained about the injustice we endured in our lives. He taught me how to move forward. If it had not been for Junior's courage and selflessness, I don't think I would be where I am today. I wouldn't be here surrounded by the love and support of my wife, four children, eleven grandchildren, and now three great grandchildren. I can tell you...seventy-three years ago...we never saw our lives turning out to be anything but tragic. Without God, we would have never made it through. God is real and God is always with us. It took me growing up to finally see that.

I hope you, Jane, always feel the love my family feels for you. I have known you now for seventy years, and you have become more like a sister to me than an in-law. I remember the day Junior met you. I had never seen him so in love with anyone before. He came home in a daze staring at the ceiling in his own daydream, dreaming about the new girl in town. MeeMaw was so proud the day he brought you home to meet her. She was so proud of Junior and the man he was becoming. And she was even prouder the day y'all were wed. Even during MeeMaw's final days in 1960, you were there for her. You were a daughter to her. And you became everything to Junior, and you made him the happiest man in the world. And for that...I thank you. You gave him the life he deserved. He loved you; you were his forever.

So, as we end today's service with the burial of Henry Gene Clark II, take a moment to reflect on your own individual tragedies, or as Junior called them, your unseen scars. Those tragedies don't have to define you. You can move past each hardship and live a life worth thousands of lives just as Junior did. Don't feel sorrow for Junior as he would not want this. He would want each of us to carry on with a sense of peace knowing that he is now surrounded by my mother, father, and twin brother."

I stepped away from the casket that would forever hold the remains of my brother and walked slowly towards the welcoming arms of my wife. She, along with Jane, had known parts of my brother's and my story but not everything in such detail. Not that Junior nor I were ashamed or uncomfortable telling the tale earlier, but rather found it unnecessary.

"I am so proud of you, my love." Leanna whispered in my ear before kissing my cheek gently.

"Thank you, dear," as my arms tightly held her around her waist.

I finally let go of her and looked into her hazel eyes that reminded me so much of my Momma. It is amazing how a pair of eyes from my childhood that provided me with so much comfort during my early years on this earth can continue to provide me comfort with the eyes of my wife. Every time I look at her, everything in this world makes sense again. And every hardship we have faced together, I owe it all to her, my better half.

I turned my attention over to Jane who bravely held herself together through the story of Junior and me. I held my arms out to her to offer her my comfort and love. She smiled so softly as she always did with the very smile Junior would go on about as a young boy.

Jane hugged me tightly while she whispered in my ear, "Thank you, Jamie… yo—your words –thank you—he will never be forgotten—" Her voice trailed off as she lost control of the tears that welled in her eyes.

"You will always be our family—no matter what—" I hugged her tighter.

I felt the eyes of everyone who surrounded us in that moment, but I didn't care. She is my sister—my family. I knew that now it was my job to protect and be there for her until the day I join my family and leave this world behind. There was not a shadow of a doubt that Junior would have done the same for my Leanna if given the opportunity.

I released our hug and stared into her weeping eyes, "Come home with Leanna and me for a few hours. Leanna prepared a roast for dinner, would love for you to try some…"

Unseen Scars

"I—I would love to..." Jane smiled honestly as she wiped away the tears with the handkerchief she held tightly in her hand.

I held firmly on to Leanna's and Jane's hands while we watched the casket being lowered into the ground where it would remain forever. I could not help but cry.

It's strange, you know. Processing the death of a random stranger comes so quickly to all of us. We aren't affected by the death of someone when we have not had a chance to meet or to know them on a personal level. But—when we know that person and have memories with them—the death affects us differently. It takes longer than a few days to process the loss of a loved one while being faced with difficult decisions regarding their funeral. But—every gravestone or urn that holds the body of a person—holds someone else's Junior. So, why do we walk past people every day as if they don't exist in this world. If each of us took a moment to smile or say hello to every passing stranger, maybe life would be valued more.

My four children, one by one, hugged my wife and me once the funeral concluded. I couldn't help but feel a little emotional seeing the sadness that lurked in their own eyes. They, along with my grandchildren, had never heard details of Junior's and my childhood. Our two daughters, Katie and Claire, met with us first with their welcoming smiles which were inherited without doubt from my late mother. Leanna always argued that Katie inherited more of her family's features, but I always saw my mother's smiles in each of them. Our sons joined us next. These two were the best of friends even with their polar-opposite personalities and the ten-year age difference between them. Leanna and I thought we were done with having children after having Claire. Three children, one job, and a three-bedroom home when Anthony came into our life. Our two girls were thrilled at the announcement of another sibling, but David (our eldest son) was annoyed at the possibility of sharing his room with a brother or sister. David was ten—the same age Davie was when he lost his life—when Anthony came along. But eventually—they became inseparable.

We made plans with our children to come over following the funeral to have dinner with us. Their children and grands were leaving soon, each one with their own lives to rush home to. They all lived in different parts of North Carolina, apart from Cameron (our youngest grandson) who was currently stationed in Texas while serving in the United States Army. It is a blessing to be able to sit back and watch the growth of your family as the years go by. Leanna and I never thought Anthony would ever settle down and get married. He had such a carefree and spirited personality, like Davie, but he found a balance when he met Diane and we were blessed.

Junior and I were so fortunate to have the families that surrounded us, especially in Junior's final days. His three sons (Johnnie, Jack, and Jerry) came together with their wives and their own children filling his room with love and peace as he passed. And today they were doing the same thing, but this time for Jane.

Jane and Junior never had an easy life together. Junior was a military man, which I never foresaw for his future, especially after watching that lifestyle destroy our father. But Junior always said he felt that was his calling in his teen years. He left for the Vietnam War as a twenty-three-year-old Infantry grunt in the United States Marine Corps soon after marrying Jane and while expecting their first son, Johnnie. Junior had decided early on that he was not going to name his first son after himself or Daddy. He decided that Pa deserved that honor more than Daddy did. Originally, Junior was only going to serve in that war and then quickly get out of the military to be home with Jane and his son. But Junior came home and realized that he missed that lifestyle. They moved all over the world but would always call North Carolina their home. All of their sons eventually joined the military to carry on their father's legacy.

As for me, I left for Vietnam serving in the Army; but I came home after a year and a half having been shot in the leg by enemy fire. I was thankful that was all the damage I endured. Junior and I decided to sell Edith and Walt's toy shop once we became of age and spent the money to buy a new shop up here in Raleigh to continue David's Toy and Joke Shop locally. I still work there today and will hopefully hand it down to our children once I pass as well.

Life turned out okay for us Clark boys. MeeMaw took us in as her own following that night. She continued to raise us until she passed in 1960. When she died, it felt as though we were losing our mother all over again. Thankfully, we had our wives with us during that time to support us during our grief. Our old home was demolished in an attempt to rid the city of the memory of what happened that day on April 30, 1946. But the memories will forever stay with my family.

The truth is: I don't want what happened to be forgotten. I want people to remember our family and the tragedy that struck us unexpectedly. But I want people to know how happy we were prior to the war. I want people to understand the importance of mental health and how quickly it can change a person from who they once were into someone unrecognizable. Remembering the past is not a negative, but rather a way to learn to ensure the future becomes better. And that is what Junior and I accomplished: a better future.

"Dear?" Leanna's voice broke my thoughts. "Let's head home...the kids said they would meet us there, and Jane's boys are taking her there now. I knew I should have bought a bigger pot roast."

"We will make it work..." I smiled at the gravestones before me—my entire family lay there in front of me. An empty plot between Davie and Junior awaited me to join them on the other side. "We always have..."

I smiled as a strange feeling of peace began to flow inside of me. Images of the long-anticipated reunion for Junior that waited just through the golden gates. The laughter from my twin brother seemed so real to me as I stood there, it was as though he were standing right next to me. I could just see them all so vividly in my mind. I prayed for Junior's peaceful transitioning, and that fog that once filled his mind with confusion and anxiety be lifted and replaced with clarity and memories. And I began to hope my father was there with them now.

Until the day I join them, I have my job laid out for me here on earth: ensuring our family is safe and happy before the day I leave to join in on their reunion.

In my hand, I held the 2-blade imperial pocketknife owned by my brother. I put it in my pocket to remind myself to give it to Jane once we returned home. I grabbed hold of Leanna's hand, and we made our way through the cemetery with an undeniable sense of peace, until—

"Excuse me—sir," said an unfamiliar man's voice from behind.

It was the same stranger I saw through the crowd at the beginning of Junior's service. I still could not place him nor his wife in my memories. He must have been a few years younger than I. I knew those eyes, but from where? His wife had a polite smile across her face as she was holding on to her husband's arm.

"I'm sorry—I know you have no idea who I am—" The man spoke. "My name is Thomas Adler, and this –this is my wife, Cynthia. I was—"

"Tommy..." I breathed.

"Yes..." He looked relieved at my memory of him. "Thomas—Clark—Adler. I was—"

"Uncle Tommy's boy...I can't believe it—" I became emotional again as I reached over to give him a hug. I couldn't believe he was here. Joan had never reached out to us after Daddy came home or after everyone's passing. And with time, we moved on.

"Cynthia here has always mentioned that I should try to find you and Junior—" He began to explain. "I finally decided I should give it a try, so I got in touch with someone in Charleston who told me that your family relocated to Raleigh after the war. So, I called up here and learned of Junior's passing. I had to come and pay my respects, and I thought maybe I could introduce myself...and explain..."

Thomas explained to Leanna and me about how once Joan learned of Uncle Tommy's passing, she began slowly falling apart. Thomas was only four years old when Uncle Tommy died. Joan began to pretend as though Uncle Tommy never existed and focused solely on raising Thomas. Of course, Thomas had questions about his father which Joan would always refrain from answering. She didn't know how to talk about Uncle Tommy or our family to an innocent little boy. She wanted Thomas to remain innocent and unscratched by the unfairness and unforgiving cruelty of this world. She raised him as a single mother until the day she passed in 1972. That was when Thomas first learned of his father, Thomas John Adler, while going through his mother's belongings. He found letters and photos dating back to 1941 and quickly realized the uncanny resemblance he held to the man in the photos. From reading the letters he learned of the identity of his father and of our family, but it took him years to find the courage to find us.

I listened to Thomas's story without interruption. I was still in shock that he was even here. Throughout the years, I would often think about Little Tommy and the possible life he led. I never believed that there would ever be a day that we'd meet face to face.

Out of his coat pocket, Thomas pulled out the medals earned and worn by Uncle Tommy through the war until the day of his death. They were identical to the ones owned by Daddy.

"This though…is something I have had by my bedside table ever since I found it in Momma's belongings." He explained as he searched through all his pockets.

Pulled from his coat pocket was a dated photo. A photo of Uncle Tommy and Daddy, arm in arm, dressed in their camouflage while holding their guns off to the side with their helmets hanging off the barrel. Each of them with a cigarette in their mouths. I had never seen this photo before. The photo was dated April 1945, the very month Uncle Tommy died.

"I thought you'd want to see this picture…" Thomas smiled at me, as I studied every detail of the photo. "If you needed any—proof that I am who I say I am—"

"I know it's you—you look just like him…" I gazed back at him with amazement.

"I even have his toes!" Thomas laughed.

"His long toes!" I remembered that from his letter to us announcing his birth.

"Yes!" Thomas replied.

"Come home with Leanna and me…" I suggested. "We're having our family come over for pot roast. We'd love for you—"

"Oh, no—We'd hate to intrude. It seems more like a famil—"

"—you are family… You always have been…" I told him. "Leanna cooks an amazing pot roast; you'd both really enjoy it. Plus, Jane,

Junior's wife, would love to meet you. She knows your father and mother through our stories. It is not intrusion at all."

"Oh, I really should have made a second pot roast—" I heard Leanna whisper.

"Well—thank you, we'd love to!" Thomas exclaimed as tears slowly escaped his eyes.

I wrapped my arm around Thomas just as my father and Uncle Tommy did in the photo, and we made our way together to the parking lot. Cynthia and Leanna followed behind us chatting away about each other's dresses and different meals they have cooked in the past. They talked as though they had known each other for years.

And just like that—life moved on again. Life will forever move on, past tragedies and deaths that we all experience along the way. And it forever will move on. Even after my death. My children will continue to live on and theirs will too. And that is how life will forever be. And that is how life should be. A continuation of family bonded together forever through love and memories. Memories will be shared and passed on, generation after generation. None of us will ever truly be forgotten in death.

And until the day I join my family again, my past will forever remain the unseen scar that I have pushed through with great success.

Acknowledgements

I want to thank my husband, daughter and family for their unwavering support and encouragement throughout this lengthy journey. Special thanks to my mother and my grandmother lovingly nicknamed, Bull, whose insights and feedback helped shape this story. And to all those who continue to fight battles, both seen and unseen, you are not alone.

S.B. Labate is a wife of 6 years to her high school sweetheart and mother of their beautiful daughter and two rambunctious fur babies. She is a Registered Nurse of 7 years. Throughout her childhood, she loved to tell stories in her numerous writing classes but eventually traded in her pen for a pair of scrubs. While her husband was deployed in 2020 with the United States Marines, she picked up her pen again and began a story that was thought of all those years ago in that middle school writing class.

This is her first book.